PRAISE FOR

EDITOR'S CHOICE, *The Historical Novel Society,*
Shortlisted for *The Selfies Award* 2022
and *The Chaucer Award* 2022 and 2023;
Finalist in *The Wishing Shelf Awards* 2022;
Quarter-Finalist in *The Booklife Prize* 2022 and 2023.

"Stunningly authentic." The Booklife Prize

"A yarn fit for a Norse saga. Full of action, poetry and heart; a thrilling voyage through the vibrant world of the twelfth century." Matthew Harffy

"Absolutely brilliant. A tour-de-force of storytelling, Viking lore, and the rugged landscape of Orkney." Deborah Swift, *Italian Renaissance* series

"If you're a lover of Viking history this book will tick all the boxes. A great read." Kath Middleton, book blogger

"Ms Gill blends fact, fiction and legend to create believable characters who straddle the real and mystical world in a truly enthralling story." Annie Whitehead, *To Be a Queen*

"A stirring coming-of-age tale forged in love, inheritance and adventure - in The Ring Breaker *Jean Gill skilfully brings the poetry and magic of the Viking world to life."* Emily Brand, *The Fall of the House of Byron*

"A skilfully written, beautifully researched coming-of-age story set in Viking Orkney." Lexie Conyngham, *the Orkneyinga Murders series*

"Viking voyages, political scheming, love affairs, runes, and sea battles - what more could you want from a story? You root for the characters and learn en route, but the pages turn easily and you can expect to read late to finish this one. Now I'm waiting for the next book eagerly!" Grace Tierney, *Words the Vikings Gave Us*

"To read Jean Gill's historical novels is not so much to see into history, but to live it and breathe it with a feeling of utter authenticity." Paul Trembling, *Local Poet*

"**Made me want to read on... just one more chapter... and then another, and another. Late into the night!**" B A Morton, *Crime on the Tyne series*

"**Top quality literary historical fiction;** *a cracking story with action and adventure based on real events, plus a touch of magic. Highly recommended.*" J.G. Harlond, *The Doomsong Sword*

"**All human emotion is there, often in full conflict at times: jealousy, duty, deceit, loyalty, brutality, love, power struggles and comradeship. You might not be able to draw breath at times.**" Alison Morton, Roma Nova series

"*An amazing sea adventure that reeks of suspenseful and enthralling tales told in a Viking hall.*" Kristin Gleeson, *The Women of Ireland series*

"*A voyage that will bring murder, terrible storms and sea monsters, clashes both in battles and cultures and mystical encounters, but perhaps the greatest risk of all is treachery from within the ranks.*" Jane Davis, *The Bookseller's Wife*

"*A compelling narrative ... not only* **brings readers into the lives, dangers, intrigues and heartbreak of (Jean Gill's) characters,** *but also provides* **a memorable portrait of actual Viking life for both men and women, as they struggle to survive on land and at sea.**" Jannie Meisberger, Voice Actor

is dead and the child takes the surviving parent's name e.g. Sweyn's father was murdered and he is famous as Sweyn Asleifsson, Asleif being his mother.

- Hlif (Hlifolfsdottir) – one 12th century runic message in Maeshowe is signed 'Hlif (female name), Rognvald's housekeeper'
- Ingeborg (Inge) Asleifsdottir – Sweyn's sister, married to Thorbjorn Klerk, then to Thorfinn (Finn) Bessasson as mentioned in the Orkneyinga Saga
- Thorfinn (Finn) Bessasson – Lord of Stronsay, Inge's husband
- Sweyn Asleifsson – sea-rover extraordinaire, Inge's brother
- Thorbjorn Klerk – guardian to the young Jarl Harald, clerk and advisor to Jarl Rognvald
- Jarl Harald Maddadson – foster-son to Thorbjorn and Jarl Rognvald (see family tree)
- Jarl Erlend – claimant to Orkney
- Jarl Rognvald of Orkney (born Kali Kolsson)
- Margaret Hakonsdottir – mother of Jarl Harald, with her first husband Maddan (Earl of Caithness), then lived 'in sin' with Sweyn's brother, Gunnr
- Ingegerd (Giri, *Bleating Booty*) – Sweyn Asleifsson's wife
- Bishop William – Jerusalem-farer, Bishop of Orkney, later nicknamed 'the Old'
- Botolf – Icelandic skald living in Orkney
- Eindridi – Jerusalem-farer, Norwegian noble who inspired Rognvald to go on pilgrimage to Jerusalem
- Frakork Maddansdottir – 'the witch', alleged murderer, Sweyn's enemy, grandmother to Thorbjorn and Olvir Rosta, great-aunt to Erlend (see family tree)
- Gunni/ Gunnr Asleifsson – brother to Sweyn and Ingeborg (Inge), exiled for living 'in sin' with Jarl Harald's widowed mother, Margaret

- Hlifolf – the cook who killed Jarl Magnus (later Saint Magnus) on Jarl Hakon's orders
- Holbodi – Lord of Tiree, who sheltered Sweyn during one of his periods of exile
- Jón Fót / Jón Fót (leg/foot) Pétrsson (Jón Halt-foot) – Jerusalem-farer, married to Rognvald's sister and wounded in the leg/foot by Rognvald in the years they were enemies.
- Ingeborg – Rognvald's daughter
- Jarl Hakon of Orkney – predecessor to Jarl Rognvald, co-ruler with Jarl Magnus, whom he had killed
- Jarl Paul of Orkney – successor to Jarl Hakon, 'disappeared' by Sweyn and replaced by Rognvald
- King of Norway – Haraldr Gilli (king from 1135-1136). Then three of his sons co-ruled as kings of Norway until 1155
- Kol – Norwegian father of Jarl Rognvald, first builder of St Magnus Cathedral
- Olvir 'the Brawler' Rosta – Sweyn's enemy, grandson to Frakork
- Rognvald's wife – one of Rognvald's poems mourns his lady but she is never identified
- Saint (ex-Jarl of Orkney) Magnus – Rognvald's maternal uncle, murdered on Jarl Hakon's orders
- Other Jerusalem-farers – The leaders: Magnus, the son of Hávard, Gunni's son; Swein, Hróald's son; Thorgeir Skotakoll, Oddi the little, Thorberg Svarti, Armód the skald, Thorkel Krókauga, Grímkell of Flettuness, and Bjarni his son; Erling, Jón, his brother-in-law, Aslák and Guttorm.
- The Maeshowe rune-carvers – Hlif, Eyolfr, Kolbeinssor, Vemundr, Ottar, Ogmundr, Arnfior, Oframr Sigurdsarsonr, Helgi, Hermundr 'hard', Arnfithr 'food'.

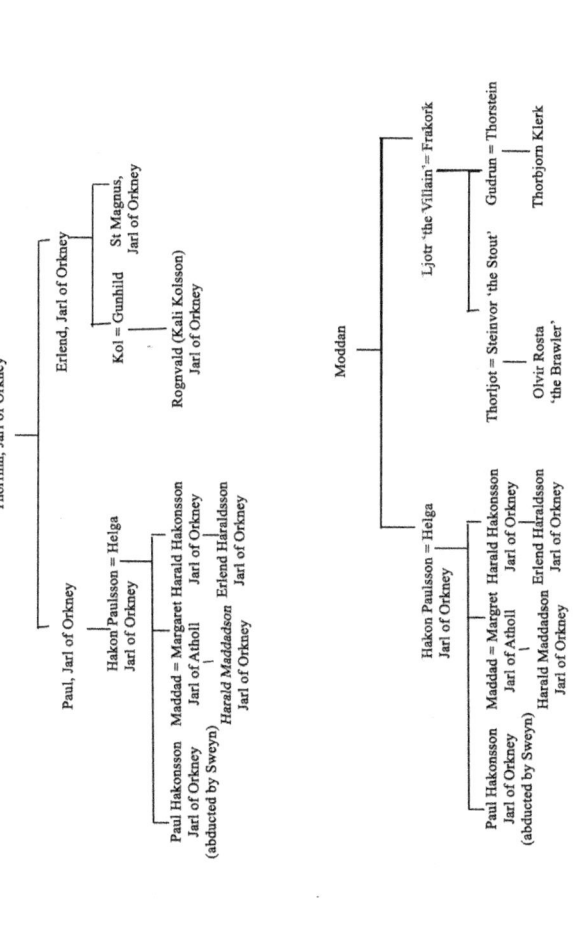

MAIN FICTIONAL CHARACTERS

- Skarfr (Cormorant) Kristinsson – orphaned ward and apprentice to the skald (poet) Botolf
- Hlif – (developed from one Maeshowe inscription) orphaned and cursed, daughter of St Magnus' murderer, Hlifolf, ward and housekeeper to Jarl Rognvald
- Brigid – woman kidnapped from Ireland, working with Fergus in Botolf's longhouse in Orkney, caring for Skarfr
- Fergus – man kidnapped from Ireland, working with Brigid in Botolf's longhouse in Orkney, caring for Skarfr
- Mamma Maria – powerful Sicilian widow
- Mouthy – old Orkneyjar sea rover

PLACE NAMES

As Skarfr and Hlif realise, geography changes with point of view. A person can face north, as is the convention in the so-called 'western' world, or face south, like al-Idrisi, and see the world differently. Place names are determined by language. As a UK citizen living in France, a kind of voluntary exile, I'm very aware that international place names don't even sound like the ones I thought everyone knew. We don't say *London* here; we say *Londres*. More frustrating still, if I say *London*, I get blank looks or am even considered stupid.

This experience has influenced my choices for place names in *Hunting the Sun*. For those parts of the story taking place in the Norman Kingdom of Sicily (*Sicilia*), I have used some Latin/ French names for flavour, (*Melita for Malta*) sometimes translated into English. The wonderfully named *Sea of Darkness* comes from the Latin *Mare Tenebrarum* for the Atlantic Ocean.

For the chapters set in Orkney, I have mainly used Norse names and have aimed for consistency within the world of *The Midwinter Dragon*, if not in all my choices. I have kept many modern English names where I saw no reason to change them.

In the 12th Century, Orkney was an earldom (jarldom) ruled by two jarls and part of the kingdom of Norway. The Jarls of Orkney also ruled over Shetland/ Hjaltland and Caithness / Ness, the north-eastern tip of what we now call Scotland.

The old letter ð, pronounced 'th', is often represented by a letter 'd' in modern spellings, so the god known to us as Odin was Óðinn in old Norse, pronounced Othin. The choice made is not consistent and the most common representation of Norðymbralanda seems to be Nordymbralanda, although we spell and pronounce the modern name, Northumberland. Steering a straight course was not easy and even Bernard Cornwell says he can't claim to be consistent, so I am in good company. Here are the modern place-names for old ones used in my series so far.

PLACES: OLD AND MODERN NAMES

MIÐJARÐARHAF/ THE MEDITERRANEAN SEA

SICILIA/ THE KINGDOM OF SICILY

Melita – Malta
Ifriqiya – North Africa (Tunisia and Morocco)

HISPANIA/ IBERIA/ AL-ANDALUS – SPAIN

THE HOLY LAND

Jórsalaheim – Jerusalem
Mikligard/ Constantinople

NORÐVEGR/ NORWAY

Biörgvin – Bergen

ORKNEYJAR/ ORKNEY

Brogar – Brodgar
Byrgisey – Birsay
Egilsey – Egilsay
Gareksey – Gairsay
Hamnavoe – Stromness
Heraðvatn – Loch of Harray
Hrolfsay – Roussay

Hrossey – Mainland
Kirkjuvágr – Kirkwall
Orkhaugr – Maeshowe
Papey Meiri – Papa Westray
Pentlandsfjord – Pentland Firth
Sandvik – Sandwick
Scalpeid – Scapa
Skalpaflói – Scapa Flow
Skarabolstadr – Scrabster
Steinnesvatn – Loch of Stenos
Strjónsey – Stronsay
Vestrey – Westray

Suðreyjar/ Hebrides, Southern Isles, Isle of Man
(sometimes the kingdom of Man and the Isles, sometimes directly ruled by Orkney or Norway)
Hjaltland/ Shetland
Skio/ Skye
(sometimes the kingdom of Man and the Isles, sometimes directly ruled by Orkney or Norway)

Ness/ Caithness

Lambaburg – Bucholie Castle
Vik – Wick

THE LAND OF ÍRLAND/ IRELAND

THE KINGDOM OF SKOTLAND/ SCOTLAND

ALBION/ ENGLAND

Nordymbraland – Northumberland
Cornweal – Cornwall

Dovre – Dover
Dunholm – Durham
Grimsby – Grimsby
Jorvik – York
Londres – London
Norich – Norwich
Tamyse – (River) Thames

Novgorod / Russia
Snaeland/ the Old Country/ Iceland

For Mathilda,
who wants to go sailing

CHAPTER ONE

SKARFR, PALERMO, SICILIA

February 1151

'I saw your wife in the Tiraz,' stated George of Antioch, Emir of Emirs, Commander of the Sicilian fleet. He looked like a Bible prophet from a Book of Hours, his white locks floating in the breeze and his bearded chin jutting out in accusation of the tall Northman imposed on him by King Roger.

Such innocuous words. A woman visiting the royal silk workshop known as the Tiraz. Innocuous words. Unless a man was aware that the silk workers earned more of their income from lying on their luxurious sheets than from weaving them. No respectable woman would visit such a place, not least from fear of catching her husband in flagrante.

The men nearest their emir paused in conversation and stopped selecting their weapons prior to a routine training session in the courtyard of the king's palace in Palermo. The hush rippled outwards.

What would be the response from this foreign warrior, who'd proved himself over and over in the five months since his dragon ship had left for the Holy Land without him? He'd proved himself as a warrior, as a sailor and as a navigator, and could make passable conversation in the three languages considered civilised in this most sophisticated of kingdoms. And still George baited him.

'I do believe this man trusts his wife,' the Emir sneered, including all within hearing in the mockery of such innocence. 'Do you, Skarfr? Do you trust your wife?' One corner of his mouth creased upwards in a cynical half-smile.

Skarfr knew there was a trap but he couldn't work out what it was. He wanted no part in these games, especially with the boy listening. 'Yes,' he said, adding, 'As all men should.'

The smile hardened. 'There is a difference between trust and complacency. One has been earned and the other is ignorance or cowardice. I've told you I saw your wife at the Tiraz,' he repeated. 'You can no longer hide behind ignorance.' He made the sign of the horns above his head, drawing more laughter.

The Northman understood full well the implication of the crude gesture but before he could reply, George's second in command, Philip of Mahdia, interjected, 'As long as you only *saw* her there.' He gyrated his significant belly suggestively to make his meaning clear.

Raucous laughter and insults to his manhood threw the provocation back at Philip in the traditional banter all eunuchs endured. The Emir's second in command had his compensations for such abuse, not least of them the privilege of insulting George with impunity.

As the laughter died, the tension increased. George was still staring at the Northman.

'I wouldn't want my wife to visit the silk workshop,' he persisted.

'In case she saw you there,' quipped Philip, once more showing the Northman a way out of the confrontation.

However, to make a crude jest at his wife's expense was more difficult for Skarfr the Northman, not only because of loyalty to his wife but also because of the boy at his side.

The men waited.

When Skarfr finally spoke, it was not to George but to the boy, whose face was screwed up in puzzlement. 'This too is training, Seaborn, to have words flung at us like stones, and to defend ourselves without the anger which clouds judgement. How do we defend ourselves?'

His brow clearing, the lad held up his small wooden shield in front of him, with two hands. The metal boss flashed sunlight into George's eyes, making him blink and step backwards.

Encouraged by his success, the little warrior growled, 'Graaaaagh!' in fierce imitation of a battle cry. Skarfr hid a smile and adjusted the child's hands, so he could hold the shield with his left hand and a dagger, also wooden, in his right.

To his men's delight, the Emir bowed his head in a lightning change of mood, and held his sword out-stretched, hilt first. 'Faced with such an intrepid enemy, I have no choice but to surrender,' he said, shaking his head sadly.

'Sea-born, tell the Emir what your mother would be doing at the silk workshop,' Skarfr told the boy.

The shield was lowered to reveal a beaming face. 'That's easy, Sire. She was buying silk! She's a trader.' The pride in his voice would have disarmed men made of steel, not just wearing it.

This time the laughter was with Skarfr, not against him.

George sheathed his sword and shook his head again. 'Why didn't I think of that?'

'Because you don't know my mother.'

'That is undoubtedly true,' conceded the Emir, apparently finished with his jibes and disdaining the opportunity to make 'know' suggestive. But then he added, 'I wonder if the man you call father really knows her either,' and he straightened to better aim his words at Skarfr.

Riding the attention, Sea-born took the opportunity to explain. 'He really is my father now and I don't look like my parents because I'm a foster-son, born from the sea when—'

'The Emir knows the story,' Skarfr interrupted his son gently.

'Oh.' The child's shield drooped. 'More *training words*.'

'Yes,' agreed Skarfr. 'And after the training words comes the action. You go over there by the wall and watch carefully what we do, so you can tell me afterwards. You can make the movements with your dagger but don't throw it.'

As Sea-born went to his place, safely out of range of both words and weapons, Skarfr looked a query at the Emir, who nodded and took up a position more commanding but equally distant from the action as the boy's. After all, this was what the king wanted from his emir: that he should extract every iota of military know-how from the Northman to better prepare his own forces.

This was what made Sicilia the power which had defied both Byzantium and Christendom: the king's collection of skilled men. Whatever their reason for landing on the island, few left, whether they were doctors or philosophers, warriors or map-makers. King Roger tailored his rewards to the man, as he had done for a Greek youth fleeing from a jealous ruler in Ifriqiya, the man who now had a white beard and was Emir of Emirs.

George raised his voice to address his sailors. 'This is today's situation. Your ship is engaging with the enemy. They saw you coming and their mast is laid down in its cradle so you can't easily damage sail or mast. You have hurled whatever missiles your ship carried, whether quarrels from fixed ballistas, short javelins, stones, fire-arrows, rotten fruit, or your mother's stale bread—' Pause for the expected laughter. 'You get the idea. You are within boarding distance. What do you do?'

Now he had experience of sailing a dromond, not just of attacking one, Skarfr knew how close the two ships had to be to send grappling irons across the gap between them. At least when both ships were multi-decked they were equal in height. Boarding the dromond from the Orkneyjar dragon ships had required more inventive tactics. *His* inventive tactics.

The saga story of a man climbing the sheer wooden side to lower the anchor, then ropes to his fellows. A story of vicious hand-to-hand fighting and of a few hostages, including one small boy, who found his enemy less cruel than his birth-father, who never went back to his people. Sea-born's story.

Answers to George's questions flew thicker than imaginary

missiles across the training yard. The gist was that men in ships with a spur on the bow should use it to ride over the oars and destroy them. In the few old ships with rams, blunt force was an option, as long as care was taken not to jam the two ships and sink with the enemy. But most battles would be won or lost in close combat.

'Put the ships in a clinch tighter than you had with your first girl,' George summarised. Pause. Laughter. 'Use the grappling irons, tie a rope or chain to axe or spear, whatever sticks to the other ship. Then board!'

The men roared a battle-cry.

'And,' continued George, 'our Northman is going to work on your hand-to-hand fighting. Which weapons, Skarfr?' Now training had begun in earnest, George had lost interest in harrying, and treated him as he would any skilled shipmate.

'All of you, take up a spear or axe, and a shield,' ordered Skarfr. He had no intention of cracking jokes, having learned from previous attempts that Orkneyjar humour did not translate well. Practical skills, however, worked in any language. 'The armed warriors and men on the open deck board first. Half the oarsmen come up to the top deck and pick up their shields from the bulwarks. They're the reserve, if needed.'

He picked up an axe and a shield, demonstrating his words. 'We practised how to swing and cut with an axe, which you can use on the rigging as well as on the enemy. The spear has the advantage of length and can secure the grappling of the two ships. But both weapons can be used before you're within reach of your enemy's hand weapons.'

He whirled and embedded the axe in a wooden post. The men nearest him flinched. 'And it's unexpected. Even if you know an opponent can throw spear, axe or knife, you won't know it's coming if he's fast enough in shifting his grip. Watch.'

His back to the men, he showed in slow motion the swing and shift that turned into a throwing hold.

'Now you do it too,' he yelled. 'But stop short of the throw if you want the next part of training. I'm not much use with an axe in my back.'

Again and again, Skarfr swung and shifted, until the movement was memorised in the men's muscles and all they needed was greater fluidity and speed.

George inspected the men while they sweated in their motley armour, pointing out holes in a padded jacket, an ill-fitting helmet or a sloppy stance. The oarsmen wore less armour than the warriors but all the protective gear was supposed to be battleworthy, like the weapons — and the men themselves. Any puffing or red faces drew the Emir's acid comments. Behind his back, the men joked about who'd come under 'Greek fire' in training and they didn't mean the fearsome Byzantine weapon, an evil-smelling substance that turned sea-water to flames. Or so Skarfr had heard.

He too inspected the men but he stuck to the objective of his lesson and gave as much praise as criticism, pointing out those worthy of emulation.

Then, just as some were getting blasé, he made them pause and told them, 'None of you would beat an Orkneyman with axe or spear because there is an element lacking in your training.'

All eyes were on him.

'Watch,' he said again. He whirled the axe from right to left, changed grip, and threw. The axe bit deep into the wood and splinters flew. But they'd seen that already.

Skarfr took the axe in the other hand, swung it right to left, changed grip, and hurled it with his left hand. It flew just as true and stuck just as deep.

'Work your other arm and hand,' Skarfr told them. 'Orkneymen use both. Most of you favour one arm and hand — your muscles are more developed on that side as well as being revealed by your stance and action. Be unpredictable.'

As before, Skarfr turned his back on them so he could model the action with the opposite hand from his first demonstration. But then he alternated facing them and turning his back, always completing the motion in his left hand, so they could use whichever arm they wanted to work on — or both.

George could no longer identify those unfit, as everyone was panting except Sea-born, who swung his arms with boundless enthusiasm, like a storm-blown windmill.

One turn each at the post, first throwing with one hand, then with the other, was the last exercise and Skarfr left them to it, while he sorted the remaining weapons into piles to be returned to chests on the vessels they came from.

The second most powerful man in the courtyard bent over a pile of spears and took the chance to murmur, 'If you have the boy gelded, he could go as far in the king's court as I have. There is a monastery on the coast of Ifriqiya, where the monks are skilled in the process.'

A man did not remind Philip of Mahdia of the stories circulating about how many children died in 'the process'. Besides, it was true that the king favoured eunuchs. Their loyalty to the throne was more reliable and, without progeny, their ambition was limited.

'It is not our way,' Skarfr replied, wooden-faced, carefully *not* imagining Sea-born as a eunuch. The innocent subject of Philip's proposal was out of harm's way, hurtling along the length of the yard then stopping short and jabbing his wooden dagger upwards, his mouth working in silent ferocity.

About eight years old, was Hlif's best guess, older than she first thought, as she watched Sea-born recover from malnutrition and abuse. Old enough to be a useful ship's boy but young enough to accept wooden practice weapons. Old enough to have suffered and young enough to accept the shelter of his mother's arms. *His foster-mother's arms*, Skarfr corrected himself. Why did he think of Sea-born as Hlif's child but hold back some part of himself as a father? The gods knew he did his best for the child they'd given him. But there it was. Sea-born had another man's hair and eyes, even if he'd clung to Skarfr rather than follow that other man back to his Muslim people.

The Emir broke into his thoughts. 'You've made yourself useful in the training yard but it's a different matter at sea. We sail tomorrow at dawn to practise on the open water and I want you to navigate my ship. Bring your sunstone, bring your helm, weapons and wear full armour — and leave the child behind.'

I'm the one who's only useful as a ship's boy, thought Skarfr ruefully, rubbed the wrong way by the continual demand that he should prove himself. No longer Jarl Rognvald's finest warrior and skald. Condemned to George's harassment. The Emir's emphasis on what he should bring for what was just a training exercise was patronising, no doubt meant to ridicule him for being earnest and over-prepared, a beginner. The sunstone was merely another potential source of humiliation.

'You won't need a sunstone if the weather's like this,' observed Skarfr, jerking his head towards the yellow circle overhead. He left a small pause before adding, 'Sire.'

Two white brows drew together, noting the near-insolence. 'If necessary, you'll navigate blindfolded and shut in the captain's tent to show what you can do. Or what you can't.'

Faced with this impossible prospect, Skarfr grinned. Nothing could make him more ridiculous than the initiation tasks he'd been set in the last five months. The worst was when he'd walked for an hour to arrange lodgings for a lady in a holy community. Holy the community might be but it consisted of lepers. The doorkeeper had laughed with dark humour and hidden face at the name of the 'lady', whose afflictions rivalled his own.

'As God wills,' returned Skarfr, knowing the pious George could have no riposte. 'Sire.'

The Emir grunted and marched off.

Skarfr touched the hard metal shape of his hammer amulet through his tunic and shirt and sent an urgent plea to Thórr. *Clouds,* he prayed, *and true direction.* If the Emir learned that this would be the first time Skarfr used the sunstone other than for practice, sharp 'training words' could be expected.

CHAPTER TWO

SKARFR, PALERMO, SICILIA

Flushed and satisfied with the morning overall, Skarfr was indulgent with Sea-born as they lingered in the yard so the boy could demonstrate what he'd learned. Skarfr overlooked a few errors in the boy's stance and grip, preferring to comment on all that was well-replicated. He would not beat knowledge into the boy as had been done to him and he was proud of his foster-son, whose exuberance was even higher than at the start of the day.

'You behaved in a fitting manner this morning.' Such words did not come readily to his tongue as he'd never heard them addressed to him when he was a boy, but they had more impact than a gift of a carved dragon ship or wooden shield and Sea-born glowed with the praise.

The boy was keen to show he'd understood everything he'd observed. 'Once you've thrown the axe, you are vulnerable. And so you must throw to kill, and keep your dagger ready, in case you didn't.'

'Yes,' agreed Skarfr, surprised and pleased by this summary of his lesson. They walked through a passageway that linked one palace tower with another, where their ways would part. Skarfr was expected by the map-maker al-Idrisi and Sea-born had lessons to go to, with the monks of St John of the Hermits.

'And you will kill those men for their hurtful words, when the time is right,' Sea-born added, 'as I will kill the man who called himself my father.'

Surprised once more, but *not* pleased by Sea-born's astuteness, Skarfr began to explain why killing was not the answer to everything but his foster-son had glimpsed a friend disappearing through the door to the street and was evidently not listening.

'Can I go swimming?' he asked.

Even in February, the waters of the Miðjarðarhaf, called the Middle Sea by the Sicilians, were warmer than the lochs of Orkneyjar ever became. Safer too than the treacherous currents and icy cold in which Skarfr had become the second-best swimmer on the islands. Second to Jarl Rognvald, who'd trained in the freezing waves of Norðvegr fjords, daring the sea caves of Doll. Jarl Rognvald, who'd saved Skarfr from drowning once, when their loyalty each to the other was untainted.

Swimming is a manly skill and good for the boy, thought Skarfr. This gentle sea would teach him well and maybe one day he would master fiercer, colder waters. If they went back home.

The homily against murder would have to wait. 'Yes,' he said and Sea-born scooted off to join his friend.

Skarfr sighed inwardly, ignoring the steps to the upper stories and ducking under a lintel to enter the map-maker's chambers. None of the internal doors in the palace were made for a man of his height and it wouldn't be the first time he'd banged his head.

Being a father was tricky. Was it harder to be a foster-father? Would he ever think of Sea-born as his son, without the qualifier 'foster'? He must talk to Hlif about the boy's reactions to taunts. And about his reactions to the powerful men who'd made those taunts.

He walked past the solid silver disc on its wheeled platform. Taller than he was and the same width, four times a man's weight. Al-Idrisi said this would one day be one of the miracles of the civilised world, a 'planisphere' showing a simplified version of his geographical work. There was nothing as yet engraved on the side facing Skarfr and his preoccupation with the Emir's jibes left little room for scientific curiosity.

She was ordering silk of course.

The words troubled Skarfr. His wife had not told him she was going to the silk workshop. She knew full well its reputation and what that meant for her own. She knew he would disapprove, if not ban the visit completely — and he had learned early in their relationship that a ban was not well received. So the Emir's implied question was festering in his mind. Why had she gone to the silk workshop?

She was ordering silk of course.

He ducked his head again and went into al-Idrisi's scriptorium, where the Muslim geographer was standing at a lectern, adding a row of black squiggles to the fleet already in neat formation on the vellum page, which was tilted at an angle to avoid smudges. Squiggles that were writing in Arabic, which didn't even look like the Christian letters Skarfr knew from Hlif's household accounts, and from the monks' illuminated books on Papey Meiri. Nor did they look like the succinct runes any true Orkneyman would use for personal matters.

The book entitled *Pleasant Journeys into Faraway Lands* was al-Idrisi's current obsession. One day this work in progress would join his others on the shelf, including a herbal which listed medicinal plants and their uses, composed and indexed in twelve languages.

Skarfr was fascinated by the very idea of written and illustrated works, which were the domain of monks and clerks in Orkneyjar. He had expressed polite admiration for the way the compendium was organised by Arabic letters, in the order they were taught to children, but he wondered whether writing made scholars lazy. Would he have memorised all the sagas and classical poetry he could recite without hesitation, if they'd been recorded in a book? He doubted it. And if any man able to read could access such treasures, nobody would appreciate a skald's skills and training.

A foolish thought. Nobody in Sicilia *did* appreciate a skald's skills and training.

'*As-salaam-alaikum*, Skarfr.' Al-Idrisi acknowledged the visitor without taking his eyes off his meticulous work. He dipped his quill in the ink-pot and continued the row, finishing on the left and starting again on the right-hand side, a careful space below the previous row. A most un-Christian way of covering parchment, right to left.

'*Wa-alaikum-salaam*,' Skarfr gave the polite response al-Idrisi had taught him was acceptable for non-Muslims to utter.

He waited until al-Idrisi had come to the end of the page, when he had to wait for the ink to dry.

The map-maker placed the quill in its rest and turned his attention to the Orkneyman.

'You have come at just the right moment. Before I make a fair copy of my notes regarding England, I want to check that they match your observations during your voyages. But first, look at this marvellous new invention.'

He indicated a glass container, a handspan in height, standing on a tabletop. Then he inverted the object, and sand began to trickle from the inverted top cup through the narrow neck to the cup below.

'Do you know how to use a sandglass, Skarfr?'

Al-Idrisi correctly took silence for ignorance and carried on. 'This is an hour-measure. When the sand has run through to the bottom glass, an hour has passed.'

He picked it up and passed it to Skarfr, who watched the top cone emptying of sand.

'Are there smaller ones to gauge a more fleeting moment?' wondered Skarfr aloud, holding the magical instrument.

Al-Idrisi laughed. 'If you ask the craftsman, he will tell you that the size of glass is not the only factor in measuring the hour. The size of the grains of sand and the width of the neck also change the speed with which the sand drops. Don't ask me how he knows what the outcome will be — you'll have to ask him.' He retrieved the sandglass and placed it carefully back on the table. 'And it needs to be on a steady surface or the rate of flow changes.'

Skarfr's head hurt from so much science. He had lived thirty years without needing any of these items that Sicilians considered so exciting. Next, they would claim they were indispensable and sell them for outrageous profits. 'But what use is it?' he asked.

A scathing look was the first response. 'Discovery for its own sake is what matters, finding out how things work.' Al-Idrisi searched for a comparison. 'Like you finding new lands.'

It wasn't like that at all. Besides, Skarfr was happy if his navigation led him to his destination. The thought of setting out to sea just to know what was out there made him shudder. The whole point of hiring local pilots was to *know* what was out there, and not get lost or shipwrecked.

'But this is also a tool with many uses,' conceded al-Idrisi. 'A man's work could be timed by turns of the sandglass. What you at sea call 'a watch' could be three turns or eight for the night watchmen in the city.'

Skarfr imagined the sandglass attached in some way to the wale or the mast, heaving up and down with the waves, the work of watching and turning it.

Ridiculous!

He didn't want to be rude to al-Idrisi so he merely said, 'It would not be practical at sea but we don't need an additional measure anyway. We can rely on the movements of the sun, the moon and the stars. A man's stomach is the best timekeeper. And on land, there are the church bells.'

'And the call to prayer for my people,' al-Idrisi reminded him. 'Which would be more precise if such a sandglass were used.'

Skarfr thought about such precision, shrugged and dismissed it. 'I don't see the benefits of measuring ever smaller units. It seems to me that such tools deprive men of their skills and weigh them down with too many things they think they need. Or else drive them to consult people who claim to be experts. Until they pay lawyers for every aspect of life.'

The map-maker's forehead wrinkled into a frown. 'If you live here long enough, you might become civilised. But, as the poet Ibn Hamdis says,

> *Take hold of the reins and with*
> *the steady pace of camels at night*
> *stride towards your goals and always reach them.*

As al-Idrisi moved to his lectern and opened the book that was his work in progress, Skarfr gathered that the somewhat obscure quotation meant the discussion of the sandglass was over.

'Now, where did we get to last time?' al-Idrisi muttered to himself. 'Ah yes, England, Seventh Clime, Second Section. I want to read this to you.'

Without wasting time on small talk, al-Idrisi put Skarfr to work. As he read from his notes, he paused occasionally to check that Skarfr found no fault with the geographical description, or to explain an Arabic word in Latin or Frankish, or to show an illustration. 'This section, the Second of the Seventh Clime contains the part of the Dark Sea where lies England, a large island in the shape of an ostrich's head. There be found prosperous towns, high mountains, perennial rivers and plains. It is extremely fertile, inhabited by brave, active and decisive men; but winter is perpetual there.'

The description continued with distances between key towns, both inland and coastal: Wareham and Dartmouth on the extremity known as Cornweal 'shaped like a beak'; Winchester, Shoreham with its shipbuilding, Dovre, Londres, the river Tamysc, Yarmouth, Norich...

Skarfr kept nodding, as he knew none of these towns or distances, but he recognised the journey the seaports traced from the west to east coast of England, the reverse of the one he'd made the previous year, sailing the strait between England and Frankish territories to reach what al-Idrisi called the Sea of Darkness.

At first, in these sessions with al-Idrisi, Skarfr had resented the geographer's corrections of his names for places. Remembering that the Miðjarðarhaf was the Middle Sea was easy enough, but other names didn't even sound like those he knew. And why should al-Idrisi's names be thought better than those his people had coined? A sea was only the North Sea if you went there from the south. To the men of Norðvegr, such a sea was the West Sea. It was as confusing as al-Idrisi's upside down maps.

Then Skarfr realised that this too was the price of exile. Not just to speak with your tongue tied by a foreign language but that even names and directions shifted shape. So many ways to be rendered foolish and vulnerable. Al-Idrisi saw *him* as the foreigner, whereas to Skarfr it was the other way around.

However, he swallowed his pride and learned quickly, so that he would be rewarded more often by al-Idrisi sharing his expertise and wincing less frequently. There was magic in book-travel and he wove the details of the geographer's work into the saga he would tell one day, of the Orkneyjar pilgrims who'd sailed to Jórsalaheim. He could see the world from different points of view, just as he could turn around to see south ahead of him and north behind, as in al-Idrisi's maps.

Even in exile, he could not help continuing to compose the great work with which Jarl Rognvald had tasked him. Every time al-Idrisi read an excerpt from his book, he fed Skarfr's dreams and brought back memories of travel across seas, sagas and seamen's tales. He wanted to hear more about Ifriqiya and Mikligard, or Constantinople as he must now call it.

Mikligard. The very name conjured up the tales told by one of Rognvald's captains, who'd been in the Emperor's Varangian Guard. For the chance of sailing against the might of the Byzantine Empire in a Sicilian war fleet, of regaining his honour, Skarfr would do whatever it took. Even if that meant hours and days of training with the Emir or listening to the dross of al-Idrisi's boring details, for the sake of the nuggets of true gold that would sometimes appear.

What saga verse he could make from a sea-battle against Byzantium.

> *Riding red-maned sea-stallions,*
> *fleet against fire flung far*
> *from prow-towers, hearts high*
> *the island warriors reach the walls.*
> *The city falls.*

He savoured the double meaning of *fleet*. Wouldn't it be extraordinary to see Constantinople fall? He must ask Emir George more about the fire-projectiles the Byzantines used on their ships. Flung from a catapult, he guessed, erected on the ship's prow. But the stories men told, of flaming seas, were beyond belief.

'Skarfr!' Al-Idrisi called his attention back and reread the last sentence. 'From Lincoln in the interior to Grimsby on the coast is a hundred miles by the river which passes through the centre of both towns and empties into the sea.'

'Yes, I remember the river mouth at Grimsby,' Skarfr said. 'The port is on the south and a ferry crosses to the new dwellings across the estuary.' *Grimsby, where Pilot was murdered and where Hlif taught him to dream-walk.* 'Hlif, my wife, said that they trade in top quality wool. And there's a trade route from Jorvik. I don't know whether it goes through Lincoln.'

Al-Idrisi's sleeve fell back, exposing one brown, very hairy arm, as he dismissed such details.

'That is enough about England.'

Skarfr volunteered, 'I know a little of the kingdom of Skotland, to the north of England, and a lot about my home islands, the jarldom of Orkneyjar.' Dazzling open skies and grey-green fields of barley and wheat, stretching without the interruption of mountain or forest between the sweetwaters of lochs and the saltwaters of wild seas. The Irish thralls, now his friends, Fergus and Brigid, tending his hearth and his farm, keeping home safe for his return.

'Yes, yes, those are in the First Section of the Seventh Clime but they are of little interest. You can tell me about these places after we put the most important features on the maps and I complete those illustrations. Let me show you Constantinople and the Golden Horn on the whole picture, as much as we have so far.'

Constantinople. At last.

CHAPTER THREE

SKARFR, PALERMO, SICILIA

Al-Idrisi picked up a sheaf of illustrated pages to take with him into the adjoining chamber and Skarfr followed, feeling it his duty to point out, 'But I've never been there so how can I tell whether you have it right?'

'This is not about where you've been but about where King Roger wishes you to go.'

'Indeed,' said a deep voice. Studying the silver planisphere, which stretched up higher than his head, was a man of medium height with wavy hair, brown dusted with grey, and a neatly trimmed triangular beard, hair and beard both well-oiled. His informal robes were richer in embroidery than Jarl Rognvald's ceremonial finery and there was no mistaking his status. He exuded power, as much through his studied nonchalance as through the presence of two bodyguards at the outer doorway, their spears crossed.

'My lord king,' Skarfr echoed al-Idrisi's reverential greeting and sketched a bow.

King Roger regularly visited his map-maker, who seemed to welcome his input rather than resent the interruption. He was studying the reverse side of the planisphere. When Skarfr joined him, he could see that the astrological signs of the zodiac were engraved on the silver surface. The design had begun to take shape.

Sunlight through the narrow window was reflected from the planisphere and etched the king's face with silvered planes and dark lines, cut deeper than the stars of Gemini or Scorpio on the metal surface Lines carved by grief.

They said he still mourned the wife he'd lost fifteen years ago; it had been unthinkable he should marry again, nor did he need to, his line assured by four healthy adult sons. But the unthinkable had indeed happened and forced his dutiful second marriage. When the third son died — his eldest — the king chose a bride of suitable lineage and set to the work of begetting more heirs. Two years later, the young queen Sybille was pregnant and the realm could expect a new prince in the autumn. Or, with less joy, a princess.

Small wonder that King Roger, the second of his name, brooded on mortality and was obsessed with his legacy, that of his kingdom and that of a scientific project that would carry his name into the future.

'You've started the celestial representation,' he observed.

'Yes. I want the terrestrial map completed before I transfer its main aspects to the other side of the planisphere,' said al-Idrisi as he knelt to lay out the parchment pages on the floor. With his expert eye he put the map together, with Sicilia and the Middle Sea at the centre.

Skarfr had spent enough time with al-Idrisi to recognise the shapes of the coast hugged by Rognvald's ships on the long voyage from his home in the north, somewhere off the bottom of the vellum pages, up southwards towards the strait which led to the Middle Sea.

Never having seen a map before this one, he'd once asked al-Idrisi why south was at the top. In his mind's eye he'd always imagined north at the top of the cardinal direction points. Not for the first time, Skarfr had been treated to the downturned mouth which meant, 'Your ignorance is beyond belief.' But al-Idrisi's tone had been that of a kind teacher when he'd replied, 'That is the correct way. All the great geographers in the Arabic tradition have represented the world in such a manner. As have the Chinese.' All Skarfr knew of the Chinese was that they traded silk but he knew better than to ask too many questions. The map was the thing. And the map was a marvel.

Surely, al-Idrisi had flown in a bird's form over land and sea to present the craggy rocks, harbours and river mouths from above, reduced to black outlines and filled in with at least six colours. Skarfr's spirit bird, the cormorant, would see the world in such a way as she flapped overhead. But a cormorant did not soar over mountains and al-Idrisi had read aloud from his book about peaks that took days to climb and cross, higher than the fjord cliffs of Norðvegr, the realms of ravens and eagles.

Skarfr glanced at the map-maker, could imagine his golden skin changing to feathers, his curved nose sharpening to a beak and the leathery hands clutching an invisible branch in their talons. But he knew better than to express such fancies to this man of science, who was also a Muslim. One who subdivided all animal and plant life into categories, denying what was self-evident to Skarfr: that the gods took what form they chose and might be in any tree or creature. From ash and elm were born man and woman, and the sap rising linked every living being.

Here in Sicilia, a wise Northman would keep such thoughts to himself. As if Bishop William of Orkneyjar were looking over his shoulder, he would attend the White Christ's church as a king's man. And as one who followed the White Christ in the Sicilian manner, he would show outward respect for the heathen ways of the majority of the king's subjects, for their mosques and muezzin calls to prayer. Outward respect and inward pity, for they were damned.

Showing no concern over his damnation, the turbanned geographer pointed to the upper coast of the Middle Sea. 'Here we are, and over here to the east is Constantinople, on the gulf called the Golden Horn.' He traced the sea route to the left. 'Two years ago, Emir George raided the Byzantine Empire's holdings in the Gulf of Corinth—'

The king's deep voice added, 'And in Corinth he claimed the holy relics of Saint Theodore for Sicilia.'

'Then he ventured as far as Thebes to bring back honour and riches,' continued al-Idrisi.

'And silk workers for the Tiraz,' murmured Skarfr.

King Roger gave one of his rare smiles as he crouched on the ground, peering at the map with them. 'May God reward him for that alone,' he said, 'but his many successes were not capped with the one most desirable and most difficult. His attempt last year on Constantinople itself was not without impact, with arrows fired on the very palace of the Emperor and villas sacked, but he could not land even one of his forty warships.'

'The harbour is defended by a bigger fleet?' asked Skarfr, looking at the horn-shaped gulf on the map. He'd never taken part in a sea battle against more than one ship and the prospect rippled the dragon tattoo on his arm in anticipation. Would it really come to pass?

Riding red-maned sea-stallions.

The other two men exchanged looks. 'They don't need a bigger fleet,' said the king. 'They will lift the chain across the harbour mouth and in the time it takes us to cut through the metal, the Emperor's fleet will form a line against our crescent. If we sail close enough, they will set the very sea on fire and we will lose all our ships and all our men.'

'That's not possible,' said Skarfr, but he could see from their faces that it was. The tales he'd heard were not just sailors' exaggerations. 'What is this thing they use?'

'A Byzantine secret. Those who have seen it and survived say dragons shoot flame from the prows of their ships. Each dragon has two or three keepers and at the signal, they call the flame to life.'

'Then we should capture one of their ships and harness their dragon's power,' said Skarfr.

The king shrugged. 'It has been done. All we found in the dragon's place was a siphon and bellows, powders. But we could not reproduce the deadly capacity to fire the seas. Nor do we know how the keepers kindle the flame. This is why I want new thoughts when we sail against Constantinople this year. *Your* thoughts and skills. Your jarl spoke of your skills as a warrior.' He glanced at the dragon on Skarfr's arm. 'We need a miracle.'

'I will serve you as I promised, Sire.' Every hair on Skarfr's body prickled with omen. Was this honour meant for him? He so much wanted it. Surely he could make it so! 'But I am still learning about the kingdom I serve. What is your grievance against the Empire?'

The king stood, his jaw clenched. 'The heretic Manuel Komnenos,' he spat the name, 'disputes our territory and our very right to the anointed rank of king. He allies with Venezia and the Germans against us, allowing the false Pope, Eugene, to wage war against our mainland territories. We are attacked on all sides, accused of cowardice and heresy for protecting our citizens of many faiths, for resisting the pressure to join in a doomed crusade in the Holy Land. And yet he, the greatest heretic of them all, gains favour by hosting pilgrims and crusaders. Nobody comments on how convenient it is for Byzantium when crusading armies fall prey to Seljuks and Turks when they leave the poisoned hospitality of Constantinople. Don't ask me why we must rise against the Empire! Ask yourself how we shall win!'

Breathing shallowly, the king turned to his map-maker, making a visible effort to regain his composure as he spoke. 'Lord Skarfr has been invaluable in our project this winter. His knowledge and understanding have added precious detail to our book and to our maps.'

Skarfr had not been praised in such a way since his liege lord had sentenced him to exile in Sicilia then packaged him as a gift to King Roger. It did not bode well. But he *had* gained fat purses from the work he had done so far and he'd been well treated by the king. So far.

'The Emir tells me that Skarfr's skills as a warrior were not overstated by his jarl.' King Roger added, 'Or by his wife.'

Skarfr remembered Hlif adding to the array of qualities he was supposed to have, as listed by Jarl Rognvald. Such praise still made him feel as if he were a ghost at his own funeral pyre, listening to his eulogy. Except that the living were expected to live up to their reputation, however exaggerated.

There was no escape and when the king addressed him directly, Skarfr met his eyes, wondering how to answer politely without making any commitment.

'Men of talent come to these shores for many reasons.' Roger gestured to Sicilia at the centre of the map on the floor. 'Usually, they think they are heading elsewhere. But, inevitably, they find that they were mistaken.

'You are such a man of talent and, when the Emir trusts you as a navigator, which I'm sure will be as easy for you as the other tasks you've undertaken, you will have a place of honour in the fleet. It is springtime and our ships will sail very soon. I want you to play a key role in our campaign in Ifriqiya. Later in the year, you will be a leader in our campaign against Byzantium.

'And between campaigns, in summer and in winter, you shall have honour in our court, with the freedom of the library. The poets have invited you to join them, to discuss their work and your own. You will find an intellectual life here that will inspire you.'

The king paused.

Honour. Riches. Sea battles and foreign lands. The stuff of sagas — and wasn't his destiny 'to make sagas', as the cormorant had prophesied to his mother? *Poetry too* — in a foreign tongue, his own voice silenced.

There could be only one response. 'I am overwhelmed by your words.' Skarfr was courtier enough to bow. 'My gratitude is deeper than I can express.'

He hadn't said yes. But he hadn't said no.

A king did not anticipate or accept 'No.'

'Then that's settled,' said Roger. 'I shall return tomorrow.' He nodded to his companions and, his long robes swirling, he swept out, followed by his impassive bodyguards.

There was much food for thought, but of one thing Skarfr was certain. No fire-breathing Byzantine prow-dragon could bring about his doom. Dragons were his creatures, ever since his victory over the beast in an ancient Orkneyjar tomb. The tattoo on his arm was his talisman and, whether miracle or magic, he'd proved its power often enough.

CHAPTER FOUR

BRIGID, NESS

Babies were born every day but rarely lived after spending two days in the mutual torture of an ageing mother's labour. Thanks to the skills of the women servants in Lord Thorbjorn's holding on Ness, not only did the baby survive but so did the ageing mother, Brigid. Equally triumphant and terrified, Brigid gave thanks aloud to both her namesake saint and to the goddess Brid, to be on the safe side, as the baby latched onto her nipple.

'You were shouting other names these last two days,' pointed out Ellisif drily, 'and none of them to be said in polite company.'

Brigid managed a weak smile. 'Once again, I owe you my life,' she told the woman who protected all the servants from their master's dark moods and who'd acted as her midwife. 'Both our lives.'

The other woman present reached out a tentative hand to touch the newborn.

'She won't bite, Wulfhild,' Ellisif told the fey girl who was more at home on the bogland that surrounded them than in such a domestic situation.

'So many colours,' Wulfhild marvelled, 'Blue and purple and shiny, not like she'll be one of us when she's grown.'

'Well, you've seen her father as well as her mother and she'll be blue-eyed, black-haired Irish before she's crawling. You mark my words.' Ellisif's words were sharp but her eyes were soft as she contemplated the commonplace miracle she had brought into the world.

'She's beautiful,' murmured Brigid, as the brief surge of birthing energy left her and exhaustion took its place.

'Rest now,' said Ellisif. 'We'll look after your daughter. She needs to sleep too.' She gently detached the baby from the nipple and wrapped her tightly in a simple brown woollen shawl.

Brigid shut her eyes, warm under her own blue and green checked shawl, as big as a blanket, a gift from Ellisif when she'd joined this complicated household. She trusted Ellisif and Wulfhild with her own life and even with her baby's. Their loyalty to each other had been tested time and again, servants standing together against the harsh landscape and the dangerous tempers in the big house.

There was something important Brigid needed to remember before she dropped into the sleep she desperately needed. Something important for her baby...

Fergus. She had to get word to Fergus that he was a father. But he must stay away for his own safety. Stay away because of That One.

Thorbjorn.

She forced her eyes open.

'Is he home?'

The women exchanged glances. No need to name him. 'No,' Ellisif soothed her. 'He's staying with Jarl Harald. They'll be making the most of their last hunting weeks before the return to Orkneyjar. Another few weeks and we'll be rid of him for the summer. Don't fret yourself. All will be well.'

Of course. It was February and they only had to survive until March, or April at worst, when the weather would be calm enough for Orkneymen to sail from their winter homes on the mainland of Ness back to the islands of Orkneyjar. Jarl Harald would have to leave his hunting and inland forests in Ness to return to his realm of wide waters, barley-fields and belligerent karls. And with Jarl Harald would go the man who was his foster-father, advisor and clerk: Lord

Thorbjorn, whose departure would be marked by a collective sigh of relief from all who had to call him master. Not least, the thrall, Brigid.

'He might not come back here at all before going with the ships,' said Wulfhild brightly.

Ellisif shook her head at Wulfhild but said nothing.

Brigid could hold onto thought no longer. She shut her eyes again, began to drift. The last words she heard were, 'He'll no leave without his ship, you wee daftie. And that's upside down by the big house.'

All will be well, she told herself.

Each time she put her baby to the breast, Brigid told her the good and the bad of the life she had come into.

'You are fortunate to be a girl, little one, for that means he'll let you live.'

The baby was less fortunate in being born to a thrall for that status was her only inheritance, from the moment she first mewled. A thrall had no rights, no possessions. A thrall *was* a possession and a thrall's child belonged to the master. Brigid had forgotten what 'thrall' meant until, for a second time, she lost everything.

For now. Skarfr will return.

She told the baby, 'But Skarfr is your master by the Orkneyjar law, a kind man, a friend, who gave your Daddy, and me the running of a beautiful farm, with a cow called Rauðka, named for her russet coat, who gives the creamiest milk in the whole of Orkneyjar.'

What had happened to Rauðka when Thorbjorn had set fire to Skarfr's longhouse in the spring? Was it possible she was still alive?

All will be well. Brigid shook herself. *Sure, she's alive. A neighbour will have taken her in and be looking after her. There's always someone kindly, no matter how bad things get.*

The baby suckled contentedly on what she obviously considered to be the creamiest milk in Ness.

But the baby should know the bad, too. That was how you survived, by facing your situation. Skarfr was over the sea on pilgrimage and would not be back for years.

But there was always good. Fergus had not been taken and had not died out on the bog, as Ellisif had led Thorbjorn to believe. He was alive and well, God willing, seeking help and waiting until they could be reunited. Brigid had to believe that. Hope was all she had left.

'Sure, and your Daddy told me that the lady, who was rescued by your Daddy and Skarfr from That One, has found herself a good man. A man it's a pleasure to work for, so your Da' will be just fine on Finn's island. Strjónsey it's called, a gem of a place where people are always kind to each other and work hard. Just right for your Daddy.'

The bad insisted on intruding in her thoughts. Thorbjorn claimed ownership of Fergus too and would kill him if he found him — *when* he found him. Fergus could not stay hidden forever with Inge and Finn. Somebody's tongue would loosen, letting slip something about the Irish thrall who'd shown up only recently, who did not belong to Finn and Inge as he claimed. Finn's accent and thrall's manner would betray him. And then That One would kill him. As he would have killed Baby, had she been a boy.

Brigid would ask Ellisif about christening Baby with a proper Irish name in secret. She dared not do so in public. She must seem to defer to That One in everything. To keep them safe. He'd said girl thralls were always useful.

And that, Brigid told Baby, was the last and biggest bad thing. Girl thralls are always useful.

CHAPTER FIVE

THORBJORN, WICK, NESS

Thorbjorn looked away from the hounds' messy enjoyment of their reward for a successful hunt. In their appetite for deer innards, there was no distinction between the swift, elegant deerhounds and the tenacious mastiff. However, in a boar hunt, the mastiff excelled, muscular and strong-jawed, able to sink its teeth into a flank and not let go, and fast enough to avoid the lethal tusks.

Fast enough so far, anyway. A boarhound's courage was that of a warrior, and there would always come a day when the warrior was wounded, then died in battle. *When the Norns decide it is time.* Meanwhile, there was fresh meat.

Or, for Thorbjorn and Jarl Harald, meat roasting over a campfire in a forest glade. One of their attendants broke off a hunk of charred venison with his knife and passed it to the Jarl, then another to Thorbjorn. The flesh was flaking on the outside, still bloody inside, and Thorbjorn understood the dogs' hunger and satisfaction. A difficult chase and an efficient kill gave a man an appetite.

'I chose well, didn't I.' Harald' smugness regarding his dogs' performance was no less irritating for its repetition over several months.

Once again, Thorbjorn refrained from pointing out that *he'd* chosen the dogs, at Harald's request. Advising his foster-son was as frustrating in the personal domain as in the political one. He grunted, an all-purpose response open to interpretation.

As he'd predicted, the dogs' names showed the same lack of imagination that Harald brought to ruling Orkneyjar. The young deerhounds were White-ear and Swift-paws; the boarhound was Strong-jaws. Not exactly poetry but, after a horn of ale, Harald could rhyme Swift-paws and Strong-jaws in lines that kept him entertained, if not his audience.

Winter lulled a man into small pleasures and small feuds, made him either contented as an old hearth-worm, or bored and restless. Once the year had turned, Thorbjorn felt the call of the coming spring and of matters bigger than chasing animals or disputing the money paid for poor-quality ship repairs. He'd had enough of ship repairs: the endless cleaning, patching, re-caulking, replacement of planks and nails. He wanted to sail his gods-blessed ship, not inspect it one more time. And he hoped Harald felt the same.

'Another six weeks or so till the weather calms,' Thorbjorn said, 'and we can sail for Orphir, find out what's been happening in Orkneyjar.'

'Nothing's been happening, Thorbjorn. It's winter for everyone.'

'And everyone is preparing for your return, whether by offering welcome or assault. You need to be ready too, have plans for what's coming.'

Harald picked meat out of his teeth with a fingernail, his words garbled as he retorted, 'That's what I have you for, *advisor*.'

'I won't always be there,' Thorbjorn said quietly. Was it a breeze or the Norns who made him shiver? He had to make Harald understand who the key players were in this game of jarls and why their actions mattered.

'What do you think Erlend is doing now? And Sweyn?' he prodded his foster-son.

'I'm not stupid! And I'm getting too old for your political catechisms.'

Thorbjorn waited and sure enough, Harald could not resist the challenge to prove himself.

'Erlend is in Norðvegr seeking support from the King for his claim to co-rule with me. If he gets it—'

'*When* he gets it,' corrected Thorbjorn.

'*When* he gets it, he'll take his ships back to Orkneyjar, go to the Thing in Thingwall, announce his claim to take Rognvald's place as Jarl.'

'And what will we do?'

'Throw him a feast and drink a lot! *I* ,' said Harald, with heavy emphasis on *I*, 'am happy to share the throne with Erlend. One: his claim is better than Rognvald's. Two: Rognvald will be away for years on this stupid pilgrimage, if he comes back at all. Besides, Rognvald would never have become jarl without support from the King of Norðvegr, so if the king chooses Erlend instead, that's settled.'

A simple summary but it would do, apart from giving due credit to the Orkneyman Thorbjorn most hated. He added, 'Rognvald would never have become jarl even *with* the backing of King Sigurd of Norðvegr, if Sweyn had not used trickery on his behalf.'

Sweyn, the golden-haired raider who made up his own rules and had robbed Thorbjorn of his fair share of booty when they'd sailed together. Sweyn, who laughed off exile and was always reinstated. Sweyn, his ex-brother-in-law.

'You know they call him the jarl-maker?' Harald asked.

Thorbjorn couldn't tell if the question was disingenuous or malicious. If the latter, then Harald was finally learning. 'Yes,' he said, through gritted teeth.

'Well,' Harald considered the matter of Sweyn. 'Sweyn hates me because I've exiled his brother. But that's not a killing hatred. And he won't back Erlend — he hates him even more. A long family feud, so that's more serious hate. So I don't need to worry about Erlend wanting rid of his co-ruler. He won't get the lords and karls to turn against me. And I have you.'

Was Harald really so blithely unaware that the family feud touched him too, wondered Thorbjorn? That his advisor and Erlend were cousins? What if *he* decided to become a jarl-maker and transferred his loyalty from Harald to Erlend?

He sighed. 'Yes, you have me.'

That was more certain than Sweyn's actions. The raider could be relied on to put himself first and to back only temporarily whoever would best serve his self-interest at the time. If Erlend promised Sweyn suitable rewards, family pride could be swallowed and if Sweyn became Erlend's ally, was Harald truly safe? Sweyn had made one jarl 'disappear' in the past. What was to stop him repeating such sleight of hand?

I will stop him, Thorbjorn vowed. *I've worked too hard with such unpromising material to lose the power I've earned. I'm not giving it up.*

He looked at the unpromising material. He'd grown used to Harald's poorly co-ordinated, goggling eyes, his malformed face and low brow. But he would never grow used to the low level of intellect. *This* was why he had no wish to be jarl himself. He loved learning for its own sake, his scribe-work, his philosophical debates with the abbot, just as much as the thrill of sailing or fighting.

He sighed again. Winter was *boring*. He would return to his estate, seek entertainment there before he left Ness in the spring. Maybe there was a woman who could distract him.

CHAPTER SIX

BRIGID, NESS

'We should have just done it without telling her. This is too hard for her, and she will break.' Brigid could barely take in Wulfhild's words through the mist of pain. Worse than being chained in and kept in Thorbjorn's stable when he captured her. Worse than sending Fergus away after all he'd been through to find her. Definitely worse than childbirth, which faded to nothing when she looked at the precious result.

She wiped the milky mouth gently, murmured 'Fásach, *mo chroi*,' and held her baby for what could be the last time. How could Ellisif have used her midwife's right to name the baby in the sight of God, only to ask this terrible thing of Brigid now? Fásach, meaning *wilderness*, after the wild land around them that was a haven for the women. Born in the wilderness against all odds, a survivor, like her mother.

'It is her right to know, to choose.' Ellisif's eyes were brimming as she replied to Wulfhild.

To Brigid, she repeated what she'd already told her, letting the cruel words sink in, giving Brigid time to hold her baby. 'This chance will not come again and the girl's body is full of love and milk that she cannot give a dead baby. She will give them to yours with all her heart.'

'Fásach,' said Brigid weakly, 'she is named Fásach.'

Ellisif was inexorable as fate. 'It is God's will that she came to me for her delivery and that we could not save her child, a little girl. She will take your baby to the village on the coast, as her own. Fásach will be safe there. We don't know what the master will do when he comes back and his man has come to say he's on his way, that we must prepare the household. Do you want Fásach's life to depend on his whims? Now and all her life?'

The physical drain on Brigid from childbirth and sleepless nights, from suckling a baby and worrying over her, had taken their toll.

Wulfhild started singing something about baby Moses floating down the stream in the bogland, which did not improve Brigid's clarity of thought. Sure, and they would all go as fey as Wulfhild, with time, especially when That One was in residence, with his dark humours and cruel imagination. He'd said he would let the baby live if it was a girl but what sort of life? What if Brigid's hopes were impossible? What if Skarfr did not return, what if Fergus could not join her, if she and Fásach were That One's thralls for all their lives?

No, she thought. *Our family will be together one day. But I must do what's best for Fásach until then.*

'Who is she?' she asked, giving tacit consent to Ellisif's plan.

'A fisherman's wife, quiet-living, with food enough and a cot in the village by the shore. This was her first baby and much wanted.'

'Take me to her,' said Brigid. She passed her sleeping baby to Ellisif and wrapped herself up warmly, then took Fásach back without waking her, and made the usual cocoon for the baby in her little blue and white shawl.

Ellisif's gifts, thought Brigid, a bitter taste in her mouth from this terrible choice presented to her as God's will.

Ellisif led the way from the small dwelling Brigid shared with the two women who'd accompanied her here from Orkneyjar, to her own identical home.

In the dim rushlight, Brigid saw the young woman, white-faced, red-eyed and tear-streaked. Although she'd been washed and cleansing herbs strewn around the earthen floor, the copper-scent of blood hung in the atmosphere. Her eyes were open and she gripped a cloth bundle so tightly her knuckles were as white as her face.

'You're Brigid,' she said. Although she spoke to Brigid, her desperate eyes were on the sleeping baby.

'I am, so,' said Brigid softly, cradling Fásach in one arm. 'I feel for you in your loss.'

The fingers tightened on the motionless bundle. 'Ellisif has explained your need. I'm Ada.'

Brigid's mouth was dry. 'This is Fásach. Tell her who she is and that her mother loves her, will always love her, and will come for her when she can.'

Ada said, 'Farsight.' A flash of hunger in her eyes was the only response to the prospect of Brigid reclaiming her baby. No promises were made.

But what choice did Brigid have? 'Fásach,' she corrected, taking a last look at the tiny eyelashes fluttering under the fold of blue and white wool.

Ellisif took Fásach from her, unpeeled Ada's fingers from the motionless bundle she clutched, and placed Brigid's baby in its place. The fingers clenched again, then relaxed, a lighter touch, on a living bairn. Ada closed her eyes, as if she'd been given permission to sleep at last and, carrying the dead baby, Ellisif signed that they should leave.

It was not fair that this brave woman, who schemed and lied in That One's face to keep them safe, should carry such a sad burden. Brigid took the bundle from her and stumbled back to her own house. There, she lay down again, with the stillborn at her side. Deathly cold penetrated her body, turning her blood to ice, freezing her heart.

Ellisif bent over her. 'No, dear one. You shall not follow this baby who is not yours. You must grieve Fásach but she is not dead. She will bloom. She will learn to crawl and then to walk, say her first words, and you will see her in your mind's eye.'

The ice melted in a deluge of sobs. Brigid did not notice Ellisif take the stillborn away, barely heard that the corpse had been buried in a simple wooden box at the edge of the bog, marked with an upright stone so the peat-cutters would not dig there.

Slipping into a grief-induced delirium, Brigid asked about her baby Fásach, why she wasn't buried in the churchyard so they would find each other in heaven.

'You remember — she was born dead. The Church would never allow an unbaptised baby on hallowed ground.'

Brigid searched her scrambled memories. 'I thought you baptised Fásach, as is a midwife's' right.'

'Oh, I did,' said Ellisif, smiling, 'Fásach's soul is safe.'

Keeping to her bed, Brigid took whatever potions she was given and woke each time with swollen eyes, a dry mouth and little appetite.

When Brigid opened her eyes after being shaken roughly, she found a man bending over her, and thought she was still in the land of nightmares. However, as she focused, she realised the master was home. And she remembered that it was important he knew her baby had died.

The face withdrew to a distance that was still uncomfortable for her but less threatening.

'Dead,' Lord Thorbjorn said, disgusted. He looked at Brigid, assessing her, then asked his trusted housekeeper, 'She's a tricky one. She's not hiding the baby from you?'

'Oh no, Sire,' said honest Ellisif. 'She couldn't hide the baby from us. I delivered her myself and buried the baby. It was born dead, so we couldn't baptise it, you see.'

The lines of distaste either side of Thorbjorn's nose deepened. 'I'll believe it when I see the body. This thrall is more devious than you can imagine.'

He turned his attention back to Brigid. 'Show me the corpse.'

The sting of his hand across her face was so unexpected she

nearly lashed out in response but she could see Ellisif behind him, shaking her head. Ellisif, whose caution would keep them all alive.

'She has been in bed all this time,' said Ellisif. 'We buried the baby and she hasn't seen the grave.'

Brigid turned her instinctive gesture into a grab for her shawl and she sat up. The shock of the slap had made her more lucid than she'd been for days.

'I will see her now,' she said.

There was no need to feign grief as she followed Ellisif to the burial site, watched one of Lord Thorbjorn's men dig up the little box, open it and grimace at the unwrapped contents.

The master glanced at the object revealed and ordered, 'Throw it back. And,' he addressed Ellisif, 'get the thrall back to work. She's had enough time lazing around.'

He started walking back to the settlement, talking to the other man who'd accompanied him. 'I have more important things to think about than thralls or old grudges. Orkneyjar is on the brink of war. Get the men out of their winter burrows and into training. Fast. We'll leave as soon as the weather changes. And the ship had better be ready to sail.'

The man holding a spade and a dead baby looked at Ellisif, who raised an eyebrow. Carefully, he wrapped up the little corpse as best he could, laid it back in the wooden box and replaced the earth on top of it. Once the stone marker was back in place, he looked at Ellisif again and she grunted approval. Only then did he speed off after the other men.

Left alone, the women stood for a moment, breathing heavily.

'He's going soon,' said Ellisif.

'War in Orkneyjar,' said Brigid. 'He might not come back.'

Ellisif grunted again.

They would survive until Fergus could come for her. And Fásach was safe.

CHAPTER SEVEN

INGE, STRJÓNSEY, ORKNEYJAR

Men grow so fretful during winter, thought Inge, as a blast of cold air swept through the hall from the open door, wafting smoke into her eyes from the peat fires that kept the longhouse warm but fuggy.

The door banged shut as her husband, Finn, marched back to join her where she sat on a stool, mending one of his work tunics by torchlight.

'Still raining?' she asked, oversewing the edge of a woollen patch with neat brown stitches. This was the seventh time he'd looked outside and returned sighing, so the answer was not surprising.

'Tipping down.'

Inge looked at the bone needle darting through the fabric, the simple in-and-out pattern that bonded two different pieces of cloth and she was pleased with her work.

Maybe she was more appreciative of domestic calm because of the years she'd spent locked in marital combat with Thorbjorn. Even *thinking* his name made her shudder. That was another reason to be grateful for winter; Thorbjorn was on mainland Ness with Jarl Harald, far enough away from Finn to keep safe the dear man who'd helped her trust again. She looked up from her sewing to find him watching her, his eyes soft.

He reached out, stroked her cheek with the back of his hand. 'I thank the gods,' he murmured.

'And I,' she replied, her heart full. But she touched the amulet around her neck, warding off evil. It was better not to draw the gods' attention in case they mistook happiness for complacence.

As if in response to her thoughts, another gust of icy wind swirled the smoke into a troll-shaped cloud as the door swung open again and a man was silhouetted against the driving rain.

Inge blinked then recognised their quiet thrall, just as Finn said, 'Fergus, will you join us?'

Fergus took something from his cloak and tucked it under his arm, then shook the rain from the garment and then spread it on a bench, near enough the fire at the back of the hall for it to dry, but not so close to his lord and lady as to be presumptuous.

'Thank you, my Lord,' he said, sitting on a coarse blanket and revealing what was cradled in his arms. The tiny lamb bleated and Fergus shushed it in soft Irish. 'We lost the dam, and this one will need hand-rearing,' he told Finn and Inge, 'but she's determined. She'll come through.' He let the tiny creature suckle on his little finger. 'And there's three pairs of twins born, ewes and lambs all healthy. I've repaired the pen in the top field and they've shelter there.'

Finn sighed. 'Birthing can't wait for fine weather, more's the pity.'

'So it is.' The lines scored in Fergus' swarthy face deepened and his voice was sombre.

Inge knew he must be thinking of another mother-to-be. She left her mending on the stool, fetched a bowl of milk and brought it back to warm beside the fire.

'Let me?' she asked Fergus, who passed her the lamb, which protested at leaving its cosy nest and then snuggled in beneath her breast.

Inge dipped a finger in the milk and felt the suction of the mobile lips that drew life itself from her offering. A small miracle. Childless, reviled as barren by the man she preferred not to name, Inge let the warmth of their two bodies nourish them both, woman and lamb.

She settled into a rhythm of dipping her finger in milk and feeding the lamb.

She glanced at her husband, who gave silent assent. Spring was coming and they had talked over this matter many times.

'Before you go back to the sheep, Fergus, we must speak of the future, *your* future,' she said.

The thrall took the words as he would a blow, flinching instinctively but enduring them, waiting to learn their import.

Inge continued quickly, 'My debt to you is beyond payment. You risked your life to save mine and Lord... Thorbjorn has taken a terrible revenge on Skarfr and on you, because of me. Spring is coming and he will return to Orkneyjar.'

'I have nowhere else to go or I should not endanger you now,' Fergus' tone was as close to bitterness as he ever came.

'We know that, man, and you're staying here until Skarfr returns. You're as good a worker as any I've seen so it's no charity.' Finn's bluff interjection cleared up any misunderstanding and Inge carried on.

'When Lord Thorbjorn returns, we will get news of your wife and your child.' She would not add 'if they live'. His belief that his wife would bear a healthy baby and they would be together again one day was all that kept Fergus setting one foot in front of the other each day. That, and working with the farm animals.

Fergus nodded.

'Thorbjorn is a cunning man and he will learn you are here, just as we will learn about Brigid, so I think we should prepare to fight him by law instead of by stealth.'

Finn stated the case, baldly. 'Thorbjorn says you and Brigid are his thralls and he has a paper to prove it.'

'He lies!' Fergus couldn't hold back the retort.

Inge took a deep breath. 'In law you have no rights, no opinion, no relations, and no child. But I know someone who is as cunning as Thorbjorn, maybe more so, who can turn his arguments against him if we take the case to the Thing. And if we win, if Thorbjorn is found wrong, by the council's vote, he will be forced to let Brigid and your baby stay with us. He will have to respect the law, as the Jarl's advisor. If we don't do this, you'll have to live in hiding, while Thorbjorn has Brigid, until Skarfr's return, which could take years, and even then, he'll have to argue the case in law.'

Hope warred with fear in Fergus' eyes. 'And if you lose?'

Inge hesitated and Finn spoke for them both. 'Then you will have to go with Thorbjorn as his thrall. Brigid and your child will also be declared legally his thralls. His property, to do with as he pleases.' He paused. Everybody present knew what a vengeful Thorbjorn could do. 'And when Skarfr returns, he will have little chance of appeal against the Thing's verdict.'

In the unlikely event that any of you still live, thought Inge. Thorbjorn would do whatever he thought would most hurt Skarfr. Unless of course one of his red rages took him. Then he would kill.

Fergus didn't hesitate. 'Do it,' he said. 'Go to this person. Make your case. If That One kills me, perhaps I will see my family before I die. If not, it shall be after death, one day.'

He stood up abruptly and grabbed his cloak. 'The sheep need me,' he said, and they let him go. The door banged shut, the foggy atmosphere returned and Inge gently wrapped the sleepy lamb in the warm blanket Fergus had left beside the fire.

'I'll look after her,' she said. 'She'll be fine.'

She sat beside Finn once more and took up the mending while she spoke.

'The goat-girl can tend the lamb while you're away,' Finn said. 'We'll set sail when there's a calm spell. I need you with me when we talk about the other thing, not just about Fergus. And it looks more natural for you to pay your brother a visit and me go with you than for me to go on my own.'

He hesitated and Inge's heart sank. He was having second thoughts again about 'the other thing'.

'I will do as we agreed but I have no grudge against Harald,' he told her. 'I cannot bear to think of what Thorbjorn did to you.' The veins stood out on his forehead and his fists clenched 'I would rather make him pay, man-to-man, than go through all this politicking.'

Of course he would.

'I know,' she said. 'I wish it could be so manly but Thorbjorn is a *níðingr*, without honour, a forked-tongue.' *And would kill you, even in a fair fight.* 'He would turn your challenge against you by smearing my name. You would not reach him but would be exiled instead. Thorbjorn would still be in power, crowing. I would have nobody to keep me safe or to help me pay my debt to Fergus.'

Finn's brows met. He didn't like it but he was listening. 'Harald has treated your family badly,' he conceded. 'He should not have exiled your brother.'

'No, he shouldn't have. We owe Harald no loyalty.' Inge pressed her point. 'And to bring Thorbjorn down we must bring Harald down. His advisor will fall with him. Erlend is ready and waiting to become jarl, and the King of Norðvegr has given full approval. If Erlend gets Sweyn on his side, the Thing will confirm his accession.'

Finn nodded. 'Harald will have to accept it — for now — to avoid confrontation with Erlend, who has more right to the throne than he does, and is Norðvegr's choice.'

'Rognvald was Norðvegr's choice too,' Inge pointed out. 'But Rognvald is not here.'

'And we can strengthen Erlend until the day comes...'

'Yes, until that day comes, husband,' said Inge. Until *both* her brothers made Erlend invincible and pushed Orkneyjar to approve *one* jarl. Harald could run and hide, or die. And his advisor with him. She tied off the thread and bit the trailing end close to the fabric, to finish the repair.

'You have sharp teeth, wife,' observed Finn.

She smiled. 'Let me persuade Sweyn where his interests lie.' And talk to Margaret, the outrageous grey-haired paramour of Inge's younger brother, Gunnr. Margaret, mother of Jarl Harald, who'd been (briefly) the respectable widow of the Mormaer of Ness, before flinging modesty to the winds and sailing off with Gunnr. Now she was stuck with at least one small child and her mother-in law, along with Sweyn's ever-moaning wife, on the Isle of Gareksey. Margaret didn't even have the benefit of her immorality as Harald had promptly exiled Gunnr for 'abducting' his mother.

Not only men grew restless in winter and found politics a distraction. Margaret had every reason to spite Harald with a plan to gain the throne for Erlend. She was also sure to have the legal knowledge they sought. More cunning than Thorbjorn, her mind honed by years governing Ness at her husband's side, Margaret lived by her own rules even more than Sweyn did. And Inge was keen to learn from her, in ways she was not going to discuss with her husband, as well as in matters of law.

CHAPTER EIGHT

HLIF, PALERMO, SICILIA

For however long they would be in Sicilia, this was home and Hlif wanted to imprint something of their family's identity on this foreign building to make it so. Something that wrapped Skarfr and Sea-born in the fierce warmth of her love, that warded them from the evils only she could see. Not just a woman's touch but a wise woman's touch was needed, to keep at bay the soul-stealing shadows that flitted through darkness, glimpsed but elusive. They faded to nothing whenever she tried to fix them with a stare. She was no child now to seek their invisible mockery, jerking her head at snake-speed to catch them and always failing. When they wished to be seen, she would not be able to shut them out, but for now she could ignore them.

Hlif began her daily ritual. First, she ensured that they could light lamps when day was done by topping up the oil in the table lamps. Then, cursing her small stature, she stood on a stool to replace the two candles in the wall sconce. To light the lamps, there were still a couple of tapers by the hearth, where she kindled the embers into enough life to heat the cookpot later on. She shifted the smoothing iron nearer to the heat, in the unlikely event that some crumpled clothing would annoy her enough to tease out its wrinkles. Regardless of practicality, the shape of the iron pleased her better in profile. Less aggressive, less like a shark's fin. She shuddered, not allowing herself to remember the sharks.

She must ask Amina, the maid, to bring up more sticks and logs. She still found it sinful to waste wood in such a manner. Here in Sicilia, there were many trees but no peat to use as fuel. In Orkneyjar, there were so few trees that even shipwrecks and driftwood were salvaged for repairs and renovation.

Plenty of trees or not, Hlif was as frugal with wood as she could be, if she were to keep a fire lit at all. Their living quarters also benefited from the fire in the servants' quarters below, which in turn drew heat from the byre on the ground floor, where two goats and a donkey made their home, and which opened in a stable door onto the street. Below the byre were musty cellars, cavern-like in temperature and construction, and empty at present. But Hlif, ever the trader, had plans.

As he'd earned ever more respect and purses of gold, Skarfr could afford to move to a bigger house in a more prestigious location, with a manservant and a maid. But old habits died hard and Hlif preferred to carry out some domestic tasks herself, however much this annoyed her maid. Nothing that lessened his workload annoyed their manservant, Pietro.

The wooden shutters of the two windows were open and pinned back in their iron clasps, rattling slightly in the February wind. The cold air entering was cleansing and the silvery early morning sunlight was further compensation for the chill. Windows were still a novelty for Hlif, accustomed to a longhouse, and she leaned out to take in the view of the city from her vantage point of the third story in this stone house adjacent to the king's palace.

Uneven stone steps, slippery in rain, led up outside the house, which had doors at two levels, first to the servants' quarters, further up to the family rooms. These consisted of living quarters and two windowless bedchambers nestling back wall to back wall against the twin house in the next street. What luxury to give Sea-born a bedspace separated from his parents by more than a curtain!

Although a wise woman like Hlif could create privacy where

none seemed possible, in dreams if need be, she appreciated this gift of Sicilian architecture almost as much as windows, a chimney and a cellar. All were luxuries she would never have imagined from what she'd considered the comfort of Jarl Rognvald's *Bu*, the ruler's hall in Orphir, back in Orkneyjar.

Her gaze traced the route from the bottom of their steps into the street below and further afield across clay-tiled red roofs to the harbour and sea glinting in the distance.

So much noise! Mules and donkeys braying as they carried their burdens to and from the docks to the citadel; yesterday's incoming merchant ships unloading, and departing ones stocking up. The ring of hooves on cobblestones when noblemen rode through the streets.

What if there were paved streets in Orkneyjar? Hlif dismissed the idea as an expensive waste of craftsmen's time. Ships did not need paving and hard earth was smoother for carts and even for shod feet. She smiled at the memory of running barefoot on damp tracks and dune-fringed beaches.

Men were shouting and banging, hammering and haggling, in workshops and trader homes, where business was conducted through the ground floor windows, with queues forming for some of the more popular local sellers.

Orders rang out and metal clanged. She fancied she could hear the king's warriors training, out of sight in the castle yard, Skarfr's voice giving precise instructions, focused on teaching others the skills he'd paid sweat and blood to learn. He was in his warrior's world and would not be thinking of her.

A pang of something akin to loneliness knifed her heart. A moment's self-indulgence, feeling the pain of what it would have been like if nobody had defied the curse laid on her. *Daughter of the saint-killer.* Pain followed by a deepened appreciation of what Skarfr meant to her and she to him, of having found each other and not letting go.

How strange, this dance between separation and connection. This marriage, born of loyalty between orphans and grown into the matching of two planks in a clinkered ship. Flexing in rough seas, stronger together and well-weathered, but no doubt with more storms to come — and repairs required occasionally.

Enough time-wasting!

She dusted the stools and the solid wooden kist containing their clothes and personal belongings which also served as a table. She swept the floor and strewed dried herbs against mice and fleas. Lavender, mint and rosemary were as common as trees in Sicilia.

When all was as it should be, she was ready to add the finishing touches. The iron hooks in the white-plastered stone wall had been accusing her of laxity for weeks and just yesterday she had found the perfect wall-hanging. She cut the string around the baled fabric and unrolled it on top of the clean kist, which it overhung by the width of two tawny lions in heraldic pose, pawing the earth beneath palm trees.

The shopkeeper had explained to her that the oriental oasis depicted King Roger's royal menagerie and its residents, winged and four-legged gifts from leaders of the outlandish countries that were trading partners. In addition to the lions, there were leopards and bears, hunting dogs and harts, horses with horns and with noses that swung like snakes from their faces, plus birds with all manner of beak and plumage. If Hlif could not have crashing waves, cliffs and cormorants, in muted greys, greens and sea-blues — and she knew she could not — then the more extravagant the eastern scene, the better. Vibrant reds, golds and greens made the white of hounds, hart and unicorn glow like moons.

Jumping onto a stool, Hlif hung the glorious work in place and stepped back to admire the effect. It was doubled in the small mirror she'd hung on the wall opposite, another exotic treasure from a Sicilian merchant. *This* was what travel offered. She couldn't wait to see Skarfr's reaction and to talk about the creatures with Sea-born, who might even have seen some of them in his life before he became their son.

Hlif moved her stool back, within hand-holding distance of anyone who sat on its neighbour, Skarfr's preferred seat, nearest the hearth. By such small arrangements of furniture did she enable the contact that nurtured her marriage.

Then she opened the kist and took out her leather pouch, pulled out a handful of wooden die and cast them onto the kist's wooden surface. Some landed with an engraved rune uppermost. These she kept and the others she returned to the pouch. She looked at the runes a long time, reading their potential and their warnings. Then she returned them to their hiding-place and fetched her cloak. She was going to buy oranges and take them to the Tiraz.

CHAPTER NINE

HLIF, PALERMO, SICILIA

Even in February, the gloom inside the Tiraz made Hlif blink as she pushed open the heavy oak door and slipped through the anonymous doorway in the forbidding, windowless stone wall.

The silk works ran along the ground floor of a wing of the palace, long and low, purpose-built by the Muslims who'd once been the rulers of Sicilia. Conquered by King Roger's father, their people stayed on as valued citizens, skilled workers and administrators. Hlif would never get used to seeing more robes and turbanned heads around her in the city than there were Christian folk but she was not afraid any more. Those dressed in such a fashion often bowed their heads to her and politely wished that God would be with her. She would return the greeting, worrying not one iota about which God was meant.

'Oranges,' she said to the two eunuchs blocking further access to the hallowed series of rooms on the ground floor to her left, where silk was manufactured, and also to the much less hallowed chambers up the stairs in front of her. The secrets of the Tiraz, below stairs and above, were closely protected by King Roger's most trusted guards and the door to the street, through which Hlif had entered, was little used. The men who frequented the Tiraz came from within the palace, through the passageway to the right of the guards.

However, this was not Hlif's first visit and she'd gained the guards' trust with her little gifts and transparent innocence.

Where was the harm in an odd little foreigner befriending one of the silk workers? The girls had little enough contact with the outside world in their cloistered lives.

Cloistered. How funny to liken the Tiraz women to nuns and yet, they did face similar constraints.

If her friendship was welcomed by the silk workers, so were the treats she found for the guards. She had overcome her distaste at their unmanned condition and learned their names, Nayal and Abdul. She knew which of them had a penchant for almond-paste and had even patched a quilted jerkin for another, when she spotted a hole beginning to fray. These poor men had no wives to do their mending, and seamstresses charged an arm and a leg for the simplest repair.

'For Rachel.' She showed the basket full of the blood-red fruit, newly in season and one of Hlif's favourite discoveries about this island. These were the last ones available, unfortunately. Not because harvesting was over, the fruiterer had explained to her, but because the orange-grower could not spare the time to bring more from his farm in the south-east to market here in the north.

The well-trodden stone stairway at the entrance led up to bedchambers and what could politely be termed convivial rooms. Snatches of lute music could be heard faintly through the ceiling, then an anguished groan from above made Hlif pause.

Feigned, thought Hlif, identifying the dying crescendo before going through the door into the silk works.

Rachel worked as an embroiderer in the room nearest the door to the outside world, the one with the most daylight. Skeins of dyed silk hung drying from a row of hooks on one wall, beside a huge chest with small drawers, like that in an apothecary's shop. In the drawers were reels of threads, buttons, beads, jewels, ribbons and laces; needles of iron, brass and steel, all with different-sized eyes, some of them sharp crewels and some blunt-tipped for tapestry work.

Hlif could never resist opening a drawer to see what treasures were inside. Even when Rachel was working with some of these decorations in plain view, Hlif was attracted to those hidden. As if each drawer whispered, *Open me.*

Panels of woven cloth were folded neatly and shelved on the opposite wall. Closer inspection showed they were sorted by colour, next by size and finally by pattern, with the cheapest, plain weave at the top. Although the multi-coloured fabrics were eye-catching, on a shelf of their own, Hlif was always drawn to the blues and greens.

Usually, Rachel was embroidering plain cloth with gold, silver or brightly coloured threads, or sewing on jewels or beads but to rest her eyes, she sometimes took a turn at the loom in the next room, as today. When she saw Hlif in the arched doorway, she finished one last throw of the shuttle, which drew the weft thread through a dizzying pattern in and out of the warp.

'It's gorgeous,' said Hlif, admiring the damson roundels appearing on the heavy silk background. Brocade, in the damask style.

Rachel glowed, as if she'd been visited by angels — or become one. The sheen on her olive skin and crescent of black hair showing below the practical cap, was as silken as all around her. Her oval face and long straight nose showed the same classical perfection as her weaving and when she looked up at Hlif, her dark eyes were lit with passion. 'I feel like this is my purpose in life,' she said. 'to create something beautiful. And when I'm lost in my work, nothing else matters.'

'I wish I had your skill,' said Hlif, a moment's envy suppressed instantly in pure admiration.

Like all Orkneyjar women, Hlif could use a loom but her weaving was basic. She knew how to set up the vertical wool threads of the warp so they were nicely weighted and held in place. And she could weave the weft yarn in and out the warp. But that was all. She knew nothing of how to set up the warp so that these exquisite patterns appeared.

Hlif had bought fabric from more skilled weavers than herself in Orkneyjar, women who could create twills and diamond patterns in two colours of wool but the Tiraz loom-work seemed like magic.

Today, Rachel was making silk brocade by adding an extra weft thread to build up a pattern in relief on the fabric in a contrasting colour.

Once, to satisfy Hlif's curiosity, Rachel had taken her through all the rooms, to the one where the process began. They'd walked from the room where Rachel competed for the window light with her fellow embroiderers, past the looms and weavers, past the small dye vats which made Hlif hold her nose at the sharp tang of urine, past the spinning wheels.

Without lifting their heads from their work, the silk workers bade *Good-day* to Hlif. The Master Craftsman was inspecting the quality of work on one of the looms and frowned when he saw Rachel leading Hlif into the inner sanctum.

'Good-day, Master Thomas,' Rachel said brightly. 'This is one of the girls we can call on for extra help with boiling it. She usually does laundry. I'm just showing her where the work will be.'

Embarrassed by the lie, Hlif bobbed a curtsey and hid her hands in her long sleeves, hoping they didn't look red and chapped enough to fit the part. She definitely needed some new clothes if she could be taken for a laundry-woman.

Master Thomas grunted and returned to his scrutiny of how even the weave was on a loom, counting threads aloud as he checked the pattern.

Rachel rushed through some rooms, all empty of people, so she could start her explanation from the beginning.

'This,' she waved her arms dramatically, 'is where silk begins.'

All Hlif could see were wooden shelves with trays on them, and two trestle tables down the middle of the otherwise empty room.

'In late March or April, the white silk-fruits grow on the mulberry trees, are harvested and then they're brought here.'

Hlif asked, 'White fruits?'

Rachel's eyes flicked sideways, as they had when she'd justified Hlif's presence to the Master Craftsman. 'The size of an egg,' she said. 'They are boiled in those vats.' Empty barrels stood in the next room. Disappointed at how ordinary it all was, Hlif walked on, noting large wheels and spindles, a stool beside each one. They reminded her of the spinsters she visited in Orkneyjar when she needed yarn for the weavers. But how could you spin fruit?

'For spinning?' she asked.

'Not yet. This is for pulling the silk thread from the fruit. The worker brushes the fruit to find a thread and then pulls and pulls. Once she finds the thread, the fruit unravels completely. She attaches the end here.' Rachel pointed to a wooden reel.

'Then she turns this wheel to spool the thread onto the reel. A good worker can get a thousand feet of top-quality thread from one fruit without breaking it.'

The word 'quality' always made Hlif's ears prick up as it could save her money in future trading. 'What thread is not top quality?' she asked.

'How we care for the fruit makes the thread good.' Hlif sensed that Rachel was keeping trade secrets of her own behind this vague reply. 'And the outer husk of the fruit is what we call floss, very fluffy, which can be spun but is not as fine a silk. I can show you what to look for in the finished fabrics, which is more important to you.'

Hlif passed from the empty rooms where thread was harvested, spooled, washed, spun and dyed, to those she knew, where thread turned into fabric, and finally back to the embroiderers' rooms.

'It must take many fruit to make a gown,' she observed.

'About three thousand,' said Rachel. 'Which makes a pound of silk.' Now that was useful. Hlif added this to her store of trading knowledge.

Rachel unhooked a skein of red silk thread, held it up for Hlif to admire. 'So fine and light but so strong.'

Like women.

Another half-suppressed noise from upstairs filtered down during an interlude in the lute's melody.

Genuine, she thought, surprised. A woman did not grow up in the Jarl's *Bu* in Orkney without receiving an education in noises through the curtains which separated couples from children at night. Modest clothes by day were no bar to private passion in bed. It seemed that in the harem, as in the most unlikely marriages, pleasure could be found.

Eros they called such pleasure, the silk workers who'd been seized in Thebes three years ago by Sicilia's Emir of Emirs in his coastal raids against the Byzantine Empire.

Wherever the Tiraz, the work remained the same for the Theban women, who'd brought their Byzantine techniques and patterns to the king's silk works in Palermo. Along with their more sensual talents.

'You brought oranges.' Rachel smiled. 'We should take them upstairs.'

Hlif nodded. They understood each other.

CHAPTER TEN

HLIF, PALERMO, SICILIA

The guards stopped Hlif and Rachel at the entrance.
'Not going outside today, Rachel?' Nayal asked.
'No,' she replied with a smile, pointing at Hlif's basket. 'Oranges for the girls.'

With that, they headed upstairs for some privacy.

Rachel was one of the few silk workers with permission to go outside the palace onto the street, where the artisans' quarter gathered together leather-workers, cordwainers, tailors, seamstresses, and an armourer, among other craftsmen. With the king's permission and a suitable weight in coin, silk cloth could make its way from the royal monopoly of the Tiraz to any of the craftspeople who might need gold-shot rosettes for a pair of shoes, embroidered samite for a cloak, or Saracen designs on brocade for a decorative alms purse.

The two women had met when Rachel was making just such a delivery to the seamstress, at the moment Hlif was disputing how much silk would be required to manufacture a man's shirt and a woman's overdress, or bliaut, as they called the more fitted version fashionable in Sicilia, to dress up her good linen undershift. The seamstress was horrified at the very idea of cutting both garments from the same fabric when the couple concerned were courtiers.

And she had sworn in all three of Sicily's main languages at the thought of Hlif wearing 'that old thing' under any fine new silk garment *she* created.

Hlif was not new to haggling and had turned to the young woman who'd just entered the shop, accompanied by an enormous armed man. Luminous dark eyes were all that was visible between a burden of silks in rainbow hues and the cream veil which was pulled low over her forehead and fell in a soft drape around her slim shoulders. Hlif approved of the modest head-covering. She struggled with the trend at court for even married ladies to wear their hair unbound, threaded through with jewel-studded ribbons.

'How much of that would make a man's shirt?' she asked the silk-bearing nymph, pointing to a medium-weight dark blue fabric peeping out from its place in the folded pile.

The eyes, accentuated in black kohl lines, glanced from the dressmaker to the customer. 'That depends,' hedged a voice muffled behind its informal mask.

'I would say two yards,' Hlif told her helpfully, 'as there's no difference whatsoever between the amount needed for silk as for linen. And I know to the last inch what's needed in linen.'

Hands roughened by loom work put the pile of silk down on the dressmaker's table, blocking the artisan's face and revealing the silk-bearer's olive skin and Greek features; slim, straight nose, sharp cheekbones and longbow mouth, wide and curved.

The silk-bearer looked puzzled. 'We measure silk in pieces or by weight,' she told Hlif. 'Let me show you this piece and you will see that there is enough material here for your needs.'

The seamstress rose to her feet so she could be seen above the silks, her face reddening at the unwanted intrusion.

Rachel smiled at the artisan and pulled the deep blue silk out without disturbing the neatly folded pile. She shook the fabric loose and what had seemed no more than a scarf's worth of material floated into yards and yards. The silk worker might be ignorant of the new wool measures Hlif had learned from English merchants but she knew about this precious fabric.

She wafted it towards Hlif where it clung like the sea, wrapping her in rolling waves. She felt beautiful.

'But,' said Rachel, 'this bliaut does deserve the best underdress.' She wrinkled her nose at Hlif's serviceable linen garment: it had been only recently washed and bleached in the sun, even though it had crossed three seas on a dragon ship!

'It is very hot here in summer.' The seamstress's eyes gleamed as she made the most of the opportunity given to her. 'An undershift in the same raw silk as Rachel's veil would be perfect.'

Hlif watched the light play on the cream silk; she was weakening.

Then the artisan said, 'And pearls on the bliaut's neckline and sleeves, picking up the cream of the underdress.'

The dream-bubble popped. Pearls indeed! 'No, that's too fancy for me, but we can talk about the bliaut and a man's shirt. Maybe two different fabrics, depending on the price.' After all, Skarfr's colouring was as unlike hers as could be. His cormorant-black hair and puppy-brown eyes were a striking contrast to her frizzy red hair and freckled skin. So unusual was she here in Sicilia that youngsters would run up to her for a dare to see if her freckles rubbed off.

She folded the blue silk slowly, to feel it run through her fingers, then, with a sigh, put it on top of the pile. Her best beads were turquoise and they wouldn't show up against such a cloth.

'I need something more practical,' she said. 'But still silk.'

The silk worker's beautiful almond-shaped eyes studied her. 'Come to my workshop in the Tiraz and look through the fabric.'

After the dressmaker made an inventory of the precious fabrics Rachel had delivered, Hlif followed the silk worker through the side door, past the Tiraz guard and into the secret world of women and weaving, gossamer and grandeur.

In the month it took the seamstress, in between more important commissions, to sew a cream chemise and a green bliaut, the two women came to an understanding.

Rachel was paid for her Tiraz work in lengths of silk, more than she could wear, but, as royal property herself, she was watched carefully by the guards. Her contact with the world outside the Tiraz was limited to those artisans who worked with silk in the adjacent ateliers, or clients who visited the silk works to benefit from any of the silk workers' services. Such clients were, by definition, the king's men, or the guards would not allow them entry. And the king's men would never risk furthering Rachel's one ambition.

Hlif's instinctive revulsion on hearing of those other services quickly adjusted to a more practical view. Rachel was a palace thrall and must do what was asked of her. As must many women who were not thralls but who were not free either. Hlif knew of many respectable women expected to do their duty by the thoroughly undesirable men they'd married, to end blood feuds or merge properties.

Now she thought about it, she had some tips to offer the younger woman on how to make those other services irresistibly pleasurable for the client while minimising any discomfort for the lady generously providing them. Without, of course, disclosing more private matters, such as the heightened sensuality she offered Skarfr when she led him through the veil between worlds. She intended to keep her powers as hidden as her hair in this foreign court to which she and Skarfr had been exiled.

After mutually educational discussion of everything from skin unguents and perfumes, to using red veils to warm the candlelight, to the careful placement of cushions, Hlif had made an offer regarding Rachel's personal store of silk. She was confident that Skarfr would be willing to keep his share of the bargain she struck, especially when he was presented with such a beautiful shirt as a surprise present.

'Come upstairs,' Rachel had told her that first time.

This too was now an expected part of Hlif's visit, when she would collect some of the silks and hide them under whatever produce she'd brought in her basket, neatly covered with a linen cloth so as not to sully the fine fabric. Not that she was doing anything illegal or even wrong, as Rachel's payment did not belong to the royal monopoly. But Hlif had a feeling the king would not be too pleased if he knew what Rachel wanted in exchange. Nor would the Emir of

Emirs, whose white hair and formal robes Hlif was certain she'd glimpsed disappearing behind a curtain. Upstairs.

As they passed the curtained doorways along the passageway, Rachel was wise enough to speak only of what was public knowledge. 'We are busier than ever at the moment, preparing for the Easter coronation and then for the baby princeling in the autumn. Every courtier wants new finery for both events. We can't make silk fast enough and our needleworkers are damaging their eyes embroidering into the night by candlelight.'

Hlif held her basket of oranges carefully, its linen cloth lining hiding the two silk garments below. Rachel had finished sewing braid onto the keyhole neck of Skarfr's shirt, cuffs and hem. She'd also insisted on stitching a simple wavy line in gold thread around the edges of the bliaut. Despite Hlif's protests that it was above her rank, she secretly thought it rather fine and was happy to be persuaded that it was perfect for special occasions.

She too kept her tone innocuous. 'We're lucky to be here to see Guillaume crowned as co-regent! What an occasion that will be and the people gain a new king without having to mourn the old one. And our new silks will be perfect!'

'You will need more than one new outfit,' warned Rachel.

'Maybe. We shall see.' It wouldn't do to become accustomed to such luxury.

One heavy red brocade curtain lifted as they passed and someone young, heavily scented and swathed in a light silk robe paused in the doorway, a lute dangling gracefully from one hand. Although the stance, coquettish tilt of the head and black-rimmed eyes were feminine, there was something masculine about the body suggested under the fine silk. Lines rather than curves.

Around the person's neck dangled another instrument, one Hlif recognised.

CHAPTER ELEVEN

HLIF, PALERMO, SICILIA

'A guimbarde!' she exclaimed, and the musician's hand reached for the bamboo mouth harp.

Surprise widened the dark eyes. 'Not many people know that name! Here, I am Mikael.'

'My husband played such an instrument in Narbonne and keeps it still,' Hlif explained, trying to ignore the state of undress and flushed face of the person she'd now identified, from the timbre of his voice, as a young man. 'He says it's a reminder of a chance meeting when he was playing his flute in a public square and it was a gift from a stranger.'

The youth smiled, 'I remember it well. Tell Skarfr that Guimbarde wishes him well. All roads do indeed lead through Sicilia.'

'Guimbarde?' she queried. 'The instrument?'

'By that name he will know me.'

'I don't pay you to gossip,' complained a voice from the interior, unmistakably male. 'More wine, you said.'

With an apologetic smile, Guimbarde emerged fully from the room, dropping the curtain behind him. He brushed past the women in a cloud of silk and perfume. Hlif and Rachel continued along the corridor until they reached the curtain that opened to reveal Rachel's bed, stool and kist. A water-filled basin and ewer were on a second stool, a linen cloth neatly folded beside them.

'Hlif, my friend,' Rachel said as soon as they were alone, sitting on vast cushions strewn about the bedchamber. Even the shadows were red as blood oranges, thanks to the veil suspended between them and a flickering candle. 'I might have more than silk for you,' she whispered. 'But it is dangerous, very dangerous. Wine makes our patrons talk too much and we know many secrets. But if such a secret gets out, a man might guess at the source. So, we must be very careful and you must tell nobody. Not even your husband — for his own sake. Promise.'

'Until you tell me, I won't know what I'm promising,' Hlif objected. It was not her way to hide something from Skarfr. Apart from the surprise gift. And apart from her visits to the Tiraz to source the fabric for the surprise gift. And apart from the meetings with Rachel because she couldn't talk about those without spoiling the surprise. Today, she would be able to pick up the shirt and the bliaut and tell him everything.

Rachel showed her two beads that glowed red in the warm light.

'The man I told you about, he gave me these,' whispered Rachel. 'He was drunk and bragging, as men do, so he showed me this too and said he found it himself, knew where to find more.'

She held out a piece of rock. 'I told him how wonderful he was, begged to keep this, told him the powers of amber to give eternal youth are stronger in its natural state so I would hide it next to my skin and stay beautiful for him. I could see he was excited by the thought and I played on this feeling.'

Hlif hoped her friend would abbreviate this part of the story and was relieved when Rachel's next words were, 'When I told him how impressed I was that he'd travelled to the Baltic Sea, he couldn't resist correcting me and he told me everything. When he visits his wheat-fields on the plain of Catania,' she whispered, 'he goes to the River Simeto. The amber washes up on its banks. Especially after a storm.'

'The plain of Catania,' said Hlif thoughtfully, 'where the blood oranges are grown.' What if she could combine her love of the fruit with this other project? She could visit an orchard and bring a bag of oranges home with her. 'But how could I find this place?'

Rachel's teeth gleamed in the warm light like yellow amber beads. 'From the town of Paternò, which you will know by its Frankish tower on a hill, go south-west for nine miles until you reach the river. There you will see a place where the river is wide and divides into channels, silted up to make many muddy shores. Take this so you know what to look for.'

Hlif palmed the unassuming little rock, surprised at how light it was. She would look at it more closely in daylight, in the privacy of her own home.

But the danger! She would need Skarfr with her for protection but she could find no good excuse for asking him to leave the king's service on such an ostensibly mundane errand.

'It's not possible you got so much information without him suspecting your motives,' Hlif mused aloud.

'You underestimate me — and he was too drunk to remember a thing when he woke up.' Rachel passed Hlif the two beads. 'See how beautiful they are.'

Smooth to the touch, enough alike to make a pair of earrings or small brooches. Hlif held one between thumb and forefinger, watching the light pick out white fissures and tiny bubbles of yellow.

'The Byzantines say amber forms from tears shed by the sisters of the doomed sun-god,' Rachel told her. 'They turned into trees and still they weep. And each tear catches the sun, as their brother tried to do — and died trying.'

'Always the women who cry,' observed Hlif. 'Even goddesses. My people say Freyja's tears fell as gold and amber.'

'What was she crying over?'

'Her husband's absence.'

'I would not mourn for a man!' Rachel hissed.

'I would.' Skarfr would put to sea soon, Hlif knew, and she would miss him. But at the thought he might not return 'missing him' were not big enough words. There were no words big enough.

'You have a good man,' Rachel said quietly. 'And all I ask in exchange for my secrets is his help, which will be easy and cost him nothing.'

She outlined her plan, so easy, so foolproof. Unless they were caught. Hlif remembered Skarfr helping another woman in a daring rescue much riskier than this one. Yet all had gone well. Inge was safe and Skarfr had suffered no repercussions. Skarfr would no doubt sail amicably enough with Thorbjorn again in the future, his revulsion dulled by time and distance, but Hlif would never forgive the man for his assault on her. And here was another such man. Hlif had no doubt she could portray the amber merchant in terms that would make Rachel's case, and that Skarfr's chivalry would be roused.

However, she preferred to be cautious when it came to promises on another's behalf. 'I will ask him,' she said, 'and I am hopeful he will agree but he is his own man. Also, our own plans to leave Sicilia are vague. I will choose the moment to approach him and will let you know.'

Rachel retrieved the amber beads and clasped Hlif's hands in her own. 'I know you will win him over. You are my only hope.'

Hlif tucked away the raw stone in her scrip. It seemed that there would still be one secret Hlif kept from Skarfr.

Rachel studied Hlif critically. 'Let me pluck your brows and your forehead, and make up your face,' she pleaded, not for the first time. 'You would be so beautiful.'

'No, thank you.' Hlif was adamant. She knew how others saw her. 'I'm used to being plain.' Which wasn't quite true but she did not think paint would improve her looks. It would only attract attention from the wrong kind of men and she had enough to contend with as it was. Always being underestimated was annoying but she had no option other than to use men's prejudice to her advantage. No, she would not take Rachel up on her offer but would remain the little Orkneyjar trader with the freckled face, sharper than anyone suspected.

And Skarfr thought she was beautiful.

She didn't like keeping Rachel's secrets from him but she *had* promised. *Just for the time being,* she told herself, standing up to leave. And at least she would have the pleasure of giving him the shirt.

As she reached out to open the red brocade curtain, she was startled for a second time by a man barrelling through a doorway. He pushed her aside as easily as the curtain. She stumbled and righted herself, biting her lip over her outrage. This was not her house, and her friend would not appreciate fuel added to the fire of a man's temper.

'Who's this?' he demanded of a white-faced Rachel, who put a defensive hand in front of her face, flinching and ducking her head like a dog trained by beatings. His clothes shouted of his wealth in a mish-mash of ill-assorted colours and sparkling decoration, with jewelled buttons and gold thread wherever space could be found. Hlif dropped her eyes, feigning modesty and hiding her anger.

Even on his shoes! she thought, risking a glance up as far as the belt cutting his belly in two like a cooper's ring around a broken beer tun. A row of amber beads studded the leather belt and with a jolt, Hlif realised who this was and that his temper could be lethal. Not even the warm lighting of Rachel's niche could soften the ugly expression on the man's greasy face. How much of their conversation had he heard?

'She's a friend,' said Rachel in a small voice, not looking at Hlif as she corrected herself hastily. 'I mean, she's a client, collecting a commission.' She pointed to the wrapped packages tucked under Hlif's arm.

How could such a fine, skilled woman — a talented, beautiful woman — shrink inside herself this way in the presence of such a pathetic man? But Hlif knew how, knew all the ways, whether brutal or subtle, by which dependency was induced. Until a woman — or a little boy — was grateful for scraps of food or kindness. Skarfr had been such a boy. Perhaps Sea-born had been too.

She faced the full brunt of the man's attention. His gaze swept her from veiled hair down her plain blue pinafore overdress to her worn leather boots. He did not seem impressed.

'She's an outsider,' he observed. 'With no business in the Tiraz. Should you need a friend,' and his sneering tone said that she shouldn't, 'keep to your own kind, a woman of the Tiraz. And soon, you will need no other clients. I have given you my word.'

Hlif hid her shudder at such a 'promise' and made one of her own. Soon, Rachel would choose her own visitors and have her own home. If Skarfr was willing — and he would be!

'You can go now,' the man told Hlif. 'You got what you came for.'

She looked at Rachel, 'Yes, I did,' she said, sending an unspoken message of support.

'She brought me oranges,' said Rachel, indicating the overflowing bowl.

'I can bring you more.' The tension in the room was unbearable but Hlif was sure he hadn't heard the plans she and Rachel were making before he entered. Either that or he was skilled at feigning ignorance, which she doubted. His ignorance was self-evident..

The man pushed her through the curtain. 'I can bring her oranges,' he said. 'Don't come back. If you need clothes, order at the shops like everyone else does.'

The curtain dropped behind Hlif with a whoosh of air as doom-filled as any prison door being slammed and locked.

CHAPTER TWELVE

SKARFR, PALERMO, SICILIA

Skarfr had never owned a shirt as fine as the one laid on the kist for his inspection, but he never knew what to say when receiving gifts, even from Hlif. Perhaps *especially* from the woman who knew him best of all. Platitudes seemed inadequate. But, as George had pointed out, did anybody really know another person? What did such a gift mean? Remorse? Guilty conscience?

He shook off the doubts created by George's insinuations, by secrets. Hlif had spent time and thought on a gift for him. She'd been in the Tiraz to buy silk.

But he'd hesitated too long and her smile faded. 'You don't like it?'

Skarfr summoned his fiercest expression. 'When a völva gives a warrior a shirt, the sagas warn us to hesitate before trying it on.' He held up the shirt, inspected it closely and sniffed it.

Hlif laughed, which had been his intention and Sea-born asked, 'What in the gods' names are you doing?'

'Don't use such expressions,' his mother rebuked him as a matter of course. Then, 'Your father is making a very clumsy joke because of an old story, in which an Orkney jarl was poisoned by a shirt, meant to be a gift for his brother.'

Sea-born laughed too. 'You would have to be a witch to make such a shirt!'

Hlif and Skarfr exchanged glances, their rapport complete again.

'That's what a völva is,' Skarfr explained.

'Are those *training words* too?' asked the child. 'To test Mother?'

Skarfr's gut clenched. Now who felt guilty? 'No,' he said, reaching out to pull his wife into his arms. 'Where there is trust, there is no need of testing.' Letting Hlif wriggle out of his embrace, he stripped to the waist and donned the silk shirt, striking a heroic pose, his chin high and his eyes fixed on some invisible adventure.

'Perfect,' was Hlif's judgement as she reached out to stroke an unruly fold, smoothing it flat over his chest. Her hand stilled for a moment, just long enough for her to see the reaction in his eyes.

'It feels nice,' he murmured, then clarified. 'The silk.'

Now it was her turn to tease. 'That should motivate you to wear it.' Then she turned her attention to Sea-born and demanded, 'What's this about *training words*?'

'The Emir said he'd seen you in the Tiraz and that I could be anybody's son with a mother like that and he made Father's eyes go hard but they were just *training words* to make Father fight better in the yard.' For good measure, Sea-born added, 'But we explained that I'm your foster-son so I don't look like you.'

Hlif's storm-grey eyes turned just as stony as Skarfr's were alleged to have been. . Before she could suggest, in front of Sea-born, that killing the Emir was too good for him, he added hastily, 'And we both showed the self-control that is necessary for a warrior to succeed, which is why,' he stated with heavy emphasis, 'the Emir used such training words to hone our minds sharper.'

Hlif pulled Sea-born into a hug, and spoke over his head with gritted teeth, her eyes flashing at Skarfr, 'Of course that was the Emir's intention and we must respect a man so high in the king's favour. Both my warriors have behaved with honour.' She pulled Skarfr into the circle of her arms, Sea-born warm and wriggling between them, his tolerance waning.

'We will speak of this later,' she warned her husband, running her fingers lightly down his silken back, as if he were a cat.

No wonder her bad-tempered, one-eyed ginger monster purrs so much, thought Skarfr, as Sea-born made his escape, leaving the door ajar in his hurry to get down to the docks and watch the fishing boats come in. One of the boy's jobs was to bring home a carefully selected specimen from the catch of the day for the family's evening meal. Hlif had taught him well and he took his work seriously, from haggling over the price to dispatching the chosen fish.

Skarfr felt the change in her hands, pressing against his skin through the silk, before he saw the distant look in Hlif's eyes.

'You will wear silk when you next see Rognvald,' she pronounced, with the resonance of prophecy.

Skarfr shivered. 'Hlif,' he said gently, tracing the curve of her cheek with the back of his hand, calling her back to him.

She started and answered his unspoken question. 'I'm sorry. I don't know when that will be.'

'It's all right,' he said. 'I don't want you throwing rune dice to learn our fates. When the Norns speak through you, we have no choice but to listen, but we should not anger them by seeking to harness them like horses.'

She ducked the topic of rune dice. 'Do you think of it? How it was to be Jarl Rognvald's man? How it could be so again?' she asked him. 'Especially when you are treated as you were today by men who could never earn your respect, whatever the king thinks of you?

He shrugged. 'I told Sea-born the truth. The Emir and Philip do what they think best. They seek to harden and test their men. And Rognvald sentenced us to exile.' She started to apologise but he interrupted her. 'No, it's not your fault. Jarl Rognvald was wrong to stand between us.'

'He will have time to learn how wrong he was and then you can take the place you choose among Orkneymen, with all honour restored.'

'King Roger wants to add me to his collection of foreigners who break their journey in Sicilia and never leave. He's offered me honour, wealth, a place in his fleet, a place in his court, work with al-Idrisi, the library, poetry…'

Hlif chewed on her lips, then released her breath in a long *humph*.

The habit puffed out her cheeks like a stone cherub blowing the trumpet on a church column.

'Everything you could want,' she acknowledged. 'But in exile. Whereas with Rognvald you could live in your own language, and go home.'

Skarfr nodded but Hlif's tone had been that of a supportive wife, not a seer. Was he doomed to spend his life — their lives — in exile? Navigating the crests of fantastical discoveries and the depths of ignorance? Or rather what seemed ignorance in Sicilia, where his Orkneyjar ways and words made him 'foreigner' or worse, no longer Jarl Rognvald's finest warrior and skald.

His skills were quickly gaining him respect as a warrior. Too quickly, to judge by the morning's 'training words', which suggested that King Roger's approval must be paid for in the usual balance of status and envy created by small-minded men grappling for power. Skarfr did not want power in Sicilia, nor even in Orkneyjar and the Emir's envy was misplaced.

The king's approval and purses of gold coin had not been won by Skarfr's skills as warrior and navigator — the latter yet to be proven. Instead, the time spent with Roger and his Moorish map-maker al-Idrisi had created a bond between the three of them as Skarfr gave details of his journey by sea from Orkneyjar to Sicilia. He watched his words turn into Arabic squiggles as evocative as the lines showing the coast of his native islands.

The intellectual joy of his time with the cartographer was the closest Skarfr came to using his skaldic talents but it was not enough. On the many-tongued, cultured island of Sicilia, he was dazzled by half-understood poetry in Arabic, Frankish, Greek, Latin and even Hebrew. But the only place Orkneyjar Norn was spoken was in his own home. For the second time in his life, Skarfr's poetry could not be spoken in public.

Yes, he missed Rognvald. The spontaneous skaldic contests among peers, the courage and camaraderie, the adventure. The low dragon ship skimming the water, part of the sea in a way these two- and three-decked Sicilian dromonds could never be.

Exile had not been his choice, had not been *their* choice, but a punishment.

'I have a trading plan,' said Hlif. 'We'll put the money you earn to work and make more money. Then, when we are rich enough, we'll sail after Rognvald.'

Of course she had a trading plan. As Rognvald's ward and housekeeper, she had provisioned the entire pilgrim voyage from Orkneyjar to Jórsalaheim for a fleet of fifteen ships. Skarfr smiled and the last shred of doubt planted by George of Antioch was removed. His wife was not like other women and he was glad of it. She had gifts from the gods, was a völva and a seer and she was a trader. If she chose to visit the Tiraz and buy silk for shirts, then he had no reason to question her judgement.

'Yes,' he replied. 'When I have fulfilled my promise to the king. The fleet is readying now for spring and summer raids, Ifriqiya and Constantinople. I will bring riches back to you — gold and jewels.'

A shadow flickered across her face but if she felt a woman's fears when her man went raiding, she did not speak of them. She knew she had married a warrior.

'Tomorrow I must sail with the Emir.'

He could never hide his feelings from her and she responded to what he had not said.

'It's the first time and he wants to test you before the raids. To test you and the sunstone.'

He nodded.

'All will be well,' Hlif told him.

Speaking as wife or seer? He couldn't always tell but was happy to accept a positive reading of the future, with or without rune dice.

He shrugged. 'No doubt there will be *training talk* and if I pass this test, there will be others. Men have told me that we can't go raiding until after the *mattanza* — some festival during the tuna run — and that I must take part at least once or be called a coward.'

Hlif laughed. 'I have heard talk of the *mattanza*! Quite a festival. And I think you can manage to catch fish without risking your life.'

He matched her tone. 'Of course, but we must make it into a big event so our womenfolk think more of us. That's why you have to stay home, not come and watch, so I can brag about how dangerous it was.' Skarfr did not say that tuna could be a hundred times the size of salmon, or that a man who tumbled from the circle of boats into the water, had little chance of surviving in the frenzy of netted fish. He could *try* to hide some of the risks he took, however perspicacious she was.

The silk shirt rippled as he reached for her again. 'We can also talk later of your visit to the Tiraz, which must have been... educational.'

Her expression became serious. 'Yes, I think my teaching was considered helpful.' she told him. Then he saw the laughter lighting her sea-grey eyes. 'I am willing to share my expertise with you... later,' and this time her tone was a promise.

All too quickly, the sound of Sea-born singing in Arabic as he mounted the stone steps to the living-quarters reminded Skarfr that he'd meant to talk to Hlif about the boy's grudge-bearing against his first father and against the Emir. It could wait.

CHAPTER THIRTEEN

SKARFR, THE WHALE ROAD

The gods had granted Skarfr lowering clouds, piled like dirty eiderdowns in a sunless sky but George had not been joking about a blindfold. When the flagship of the Sicilian fleet set sail from Palermo harbour, its navigator was sitting on the top deck inside the wooden fortification midship which protected the archers, and his eyes were bound with a black band. The fact it was silk did not make Skarfr feel any less irritated. He closed his eyes, the better to see with those inner senses that every sailor developed.

Despite his height above the waves, Skarfr could feel the change in movement when the ship left the shelter of the harbour for the open sea. If this had been an Orkneyjar dragon ship, he'd have felt the heave of the waves through the clinkered planks and known the current. He'd have been so close to the ocean that the spray wetting his face would have created a wind tell. The coldest side would be where the wind came from. And he knew those seas so well, their prevailing winds and currents, that he could have navigated without the fickle sun or gods-touched, blood-cursed sunstone. With one hand, he cradled the leather pouch dangling from his neck, in which the precious instrument was concealed. A legacy from a pilot who'd been murdered for the sunstone.

Philip interrupted his thoughts. 'You wanted to know more about the fire missiles used by Byzantine ships? Now's a good time. We'll be sailing for a while before the Emir asks you to show your skills.'

A deliberate distraction so he'd lose track of the course they were on? Skarfr breathed in the scent of land, and heard the cries of birds, on his left. They were heading west. He visualised al-Idrisi's map. West, hugging the coast of northern Sicilia. People often spoke of the briny tang of the sea but only sailors grew sensitive to the scent of land, a whiff of trees or smoke, or a barely perceptible change in the air currents from the land direction. Was this how a dog sensed the world when it raised a nose to catch the wind?

He flared his nostrils even as he replied to Philip. 'How could we combat this weapon?'

The stench of gutted fish and the sound of working men calling to each other. They were passing the coastal fishing villages.

'Soak everything in vinegar and urine,' Philip said. 'Stay beyond the reach of the flame-throwers, use archers and catapults, hurl everything that will damage their ships from afar, attack the side of their ship that has no flame-thrower — but they've grown wise to that and no longer mount them only on the prows. And their line formation means each ship protects the sides of the others.'

Philip paused in rattling off his response and his next words were slow and weighty. 'Twelve years ago in a special meeting, the Pope declared Greek fire a weapon too destructive to be used against Christians. *That's* how terrible it is.'

Then the eunuch's tone regained its usual cynicism. 'In the same meeting, he banned clerics of all kinds, monk and nuns, from marrying. How successful do you think either of those edicts was?'

Without waiting for Skarfr to answer the rhetorical question, Philip had said, 'Exactly. Byzantium has perverted war as it has perverted Christianity. They are heretics.' This observation was made with the detachment of one who was not pious, or at least not pious in following the White Christ and his mother. Unlike the Emir. And yet the devout Emir was decorating the interior of his magnificent new church in the Byzantine 'heretic' style, and King

Roger's palatine chapel glittered with gold mosaics set in niches created by Muslim architects.

Beneath all this surface tolerance of other beliefs in Sicilia lay tensions that Skarfr sensed without understanding them. He was accustomed to fitting in with Christian observances. Fish on Frigg's day and church on Sunnudagr did not disturb his own gods. But he had never felt threatened by this ambiguity as he did in Sicilia, when a derogatory comment on a man's religion might come out of the blue.

Was this how Philip felt? Skarfr suspected the eunuch held a mixture of beliefs, but such thoughts were best left unspoken. Much was best left unspoken on an island where the court was Christian and most of Roger's subjects were Muslim. The tensions that lurked below the surface had teeth.

'Distance,' repeated Philip. 'Keep at least ten oars' length from any Byzantine ship — about a hundred feet. Or have a good reason for your sacrifice.'

With that thought Philip left Skarfr to his blindfolded observations. Or rather to some lines of verse.

> *The sea-stallion's smooth gait spurred to galloping*
> *by fast fillies, whitening the wide blue—*

He was trying to think of the best kenning for 'sea', unhappy with images of ploughed fields or whale roads when juxtaposed with horses, when he was interrupted by the Emir shouting to the oarsmen.

The instruction to pause the bank of oars on the left came as no surprise to Skarfr. He'd studied al-Idrisi's maps and made enough sorties as the lowliest of oarsmen during the winter to know that heading west was the Emir's likeliest direction. Westwards from Palermo would take the fleet across the Middle Sea between the coast of Ifriqiya and that of Hispania.

The Emir must know he would have to remove the blindfold to enable Skarfr to use the sunstone. Until then, all he had to do was to keep his sense of direction and how much time had passed, then he'd have a good idea of where the sun was in her journey across the sky.

When he squeezed his eyes tightly, miniature suns and black flecks danced inside his eyelids. He remembered learning how to use the sunstone, the way it caught light and Pilot's injunction not to look directly at the blinding sun. As his subjects were told not to look directly at Manuel Komnenos, the Emperor of Byzantium, whose sanctified gaze could be deadly.

> *Hunting the sun, the wolf Sköll scents burning,*
> *his own charred fur a warning*
> *that World's End is within his reach.*
> *Yet he races ever faster in*
> *the wolf-hours of his doom*
> *towards the fire-storm of the final fight.*

Men cursing jerked Skarfr's attention back to the present and he added his own swearwords to those around him as he realised why the ship was bucking against its crew's actions. George had made them turn the ship in circles, so that a blindfolded man who did not know this coastline would lose all sense of direction.

'Take his blindfold off,' commanded the Emir. The ship was stable again, moving gently with the wind.

The wind? Skarfr racked his brains to remember which way the wind had been blowing when they left the harbour. But he knew that the Middle Sea winds played a fickle game, rebounding from the many coasts. Sailors used to the fierce, predictable winds of the Dark Sea could be lured to their deaths by the deceptive calm and dangerous currents if they did not respect the vagaries of the air gods here.

Sounds from the other ships were no clue either, tacking and zigzagging in random directions like ducklings scattered by a cat. And he was expected to demonstrate what this gift from the gods could do as if it was a jester's trick at a feast. Did they not know, these Sicilian Christians, that for all such gifts, a price must be paid?

From the Starkaðr's three lives to the Volsung sword, Óðinn's gifts came at a terrible price.

That was why Skarfr prayed as always to Thórr not Óðinn, and hoped that the Great Protector would allow a more human dose of success. Immortality and endless wealth were not in his prayers. He bowed his head and silently repeated the words Pilot had used. Let the Emir and his men imagine he was praying to the White Christ! *Mighty Thórr, now glorious Sol is veiled, may the wily wolf Sköll catch her chariot, to show an unworthy pilot which course to steer. Let Skarfr the Navigator see the wolf chase Sol.*

All eyes were on him as he raised his arms and slowly moved the sunstone around his head in a circle. He looked through it at the leaden skies, focusing on the black spot that was Sköll chasing the second black spot, the sun that appeared by magic when the heavens were viewed through the sunstone. The two spots grew nearer to one another until the wolf caught the sun and Skarfr cried out, 'The sun is in that direction!'

He guessed he was pointing south-east but he could not be sure of how long they'd been sailing.

The Emir, however, knew every contour of this coast and knew exactly where the compass points were. Like all expert sailors, he could estimate the time sailed and could calculate where the sun must be. He had no need of the sun to steer his course but he could judge the sunstone's accuracy — and Skarfr's.

'Our navigator is right.' George's voice boomed out. 'His sunstone belongs to Sicilia now!'

Skarfr ripped off the blindfold and blinked. Then he closed his fist tight around the crystal and thrust it back into its leather pouch.

Philip's black eyes followed the movement and then he looked away again, as had two men at table in a hall, the day before they murdered the first pilot. For this very sunstone.

'The sunstone is my inheritance,' Skarfr said. 'It only works for its true master and takes vengeance on anyone who comes by it illegally.'

The Emir grinned. 'Then it is as well that Sicilia owns Skarfr the Navigator.'

Before Skarfr could find a polite rebuttal, a familiar voice piped up, 'I told you my father had mastery of the sunstone. And it's magical.'

'Don't scold the lad,' George said. 'I changed my mind. He can be of use on this voyage.'

Skarfr's stomach clenched with foreboding. How had the Emir — or Philip — reached Sea-born? It wouldn't have taken much persuasion to convince the boy to come sailing. 'I thought we were practising skills for attacks at sea and going home today?'

'I've changed my mind about that too.' The Emir's mood was buoyant and his smile disingenuous. 'We've provisions enough to reach Ifriqiya so that's where we're going.'

So *that* was why the Emir had been so insistent on Skarfr wearing full armour and bringing his helm. This was no training exercise.

Ifriqiya. Wealth. Honour. And a small boy to protect, against his own commander and crew. Hlif would be incandescent with fury at the insult to him and to her in the lack of notice, and at him bringing Sea-born to war. He could only hope that he and Sea-born would return safely to Palermo to account for their dereliction of duty. They would be away, not for a day, but for months.

CHAPTER FOURTEEN

HLIF, PALERMO, SICILIA

Hlif had left a couple of loaves at the bakehouse, to go in the oven after they'd risen, and to be collected before the midday meal. She'd grown used to leavened bread and city sophistication, and no longer made bannocks over the home fire. The two tiny redemption chips were in the scrip attached to her belt, beside a much more valuable stone and some coins.

No doubt her maidservant Amina would have carried out the task, rather than going about the household chores with pursed lips but Hlif enjoyed going to the bakehouse and dawdling beside the shops she passed on the way back. Accustomed to the bare necessities of leatherwork, wool, pottery and smithware in an Orkneyjar village, she was like a child with sweetmeats, eyes bigger than her stomach as she lingered by the haberdashery.

How could such a plethora of buttons exist? Wooden, bone, embroidered or even jewelled. And as for the ribbons — a silken rainbow of colours, thin as laces to weave through the new court fashion for loose hair, broader to decorate sleeves and necklines, or wide enough to sash a gown and enhance a slim waist. She succumbed to the *'Buy-me'* glamour of a turquoise snood, sparkling with gold threads. Something to wear at the coronation, she told herself. Buying it was almost a duty.

Then, driven by her extravagance to make amends by furthering her trade project, she headed for the fruiterer to discuss why the supply of oranges was so erratic.

The shop door was closed so she reached for the ornate brass knocker, shaped like a lion's head, but hesitated. She could hear men shouting within but could not make out what they were saying. While she debated whether to call back another day instead, the door jerked inwards and two men pushed past her, with no hint of apology. They left a fleeting impression on her of burly physiques, black hair, brown eyes, workmen's clothes and the odour of sweat laced with wine.

As she recovered her balance and watched them swagger down the street, one turned and gave her a long, hard stare.

She stared back, memorising his every feature. Black bushy eyebrows that joined in one straight line above wide-set eyes in a slightly flattened face. The nose a snub. More otter than hawk and an impression of cunning about an unsmiling mouth, something calculating in the compression at one corner. She would know him again. Although she had no reason to think it might matter.

Slowly, holding her gaze, he put a finger to his lips, then, with frightening speed, he sliced the same finger across his throat. The threat was clear but Hlif had no idea what she was supposed to keep quiet about.

He smiled at her, showing a full set of very pointed teeth, before he clapped an arm around his fellow and sauntered off, as if his gestures had been the most common of civilities.

Her legs shaking, Hlif managed to get a faint *rat-a-tat* out of the lion and the fruiterer opened the door, ashen-faced.

'Who were those men?' she blurted out. 'Are you all right? Did they hurt you?'

If anything, he blanched further. 'You don't know what you're talking about,' he snapped.

'I heard shouting,' she persisted.

He waved an arm, in an attempt to convey, '*It was nothing*'. 'They protect my shop,' he explained, his gaze skittering about the room, alighting everywhere but on her, 'and I was late paying them because of a problem with the delivery of oranges.'

'It's good you have protection,' acknowledged Hlif. 'It is the same in my country. It is the Jarl, our ruler, who protects his vassals, and each minor lord protects those who work his land. In return, dues are paid to the overlords.' Her attention had already moved on from protection to the shortage of blood oranges which had caused the altercation. Here was the opportunity she'd been looking for.

'It's not quite the same here,' said the shopkeeper drily, looking at her as if she had three heads. She was used to such looks. He muttered something that sounded like 'shafted twice over' and Hlif suddenly pictured the Orkneyjar bondsmen grumbling about tax increases to pay for Rognvald's cathedral; and Sweyn skimming so much of the crop from his land on Ness that the peasants had complained formally to the Jarl and war had resulted, however briefly. Not every lord was as fair in shouldering his feudal responsibilities as Skarfr, or in asking only for the work and return that was proper.

And at sea, the captain should ensure fair distribution of the spoils they garnered. A sudden doubt hit her. When they set sail later in the year, would George and Philip give Skarfr a fair portion? Or would they cheat him and laugh in doing so, as Sweyn had robbed Thorbjorn of his share in plunder. Was she so filled with nostalgia that she'd forgotten the greed and violence that were also part of Orkneyjar life?

'It is not always fair,' she conceded, changing the subject. 'Why can't you get oranges all the time? I might be able to help you.' The mouth-watering fruit had become a passion for Hlif, not just a pretext for visiting the Tiraz so often

'You?' replied the fruiterer, almost smiling at the absurdity of the suggestion. She was used to that too. Always having to prove herself, being twice as knowledgeable about her business as her competitors — usually men.

'If you tell me the problem, we shall see if I have a solution,' she said calmly.

She learned that the orange-grower, whose name was Gian, lived a day's journey away and could not afford the time to send his crop to market more than once every two weeks, when his man could travel in the safety of company. He was also limited by what one wagon would carry so Hlif must wait for her oranges until the following Óðinn's day and be first in the queue to ensure she bought some.

'You have more demand than you have oranges?' asked Hlif, musing.

'Much more,' was the reply.

'And the grower, Gian, has harvested more than he can transport to you?'

The fruiterer nodded. 'The harvesting season is short, from February to early April usually. He has many orange groves and men working for him. Gian gets a better price here in Palermo than he does locally, where others also grow the oranges, but he has to accept the lower price if he can't travel, or the crops would spoil.'

'Hmm,' said Hlif, considering how she could weave the information into her plan. 'Would you put a box of the new arrivals aside for me on Wednesday?'

'I can't—' he began.

She interrupted him with a winning smile and a coin. 'It seems fair to give you half-payment in advance.'

He took the coin and the bargain was sealed. In Hlif's experience, the first step in successful trade was trust and this was a good start to what she hoped would be a business relationship beneficial to them both. The second step was of course making sure you weren't cheated, which is why she wore weights and a measuring string attached to her housekeeper's belt.

Now that her plans were taking shape in such a practical way, she would talk them all through with Skarfr, tonight, and seek his support for the parts which did not concern oranges.

A sudden shower ended all thoughts of further shopping and Hlif dashed back to the shelter of her house, pausing at the ground floor entry to let Amina and Pietro know she had returned. As expected,

Pietro rebuked her for going out unaccompanied but showed no real concern. He barely broke off from entertaining Amina with an anecdote concerning a hunting-dog and two cockerels to greet his mistress. His dark eyes sparkled, black hair flying as he threw his head back and laughed. His hands flew at each other and jabbed, like fighting-cocks.

As usual, he was happy to lounge around unless he was given a direct order. Like one of his allegorical cockerels, strutting and flirting his tail-feathers for the world to admire. Hlif would wager a basket of oranges that the fine-feathered rooster would not be alive at the end of the parable. An easy life suited him fine. However, Hlif found him reliable enough if held to account and the last thing she wanted was an over-diligent guardian watching her every move.

And although amused despite herself by Pietro's charm, Amina did indeed purse her lips at having missed out on an enjoyable outing. Amina rarely gave the impression she enjoyed anything in life and wore a permanent air of disapproval, to a greater or lesser degree, according to how inappropriate her mistress' behaviour was.

Amina was so different from Skarfr's thrall Brigid, whose warmth could not be extinguished, even in the dark days of the skald Botolf as master. Brigid had mothered the orphaned boy and added a woman's touch to the warrior's home as Skarfr grew into his inheritance. Home-longing swept through Hlif for the smoky longhouse, the flames guttering in the hearth while the soft rain misted the view of fields outside. For Brigid's bannocks, fresh-baked, and Fergus' tales of Irish monsters and miracles. That was one reason Hlif liked the bakehouse. The smell reminded her of home.

From dawn onwards, loaves of shaped dough were scooped up one at a time on the baker's long-handled peel and arranged as a batch in the middle of the hot oven, a dome-shaped stone like a vault, above a log fire — more Sicilian extravagance! But the crackle and flames did contribute to the sensuality of the scene in the Sicilian bakehouse. The baker's face was always flushed as he thrust the risen dough into the dark oven and removed the baked loaves, golden and crusty. Sometimes, a piece of bread would fall off and he would offer it to Hlif. 'Taste this,' he'd say and she never said no to a warm, crumbly mouthful. However, today, Hlif would not be greedy. She would send Amina to collect the bread, to make up for the missed outing earlier.

As she carefully mounted the slippery stone steps towards the first story entrance, one hand holding her damp hood away from her eyes so she could watch her footing, Hlif wondered whether Brigid and Fergus felt about Orkneyjar as she did about Sicilia. Could one place be both home and exile, to different people? How would a Sicilian feel in the Jarl's stronghold in Orkneyjar?

She let herself into the family's living quarters and set her cloak to dry on a stool by the fire, thanking Sicilian sophistication for the chimney that allowed smoke to escape into the sky instead of blackening the walls, as happened in their longhouse back home. Even with the chimney, the odour of damp wool rose from the steaming cloak, filling the Palermo room with Orkneyjar sheep.

Hlif shook off the home-yearning along with the raindrops and unloosed her hair. Her coif was wet in front from rain dashed under her hood by the capricious wind so she put it beside the cloak to dry. In Orkneyjar, the rain gentled her frizzy hair but Sicilia's harsh downpours made it bush out even more when wet. She brushed it fiercely to tame it as best she could before trying Rachel's suggestion — smoothing it down with olive oil. She was about to try on the snood when there was a knock at the door.

Only strangers knocked and nobody had called on Hlif and Skarfr — until now. But hospitality was the gods' law, tested by Óðinn in many guises, and, even in Sicilia, you always opened the door to one who knocked, however fast your heart was beating.

CHAPTER FIFTEEN

HLIF, PALERMO, SICILIA

The wind caught the door as Hlif opened it and she stepped backwards, thrown off-balance. She had the impression that the visitor flew into the room, his robes flapping. Not one-eyed and not hiding his visage under a broad-rimmed hat, this was no god testing humans' hospitality. The caller's face was rain-spotted underneath a damp turban. His eyes widened with shock on seeing her and she suddenly realised what she must look like, as wild and loose as her hair. As was her right in her own home!

But she reddened anyway, regardless of how unfair to her the situation was.

'*As-salaam alaikum,*' al-Idrisi greeted her politely.

'*Wa-alaikum-salaam,* my Lord,' she said, remembering her manners. 'You caught me unawares.' As if that wasn't obvious! 'But do come in.'

Rushing in behind the king's geographer came Amina, breathing heavily. Nobody would climb the steps without Amina spotting them and of course the servant had realised that a chaperone was required.

'Shall I make some peppermint tea, my Lady?' Amina asked tactfully and offered a stool to al-Idrisi. He sat down heavily.

Surprisingly grateful for the prompt, Hlif said, 'Yes please,' and 'Do excuse me for a moment,' to her visitor.

Behind the curtains that separated the bedchamber from the living area, Hlif extricated her spare coif from the clothes kist and quickly coiled her hair up underneath it, tucking away any rebellious strands. Modesty restored, she returned to her visitor and took the second stool which Amina had placed at a polite distance from al-Idrisi.

Amina had brought some mending with her and was seated discreetly in the background, her eyes on her sewing.

All ears, thought Hlif, not sure whether she would have preferred privacy or not. Clearly, al-Idrisi was more comfortable with both Amina' presence and with Hlif's circumspect hair-covering.

These Sicilian men, sighed Hlif inwardly, *whether Frankish or Muslim, are too worried about a woman's ungodly attractions to talk and listen in any sensible manner. Imagine sailing with such a crew! Well, spit it out. Why have you come here to talk to Skarfr?*

'I'm afraid my husband is away with the Emir's fleet today and I don't know when he'll be home,' she said, trying not to grimace as she sipped her peppermint tea, strong and sickly-sweet in the Sicilian manner.

'My lady, it is you I've come to see. The king visited this morning and told me not to expect Lord Skarfr tomorrow, nor the next day.'

Hlif's hand shook as she lowered her ceramic cup to her lap and cradled it, suddenly aware of its fragility. 'Has something happened to my husband?' she asked.

'No, no,' al-Idrisi hastened to reassure her but her nerves had only a moment to calm before he added, 'They are not training. They have sailed for Ifriqiya. He will not be back for months.'

The blood rushed to Hlif's head. 'Without telling me!' *How could he!* He'd even protested when she put a small pot of charcoal into his pack, saying if he was wounded in training he'd come home for healing. Thank the gods she'd insisted. At least he'd have something to rub on cuts. She forced her mind away from worse possibilities and tried to concentrate on what the map-maker was telling her.

'That's why I came,' said al-Idrisi. 'I'm sure he didn't know. He told me he would come to me tomorrow to continue our work and

Skarfr has never let me down. Of course, the king knew the fleet was sailing but he implied that the Emir kept the true destination quiet, to avoid word reaching the shores of Ifriqiya ahead of our ships.'

'But, not telling Skarfr!' Hlif had no words to convey the lack of respect the Emir had shown — and for a warrior worth all the rest of the crew put together.

'It's very annoying,' agreed al-Idrisi. 'Especially as I wanted to check the main trading items in the places at which Skarfr stopped on his voyage to Sicilia.'

'On *our* voyage to Sicilia,' corrected Hlif. 'My husband is second to none in describing coastlines, winds and tides, or in battle strategies on sea or land, but I think you'll find I know more about trade than he does.'

Al-Idrisi glanced away, embarrassed. 'My dear lady, I am sure you have purchased some pretty trinkets on what must have been a very tiring expedition for you, but my work is a scientific treatise.'

'Indeed.' Hlif nodded her understanding of how inadequate a woman's contribution would be to a scientific treatise. 'How impressive such a work must be. Perhaps you would give me an example of the trade details you record?'

Al-Idrisi beamed at having a listener, any listener. Then he shut his eyes, lost in some inner world, before reciting,

'In the Qamnuriyya, one sees Manan Mountain, which rises from the ocean. It slopes steeply, with a high summit, and the earth is red. Sparkling stones are found there, which dazzle a man's eyes so much that when the sun shines, their reflective pulses and their red brilliance avert human gaze.'

Hlif gave a guilty start. *Red stones!* Was al-Idrisi reading her thoughts?

Al-Idrisi was already bestowing another snippet from his book upon her. 'Tulmitha is well-populated and regularly visited by ships which bring superior quality cotton and linen in exchange for honey, tar and butter. These ships come from Alexandria.'

'Where is the Manan Mountain?' she asked, feigning idle curiosity and hoping this was not another name for the Sicilian peak

Rachel had described. She hadn't made it sound so close to the sea. Had the words of drunken pillow-talk been that specific? Or recalled exactly? And how could a woman know where any place might be when the names changed from one language to another!

'And where is Tulmitha?' she added, to cover too much interest in red stones. She was pretty certain she'd never been there either, wherever it was, but she'd heard of Alexandria.

Al-Idrisi's eyes snapped open. 'Manan Mountain is in the Second Clime, First Section and Tulmitha is in the Third Section of the Third Clime,' he answered.

'Oh.' None the wiser, Hlif realised she would not be able to help the geographer after all. The work was indeed too scientific.

'Ifriqiya,' al-Idrisi clarified.

Where Skarfr is sailing. The word gave Hlif enough courage to say, 'I would love you to show me where that is, on one of your maps.' She could only dangle the bait and hope.

'I don't know...' began al-Idrisi, sucking his grey beard. Hlif was always puzzled by the way Muslim men hid the hair on their heads so carefully while sporting thickets from their chins.

At that moment there was a knock on the door and Amina left her darning in order to answer it.

'Mistress, a messenger from the monastery school,' she called over her shoulder, blocking entry until Hlif gave assent.

In came a bedraggled schoolboy, dripping on the floor tiles as he carried out his errand. 'Brother Paolo wished you to know in case you didn't already that Sea-born — your child — which I'm sure you do know already so I don't know why he put those words in — was collected from school by the Emir's men to go sailing with his father — and he's so lucky — I wish I could go to Ifriqiya because I'm not too young whatever they say — and they said he's gone to Ifriqiya.'

Hlif dropped the cup, watched it smash into pieces on the tiles, the tea dregs green and dark as an angry ocean. Unthinking, she retrieved a small piece and winced at the fine cut.

'I'll do that, my Lady.' Amina fetched a broom and swept up the broken shards as Hlif licked beads of blood from her finger.

Al-Idrisi grimaced, whether with distaste or sympathy Hlif could not tell. His manner was so different from Orkneymen's.

'Thank you,' she said, fishing in her scrip for a small coin to give the boy. 'Your mother will be very glad you're not going to Ifriqiya. Go home now and give her the biggest hug a dirham can buy.'

The young messenger blew back into the rain as quickly as he'd come and no doubt even more confused.

Hlif picked up the thread of her conversation with al-Idrisi as if they had not been interrupted, as if he had not been about to deny her the chance to follow her husband and son, if only by tracing a route on coloured vellum. She could be with them in spirit.

'Almería...' she began and shut her eyes, the better to visualise the docks where she'd haggled for a barrel of fish, the Moorish citadel dominating the port, recently taken by the Genoese. She recalled the arguments between the two pilots with Skarfr and Jarl Rognvald, over whether they should explore Almería's river, or sail around the east coast to a different river where fabulous riches awaited them. Skarfr's insistence that they should find this mythical river, reported to be so long that they could sail up it for months, had already caused one of the Captains to leave the company and head directly on the known sea-route to Narbonne. Not that Captain Eindridi was any loss, but he'd taken five ships with him.

Skarfr. The light of adventure in his eyes. Making sagas whether he realised it or not.

This was only one of the reasons she loved him.

She shook herself. None of that was what al-Idrisi wanted her to speak about so she tried to emulate his factual tone. 'Outside the city are orchards, gardens, country homes and vineyards belonging to the residents of Almería.'

'Good. Almería is in the in the First Section of the Fourth Clime. Continue. You said you knew about trade. Tell me of Almería's trade.'

Hlif risked a glance at the geographer. He was nodding, so she shut her eyes again and continued. *Thank goodness for Rachel!* 'From Muslim times, Almería was a major producer of silk fabrics, including brocade, red taffeta, Ispahan designs; also those ornamented with precious stones, pearls and beads, decorative hangings and slippers.'

She opened her eyes to receive the verdict.

Al-Idris waved an arm airily. 'Of course, there is nothing there I did not know and your expression is poor. It is also important to be exact — the Muslims were Almoravids, may they be cursed.'

Hlif found it difficult to believe that Skarfr had expressed himself any better than she had *or* known as much but she held her tongue.

'But,' al-Idrisi concluded, 'I think you know enough to be useful in checking what I have written about those places you know. I am willing to teach you enough to understand the structure of my book.'

Hiding a smile, Hlif thanked her new teacher. 'I can come to you tomorrow morning, when Skarfr was supposed to come.' Hlif was at her most businesslike. 'I can give you all the trade information I have and I would like to learn from you about Ifriqiya and the places our fleet will be travelling to, what they face there.'

'Let it be so. And of course you must bring your maidservant as chaperone.'

Of course. What a joy to have Amina' sour presence to preserve my modesty.

The geographer rose awkwardly as if he had stiffened while sitting. Hlif wondered how old he was. His work was not good for his back, all that stooping over the lectern. And all that peering at details was a strain for his eyes. Maybe she could help him with more than trade facts for his book. And she had an idea as to how he could help her. With more than maps. It was indeed by God's grace that red stones had been mentioned. Or by the gods' grace.

CHAPTER SIXTEEN

HLIF, PALERMO, SICILIA

It took Hlif three sessions with al-Idrisi before he gave her an opening to put her request to him.

For two sessions she listened to descriptions of coastal settlements where she had stopped en route to Sicilia. Grimsby, Frankish villages, Almería, Tortosa, Narbonne — each town held memories that made her miss Skarfr even more. The geographical details blurred: travel distances between towns; locations and residents; trade and climates.

Skarfr had taken this imaginary route before her, in this very room, glimpsed the silver planisphere through the doorway, seen the maps laid out to dry, been challenged by the exacting intellect of this grey-bearded sage. She found no mistakes in the information recited to her but sometimes she could contribute an extra detail. For which she was rewarded with a grunt and a note added to al-Idrisi's work in progress.

In the third session, she plucked up courage to tell al-Idrisi that the lands of Skotland, Ness and Orkneyjar were missing from his book and that she could tell him all he needed to know. He was courteous, if not enthusiastic, so she forged ahead. Speaking of her homeland, she forgot the man listening and taking notes as she spoke. She also forgot his categories as she lost herself in the colours and scents of home. Dove-grey skies and sealskin seas, fields of barley rippling like gold silk in the northerly winds. Frost-hardened women with coarse hands tending their flocks and weaving the islands' wool, making everything from sails to decorative trim for best clothes. Standing stones as old as time, their power thrumming dimly between solstices and flaring into magic. Sometimes a stone would straighten and lift his head at night, walk in search of—

Hlif broke off and flushed as she realised she'd been carried away. Her account was not suitable for al-Idrisi's book and his quill had not moved in some time. However, she'd forgotten about the other person listening.

'I can see it all!' exclaimed Amina, her eyes shining, her work forgotten. Her hands were also still but because she was entranced. 'A place of such beauty and so many marvels.'

Hlif smiled at her, grateful for appreciation from such an unexpected quarter.

Al-Idrisi coughed meaningfully and Amina dropped her eyes, returned to her embroidery.

'You have given me all I need for the north of England,' al-Idrisi said, adding graciously, 'I think you want to look at the map of Ifriqiya.'

Hlif bristled. North of England indeed! But she knew better than to argue for the importance of her homeland. And she understood al-Idrisi's point of view. She had never heard of Sicilia before leaving home. Truly, a woman — or a man — had to travel widely to learn what home meant.

'Yes please,' she said, 'but first I have a proposal to put to you.'

Amina' busy fingers stilled once more, her customary expression of disapproval in place and duplicated on al-Idrisi's face.

'Oranges,' explained Hlif. 'Sanguine oranges. I've spoken to a shopkeeper in Palermo who has difficulties sourcing as much stock as he believes he can sell and he'll pay me to resolve the problem.'

'Sanguine oranges,' mused al-Idrisi. 'According to Ibn Butlan of Baghdad in his medical treatise *The Taqwim as-sihhah*, the pulp is cold and humid in the third degree and the skin is dry and warm in the second. As long as they're perfectly ripe of course.'

Why did scholars have to number and catalogue everything to make it so… flummoxing! When what mattered could be shared in simple words that a woman could understand? As if the words used were deliberately complicated to shut out anybody who had not been schooled in the same manner. To shut out all women.

But that didn't prevent her from finding the kernel in a nut — or the juice in an orange. 'They're good for health,' she agreed, 'and taste like sweet balls of sunshine. And they're ripe now, for only a few months, so I need to go to the orange grower as soon as possible, to agree a trade deal.'

Al-Idrisi looked down his nose at her. 'A trade deal.'

'Yes, I'm well accustomed to trading.'

Al-Idrisi looked sceptical but merely observed, '*The Beauties of Commerce* tells us there are three kinds of merchants: he who travels, he who stocks and he who exports. Which are you?'

Hlif had never been asked to subdivide and name all the aspects of the work she had conducted as Jarl Rognvald's housekeeper, both on land and at sea. Her mind blanked.

She began, 'I provided food for the household…' then faltered.

'Yes, yes,' said al-Idrisi kindly. 'As a woman does.

Hlif remembered Grimsby, not in relation to the geographer's categories but to her own. Stocking up on provisions for fifteen ships during shore leave while the men sailing them held pissing contests and spent their money on whores. Trying to steal a private moment with Skarfr and teaching him how to enter the dreamworld and find her there. How she missed him!

As a woman does, indeed! Nonplussed, Hlif considered the categories of trader offered to her.

He who travels. She'd certainly travelled. To Hjaltland for soapstone and Ness for wood. On this voyage, she'd acquired salt from Narbonne as well as all the provisions for a fleet of fifteen longships. *Anchovies.* She remembered haggling over barrels of them, stocking them on board, then losing one barrel in the storm. Her mind balked again at memories of the storm too painful to revisit: memories of her loss.

He who stocks. She'd stocked not only the anchovies and other ships' provisions but everything in the Jarl's *Bu* in Orphir, from cabbages to slingshots, ale to axes.

And as for exporting! That's how she'd paid for the furs and wine, brought to Orkneyjar shores by shipping partners. With homespun wool, both raw and woven.

'All of them,' she said firmly. 'I'm an Orkneyjar trader. That's how we do things. Man *or* woman.' Let him add *that* to his categories.

Then she gave al-Idrisi the sort of facts he understood. 'The Jarl's household consisted of five hundred men at sea and more than that in Orphir, when there were visitors to his stronghold. Not just food but all provisions, including armour and weapons.' *Not just as every woman does.*

The more she talked, the more she realised the scope of her responsibilities. *Why had nobody ever listed them in such a way before?* She felt a new sense of achievement. 'Not just produce and craftwork from our islands but those carried by merchants to Orkneyjar from far countries. And on our voyage, I have bargained with such merchants in their home towns to provision our ships and buy valuable goods for trade and to take back to Orkneyjar when we return from this pilgrimage.'

He gave her a sharp look then and she coloured, remembering that she was not supposed to think of going home. The king and al-Idrisi — and even Emir George — wanted Skarfr to stay here in Sicilia, call it home. With a sinking feeling, she realised that she might have to stay here but it would never be home.

Al-Idrisi dismissed her trading history with an airy wave but the very fact he returned to the topic of oranges suggested she had established her credentials.

'The orange season is short,' said al-Idrisi, still quoting from one of his books, 'but the peel can be candied and preserved. It is good for the stomach and easier to digest than an orange. Although Ibn

Butlan says the danger of indigestion can be neutralised by accompanying the orange with a glass of the best wine.'

Hlif was not averse to a glass of fine wine, and intended to find out what the process of candying involved but before putting these suggestions into practice she had to obtain and transport her oranges.

She put the easier request first, to test the water. 'I was hoping you could recommend a trustworthy captain, with a cargo ship, willing to sail to Catania. You must surely have had many dealings with one such for carrying—' she looked at the exotic items around the room '—books, or furniture or the silver disc for the planisphere.'

'Ah yes, that was quite a feat.' He sucked his beard, a habit with him when reflecting. He split the stack of finished pages in his book into two piles, as if it were already bound. Then he leafed through, careful to keep the correct order as he moved pages from one pile to the other. When he found the ones he wanted, he called her over to stand beside him and pointed to the map, which was level with Hlif's forehead.

With an impatient sigh at the inadequacy of women, al-Idrisi gestured to a nearby step-stool he used to reach the higher shelves in his library. Hlif took the hint, thinking how much easier her life would be if the lectern was at her height. But the world was arranged for the ease of tall men, and that wasn't going to change so, as always, she adapted and stepped up onto the stool.

'This is Palermo and you wish to sail east, through the Strait of Messina then south around the coast.' He tracked the route, left and then up the page. Hlif suppressed the urge to turn the map upside down and concentrated. 'Once you're through the strait into the Aegean, the prevailing wind is northerly, which will suffice to carry you south. I have done this many times to visit my family in Syracusa.'

Hlif tried and failed to imagine this dry academic playing hide-and-seek with nieces and nephews, or even discussing births and marriages while watching the sunset. No doubt he would talk about his book. Maybe indulge in an intellectual board game like *tafl*. She had seen turbanned men playing something similar in the city streets.

'And for the return?' asked Hlif, suspecting she would not like the answer.

Al-Idrisi shook his head. 'No captain worth his salt would waste time coming back against the wind. No, the usual route circumnavigates the island.'

Hlif's heart sank. 'The whole island? How long would that take?'

'Allowing for occasional bad weather, you would still do it easily in three weeks. Plus whatever time you need to conduct your business.'

How long would the oranges last? Would she have to sell them en route? What about her agreement with the Palermo shopkeeper? And what about her other project, the red stones?

She looked at the map. From Palermo to the inland plain of Catania looked so easy, so quick, just a handspan. A thought struck her. 'Would travelling by land be better?' She was so used to Orkneyjar ships and trade via water routes, that she'd forgotten that taking a cart cross-country was another option.

'You could walk it in four or five days,' was the encouraging reply.

'I'd need a cart,' she said.

Al-Idrisi looked at her with pity. 'You could take donkeys,' he said. 'Not a cart. To and from Palermo, there is a well-travelled road, even though the ruts and stones would juice your oranges before they arrived here. But across the wild lands and in the foothills of Mount Etna... folly! Also, you would need more protection than your profits from oranges would bring in. There are bandits in the interior and a woman is an easy target.'

'Then by ship it shall be!' Hlif would not be put off and if she was successful, her true cargo would more than pay for the only protection she needed. Pietro would suffice.

Al-Idrisi was sucking his beard again. 'Even though the ports and coastal waters are friendly, no ship is completely safe from pirates,' he observed.

'I have survived pirates,' said Hlif calmly.

'Then, if you insist on this venture, I think I know the man for you to transport your fruit. Captain Lemercier. He is awaiting the arrival of a Melitese merchant ship and will set sail as soon as he's loaded his share of its cargo. He offloads stock at Taormina so I'm sure he'll have room for your fruit, with sufficient remuneration. I'll send him a message to let him know of your request. Have your man call at the docks tomorrow afternoon to give your instructions.'

'I was sure you would know someone — thank you. As I'm sure you could help me with an even more difficult matter,' continued Hlif doggedly. 'The fruiterer tells me I need a trader's permit.'

Al-Idrisi was shaking his head, 'Ah, no. There you are mistaken. I cannot issue permits nor do I have any idea who can.'

'The King,' said Hlif and waited for rejection, which came instantly.

'Ah no, I couldn't ask King Roger for such a thing.'

She persisted, 'The Jarl was like your king to his own people, so, as his representative, I needed no permit, but now I must comply with the regulations here.

'I have been talking to the other traders and I can resolve this problem with the supply of oranges. I know they need cool, dry, dark storage and the cellar in our house is perfect, with plenty of room. I've calculated that I can sell a sack to the fruiterer on a regular basis for several weeks from only one trip to Catania.'

Hlif swallowed, hoped that al-Idrisi found the fruit as tempting as she did. Or even as essential for his stomach's health. 'Perhaps you would like a personal supply of oranges?'

'One a day would be most acceptable, during the season.'

How long is the season? wondered Hlif. There was so much she needed to find out but she would learn all that was necessary. She had done so before.

Al-Idrisi smiled. 'Now, shall we study the maps of Ifriqiya?'

CHAPTER SEVENTEEN

HLIF, PALERMO, SICILIA

They knelt on the floor, the better to study the parchment rectangles.

Skarfr's journey looked so easy, sailing upwards on the blue sea, to call on some islands under Sicilian rule, all outlined in black with the land in yellow. Then the little triangular sails would scud right across the Middle Sea to the coast of Ifriqiya, which looked as if a giant rat had nibbled the edges of a piece of lace. Maybe it would be as easy as that. Maybe Skarfr and Sea-born would see palm trees, sand dunes and camels, and all would be as peaceful as in al-Idrisi's book.

'They will probably sail to Mahdia,' the savant was telling her, as he pointed to a place in Ifriqiya that was but a skip-and-a-jump from a Sicilian island. 'That's where Philip was born among the Berber people.'

'Where were you born?' asked Hlif, curiosity getting the better of her manners.

Al-Idrisi did not take offence. 'Here,' he ran a finger along the full length of the Ifriqiyan coast, westwards to the narrows bordered by Hispania on the other coast. 'Ceuta.'

'We must have sailed through that strait!' realised Hlif. 'How wonderful that your map records our journey.'

'It records all journeys.' Al-Idrisi's tone was less frosty and Hlif hoped to thaw him further.

'Tell me about Ceuta.'

She sighed as he fetched the relevant pages from his book to read to her, but among the number of hills (seven) and its measurements (one mile from west to east) were more vivid descriptions. On 'the best fishing coast in the world' a hundred different species could be found, of which the specialty was the tuna. These were caught with barbed spears.

'The Ceutan tuna fishers must be strong and agile, to hold onto these giant fish by the hemp ropes attached to the spears. They are peerless in such skills. And,' finished al-Idrisi, 'the men of Ceuta also fish for coral trees and for pearls.'

What treasures! Hlif's eyes gleamed like Ceutan pearls as she listened. She recalled something mentioned by Skarfr. 'They fish for tuna here, too, don't they,' she said.

'Yes, they make a big festival of it, the *mattanza*. Not in Palermo, but on the west coast.' Al-Idrisi's shrug was expressive. The *mattanza* was not Ceutan.

By the time she went home, Hlif had broken through the mapmaker's reserve and found a constructive way of passing the mornings in long, lonely days. He'd even obtained the trading permit she needed, signed by King Roger, although she'd paid for it by suffering several diatribes on 'how to avoid being given short measure' and 'how to conduct oneself in the ritual dialogue of haggling'. She put up with it all because she'd come to like the stuffy old savant. Underneath his categories and numbers, he hid courtesy and kindness that were balm to her loneliness. Also, she felt closer to Skarfr and Sea-born when she could look at the maps and learn about the places where they might be. As if she was travelling with them.

Following each session with al-Idrisi, Hlif pictured the two of them in her mind's eye. Two days sailing to Melita, where the Emir would oversee the payment of tribute, most notably a Melitese falcon of top hunting quality, to be shipped immediately to Palermo.

With the arrival of the falcon would come news of the Emir's fleet. Although Hlif doubted that she would hear of Skarfr and Sea-born by name, she would know of any great natural disaster or battle. Then, like all women whose husbands and sons went a-viking, she would put her worry aside and busy herself with her own work while they were away. And her work promised to be quite an adventure.

While Skarfr sailed from Melita to a smaller island, once a nest of pirates and now as Sicilian as Melita and Ifriqiya, Hlif would be heading from Palermo to a distant orange grove, with her happy-go-lucky bodyguard and a cart she'd hire when the ship docked. When the Emir's men were claiming gold and spices as King Roger's dues in his Ifriqiyan provinces, using swords where words failed, Hlif would also be loading treasures. The cart would return from the farm to the port, heaped with the produce of southern sunshine and, hidden amongst the blood oranges, would be some small linen pouches. If Hlif was successful, the objects in the pouches would not be the pebbles they resembled. She couldn't wait to get on with her own project, to fill her days with something other than waiting and worrying.

After her first conversation with al-Idrisi, she'd sent Pietro to the harbour to negotiate passage and cargo for the return journey, with Captain Lemercier. Every afternoon, she checked with him whether the captain was ready to sail yet and the answer was always 'Maybe tomorrow.'

One evening, when even One-eye had deserted her to rehearse his courtship caterwauling in the street outside, she succumbed to the temptation to read the runes and find her loved ones that way. Although she squeezed the wooden die until her palm was scored, it felt dead in her hand. The runes she'd thrown were merely letters with no special meanings. She felt no frisson, nothing of the trance state she had gone into during previous readings and she couldn't force it. Why did her gift so often bring her unwanted visions and yet deny her a glimpse of those dearest to her? How dare the gods deny her this boon, when they cursed her with visions at their whim!

She had no intention of sleeping when she went to bed that night. Instead, Hlif crossed the veil between worlds and sought Skarfr in the place of the dragon, the ancient tomb of Orkhaugr in Orkneyjar where his poetry had come alive in fire and blood. Where she had first walked with him in that world only they shared.

Skarfr would have warned her of the risks and tried to stop her, but he had no such qualms about risking his own life — and Seaborn's! — on Ifriqiyan shores without so much as a goodbye. Just as she accepted that she'd married a warrior, he must accept what she was. She had just as much right to use her gods-given powers as he had to navigate a ship or fight against ten men at the same time while a sea-monster attacked him! She bolstered her righteous indignation with such fragile logic, ignoring her conscience, which told her that Skarfr was right to worry. There was a difference between accepting the visitations sent by the gods, and calling on her *seithr* to walk between worlds as if she were a god herself. A difference that showed arrogance and would attract attention from beings to whom she was less important than an Orkneyjar midge, to be crushed if she irritated them.

Longing for Skarfr swept through her. She missed his steadfastness as much as the fit of their bodies, the trust between them founded on so many years growing together, an unshakeable bond. He would never have left without telling her and her anger was foolish, a betrayal of that trust. He must have been tricked, then angry and frustrated when he realised how anxious she would be. Maybe he was reaching for her this very moment, the way she had taught him.

Her longing circled around to justify an attempt at dream-walking and so it went on until the fourth night. Even though she knew that Skarfr would be sleeping, in fits and starts, off-watch in daytime or at night, she reached for him as she fell asleep, just in case.

Each time, she failed, wandering alone in the haunted darkness of old stone. Ghosts echoed her whisper, 'Skarfr?' and sent back a raven's mockery, '*Kar, Kar, Kar.*'

Óðinn's warning? The god who'd drunk the mead of verse and died for rune-learning would not look kindly on her divination with rune-dice, or on her presumption in breaching the veil. But still she persisted, exploring a labyrinth of dark chambers that had no existence in the day world. Just in case Skarfr was waiting for her.

On the fourth night, she heard something, a mewling, just a little further on down a tunnel that closed in on her. There was so little headroom that first she was stooping and then she had to crawl to continue. The crying was louder, more desperate. *A baby! Not far now!*

The sides of the tunnel were so tight against her that her elbows were squeezed against her ribs. Her breath came in gasps, as if there was no room in her chest for air.

But she couldn't stop. This was *her* baby, the one she'd lost, the tiny beginning of life the gods had ripped from her womb and sent to the seabed. She could reach the little one and bring him back. The baby was gurgling now and she was sure it was a boy.

She lay down on her stomach in the stone tunnel that was crushing all breath from her body and forced one arm between her breasts, up in the space between her neck and her head. If she twisted her face sideways, she could stretch out, touch those tiny fingers, and bring him back with her. They would be together, mother and child.

She straightened her fingers, stretched them out. The words, *My son,* formed in her mind. Then her fingertips met sharp, agonising nail-pulling pain, as if crushed between rocks.

When the baby screamed, she felt the sound twist in her vitals, knew she was losing him again, losing everything.

As she sank into oblivion, she heard an older child, fearful, calling, 'Mother?' She knew the voice so well, had made him a promise. *Sea-born.*

You have to choose!

The voice that roared in her head, pounding like her blood, could be monster or god. It no longer mattered. Her head swam. Sweat ran into her eyes, her mouth and down between her thighs. She didn't know whether she was breathing or not breathing in the darkness of otherworld but her body was being clawed backwards by *something*, her clothes ripped and her skin shredding beneath the fabric, as whatever remained of her was dragged from the tunnel into the familiar square chamber in Orkneyjar, bright with flame.

Skarfr's carved dragon blazed fire at her from the stone pillar where it lived, scorching her hair and eyebrows, searing her eyes shut in a golden blindness while she sensed her blood seeping from a thousand wounds. With the last of her strength, she pictured the little chamber she shared with Skarfr in Palermo, the wall-hanging of the palm trees and the lions.

She prayed for forgiveness, and she prayed for help, and she prayed without words for the baby she'd lost twice.

Which world she was in when she began weeping, she had no idea, but the claws kneading her belonged to a black-and-white cat and a rough tongue was licking the tears from her face. Purring reverberated through her chest, keeping her heartbeat company, steadying its wild vagaries.

One-eye had never bestowed his affection in such a manner. But he spent most of that night lying on the pillow above his mistress' head, his purring all that kept her in his world.

'He would have been born this month,' Hlif whispered to One-eye. 'I didn't think I would have to endure this grief on my own.' The cat purred comfort while his mistress cried herself to sleep in an ocean of tears, bottled up for too long.

When she woke, red-eyed and heavy-headed, the sound of mewling wrenched her guts. But it was just a hungry cat, rubbing against the bed and arching his back.

She got up to find some scraps of dried fish for him and noticed dispassionately that she *was* bleeding so she attended to rags and hygiene before stopping One-eye's complaint.

'There's always a price to pay,' she murmured. And she had paid it, knowing the cost. She would never give birth to a child. She had known that this was the price demanded by the gods for her son Sea-born. What would have happened to him if she'd succeeded in her mad quest the previous night?

Daylight brought clarity. Skarfr had been right about the dangers of using her powers. She would never read runes again, never seek the otherworld, never attract the gods' attention. After an extensive list of vows including the word 'never', Hlif added the get-out clause *unless it's really necessary* and busied herself with household matters.

She shuddered at what might have been and vowed that she would never again forget her living son in mourning her dead one. She knew all too well what it was like to grow up without a mother, as did Skarfr. Sea-born needed them both. And today she would go to the harbour again, hoping for news of her menfolk.

CHAPTER EIGHTEEN

HLIF, PALERMO, SICILIA

Happier at the prospect of something to do, Hlif sought out Pietro. She would go to the docks with him, confirm details of the passage he had booked for them on the merchant ship, perhaps pick up some bargains. There was plenty of room in the cellar.

As usual, Pietro was idling in the servant's quarters, entertaining Amina with his anecdotes and getting in the way of her chores.

Hlif came to the point. 'I want you to take me down to the harbour this afternoon, to talk to the captain myself.'

'There's no need for that,' objected her manservant.

She had clearly given him the wrong impression of her authority. 'I'm sure you have done exactly as I asked,' she told him, 'but an Orkneyjar trader agrees a contract in person, so there are no unpleasant surprises for either party.'

He looked sullen but left without further demur.

Hlif's spirits lifted. *Action at last.* She played with the scrip on her belt, feeling the shape of the red stone inside it, like a pebble amongst the jangling coins. She would bring back more than oranges and Rachel would be free.

Hlif went through Palermo's fortified exit, which was dominated by a Moorish tower well-manned with guards. The harbour formed a horseshoe shape where sea met land, with wooden walkways between berths and mooring posts. Men were loading or unloading cargo on the docks, officials were checking dockets and inventories, and seagulls screamed as they fought over food scraps or imagined treasures.

She took a trader's interest in the transactions going on as money changed hands over the newly imported luxuries. Never had Hlif seen such a truly international marketplace before. She recognised Muslim dinars and Venezian ducats among the gold coins, and English silver among the local dinars. Pawnbrokers and moneychangers had set up their stalls among the merchants, to further tempt traders. The line between an investment and a rash gamble was easy to cross and Hlif was no longer spending Jarl Rognvald's money but her own, which made her light-headed with freedom.

She kept her head, amongst tiger skins from the land of the Indus; coconuts from Siam; Melitese cotton; balsam from the Frankish south; English wool; filberts by the sack; metals marked with seals to show their quality; commodities from silk to saffron, sold by pound weight.

She succumbed to the lure of pearls from Oman, onyx and coloured gems from Arabia. After all, they were portable wealth, would fit in her pouch and would help camouflage the red stones she hoped to acquire. Then she tore herself away from the array of fine pottery, inks and paper from China, to attend to the matter of her travel. After all, she told herself, a wise trader spreads purchases over several days, to even out any fluctuations in price. It wouldn't do to fill her cellar in one day.

Pietro pointed out to her the cargo ship on which she'd booked passage, bobbing at its berth between smaller vessels. He told her it was a modern roundship he called *La Nef Marchande*, which meant nothing to her, but she noticed that it was solidly built and double-masted, with triangular sails above a lower deck that was mostly hold space, but with some oar-holes at the front of the ship. The hold was more than big enough for her needs. She approved of the option of oar-power but it worried her to see the foremast tilted in such a manner. The midships mast was straight and true so the angle of the other looked even odder.

When Pietro introduced her to the captain, who said 'They call me Lemercier', she took the opportunity to ask about this anomaly. After listening to a long, detailed digression on the choice between more rowers and more hold space, and of the need to stay close to the coast in such a ship because of its instability — something Hlif would rather not have known — she got her answer. The tilted mast coped better with fierce winds.

Finishing with a spirited account of shipbuilding around the Middle Sea, and Venezian excellence, Captain Lemercier released his captive listener.

'We will sail the day after the Melitese ship arrives,' the captain reminded her. 'You must be ready.'

'I will come down to the docks each day and check,' promised Hlif. *And hope for news of Skarfr.* 'And if I ever invest in a merchant ship, I will visit the Arsenale shipyard in Venezia.' Hlif thought nostalgically of the broad-beamed knarr merchant ships of Orkneyjar, as intrepid in the open sea as their faster cousins the dragon ships. No 'staying near the coast' for them! But she hadn't said she would choose a roundship over a knarr, only that she would visit the Venezian shipyard. And who knew what the future might bring!

The captain's eyes gleamed. 'Let me know if you do and I'll lead her first voyage for you.'

As she walked past the trestle tables that were erected as temporary stalls to sell excess stock fresh from the new ships, she realised that Pietro was no longer with her. She glanced back towards *La Nef* and saw her manservant in heated discussion with the captain, who pointed in her direction, shook his head, gesticulated wildly and finally accepted a leather pouch. Coins, no doubt.

How strange. Pietro had said all was agreed and the captain had shown no sign of discontent when speaking to Hlif.

She waited for Pietro to catch up with her.

'You did make sure we're the only passengers on the voyage?' she queried, well aware that space was limited on a merchant ship and cargo the priority. But she'd paid well for what comfort was possible as well as for hold space. Surely she was not seen as an inconvenience.

'The captain knows your requirements,' said Pietro, not meeting her eyes.

'Was there a problem?' she persevered.

He looked past her, towards the servants elbowing each other to be first at the fish stalls, where the catch of the day was already becoming dull-eyed. 'No, not at all,' he said, too quickly. A pause. While he thought of a plausible story? 'My brothers are business partners for the cargo going to Taormina and gave me some money to pass on.'

If true, that was the first time Hlif had ever seen someone argue against being *given* money, and Pietro's brothers did not strike her as trustworthy. But as long as her own passage and cargo were unaffected, it was none of her business, so she made no further comment.

CHAPTER NINETEEN

HLIF, PALERMO, SICILIA

On the third afternoon since she'd spoken with Captain Lemercier, Hlif navigated the crowds around the market at the entry to the docks, with Pietro trailing behind her. She averted her eyes from the slaves being displayed and sold like freshly caught fish. But the slaves were alive and if their eyes were dull, the cause was despair, not the onset of death. Hlif shuddered and closed her ears to the slave-trader's crude banter, trying not to put herself in the thralls' place.

She *could* have been the one in chains if the pirates had overcome the Orkneymen the previous year, rather than vice versa. Sea-born could have been her master rather than her son ludicrous thought! She would rather die than be enslaved by men such as the pirates. The sorry beings in Palermo market could at least hope to find civilised masters. If the fates were kind, the human catch of the day might even find masters as generous as Skarfr, and a hearth as welcoming as the longhouse back home, where Brigid and Fergus would be busy with lambing. Although they had begun life in Orkneyjar as thralls, Brigid and Fergus were as family to Skarfr and were freedmen in all but the formalities. The moment she and Skarfr returned home, those formalities would be completed.

Home! How she missed it.

She approached the customs officer on the stone walkway above the docks. Before she could pose the usual question, he jerked his head and pointed. 'Last galley, just docked.'

She sped along the jetty, past the moored ships she'd admired the day before and stopped at the broad-beamed arrival. Its cargo was piling up on the docks, ready for inspection: a bale of heavy red silk, damask probably, had unrolled and was being baled up again. When Hlif craned her neck to get a closer look, two burly men dressed in the palace colours intervened, standing between her and the precious fabrics.

'King Roger's tribute, my Lady. Not for sale.'

A clucking tut-tut-tut of disapproval came from a box shape covered in coarse sacking, an oddity in the midst of all the luxury goods surrounding it.

Of course! The Melitese falcon in a darkened cage.

'And not for peeking at either,' added the other guard. 'There will be the devil to pay if anything happens to that bird between here and the palace. A falcon that's gone feet-up would be the end of me and him.' He jerked a finger at his fellow.

'I just want a word with one of the sailors from Melita,' Hlif assured them and stepped back far enough for the guards' comfort, to wait for someone from the ship to come ashore. In the same way she might notice the absence of a persistent fly, she became aware that Pietro was no longer in her orbit and she scanned the bustling docks for his straight black hair and bulky frame.

Her gaze snagged on a group of three such men in impassioned debate, gesticulating their difference of opinion as clearly as its resolution with clasped hands and back-patting. As the crowd thinned around them, she glimpsed their faces and recognised not just Pietro, but all three. Then they disappeared from sight in a new wave of merchants and sailors. Perhaps she had been mistaken.

'My lady,' Pietro hailed her, no sign on his sunny countenance of anything amiss. He cleared an effortless path through those blocking his way and stood beside her.

Perhaps she had not been mistaken.

'Those men you were with,' she queried. 'Who were they?'

Without hesitation, he replied, 'My brothers.'

She waited but no names were forthcoming and something held her back from asking. She remembered a finger held to a man's lips, and a mime of a throat being cut. But Pietro worked for her, had been hired to *protect* her, so there was no harm in asking, 'Did they want something from you?'

For a moment, a different Pietro studied her from behind his usual bonhomie. A Pietro who knew the streets of this city. 'What could they want from *me*?' A certain arrogance coloured the response from this Pietro, who surely knew about the protection his brothers offered. She changed tack, unwilling to drop the subject.

'From someone else at the docks then.' She made an inspired guess. 'Perhaps they wish to offer protection to some newcomers to the city.'

His smile was all teeth with no light in his eyes, another reminder of the mysterious warning his brother had given to Hlif. 'You don't need their protection. You have mine.'

Out of the corner of her eye, Hlif could see Pietro's brothers giving a purse to one of the tax inspectors, then looming over a newly arrived merchant and more coins changing hands. Despite the crowds, the brothers were never jostled, even though people seemed oblivious to their activities. The total lack of curiosity from all but Hlif was unnatural, studied and deliberate. Self preservation in response to a threat?

'Yes,' agreed Hlif. 'I have your protection.' She shook off her sense of foreboding. 'For which I am very grateful.'

At that moment, a self-important portly man swathed in the blue and yellow fabric Hlif had seen on the docks, rolled down the gangway from the Melitese ship. A merchant.

The moment he reached his goods, Hlif ducked past the guards and addressed him, carefully standing as far away from the birdcage as she could so as to pose no threat to the precious falcon.

'My lord,' she called, 'My husband is in Melita with the Emir.'

How could she describe Skarfr for a stranger? 'He's the ship's navigator, a Northman, with a dragon tattoo on his arm.'

The merchant was shaking his head and Hlif's heart sank. She'd known the odds were against hearing news of Skarfr and Sea-born but she had hoped. The two guards had her firmly by the elbows.

Sea-born!

'And a boy,' she added desperately, 'The ship's boy on the Emir's ship is our son. You might have heard of a Northman and a boy.'

The merchant still shook his head.

What else would identify Skarfr? She racked her brains.

Over her shoulder, as she was marched away from the Melitese ship, Hlif yelled, 'He has a sunstone, a magical instrument for navigation.'

The merchant looked up from his goods and shouted back. 'Now you mention it, there was talk from the Sicilian men of a foreign navigator with some such talisman. I asked Emir George if he wanted to sell it but he said, 'Not if it's any use.''

'Thank you,' said Hlif, not caring whether the Melitan heard as long as the gods did. Skarfr was alive and if so, Sea-born must be. These Sicilians knew *nothing* about protection.

Raucous croaks overhead and a swoop of wings made her look up in time to see a cormorant barely miss the Melitese ship's masts, as it avoided the rabble of gulls which mobbed the smaller fishing boats. Perched on the wales, the cormorant stared at Hlif.

'*Aaark!* Skarfr's safe!' his spirit bird told her. 'Dive deeper than others can, fish in those depths and hold your breath as long as you must.' Then the cormorant dived between the restless ships, dropping out of sight through the churning surface like an iron anchor.

She had never doubted what Skarfr told her of the cormorant's messages but this was the first time the bird had spoken to her. Unfortunately, she was none the wiser for the strange pronouncement although she did feel less alone. Also, Skarfr and Sea-born were safe. She was sure of it.

And the Melitese ship had come, which meant her own would be leaving the next day. With a renewed sense of purpose, she instructed Pietro, 'We leave tomorrow. We'll need a pack-mule to take my kist and belongings to the ship. And your belongings. Go to al-Idrisi and tell him I will be absent for a while trading. He will understand.'

'Amina will go too?' Pietro asked, a glimmer of hope in his eyes.

'No, just you and me. I don't need Amina.' The last thing Hlif wanted was a servant truly keeping an eye on her. If there was a girl in Catania, or food and wine, or merely a place to sleep, giving the slip to Pietro would be easy.

CHAPTER TWENTY

SKARFR, THE WHALE ROAD

Skarfr tried to keep Sea-born close to him but the Emir's tongue lashed them both with insults and orders, ever more demeaning for Skarfr and more dangerous for the boy. Relegated to a rower's bench on the lower deck, his rhythm and his mother equally questioned by the oarmaster, Skarfr dipped and pulled with the ease of a man taught young how to work with his core muscles, not with his arms.

Sea-born was under strict instructions from Skarfr to report to his father after fulfilling George's commands but when he rushed down the ladder panting, with the Emir at his shoulder yelling at him to climb the mast and check the knot at the top of the mainstay, Skarfr got the message. The more he tried to protect his son, the more harshly the Emir would treat them both. Skarfr could laugh off his own humiliation but if Sea-born was to pay for showing obedience to his father first, then the rule of the sea must prevail. The captain's word was law and a ship's boy did the work of a ship's boy.

Without breaking stroke, Skarfr released Sea-born gently, cutting him loose. 'You've done well, son and can be trusted with whatever task the Emir or his men give you. We must both do our work now and shall see each other when permitted.'

The lad scampered back up the steps.

Skarfr imagined his son climbing the mast as it swayed, his arm muscles straining to pull himself higher and higher, the deck smaller and the ocean vast when he sneaked a look down (because being told not to look down ensured that every ship's boy who ever climbed a mast *would* look down). He would reach the top of the mainstay — gods willing — and grip the mast so tight his thighs would vibrate as he reached out with both hands to check the knot, re-tie it in the round turn and two half-hitches that every sailor knew.

If he loosened the rope and the huge triangular sail flapped in a sudden gust, he would have to *be* the knot holding fabric to wood, until he'd secured it again. If the sail whipped away and was too strong for him, if his legs lost their grip, he would fall.

If he succeeded and tied the rope tightly through its eye-hole in the wooden mast, he would still have to come down safely. Exhilarated and overconfident, he would relax his thighs for the descent, a hand would slip on the wet wood of the mast just as a rower missed his stroke and a cross-current slapped the bows. The ship would skew and the son cut loose by an irresponsible father would plummet into—

'Skarfr!' Once more the Emir's voice yelled from the hatch above. Skarfr felt the void in his chest where his son had lived and breathed, felt it crushing him. How could he tell Hlif? 'Are you blind, man or just stupid like that boy of yours? Xerxes is there to take your oar. I want you up here working your overpriced arse at what you're paid for.'

Skarfr became conscious of the man standing beside his bench, waiting for him to ship the oar and exchange places. He stretched to ease his back, then rushed the steps two at a time, heart thumping as he scanned midships from the decking around the base of the mainmast, innocent of a child's splayed form, then higher and higher up the mast.

Dear gods, protect him!

'Father!' yelled Sea-born, letting go of the mast to wave vigorously as he descended.

Too fast! Skarfr could not reply for the hard ball of terror in his throat but he managed to wave and look nonchalantly in another direction. He would not shame this fearless man-child. Sea-born had been a ship's monkey on vessels like this from the moment he could toddle. He would be fine. He *had* to be fine.

With only a slight wobble in his voice, he asked the Emir, 'You want me to navigate? What's the course? The current?' He glanced at the streaming ribbon on the mast. *The fates' humour — just when he'd been relieved as oarsman, the wind had picked up again. And with the mainstay sorted, the sail would be fully unfurled as quickly as a boy could jump down to the deck from the mast.* 'Wind direction's south-easterly,' he observed.

'In our favour,' agreed George. Was that a hint of approval in his eyes as he added, 'Philip will tell you all you need to know before he takes a break. It's your watch now.'

Skarfr did not point out that he was working his second watch, having already pulled his weight on the oars for what must have been four hours. The captain's word was law. Besides, behind him a high voice responded modestly to bluff praise and to a battery of orders. The tasks Sea-born was given were now of the dogsbody variety rather than life-threatening, and Skarfr's pulse gradually returned to normal. The black void in his chest filled to bursting with pride in his son, formed lines of verse.

> *At hawk-height flew the hero*
> *above the sea-mountains and foam-mounts,*
> *heart high as the sun's path and*
> *heedless of Aegir's dark deeps below.*

On a dromond, as on a longship, the navigator was at the stern but the extra width of the deck allowed for freer movement, of which George as captain made full use. Rather than sending orders along the ship from a position beside his navigator, as Jarl Rognvald had always done, the Emir ranged the deck and hovered, ranged and hovered, a sea eagle swooping on incompetence or inattention, in his element. He would then return to the stern and confirm the course to Skarfr as navigator and to the two steersmen beside him, each turning a quarter-rudder. Sometimes, he would rest in the captain's tent, also at the stern, before emerging to range the ship once more.

Amongst the gruff voices, creaking planks, snapping of sails as they tautened or slackened in the wind, Skarfr's senses were attuned to the boy's voice, responding to orders or passing on messages. The boy's voice was a flute, each note touching the heart, distinct in the hubbub.

Philip greeted him with a volley of instructions. 'When you see the island of Melita — you can't mistake it, it's the only large land mass — hug the west coast. We're heading for the harbour of Wied-iz-Zurrieq and before the harbour, the coast is all cliffs and rocks. It's the first harbour big enough for the fleet. Melita is part of the Kingdom of Sicilia and we have a garrison inland in Mdina, so in theory it's friendly territory. In practice, not everyone forgets the manner in which King Roger, and his father, claimed this land, so we'll be sending an armed party to Mdina. A show of force, to remind the Melitese why they pay tribute. And we can collect the tribute at the same time.'

Part of the Kingdom of Sicilia! Skarfr wished he'd taken more notice of the islands on al-Idrisi's maps.

'But you don't need to know all that,' continued Philip blithely. 'Take your watch now, while I try to get some sleep. If you can see the birds on the rocks, you're too close to them.'

With which cheerful thought, Philip ducked into the captain's tent, where he had the privilege of taking turns with the Emir, tucked into the bedroll within. Skarfr was left to his own devices — and George's orders. The dromond might be ten times the size of a dragon ship, a hundred men strong instead of thirty, but the principles of wind, tide and current applied in the same way.

As Skarfr discovered when he sought their counsel, the two steersmen manning the rudders were both familiar with the route and its hazards. Their reticence vanished on being asked for advice and their shared expertise soon needed few words from him to guide the ship on its course. Against the immense forces of sea and sky, the ship's crew learned to trust each other, strange though it seemed to Skarfr that he would never know the names of all the men whose lives lay in his hands. In so far as any human held such power, which would always be snatched away by the mocking Norns, whenever they chose.

As he grew accustomed to sailing the dromond, with its triangular sails and two rudders, Skarfr stopped wishing for a square sail and low keel. Running before the wind and leaving the course set was not an option. Both the variable winds and the type of sail required constant adjustments to the rigging. But he had to navigate the ship he was on, not the one he missed and make the most of the dromond's advantages. Lateen sails could be taken closer to the wind and the oar-power was strong, as was the total manpower on board.

With good-humoured teasing, members of the crew called for Sea-born to relay messages and he was sent scurrying about the ship until he was red in the face. The Emir moved more slowly but he too kept up his inspection of rigging and sails, initially raining commands on Skarfr until his new navigator proved up to the job and was given more leeway.

After Skarfr had taken two more watches, when the sun dipped in the west, George gave the orders to shelter and drop anchor off the northern coast of Melita. The rest of the fleet followed suit and, after eating their rations of dried fruit and hard bread, washed down with a swig of wine, the men crammed themselves into whatever sleeping-spaces they could find near their work-stations. Skarfr pitied the oarsmen, crammed between the thwarts, as he had so often spent his off-duty watch or a restless night on a longship. Worse still, they were in darkness on the lower deck of the dromond while he could stretch out on deck under the stars. Maybe he would feel differently if the weather gods brought rain but tonight Thórr was kind to them.

He missed the warmth of his wife beside him. For the first time since they had married five months ago, he was sleeping alone. Was Hlif thinking of him? Was she angry at him setting sail with Sea-born, without a proper leave-taking? Or would she understand that he'd had no choice? The latter, he decided. And he would return safely to explain. He *and* Sea-born would return safely.

Someone dropped a bedroll beside him, moved it close and snuggled against him. Not Hlif but the child who'd made them a family, who'd brought this wonderful, terrible responsibility into Skarfr's life.

Skarfr murmured, 'Good work.'

There was a pause, as if Sea-born were considering the judgement before giving his own. 'I know how to be useful on a ship.'

Skarfr remembered himself as a small boy, saying those very words to his hero, Sweyn the sea-rover, and being humiliated on an Orkneyjar beach for wanting to sail with such company. How different Sea-born's life must have been from his own, not learning to sail but living it as second nature, on a dromond like this. With what brutality had the lad's evident 'usefulness' been shaped?

'He showed you no respect,' stated Sea-born.

'Who?' asked Skarfr, although he knew.

'The Emir,' whispered the boy.

'Testing words and testing actions,' murmured Skarfr drowsily.

Sea-born replied in emphatic Arabic, of which the only words Skarfr recognised were 'God', 'prayer' and 'pay.' He was too tired to take in the significance of the whole but he would come to regret not asking.

CHAPTER TWENTY-ONE

SKARFR, THE WHALE ROAD

Everyone important was in the landing party that headed inland to the Mdina, accompanied by a hundred men-at-arms, some of the designated warriors from each ship. Not enough to appear threatening but quite sufficient to remind the Muslim Emir of Melita why an annual tribute was due from the vassal state to the Kingdom of Sicily. And why the merchant ship from Genoa at anchor in the harbour must show papers signed in Palermo before trading was authorised.

Skarfr was left behind to ensure that the reduced crew sailed south with the rest of the fleet, and reached the Grand Harbour safely. The haven was immense, protected by a chain across its entry which could be raised if the beacon on the look-out point was lit. *Like Constantinople.* The Sicilian fleet dominated the port and Skarfr's pulse raced at the thought of taking this war fleet against its equal in a few months' time.

This year you'll fight against the Byzantine Empire, King Roger had promised him. And Skarfr would *not* be left behind when the moment came for him to prove his worth as a warrior, not just as a navigator.

They lay at anchor in the quiet waters among the brightly-painted local fishing boats, merchant ships from Sicilia and one peaceful intruder from Genoa, whose captain would pay for the privileges of stealthy trading, if there were no papers. Ships from the city-states of Venezia and Genoa were all too likely to sidestep the proper agreements with Sicilia to trade in the kingdom, while being protective of their own monopolies. King Roger's orders to his Emir were clear should such be the case. Crippling payment in reparation would be paid or the ship would be scuttled.

The Sicilian ships had not been at sea long enough to need much maintenance but the crews carried out whatever repairs were needed, splicing and replacing frayed ropes, scrubbing decks and emptying bilges. Then, duty done, the lure of the port proved irresistible to those allowed ashore.

A new watch rota gave all the mariners in turns a chance to overnight in Valletta and discover the welcome given by the town's shopkeepers, wine-sellers and women. Those returning to the ship passed on tales and tips, firing the enthusiasm of the next shore-goers. Skarfr had no intention of leaving the ship and the usual banter passed over his head until he noticed a very small mariner about to climb over the wales and shin down a rope to join a jovial band of mariners in the local rowboat which ferried the shore party.

'Sea-born,' he yelled, running across the deck, only just fast enough to grab the boy and hold him back. The abuse Skarfr yelled at the departing sailors was met with good-natured laughter and shouts of, 'Your time will come, Sea born.'

In no uncertain terms, Skarfr made it clear to all those still on board that Sea-born's time had *not* come and any man who took his son off the ship would be lucky to keep both hands when he returned. The laughter died down but Sea-born's sullen face showed that his acceptance of his foster-father's authority was only on the surface.

The boy was only eight! Skarfr thought back to his own childhood and admitted to himself that he too had learned much from the crude talk of men at sea, long before a whore in Kirkjuvágr gave him his first taste of the pleasure a woman could bring a man.

And long before he learned the more important lesson of how he could pleasure a woman. Hlif had been his world for so long that he'd forgotten his early experiments, dismissed them as unimportant. But for this boy's sake, he must remember, so as to bring Sea-born gently to manhood, fit for a Hlif of his own one day.

But that time was a long way off! Sea-born might be curious about the sailors' crude revelations but what he was sulking over was missing out on sweetmeats and adventures. So that was what Skarfr must offer.

'You will be a leader one day,' he told Sea-born and was rewarded with a glimmer of interest in those black eyes. 'So you must have self-control as well as all the skills required.' The eyes dulled again. *Boring.*

'One of those skills is observation,' Skarfr continued. 'Describe the local fishing boats to me.'

Sea-born shrugged at a task so easy. 'Brightly-painted in red, yellow and blue, medium size rowboats,' he replied.

'There is something special about them, different, that I have seen nowhere else,' said Skarfr. 'Not just the colours.'

Sea-born peered at the boats around them. His face cleared and he grinned. 'They have moustaches and eyes painted on the prow.'

Skarfr nodded. 'I want you to find out why.'

'How can I do that?' Sea-born puzzled over the task.

One of the mustachioed boats with painted eyes drew close to the Emir's ship and a man yelled up, 'Anyone for the shore?'

Skarfr called back, 'Can you take the ship's boy fishing for the afternoon? I'll pay you for the catch and for your inconvenience, when you bring him back. He's a good boy but he asks a lot of questions.' He winked at Sea-born, whose eyes glittered with excitement.

'Go on then, before I change my mind.' Skarfr tipped his head towards the rope hanging over the wales and Sea-born didn't have to be asked twice before hurtling over the side of the ship and descending hand over fist to join the fishermen.

With aching heart, Skarfr watched the boat heading for some

unknown destination until it grew tiny and vanished. However much it hurt him, this was his job as a father, deciding when to hold the boy close and when to let him go.

A bearded crew member with a broken nose, Ahmed by name, had been watching the scene with a cynical twist to his mouth. He shook his head and said, 'We're heading for Ifriqiya. The boy needs to be prepared for war, not fishing.'

Skarfr remembered a different dromond, Sea-born picking his way across a deck slippery with blood, more frightened of the man who called him son than of the attackers who'd slaughtered most of the crew.

'He's prepared for war,' Skarfr said quietly, 'but knows nothing of peace.'

The sailor laughed. 'Peace is just the wait between wars.'

'For some of us,' agreed Skarfr. 'But we still need clothes on our back and food in our bellies, provided by men with trades and tools, not swords and shields. Fishmongers, not warmongers, will bring us a full net. But if you'd rather stick with hard bread and dried tuna?'

A mock groan was the answer. 'Not on your life! When we get home, I'm not touching tuna until the *mattanza* when we'll have enough fresh steaks to let the dogs feast on their share.'

Or the cat. Skarfr had a sudden vision of One-eye gorging on a tower of tuna steaks. Were the fish really as big and dangerous as he'd been warned? Or were these sailors' tales as fanciful as the ones they told of fish-tailed sirens who'd sing a man to a watery grave?

He touched his hammer amulet for protection, just in case, and responded lightly to Ahmed, 'No tuna here but let's hope the fish are plentiful and that my boy learns fast.'

Skarfr was sure al-Idrisi's hourglass was trickling so slowly that time seemed to stop, while he worried and waited for the fishing boat to reappear. He ran out of tasks and was oiling the rowlocks, when he heard a man shout, 'Twenty fish and a boy for you!'

With lightened heart, Skarfr lowered the agreed sum of coins tied in a cloth and went to the top deck to greet Sea-born.

No need to ask if he'd enjoyed himself — the boy glowed and was bursting with news.

'It's the all-seeing eye of God,' he reported. 'Painted on both sides of the prow. And nobody knows how it started because there were people here so long ago that they walked with the first gods. But that's blasphemy so the fisherfolk mustn't say that when there's a priest nearby.

'And,' he rushed on, 'the moustaches and how the ships are painted in red, blue and yellow have always been like that too. It's tradition. There's talk of changing the shape a bit for new boats because the shape of the Sicily fishing boats is sturdier.'

'And the fishing?' asked Skarfr.

'I took an oar.' Pride rang in Sea-born's voice. 'We rowed north to a bay where the nets were already in place and I helped lift one. Then we emptied all the fish into a barrel on the boat and dropped the net back into the sea.'

'You did well,' Skarfr told him, silently thanking the fishermen for their manner with the lad.

Over the next few days, Sea-born was given further opportunities to row with the fishermen and each time he came back with provisions, gifts and information about local ways.

'You must tell your foster-mother all about Melita when we go home,' said Skarfr. Had the child's eyes clouded slightly at the term foster-mother? Perhaps he missed Hlif, as did Skarfr himself. 'She uses such knowledge when trading. And I will tell al-Idrisi so he can add your details to his book.'

Sea-born positively strutted with his new-found importance and was brought back to earth by the crew, who gave him menial tasks on the ship and gently punctured his ballooning pride. These were good times.

When the landing party returned from Mdina, their boasts made it clear that those who'd stayed on the ship knew nothing of Melita, whereas *they* had stayed in court, met the Muslim Emir and seen his legendary mews. The Emir had personally witnessed the tribute of one priceless white falcon being caged and stowed in the hold of a ship bound for King Roger. Then, having gained all the pledges and affirmations of alliance that any king could want, and laden with gifts for themselves, the Emir and Philip had led the army to Valetta and back to the ships.

Glowing with success, Philip told Skarfr, 'King Roger's father took Mdina with only thirteen knights and look at Melita now! A jewel, a source of riches and a loyal state in the Kingdom of Sicily.'

'And Christian,' added the Emir drily. He looked weary, a grey tinge to his complexion.

'And Christian,' repeated Philip quickly, glancing away, then explaining to Skarfr. 'Melita was Muslim previously, like Sicily.' He paused. 'May God's will be done.'

Skarfr bowed his head politely, whichever god Philip meant.

When George was out of hearing, Philip said to Skarfr, 'It's not the vassal states being overtaxed on this voyage but the Emir, I fear. I hope his health will bear up.'

Sea-born made a weird noise in his throat. He had been acting strangely ever since the Emir had returned to the ship, his expression guarded, even fearful. Before Skarfr could ask what ailed him, he scampered along the deck to help coil a rope. Then he took up his position in the bow with the horn.

'Prepare to sail,' came the order and there was no more time for religion or philosophy.

With horn-blowing, full-bellied sails and a drumming of shields, the fleet left the Grand Harbour with style. After triumphing in Melita, they were heading for another friendly island. Once infested with pirates, then swept clean and Christian by King Roger's fleet, Lampedusa would be the last certain opportunity to reprovision — after what should be a speedy renewal of oaths and payment of the small isle's tribute to Sicily.

Then, refreshed and fighting fit, they would head westwards to Ifriqiya, a region hostile in climate, landscape and residents.

Lampedusa proved as easy as Philip had predicted and, apart from George's perceptible lack of energy, there were no setbacks. Next stop was Djerba, then six hours sailing with the easterly wind which blessed them, to Mahdia, the key city of Ifriqiya. Also according to Philip, who claimed Mahdia as his birthplace and knew it well, the currents on this part of the Ifriqiyan coast were exceptionally variable even for the Middle Sea.

Just when the Ifriqiyan coast was in plain view, frustratingly close, the wind turned skittish and changed direction, flapping the sails as Skarfr tried without success to set a course that picked up the wind again. He cursed and the ship stalled, wallowing. Instantly, the Emir yelled the order to reef the sails and man the oars, and every ship in the fleet followed suit.

Skarfr had sailed in unfavourable winds before and there were good strong oarsmen on all the ships so he did not foresee much of a problem. Until the sky to the south-west filled with orange clouds, low and threatening, speeding towards the ship. The wind had settled to sou'westerly, gusting wildly and blowing against Skarfr's face, startling him into crying out. 'The wind is hot!'

'It's from the desert,' breathed Philip, his expression grave.

From Christian hell, more likely, was Skarfr's thought as he surveyed the apocalyptic scene around him. *The end of the world.* Surely, this was how Ragnarok would begin, with the heavens on fire. He touched his hammer amulet, ready to call on the dragon to keep him strong against whatever new assault was imminent. He grabbed a rudder from the steersman and held onto it as it bucked. The simple aim of hanging on steadied him rather than the ship, as the full force of this phenomenon hit the fleet.

The sea was black below the ominous sky, blackness that reached the company all too quickly in torrential rain that doused the daylight as if snuffing a candle. Shafts of orange sky burned through the rain and the wind blasted Skarfr's face with sand. If he'd been a new-forged blade, he would be shiny as silver and diamond-sharp.

Never had Skarfr seen such unnatural rain, depositing a thick layer of lurid mud on everything and everybody on the ship. His skin was on fire, flayed and burning. He could not speak for the grit in his mouth. His nose was crusty and he was struggling to breathe. He would silt up and die. Like the bottom half of al-Idrisi's glass, full of sand, his end had surely come.

CHAPTER TWENTY-TWO

SKARFR, THE WHALE ROAD

If he shaded his eyes as if from the sun and squinted, Skarfr could see the filthy rain splattering rust-red sand on every surface the crew had spent so long cleaning and oiling. How Loki must be laughing as the weather gods played havoc with men's painstaking work!

With one final discharge, the fiery clouds blew overhead and, although the sky remained orange, the rain ceased. Men shook themselves, tried to wipe their eyes with gritty hands, clung to ropes by sheer force of habit. The ship faltered as if equally dazed. The oarsmen had lost their rhythm in the confusion and the furled sail was useless, bunched up under an uneven coating of red dirt.

Nobody had the voice to set the pace for the oars. George's white hair was streaked with terracotta and his bushy eyebrows were fringed red, as was his beard.

'We have to row,' he told Philip, rasping out the desperate words in a voice like sandpaper.

As if in response, the oars stopped flailing, returned to the rhythm of a giant's heartbeat that enabled them to pull, dip and rise in unity. The oarsmen must have fared better under shelter than those on the top deck and someone was calling time for them, keeping the ship moving.

'We'll clean up at anchor before we launch the rowboats and attack.' The Emir only just managed to get the words out.

Philip nodded, held out a leather wineskin and the Emir took a swig, spat it out to clear his throat, then passed it back. Skarfr took his turn and then drank a mouthful, grimacing as salty grains fouled the taste of the liquid.

The immediate danger was past, the coast was once more visible and the ship's course was clear enough, so he passed the rudder back to the steersman, and reached for his pack. It looked as if it had been buried on a wet beach but the inside was dry and clean.

Skarfr resisted the temptation to check on his precious flute, his sunstone, or his pouch of coins, as he knew he'd only make them sandy if they weren't already. Instead, he pulled out his spare shirt and then hesitated.

A familiar cry drew his attention to the sea below, where black birds were diving into the sea, complaining loudly as they washed off the sand that must have caught some of them in flight or on the surface. One bird was barely recognisable as a cormorant, covered in a crust of red like a badly baked pie, but Skarfr would have known her anywhere. She landed awkwardly on the rolling waves, bobbing as she looked fixedly towards him.

'*Aaaark*,' she admonished.

Two other cormorants swam up to her and, in a sudden frenzy attacked, pecking her as she flapped and protested. She managed to twist away and dive.

Skarfr counted to four times the number a man could breathe underwater, and was convinced she must have drowned when, as is the way of such birds, she popped up again some distance from where she went under, looking cleaner.

Her two aggressors had been waiting and zoomed towards her but this time they made crooning noises and pecked her in little darting movements, as if grooming her.

'*Aaaaaark*,' she told Skarfr. '*Think of the coming battle.*'

His spare shirt in his hand, Skarfr thought of the coming battle.

The cormorant would not be here if the message were not important, however puzzling. What could it mean?

After the ship landed, the Emir would lead his warriors to the town of Mahdia, which was a rebellious vassal and the men there were likely to take up arms rather than pay their dues. So, a battle was coming and the Sicilian army must use the advantages of surprise and strength.

What would the Ifriqiyans feel when they saw such a horde coming? *Fear, of course.* If that fear could be increased, the battle would be over sooner.

In his mind's eye, Skarfr saw the cormorant again, striking fear into the other birds because she looked different from them.

'Wait!' he told the Emir, who had started to wipe his face. 'Tell the men to clean only their eyes, nose and mouth, to leave everything else, clothes and skin, red. When the Ifriqiyans see such strange men, they will surely wonder what demons have been sent against them by the gods. Their shock will double the strength of our men and weapons.'

George corrected automatically, 'Sent against them by God,' then nodded. 'It might help and it can't do any harm. A layer of mud won't hurt a man.' He sent the word along his own ship and the horn blower blew the signal for 'close formation.' As they'd practised outside more peaceful harbours, each ship was steered near enough its neighbour for commands to be yelled between them. Skarfr doubted very much whether anybody had cleaned themselves in the time available and he wiped off enough grit so he could see, speak and breathe, then finished with a desultory pass around his ears to clear them.

He looked about him at a crew of red men, their teeth unnaturally bright in mud faces, fearsome — but not fearsome enough. A memory came to him of the old warriors altering their appearance before battle.

'Charcoal!' he exclaimed. Hlif had put some chips in his pack to rub on wounds but the warriors he remembered had used its black dye for other purposes.

He quickly outlined his suggestion to the Emir. There would be enough charcoal for all the crew if each man dipped a wet finger in the black powder and used no more than that.

George gave his consent and as quickly as the charcoal could be crumbled and the linen wrap passed around the crew, white smiles turned black as men rubbed their teeth. The effect was all Skarfr could have hoped for. Let the Ifriqiyans show whatever courage they could, their insides would be quivering, in front of such monstrous creatures.

The moments before a battle were always strangely peaceful for Skarfr, even more so this time as he watched the gold and brown shores of the land passing by the ship, the blue of the furrowed waves ploughed by the prow. Axe and shield were to hand and he would wear the red mud instead of his well-oiled hauberk. Death would come for him if that was woven by the Norns, but he would use all his battle-wiles to win this victory for King Roger.

His resolve was shaken at the first sight of Mahdia, a great wall that seemed to rise from the sea itself. Two watchtowers rose high above the stone barrier, west and east of the only visible entrance to the harbour, as tall as a ship and as wide. Stone-throwing machines, mangonels and catapults, were visible on the towers. These were linked by a crenellated walkway, no doubt lined with archers behind their stone hiding-places. Skarfr had seen this solid construction in Muslim fortresses along his journey, in all the colours of unpainted earthenware. Mahdia's walls were of beige stone, golden in sunlight, but Skarfr's admiration was short-lived.

This was a defensive dream of a seaport, impregnable. Steering a ship through the narrow passage between the two towers would be suicide and the Emir was too experienced to make such an error. He must have a plan. How, in the gods' names, had he managed to conquer this peninsular city for Sicilia in the first place?

The closer they came, the further the walls seemed to stretch. The ships were already too close for safety and Skarfr braced himself for the stone shot and a hail of arrows, or even flaming missiles. But still he followed orders and steered straight ahead, into his doom.

What was the Emir thinking? When he did turn the fleet, he would have to hug the walls for a mile or more, whether east or west, and they would never survive the onslaught from the safety of those city walls. There would be no time to set up their own small catapult, which, in any case, would barely dint the massive walls.

'Straight ahead, through the entrance,' commanded the Emir.

In disbelief, Skarfr obeyed, his heart hammering. And still the defensive onslaught had not begun. The chain between the towers was winched down below the water, an invitation to enter. What if it was raised as the ship passed above, slicing the hull in two like a knife through a hunk of bread? Giving the choice between drowning or struggling ashore to be dispatched by those waiting? A strong swimmer, he would be one of those who died fighting.

The chain did not rise up as they passed over it.

The Emir sent word along the ship and down to the oarsmen. 'Hold the oars on the port side. Slowly on the larboard. We're docking.'

Maybe the enemy was waiting for more ships to be trapped on this side of the walls. Despite being on the alert for danger, Skarfr took in his surroundings with a growing sense of wonder. Mahdia's harbour was a citadel for ships, entirely enclosed by stone walls, with spurs for berthing hundreds of vessels and regular stanchions where they could tie up. Opposite the one entrance through which they'd come was another passage wide enough for one ship at a time, leading to the city, whose minaret rose above the flat rooftops.

The Emir indicated a row of empty berths. 'We'll tie up there,' he said, seemingly unaware of the robed men crowding the quayside to meet the Sicilians, all bearing curved swords.

So this was where the fight would take place, while the Sicilians scrambled onto the wharf, to be killed if they were lucky or taken hostage, if they were not. Yet Skarfr seemed to be the only one who perceived any danger and he could hold his tongue no longer. As Rognvald's champion, he'd always contributed to decisions, asked for explanations — and been given them. Never before had he followed orders that made no sense.

'These people, the Ifriqiyans, are our enemies.' He stated the obvious. 'They will kill us when we set foot on land and they have all the advantages.'

George laughed, blackened teeth in a wild red face. 'This why you should follow orders, not waste my time. *Ifriqiyans* are all different, my little Northman. Mahdia is governed by Almoravid Muslims, who pay tribute to Sicily.

Philip chipped in. 'Since the Emir conquered Mahdia two years ago.'

Without showing pride, George acknowledged the fact. 'Sicily's wheatfields conquered Mahdia. And the drought every year. Without our grain they die of famine. We stopped their supply of wheat.' He shrugged. 'They died. And we imprisoned their ruler al-Hassam. The new one will never make the same mistake.'

That is how the king rules, thought Skarfr. *Through a local leader, keeping local ways.* After *the battle is won.*

'This is Philip's birthplace,' George continued, 'and he knows its people well. The Muslim ruler of Mahdia asked King Roger for aid because the Almohads, also Muslims but extremists, are enemies of the citizens here, and have laid siege against the city from inland.'

'So we are here to help the Mahdians and fight these Almo… Almohads Muslims?'

'Yes, little Northman. Unless you want to fight all Muslims?' His tone was ironic as he looked around at his crew. The men were lowering the rowboats and ropes to access them. Most of the men wore turbans.

Skarfr flushed.

The Emir returned to his plan. 'We are expected by the Mahdians but not by the enemy so we'll march through the city and straight into battle on the other side of the city walls. The Mahdian warriors will no doubt join us.'

Philip added, 'Make no mistake. This battle is for gold and slaves, which come by camel caravan from the southern desert and are shipped to Sicily. Nobody will cut off our trade routes.'

George looked towards the fast-approaching harbour. 'We will teach the Almohads to show proper respect for the Kingdom of Sicily, the ruler of the Middle Sea!'

CHAPTER TWENTY-THREE

SKARFR, THE WHALE ROAD

Red with dried sand, grinning with black teeth, the first warband of the Emir's army was given a cautious welcome by the dignitaries and citizens of Mahdia. The men disembarked directly from the dromond down the gangplank onto the stone paving above the embankment that sloped down into the water. George ordered a few of the oarsmen to stay with the ship, a token gesture in such a secure and apparently friendly harbour. Among those staying aboard, Skarfr was relieved to see a very small person, as red and black-toothed as the rest of the crew and lively as a cricket. Sea-born would be safe.

Whatever their misgivings, the Mahdians wasted no time in directing their reinforcements from their berths to the perimeter walkway and docks, then through the entrance to the inner harbour. Skarfr had hardly any time to admire this inner sanctum for small boats, bordered by a canal that regulated water levels, before he passed through the gate to the city itself.

As ordered, Skarfr dropped back, to ensure orderly conduct among the rearguard. The azure standard of Sicily, with its chequered diagonal of red and silver squares, waved at the head of the procession and vanished out of sight as Skarfr took his place once more in the surge forward. Filling the narrow, winding streets, their boots ringing out on the cobbles, George's army grew bigger as Mahdians joined the force, tagging on behind. Armed with whatever tools came to hand, hammers, knives and axes, artisans took heart from the newcomers, and joined those better-trained, in the fight for their city.

Past the grand mosque they marched and through the city's south gate to the source of the noise that had been growing louder. War cries and drumming, insults and hurled missiles, horses and men screaming in rage and pain; the cacophony of battle.

The great army broke into a run at the gate, flowing like wine from a bottle into a line against the solid protection of the wall. And then halting, while the next line formed in front of them. And the next. Until, rank upon rank, Mahdia and its allies formed a solid block. Men changed places to ensure the front rank bore shields and weapons, while the craftsmen were further back and blocking the gateway, the last defence.

A somewhat unconventional shield wall but good enough, thought Skarfr, shouldering his way to the front. Nobody challenged his right to pass them by. He could see King Roger's blue standard, with its chequered diagonal, fluttering above turbanned and helmeted heads in the fourth rank. The Emir and Philip would be beside the standard-bearer, the centre of command and the heart of the army, so he elbowed and ducked his way to a place in the first row before the flag. Skarfr's job was to prevent anyone reaching them. Their army was on foot against horsemen and archers but had superiority in numbers and their appearance had shocked a complacent enemy into paralysis — for now.

'Appearance' in both senses, thought Skarfr, glancing at his red-streaked, black-toothed comrades.

The brightly-striped tents of the Almohads were visible across the sand behind clusters of warriors, some on horseback, some on foot, showing no sense of urgency about the ongoing siege. That was about to change.

'Father!' The excitement in Sea-born's voice ripped through Skarfr's pre-battle calm like a lightning strike.

He knew before looking behind him where the boy must be. The azure standard was waving madly, only just higher than the men's heads around it, in an attempt to catch his attention. Waved proudly, not in a plea for help. Skarfr could do nothing but hold his shield high, swing it back and forward to wave back but his inner calm was swept away in a flood of terror. He stared at the dragon tattooed on his arm, summoned its strength, knew his own mortality through fear for his son. Not his foster-son. His *son*, as much blood of his blood and bone of his bone as if Skarfr were his birth-father. And then it was too late for such thoughts.

The dragon in him roared, sending its flames through Skarfr, quenching all fear. As if his raised shield had given a signal to the enemy, the Almohads roared back and the battle began.

'Arrows!' yelled Skarfr, adjusting his shield's angle to block the storm loosed against them. With overhead shield cover so patchy, some men would be caught bareheaded.

He had no time to think about that. The hail of arrows was followed by a cavalry charge. The light, fast horses turned like dancers and showed no fear. Any normal mount would swerve just before it reached a solid object but these didn't. On they came, these courageous four-footed warriors, rearing up to smash their hooves against whatever stood in their way — and they paid the price of showing their bellies to axe and sword. Their riders jumped clear of their maimed mounts and hacked at the Mahdians.

Such was the strength of the attack, the shield wall broke in several places but men moved forward to trap those few Almohads who'd made it past the front rank. They did not live long.

The Mahdians had survived the first attack and there was a tense pause in the fighting while the Almohads retreated and regrouped. Blinded by blood and sweat, Skarfr glanced behind him. He could not see the standard. For a long moment he kept looking and his heart leapt into his throat as the flag flew once more. Sea-born must have fallen over in the crush of men around him. He was only a little boy.

The standard fluttered bravely, undamaged, high above men's

heads. Too high. Sea-born was no longer the standard-bearer. As Skarfr stared at the banner, the diagonal band wavered, turned black and bulged into a huge raven that flew up and away, taking the Mahdians' luck with it.

Like Jarl Sigurd's magical banner from the sagas, witched with invincibility for its lord and with death for its bearer. Loki's laughter rang in Skarfr's ears and he had only one thought.

The standard-bearer! Sea-born! Let other men hold back the enemy. Cursing and praying at the same time, Skarfr forced his way back through the ranks towards the flag, its device a blur as it furled and flickered. Men swore at him as he barged towards it but he ignored the aspersions cast on his courage and his mother, intent on reaching the boy.

'You're going the wrong way, Northman,' complained one he recognised, one of Philip's guards. He'd reached George's elite band.

One last shove gave him a view of the standard-bearer — *not* Sea-born, who was sitting in a huddle on the ground, his head buried in his arms.

Alive, thank the gods! Alive!

Philip blocked Skarfr, frowning. 'Get back to your position. We're going to advance now.'

'I thought the standard had fallen.' The half-truth was acceptable enough to gain a response.

'The Emir suffered stomach cramps and the boy was overly affected by his illness, let slip the standard.'

Skarfr glanced at the flag. No winged shadow marred the perfect red and silver chequered squares or the sky-blue background. He rubbed his eyes, swore at his foolish imagination, gave all his attention to what Philip was telling him.

'The lad's been like this since then, despite George being fine now. Maybe his first battle is too much for him.'

Unlikely, thought Skarfr, stooping to put a hand on the boy's shoulders.

'Son,' he said.

Sea-born looked up. Tears had washed streaks down through the rusty sand on his face but his eyes were dry now.

'I'm sorry,' he said. 'But it's too late now.'

'Forward!' George gave the order, apparently recovered from his momentary sickness, and there was no time for Skarfr to clear up whatever misapprehension Sea-born was under.

'You've done no harm,' he told the boy. 'Just do your best now. Be a man and take your turn again with the standard. Stay here.'

As Sea-born stumbled to his feet to obey orders, Skarfr was already pushing to the front, breaking into a run with his fellows towards the dead horses that marked the previous battle line.

Stay there and you'll be safe till I come back for you. Stay safe for me. My son.

He sent the words back to Sea-born as he led the Mahdians en masse against the Almohads, ducking around the horses, engaging in combat too close to allow the archers to do any damage. Pressing with sheer weight of numbers, row upon row charged at the enemy, forcing them back towards the sand dunes.

The outcome of the battle was a foregone conclusion but the number of deaths was not. Such must have been the conclusion of the Almohads because their defence was short-lived. The archers were the first to melt away into the dunes, then one warband after another retreated until the only enemies left standing were men sacrificing themselves to protect those who fled.

Skarfr would not kill needlessly. 'Let them go!' he yelled, brandishing his axe and shield at the Almohad awaiting a death blow.

'Run!' he told the man. Hesitant at first, sure he was being mocked, the man backed away then turned and ran, robes flapping.

Following Skarfr's lead, the Mahdians backed away, let their opponents vanish into the desert from which they'd come. A few chose death over failure and some were given no choice, but the battle was over.

'Why didn't you kill him? I would have!' Seemingly recovered, his eyes gleaming with battle fever again, Sea-born ran to his father, waving his dagger. Was that blood on it?

HUNTING THE SUN

'A warrior does not kill for sport,' Skarfr replied, 'And must be able to hold back the dragon inside him.'

Sea-born bared his black teeth. 'I have a wolf inside me and he is always hungry.'

Still aware of how he'd felt, thinking that Sea-born was dead, Skarfr held back the harsh put-down that came to his lips and said, 'That is because you are young, with much training ahead of you.'

It was enough. Skarfr had always known that men were different but for the first time he wondered why, and reflected on his responsibility in shaping the man Sea-born would become. His son was not like the child he had been. Sea-born showed no compunction about killing and his inner wolf seemed quick to respond. This was both an asset and a worry.

'You did well, ship's boy.' The Emir's tone was warm, the praise genuine.

Sea-born flinched and looked away, as if he'd been whipped not complimented.

More strange behaviour. If only he could talk about the boy to Hlif.

'And you fought bravely, Skarfr,' George told him.

In the heat of the moment, Skarfr spoke to the Emir as if he were Jarl Rognvald, a battle-brother. 'You earned the favour of the gods today, Sire,' he said, unthinking.

The silence had teeth.

Philip spoke first. 'There is no other god but God.'

Instead of appeasing George, Philip's reprimand to Skarfr aggravated the set of the Emir's mouth and the furrow in his forehead. 'The sentiment is fitting but the choice of words could be misconstrued,' he told his second in command. 'The Bible says, *Thou shalt have no other god but me.*'

Philip dipped his head, a gesture of appeasement. 'I defer to the right hand of the king. *Apulus et Calaber, Siculus mihi servit et Afer.*'

The Apulian, Calabrian and Ifriqiyan are my subjects. Skarfr recognised King Roger's personal addition to the Hauteville family motto, engraved on his sword and shield, but was confused by George's evident disapproval of Philip's words as well as Skarfr's.

Was there sarcasm in Philip's words? His comments were often cynical. Or was there some non-Christian nuance? Muslims also spoke of the one god. But if that were the case, why would it matter in Sicilia, where, as George himself had recently pointed out, most citizens were Muslim? Philip professed to be a good Christian, which was surely all that mattered, even if his comments could be cynical.

Skarfr found it all too confusing. He would have to be as careful as if Bishop William were listening to his every word. He smiled at the memory of the Orkneyjar bishop's onboard vendetta with the ship's cat, in which One-eye had always come out on top. As the representative of hellfire, Bishop William had never induced much fear in his congregation. The Emir's anger was a far more menacing prospect, to be avoided.

The sour note was quickly forgotten in anticipation of the most notable reward offered them for winning the battle: bathing. The Frankish and Muslim co-rulers of Mahdia led the Sicilian nobles through the arched keyhole doorway in a cobbled street of the medina into steam heaven. And this time Skarfr was among the elite, as was the ship's boy, erstwhile standard-bearer. Between brown and yellow tiled walls and tiled paths in red and white stripes, lay rectangular pools, also lined in bright ceramic patterns.

Filthy clothes were shed, then discreetly removed from the tiles, and replaced with clean robes by the barefoot slaves of the bathhouse.

Angels, thought Skarfr as he eased himself into the scalding-hot water of the first pool. Sitting on the ledge perfectly placed a foot below the surface he felt the tensions in muscles and mind flow away and vanish in steam. He even forgot to worry about Sea-born, limpet-close to his side, eyes closed in some boyish prudery. He let go of every clinging filament of *dwale,* the post-battle loss of morale that afflicted some men, even after a victory. *More* painfully after a victory because the drop was greater, from heightened senses to banality.

George sat between Skarfr and Philip, showing no sign of his earlier weakness. His soldier's muscles stood out against the first signs of flab, denying his white hair and the age spots marking his skin. 'We'll hardly need to bang on a shield after today,' he said with regret. 'Our enemies will run before us and we can load our ships to the tipping-line with the rewards on offer from our grateful townspeople. You were magnificent, Skarfr. And you, young man.'

If anything, Sea-born seemed to shrink even more into himself at being noticed. But boys were shy about their bodies so Skarfr thought it kindest to ignore him. He'd felt a little awkward himself at sharing the bath with a eunuch, even though their voyage at sea had rendered familiar the sight of Philip pissing through a tube. Skarfr was glad of the modest opacity offered by the soap suds and increasingly scummy water.

In the luxury of Mahdia's hot water and perfumed soap, slaves scrubbed the grit from the Sicilians' hair, faces and bodies while they exchanged tales of past fights and old scars.

The baths ran red as blood and desert sand mixed, and men bonded as battle-brothers.

Skarfr took the opportunity to ask the question most on his mind. 'Shall we sail against Constantinople soon?'

George laughed. 'See how keen he is, Philip? Not even pausing to celebrate one victory before planning the next! Constantinople is not Mahdia. We barely managed to loose one arrow into Manuel's inner court last year, for all our preparation, but this outlander thinks he can sit on the Emperor's throne next week.'

Used to the Emir's sarcastic style by now, Skarfr just waited.

'Politics,' Philip told him. 'The Byzantines are cunning as snakes and will fork their tongues to make allies of Sicilia's enemies. We need to tally up who is with us and who is against, so we can strike first, or our enemies will wage war on our states in Italy while we are busy elsewhere. This voyage secures trade in Ifriqiya so that is one threat removed.'

'Ifriqiya will be secure, God willing, but only for a year or so without us coming back in force,' said George drily. 'The Almohads will rally. And by conquering these territories we have also weakened them. Without our support, they cannot hold out — as you saw today.'

Philip waved away the gloomy thought. 'But they do have our support. And we have reinforced relations with Melita and our islands off Ifriqiya. So our next concern is indeed that thorn in our flesh, Manuel Komnenos of Byzantium. He controls trade through the Bosphorus and harries our ships trading in the Baltic states. We took Corfu, Thebes and Corinth and could have kept them if the Venezians hadn't given aid. He is building up to war again and to capture our territory in Italia— unless we take war to him first in his own city.'

'Not one scourge but two,' said George. 'Conrad of Germany casts envious eyes at our king and the dislike is mutual. Conrad is a laughing-stock since that failure they called a crusade and King Roger — who refused to go crusading — is seen as the key power of the Christian world. This, Conrad cannot stomach.

'Last year, King Louis of France would have supported Sicilia against the unholy combination of Pope, Conrad, Venezia and sundry north Italian states. But a king's memory is short and his own country's needs all-consuming. He will send only words in our support this year. Our only allies against Byzantium will be Moorish.'

Skarfr listened and learned, storing every bit of information that would make him more effective when he captained a ship against Byzantium.

Summer, he told himself, sure he had earned such a position by his actions in Mahdia. And he had further opportunities ahead. From Mahdia, George's men would continue south before returning triumphant to Sicilia. Ifriqiya and its wealth was theirs for the taking.

CHAPTER TWENTY-FOUR

INGE, GAREKSEY, ORKNEYJAR

From the moment she returned to the family home on the isle of Gareksey, Inge let her widowed mother Asleif take charge, while she warmed herself in another dark hall by another smoky fire, and listened to her brother Sweyn tell her husband Finn how boring winter was.

It seemed a man could build the biggest hall in Orkneyjar, where eighty men could sleep in comfort — so her brother claimed, and she believed him — and still find it too small in winter.

March is the worst month, thought Inge, *inflicting the last bite of winter's wolf before April brings true spring to the islands.*

After organisation of food and accommodation for the extra guests, her mother joined her, took her hands and studied her face. Then she pronounced judgement quietly. 'You look well. Finn is a good man.'

'And you?' asked Inge.

Asleif's mouth quirked wryly. 'Your brother prefers the peace of his splendid hall here to the lively atmosphere in the house he built to stop *Princess* Giri complaining this was too big. I have sent for her and the children.'

Sweyn interrupted his description of his last raid to grumble, 'Inge could have visited them in their own longhouse, without bringing them here and troubling Finn. Or you,' he added as an afterthought. Then he returned to his heroic account.

Asleif and her mother exchanged glances but, truth be told, Inge was no keener to see Giri than Sweyn was. If her mother referred ironically to the Irish princess Sweyn had brought home as wife, after killing her husband, Inge was even ruder, in the privacy of her own thoughts. She'd nicknamed Giri *Bleating Booty* because the moment she opened her mouth, an endless stream of complaints flowed out. Usually about Sweyn being absent but Inge was sure Giri could find plenty to criticise about him when he was present too. The routines of family life did not suit Sweyn's piratical soul.

'It will be lovely to see them again,' Inge lied. 'I bet the children have grown.' She directed the topic of conversation towards the third noblewoman on the island, in whom she *was* interested. 'And Margaret too. She and Gunnr have two children now, don't they? His exile must be hard on her.'

Asleif's expression hardened. 'You will see her too and the offspring.' Her tone and thinned lips showed her distaste at Margaret's immoral status and the bastardy of the children.

There was a good reason that Inge's brothers had separate longhouses on the other side of the small island, rather than living together in the family home, which was more than large enough for all of them. These three capable women could set fire to any house they shared, just by looking at each other. Only Asleif, the widow, made the best of life without a man but, whereas Giri blamed her husband, Margaret blamed Jarl Harald, her own son, who'd exiled Gunnr from pure spite over their 'sinful' relationship.

'I must set to work.' Asleif excused herself, refusing Inge's offer of help.

The men who'd sailed with them were at a discreet distance, towards the back of the hall, stowing their belongings by the benches where they would spend the night. The moment was ripe to broach the subject of Erlend with Sweyn and let him think it over during the days that followed.

Inge knew her brother well. Eyes wide, she insinuated herself into the conversation. 'To think the King of Skotland begged you to stay! What marvels you must have seen at the Skottish court. If only Jarl Harald showed you the same appreciation.'

Finn's eyes gleamed in the firelight, as he followed her lead. 'Harald thinks he can do as he likes, however nonsensical. What an insult to your family, exiling Gunnr! But,' he sighed, 'with Thorbjorn to support him, nobody can challenge him. Thorbjorn can't be matched as warrior or strategist.'

Sweyn took the bait, tetchy. 'Yes, he can. I took his plunder easily enough after the raid on the Isle of Man. And it's not Thorbjorn who's called the jarlmaker. If I wanted to, I could...' He broke off, giving his audience a chance to remember all he *had* done. Such as making a jarl 'disappear'.

'Maybe the challenge from Erlend will come to something,' mused Inge, stirring the conversational pot.

'No. He has nobody to pit against Thorbjorn,' said Finn.

'He sent me a message,' said Sweyn, 'said how insulting Harald's treatment of our family is, how I should teach him a lesson, intercept Harald's tribute ships when they sail from Hjaltland before Easter.'

Now that *was* surprising news and suggested that one party was already willing to forge the alliance Finn and Inge hoped for.

'Will you do it?' asked Inge.

Sweyn's face lit up with mischief, ready for adventure. That expression had won Inge's devotion to her big brother so often when she was a little girl. Until she had learned that there was only room for Sweyn and his own success on his adventures.

'I think I will,' he said. 'Spring is coming.'

'So is your family,' observed Inge as two boys launched themselves across the hall to jump on their father and wrestle with him. Sweyn was remarkably patient with such physical play and Inge suspected that once his sons were old enough to sail with him, they'd get more of his attention. Unlike his wife.

Panting and red-faced from walking so fast to reach the great longhouse and its visitors, Bleating Booty arrived and homed in on her target without so much as a good-day to the visitors. 'I thought you said you were checking ship repairs. *Again*.'

Sweyn's warm smile was a masterclass in charm. 'My mother sent word to me too that my sister and her husband had arrived and here I am.'

The suspicion etched on Giri's round, pink face didn't change. If only there had been a quirk to the sour down-turned mouth and a glint in her eye, the Irish princess Sweyn had married could have won a man's heart. Her soft curves and smooth, white skin had only been enhanced by birthing three children, two of whom were still making the most of their father's presence, ignoring their mother's complaints.

Asleif pulled a face behind Giri's back and Inge stifled a giggle. She knew she and her mother should feel sympathy for the woman but Asleif would never let her son down and Sweyn knew it. If only Giri didn't whine so, she might find more support.

'I saw Finn's ship round the headland and if you'd been making repairs, you'd have seen it too.' Dogged and self-righteous, because she *was* in the right, Bleating Booty continued prodding her husband. Sweyn's expression clouded over and an outburst was imminent when another mother entered the hall with her children.

All eyes went to the newcomer, whose beaver-trimmed cloak still swirled around her as she entered the warm hall, a babe in her arms and a toddler clinging to the fur hem as if it was his bedtime blanket. Men said she was beautiful but could never describe what made her so. Not her frizzy brown hair, now streaked with grey and coiled in two perfect plaits, pinned to her head in a coronet style. Not her nose, which tilted to one side as if her maker had moved his ruler when glueing it in place, perhaps distracted by someone entering his workshop. Not her hazel eyes, always squinting a little as if she couldn't believe what she saw. Nor the mature shape of her body in her rich clothes, although the way she wore her braided belt and swung her hips showed a confidence Inge envied.

Even if Margaret's allure defied analysis, all eyes turned to her when she entered the hall, her head high and proud as if she were a queen visiting rather than the woman currently known throughout Orkneyjar as Gunnr's whore.

Perhaps that's her secret, thought Inge, observing the others' reactions. *She lives by her own rules and cares nothing for what anyone thinks.* Like Sweyn but a woman!

Margaret had been the wife of the Mormaer of Ness, a position of power, and had borne the son who was now Jarl of Orkneyjar. As Harald's mother, she could have had as much power as when the Mormaer was alive. But instead of playing the respectable widow, she'd exercised a different kind of power on Inge's younger brother. Gunnr had fallen completely under her spell and they'd sailed away together in an open display of lust that had shocked all of Orkneyjar.

Outraged and embarrassed, Harald had exiled Gunnr, on the pretext that a virtuous lady had been abducted and dishonoured, which had only added to the entertainment value of the story — and to Harald's humiliation. As far as Inge knew, Gunnr was still entranced with his lover and the two children were evidence of surreptitious trips to his home from the Isle of Ljóðhús, where Sweyn had found a refuge for him.

The men seemed unsure whether to make the sign of the cross against evil or fall at her feet and worship. Finn licked his lips, wearing a slightly glazed expression, then shook his head like a dog in the rain, as if shaking off the strange feeling. He smiled reassurance at his wife, who didn't need it and was suitably amused.

Inge stood and welcomed Gunnr's lady with genuine respect. Some women might fear such defiant rejection of all that was decreed by church and tradition but Inge was fascinated by it. She also needed Margaret's legal knowledge.

After she'd been acknowledged with varying degrees of enthusiasm, Margaret threw her very expensive cloak onto a bench. She went into a curtained chamber and came back without the baby, who was no doubt still sleeping soundly, but under a blanket in a crib. She gave a wooden boat to the toddler and told him to play quietly by himself, which he did, without a murmur, while Sweyn's boys interrupted the adults and pestered their father for promises of future outings.

Margaret pulled up a stool to join the family circle. 'Children are as tedious as winter, aren't they?'

'It is our sacred duty to raise them well,' Giri said, her mouth pursed.

The contrast between Margaret's impeccably behaved toddler and Giri's well-raised boys grew in volume.

'That's enough!' Sweyn shouted, *probably* at his sons, who took the hint, stopped swinging around his neck and sidled off to make demands of whichever man would pay them attention.

Family gossip and building projects kept conversation flowing until Asleif called them to table and the combination of hot stew and cold ale rendered the atmosphere relaxed enough for silences. Along the length of the hall, the tables were full of the two families' retainers and, even under the influence of ale, nobody was foolish enough to make inflammatory remarks. Inge had seen many fights start between her brothers from apparently innocent questions such as, 'Who do you think is the richest man in Orkneyjar?'

As a general rule in Inge's childhood, whenever two men disagreed, no matter how trivial the topic, the argument would be settled with fists — or worse. Luckily, Finn was not such a man. He could hold his ale well and his tongue even better but when called to action, he did not hesitate. Her mother was right. Finn was indeed a good man and she was lucky.

CHAPTER TWENTY-FIVE

INGE, GAREKSEY, ORKNEYJAR

After a few days doing what was expected of her in her mother's hall, Inge paid a visit to Margaret, who'd returned to her own house with the children. She did not want to draw attention to the importance of the visit by taking Finn with her but it seemed natural for Fergus to accompany her. The regular 'thunk' of his walking staff blended with seabirds' anxious calls as they warned each other of intruders. As thralls were forbidden to carry weapons, Fergus was in the habit of using a walking staff, which doubled as a stout cudgel — when he was keeping to the law.

It came in useful now, as a more aggressive cry, a *'skree skree skree'* sound gave them warning and a great skua dived at them. Inge ducked her head instinctively and Fergus shook his staff at the cream and buff seabird, adding an Irish curse for good measure.

Inge laughed. 'I swear that *bonxie* remembers me and tries his luck every spring I come back! It fair hurts too if that beak touches you.'

They were walking eastwards from Sweyn's great hall on the west of the island, following the path beaten across the heath, along the lower slopes of Gareksey's one hill. The upper slopes made the shape of a whale's back and so Inge had always thought of their isle, as a living creature at home in the ocean. Sheep bleated and skipped out of the way, then grazed again on the tufts of newly-green grass that gave way to brown heather higher up.

Inge could see down the dunes to the boats beached on the shingle and to the sea beyond, sparkling and misty in the watery March sunshine. Inge remembered, when she was a girl, running down to the ships with her brothers in springtime, digging her feet into the sand and wanting to know why she could not sail with them. Gareksey had been Sweyn's reward for services to the Jarl but it was more Inge's and her mother's island than his, given how little time he spent there.

Two men were sitting on the ground outside Inge's house, making and repairing ropes. A pile of lobster-pots hinted at their trade, or rather one of their trades. All men were fishermen or farmers when they weren't crewing on their lord's sea voyages, and no doubt some of the ropes were for the boats that bobbed restlessly at anchor in the distance.

The men looked up, registered that these visitors were harmless, called for someone in the house, and returned to their work.

A maidservant in a serviceable dun pinafore dress hurried from the interior to greet them and take them to her mistress, whose clothing was as richly decorated as if she was expecting princes to visit. Margaret's hair was woven in complicated braids which must have taken her maid an hour or more. Inge wondered what the children did while their mother spent so much time on her appearance. She didn't have to wonder long.

'I hope you weren't expecting to see the dubious fruit of my loins,' said Margaret, ushering Inge to a stool and throwing a curious glance at Fergus, who stood to attention behind the women like a rustic bodyguard. 'They're at Giri's house.' Her face lit up in an irresistible smile. 'She likes children and I don't, so that works perfectly.'

How could Inge have thought anything could be conventional in Margaret's household? Or conversation? She was thrown for a moment but her habitual good manners came to her aid, and she merely replied, 'I'm sorry to have missed them but it's you I came to see.'

'Now that does sound more interesting than the usual dull routine. Let me just finish what I'm doing and I'm all ears.' Quick, authoritative, Margaret laid three lightweight gowns in the maid's arms, with instructions for the seamstress on fashionable alterations, tucks and edging, then set her scurrying on her way.

Inge doubted whether Margaret was capable of even basic mending or housework, and credited the servants with the cleanliness of the house, the perfectly tamped down peat fire, trimmed rushlights, and the tidiness of blankets and stoneware on shelves. No wonder the woman was bored, especially with Gunnr in exile. In a flash of insight, Inge wondered whether Margaret was equally bored when Gunnr was home. She could not imagine her brother and this vivacious, highbred woman as a couple for anything more than playing behind the bed-curtain. She suspected that Gunnr's absence and the dangers he faced in his sneaked visits kept sparks flying that would otherwise have been put out long since, in the drizzle of daily life together.

'You'll take a cup of wine?' Margaret didn't wait for an answer and produced goblets and a full jug before Inge had even said 'Yes'.

'I have a legal puzzle to solve,' began Inge. She and Finn had considered the possibility that Margaret would be reluctant to give advice that would be used against Thorbjorn, her cousin's son and her choice as foster-father for Harald when he was a child. So she paved the way carefully, ready to retreat. 'But if I succeed, Thorbjorn will not be pleased.'

Margaret beamed, passing Inge a brimming goblet. 'Then let's drink to your success! Gunnr wouldn't be in exile but for Thorbjorn indulging that spiteful brat I mothered, who grows even uglier and more irritating, the older he gets. If somebody told me that a horned goat had fucked me in my sleep and begot Harald, I would believe it. The Mormaer was paunchy and bald but not *that* disgusting.' She raised her cup and drank.

Inge blinked and gulped some wine. Clearly, there would be no objection from Margaret to besting Thorbjorn.

'I know what you and Finn have been up to with Sweyn.' Sharp hazel eyes met Inge's. 'Thorbjorn and Harald will find they've lost the upper hand if Sweyn takes Erlend's part and two jarls ruling is not always the happy situation the saying suggests. I can guess where your support would lie.'

Inge said, 'We would be happy with two jarls and peace.' She did not intend to confide her more treasonous hopes, whether Margaret guessed them or not. 'You have summed up the issues perfectly. But it is a different matter on which I need your counsel.'

'I am intrigued.' Margaret waited.

'One of Rognvald's men, away on pilgrimage, is a friend of mine. Thorbjorn bears him a grudge, burned down his longhouse and stole a thrall.'

Inge was conscious of Fergus, as still as a wooden post, listening to her every word, but she had to put the facts clearly as others would see them.

Margaret's forehead furrowed. 'That can't be very satisfying as revenge if Rognvald's man knows nothing of events. And you want recompense on your friend's behalf for the house and thrall. Were any other possessions taken?'

'There is no proof that Thorbjorn burned down the longhouse and he has a paper that he claims is a will, leaving the thralls to him.'

The frown deepened. 'You are giving me a puzzle indeed! How do you know Thorbjorn set fire to the longhouse if there's no proof? And if your friend is alive, his will cannot be acted upon. *And* you said 'thralls' but that Thorbjorn only took one.'

'This is the other thrall.' Inge gestured to Fergus. 'This man, Fergus, is witness to the burning and to the taking of the other thrall, his wife, Brigid.'

Margaret waved an airy hand. 'I don't know why you got involved. You can't use thralls in some dispute between you and Thorbjorn. You know they have no rights and can't be witnesses. Let your friend sort it out when he returns.'

Inge threw an apologetic glance towards Fergus, who remained impassive. Perhaps if he gave way to even a little emotion, the dam would break. She said quietly, 'I owe this man my life and I think there might be a way to repay him. Listen to the rest of the puzzle and let me know what you think.'

Margaret nodded, although her mouth took on an ironic twist.

'The will was not written by my friend, Skarfr, but by his foster-father Botolf.'

'I heard him at Rognvald's court,' remembered Margaret. 'A thoroughly unpleasant man but a gifted skald.'

'Yes, quite so. The Thing Council gave Botolf the use of Skarfr's longhouse and farm until Skarfr came of age, along with responsibility for the boy, whom he educated as his apprentice. Despite Botolf's harsh treatment, Skarfr was generous when he came into his inheritance and let the old man stay by the hearth, though he no longer had any right to do so and had certainly not earned his place with kindness. His last act was pure spite. The moment Skarfr set sail for Jórsalaheim, Botolf told Thorbjorn of something Skarfr had done.' Inge spoke quickly, avoiding detail. 'Something galling to Thorbjorn, and this was revealed in the same paper that gave him the thralls as a legacy.'

Fergus nodded in confirmation but Margaret ignored him completely, pursing her mouth.

'Most of that is irrelevant,' she judged. 'But you could win your case if you really think your friend would care so much. They're only thralls.' She must have seen Inge's reaction in her expression as Margaret rushed on, 'No, it's all right, I see you're determined. The case turns on whether the thralls belonged to Skarfr or to Botolf. I assume he bought the thralls...'

Inge looked to Fergus, who nodded.

Margaret tapped her finger against her cup while she thought. 'Were there other farm animals. Dogs? Cows? Sheep?'

Other. Inge knew Margaret was applying the law regarding thralls' status but the other woman wouldn't even look at the man she addressed.

'Sheep,' said Fergus, 'and a cow.' A nervous tic beneath his eye revealed the emotions he was trying to keep hidden.

'And did Botolf's will mention them?' asked Margaret, her eyes shining.

'I can't be sure,' confessed Fergus. 'I couldn't read the message. But Lord Thorbjorn didn't take the beasts.' His face flushed with shame. If he'd been able to read, the message would never have reached Thorbjorn.

'That's the answer!' said Margaret, her eyes shining.

Inge was none the wiser until, step by step, Margaret explained how she could dispute Thorbjorn's right to the thralls and assert Finn's. As a woman, she could not do so at the Council herself, so everything would depend on Finn.

'He's a good man,' said Inge, stoutly.

'If he loses, Thorbjorn's ownership of both thralls will have been ratified by the Thing,' warned Margaret.

'He won't lose,' said Inge, aware of the tremor in Fergus' white-knuckled hand as he gripped his walking staff.

CHAPTER TWENTY-SIX

INGE, GAREKSEY, ORKNEYJAR

To show she had allocated her time equally between her two sisters-in-law, Inge dutifully walked a second time with Fergus across the windswept heathland to visit Giri in the cosy longhouse close to Gunnr's, and as far from the great hall as the island permitted.

Unsurprisingly, Sweyn was absent. The hall was so noisy with squabbling children and a crying baby that Inge could not make herself heard. Giri was rocking Margaret's baby in her arms and jumped when Inge touched her gently on the shoulder.

'Will you take him a moment?' Giri asked, not waiting for an answer as she rushed over to where one of her boys was dangling the toddler's toy boat over the fire, threatening to throw it in and laughing as the little one reached out, always too slow as the toy was snatched away. Just in time, Giri scooped up the toddler before he overbalanced and scorched himself.

Inge handed the baby to Fergus and marched over to the lad who was still holding the wooden ship. She held out her hand and he placed the toy in it, which she gave to the sobbing toddler. Reunited with his prize possession, he immediately put it in his mouth and sucked the prow, which calmed him instantly.

Once more, Inge became the recipient of a small child as Giri said, 'Take this one,' strode over to her son and whacked him on the back of his legs.

His squeal of complaint was repeated when his brother helpfully punched him in the chest, saying, 'I told you to pick on someone your own size.'

'Like you're doing?' The verbal response was accompanied by a thump in the ribs and Inge, sighing, put down the small tot on the floor with his boat and placed herself between the two red-faced brothers. She grabbed the wrists of the older boy in one hand, judging it to be his turn to land a punch next, and she gave the younger her pouch as she spoke. He might or might not be entirely to blame for events but at least his hands and his mind would be kept busy for a while by a little bribery.

'Stop behaving like your father when he's drunk and take my pouch over to the table. Open it and you'll see what I brought for you both.' She glared at the older brother and let go of his wrists. 'But you'll have to convince me you deserve anything at all. I'm minded to take it all back with me.'

Their grievances forgotten, the brothers dashed over to the table, emptied the pouch, and inspected the contents.

'A comb!' said one in disgust.

'Needles and thread!' said the other.

Inge gave them enough time to realise that nothing in the pouch was of any interest to a self-respecting would-be warrior, then she said, 'Oh, silly me. They're not in the pouch at all. I must have given them to Fergus.'

Her man was grinning by now, the baby asleep in his arms, making little suckling movements with its rosebud mouth.

He hushed the boys, whispered, 'You'll have to wait until the baby's put to bed and if you wake him, you'll get nothing.'

Giri took the hint and the baby, disappeared behind a curtain and Fergus made the boys sit on the floor and wait, like well-trained dogs. Beside them, the toddler gurgled and rubbed his boat along the ground, with no rancour.

Inge savoured the peace.

When Giri reappeared, Fergus unrolled the very long bundle he carried.

This time there was no disappointment and two boys with shining eyes, making promises to be careful and well-behaved, went outside with Fergus to use their new bows to shoot arrows into an inanimate target.

'They'll be safe with Fergus,' Inge told Giri, who raised no objections. 'How is it that you have Margaret's children as well as your own?'

Giri smiled ruefully. 'It's my fault. She often leaves them here and I love them. Babies and small children are so sweet and easy to look after. But the older ones…' she looked towards the doorway, beyond which, out of earshot, two rambunctious boys were letting off steam.

'My brothers were just the same.' Inge smiled. 'And they haven't changed much as adults.' Inge felt the usual pang for her eldest brother, the one who'd drowned, but she would not sadden this visit with those memories.

'I don't know how your mother managed!' Giri said.

'Ask her,' Inge suggested. 'She likes nothing better than to give advice. If you ask her for help, she'll give it, but she wouldn't want you to think she's interfering so she'll hold back if you don't ask.'

'Do you think she might take my boys sometimes?' asked Giri wistfully.

'Definitely,' said Inge. 'And you should leave them with Margaret sometimes too. I suspect she is quite capable of sorting them out if she has to and is just too selfish to look after her own if she can offload them.'

'Oh, that's a terrible thing to say,' said Giri, then giggled. 'But it's true. Would you like a cup of wine?'

Over generous cups of wine, Inge saw a different side to Giri. She learned of the dour brute, lord of the Isle of Man, who'd been Giri's first husband. Of her relief when Sweyn had bested him in combat and her hopes for a life elsewhere, with a husband strong enough to protect her and any children they might have but not inclined to use his strength against her. That's why she'd insisted on widow's rights, making Sweyn do his duty and take the place of the husband he'd killed.

'And he's not so bad,' she concluded. 'When he's here. He's given me a home and children. He even takes my eldest with him when he sails, or asks a farmer to give him work. Not all men would do so much for a stepson.'

When Fergus returned the boys to their mother, she inspected them for arrow wounds and congratulated them on their fine scores.

'He's good with children, isn't he? It's so sad you don't have any yourself,' Giri observed.

Fergus caught Inge's eye in sympathy, and she realised that the thrall was more sensitive than her sister-in-law, despite the callous insults that were his daily lot. She knew he must be thinking of his child, somewhere, vulnerable. Just as she was thinking of the children she'd never had.

With great self-restraint, she said, 'I can always find children to care for, even if they're not mine.' Her eyes stayed on Fergus, promising him, *I will do my utmost to reunite your family.*

He nodded.

'You are too good,' said Giri.

For once, Inge thought this might be true. As she sought a less painful topic, she noticed some tablet weaving abandoned on a stool in the shadows and she went over to have a closer look. The chevron pattern was far more complex than anything she'd tried and the cards through which the wool was threaded were leather, so old that the holes in them were smooth.

'This is beautiful work,' she said, admiring the woven band formed as the coloured strands joined.

Giri blushed. 'They were my grandmother's cards. Margaret bought a belt from me. I've just finished the second she ordered but if you'd like it, I can tell her it's not ready yet and make another, in different colours.'

'I'd love that!' Inge hesitated but the urge to try making such a pattern overcame her fear she was asking too much. Inherited craft secrets like this were highly prized. 'Is there any chance I could have a copy of the pattern? I've only made simple designs but would like to learn to do more complicated ones.'

Giri's face shone. 'I'll copy the pattern onto wooden cards and send them to you. Be careful to check the numbers on the cards and I'll show you now how I turn them and also how to get the pattern reversed on the right-hand side, for symmetry.'

Time flew as Giri demonstrated tablet weaving and made Inge practise what she'd learned. Too soon, the baby began to cry and the older children showed signs of restlessness, so the women reluctantly left their craftwork and Inge took her leave. She insisted on paying for her new belt and she meant what she said when she thanked her sister-in-law for being good company and hoped they'd have many such conversations in the future.

The weather had changed with typical March fickleness. Fergus and she could barely see ten steps ahead of them and the rain slashed at them, horizontal in the driving wind. They said not a word. She pulled her hood low and battled the elements but a particularly fierce gust made her stumble. Fergus reached out to take her arm and supported her, all the way back to the great hall, as any gentleman would do. The moment they reached the door, he was her thrall once more, but Inge felt they had forged an alliance during the day. The word *friend* was inappropriate and yet it lodged in Inge's mind and for the first time she understood why Skarfr cared so much about people who were only thralls.

The week had passed quickly and when the weather was favourable, it was time for Inge to return home. She was surprised when Giri came to bid her farewell at the great hall, without the children. She raised an eyebrow and asked, 'Is Sweyn looking after the children?'

'No, Margaret is,' Giri replied with a smile.

'I'm impressed! How on earth did you manage that?'

'I bribed her. I've promised to send messages over to Hrossay inviting people I know to come and visit. She'll do anything to have new company and some gossip.' She took something out of her scrip and pressed it into Inge's hand. 'This is for you.'

A soapstone doe, carved with love. Inge felt the smooth curves of the haunches, the delicacy of the pricked ears.

Without a trace of her usual whine, Giri said, 'This reminds me of you, so feminine and so calm. I wish I was like you.' She sighed. 'Thank you for being so kind to me. I sometimes think nobody here likes me.'

Inge bit back the formulaic reassurance and hugged her sister-in-law. 'My mother has had a hard life and expects other women to be equally strong. The more you hide your feelings, the more she approves of you and lets hers show, a little.' She smiled ruefully. 'At least that's how it was for me.'

'It's not easy—' began Giri, then she laughed. 'Good advice,' she said. Was that a twinkle in her eye? Inge hoped so,

'Finn is waiting for me,' she told the Princess. 'You will find your place here. I'm sure of it. And we all put up with Sweyn.' She shrugged. 'Even the men say "Sweyn is Sweyn" and that's just how he is.'

'So I've discovered,' his wife said, ruefully.

Inge felt a twinge of conscience and might have said more but Asleif joined them, ending further conversation. She vowed to be kinder in her thoughts as well as in talk and action. She knew better than anyone how a husband could bring out a woman's worst qualities — or her best.

As she promised her mother to always use lavender strewn in the sleeping quarters, and all manner of domestic essentials, which conveyed the love that was never expressed directly, a sudden thought struck Inge. 'Where *is* Sweyn?' she asked. Surely, he had the manners to bid her farewell.

By the end of their visit, Sweyn had agreed to a discussion with Erlend on Finn's island, if Finn played mediator. He was sufficiently annoyed with Harald to be open to the idea of supporting the would-be jarl Erlend, so she was hopeful their plans would work. But it would have been good to water the seeds they'd planted in Sweyn, one last time.

Her mother raised her hands in exasperation. 'The gods alone know what's got into him this time. He's taken three ships to steal tribute money going from Hjaltland to Harald's coffers. And then he'll have to lie low in Skotland while Harald rants and raves, and probably exiles another of my sons! It's not going to get Gunnr back home any sooner and that'll set Margaret ranting and raving too. Lord knows what I did to deserve such a family.'

Giri smiled shyly at Inge and they exchanged looks of mutual understanding. No more planting seeds and watering was required. Sweyn was publicly demonstrating his contempt for Harald with his customary lack of subtlety. Such provocation could mean only one thing: Sweyn was open to supporting Erlend.

Well satisfied with the progress of both her projects on Gareksey, Inge joined Finn on board ship. As they sailed the wide channel eastwards, between the shores of Gareksey and Hrossey, the wind blew open Inge's cloak, revealing a new tablet weave belt, slung low around her hips.

She saw by the widening of Finn's eyes that he'd noticed.

Nonchalant, she said, 'A gift from Margaret,' and smiled to herself. In her pack was another gift, a little soapstone deer. It was just as well men didn't realise the power women wielded through such bonds with other women. They might resent being steered.

Gareksey faded into the distance as the oarsmen pulled in a strong, steady rhythm, Fergus among them.

'How does he bear it?' Inge asked Finn. 'Keeping faith they will be together again, staying true.'

'A man can feel like that about his wife,' said Finn, 'rare as it is.' And his gaze was steady, an open book. She reached for his hand.

CHAPTER TWENTY-SEVEN

HLIF, SICILIA

In the event, Hlif did find herself chaperoned on the journey, not by Amina but by a woman as unlike a lady's maid as could be imagined.

She'd walked across the swaying gangplank onto *La Nef*, clutching the same pack which had kept her company for months at sea with Jarl Rognvald's company. Four steps took her up to the raised platform, like a small castle above the foredeck, where one theoretical place remained on what could optimistically be called a bench. This was already occupied by a milky-eyed crone with a hunched back. The woman shut her eyes and ignored Hlif, who tried to perch on the corner of the stool left for her.

Standing-room was even more cramped, with crew members crushed together like anchovies in a barrel, getting their last sight of land before pushing their way past their fellows to go back down to the deck and take up their stations. For some, it was a last breath of fresh air before they faced the stench and swill below deck, securing cargo in the hold or manning what few oars there were.

'Sit,' said the mariner who'd ushered Hlif on board. 'And keep out of the way. My lady,' he added as an afterthought. Passengers were clearly not to be encouraged, even ones paying for hold space. Pietro was nowhere to be seen but Hlif thought it safe to assume he'd be more comfortable than she was.

Squashed beside the ancient lady on a crude stool meant for one normal-sized person, Hlif determined that she would stand for the whole voyage as soon as the ship set sail and the mariners had more to think about than where their passengers were. She'd paid more than enough to be the sole passenger, only to have her request ignored. Whether the captain or Pietro was to blame, she could not say yet but when she found out they would regret cheating her. Meanwhile, she must suffer the inconvenience.

Taking a sideways glance, Hlif's first impression of her unwanted companion was that she was some old relative, probably of a crew member, taking advantage of cheap passage to return home. Cheap passage that Hlif had no doubt paid for! And why someone who looked so wizened that she might not last the journey should be voyaging at all, Hlif had no idea.

The gulls diving at the docks worked themselves into a final frenzy over the scraps dropped when the last provisions were loaded and then the gangplank was shipped, ropes cast off and sails trimmed. The forecastle had emptied so Hlif rose and looked over the wales to the water below, where oars splashed and lifted to manoeuvre the ship away from the docks and the sheltered harbour to the boisterous winds and the open sea.

Looking down so far made Hlif dizzy. On Rognvald's *Sun-chaser* she was part of the water-world, salted by spray and riding the waves. Such close contact was indeed beneath those who sailed on *La Nef*, as if even the oak planks of the ship disdained the whale road on which they must travel.

Hlif shivered. The gods were not kind to men who challenged them and she knew too well what could lurk in the depths or strike from stormy skies. She turned away from the sea view and sought reassurance in the triangular sails, bellying with wind, in the same way the familiar square ones did when they were happy with the course set. The same breeze played with wisps of hair, teasing them out of her linen coif. She flicked them out of her eyes and took another look at her companion.

The old lady made no sound, her eyes shut and her head drooping onto her chest. Hlif took the opportunity to study her without fear of being thought rude.

She had seen few old women in Orkneyjar, having grown up at the Jarl's court. Old women stayed in their homes — now their children's homes — stirring the pot or cording wool, whatever tasks their failing eyes and joints could still attempt. Until they took to their beds and waited for the end of their days, taunted by memories of all they'd lost. There was no more honour for a woman in outliving her usefulness than there was for a man in becoming a hearth-worm, his viking days done.

Hlif remembered Mouthy, Skarfr's old sailing companion, who'd found the death he sought, in battle, with honour, sure he had earned Valhalla. She knew Skarfr wished for such a death, one day. She shivered and made a sign to hide her thoughts from Skuld, the Norn who could bring about such a fate. All knew that Óðinn liked to harvest his warriors in their prime.

What of Freyja, whose halls also offered sanctuary in the hereafter, for women as well as men? By what manner of death did a woman earn her place in the goddess' halls, where legendary cats stalked? Would Freyja's cats welcome one more? Hlif had not considered before what manner of death she would prefer but this enforced intimacy with a crone confirmed that she did not want to be old.

Aged women did not sail on dangerous journeys into disputed territories. This one, who did, had drool forming at one corner of her mouth. The hands clutching her walking stick were gnarled as tree roots, knotted with blue threads. Yet she wore lavender scent, her white coif was impeccably laundered and her gown was fine black wool, an import surely, with embroidered detail on the sleeves. No peasant could afford to wear black, let alone abuse such luxury by submitting it to the wear and tear of travelling!

In contrast, Hlif was dressed in her sensible seagoing clothes: a linen undershift and dun overdress in coarse wool, the straps pinned with two engraved silver brooches which Skarfr had given her. Her clothes were well-washed rather than well-laundered, and mostly by seawater. Regarding the old woman's clothes, Hlif revised her first impression. She would bet her rune-dice that this was no sailor's relative.

'Looked your fill, have you?' The woman's eyes snapped open though what they could see through the milky film, Hlif had no idea.

She coloured. 'I'm curious about my travel companion.'

'As am I,' was the dry response. 'A woman voyaging alone into the unknown.'

Did she mean Hlif or herself? 'I am a trader,' stated Hlif, trying to establish her status, which felt threatened by this stranger. Her own *superior* status, she reminded herself, despite the other's rich clothing, and *she* had booked a place on this ship as sole passenger. This person was an uninvited passenger, to be tolerated — or not.

Her upbringing prompted her towards tolerance and she knew, from the sagas Skarfr narrated around campfires, that you should never underestimate the power of an old woman. Hag and crone could be guises for witch or god and Hlif was sensitive to others' gifts. However, in her rare contact with old women, she had never sensed anything other than pain and frustration. Until now. There was some undercurrent here that she didn't understand.

The crone nodded. 'We are all traders, in a manner of speaking. I am here on family business.' She spoke quietly, deepening her voice so that the quaver of age was barely perceptible. Once, her voice must have commanded attention across a hall, across a crowded dockyard, across heaped bodies and screaming children.

Hlif shook herself. Now was not the time to see beyond the veil to might-have-beens.

The crone continued, fixing Hlif in that strange unfocused stare, milky-eyed and fierce at the same time. 'I'm a widow, which gives me more freedom than I ever had as a wife, and I've taken over my husband's affairs. I'm too old to be forced into remarrying, and I wasn't inclined to wear the russet veil.'

'Wear the russet veil?' queried Hlif.

The woman cackled. 'How young you are and how little you know! When your husband dies, you can supplicate the king for permission to take vows of chastity without joining a cloister. A widow fortunate enough to be granted this privilege is proclaimed a holy widow by the bishop and wears a russet veil with a dull, poor-quality robe to show her status.' She brushed her own rich black gown. 'A childbearing woman like yourself is too precious a commodity to be allowed such tranquility.'

Hlif winced, turned her thoughts from bearing children to the equally painful topic of widowhood. The only vow she'd make was that no russet veil would ever be her fate!

Courtesy required that she should say something about herself. 'I'm a trader, on my way to buy oranges,' she offered.

Any last hint of a mystical moment was shattered by a sudden stink and rattling, unapologetic expulsion of wind from the old lady, who said, 'Like King Roger's father, I know rubbish when I hear it. And that's the same response he gave when they tried to make him fight against his Muslim allies in Ifriqiya. I know why you're here and that's what I say to you.' With a hand curved by age, she wafted the stench towards Hlif.

Sagas, warnings, politeness to strangers and other childhood teachings flew over the ship's wales towards the sea, with the bad smell.

Hlif recalled Bandy-legs yelling, 'Put a cork in your arse,' and other such witticisms on the journey to Sicily but all she said was, 'You think a *fart* can impress somebody who spent months on a ship with Orkneyjar sailors?'

Once she'd begun, Hlif couldn't stop herself. 'Half the men I was voyaging with were *named* for their bloody acts and blades, so a man known as Fjert 'the Farter' ranked as low as his skill!'

She hadn't finished. 'And another thing! King Roger's father might have said no, in a *very* vulgar manner, to waging war in Ifriqiya, but King Roger himself has sent men — *good* men — on exactly such a mission and I won't hear a word against them. Give me one good reason why I should allow you to stay on *my* ship when I have no idea who you are or why you are so rude! I should ask my guard to put you off at the next port — an ass would be a more suitable mode of travel for you!' It wasn't *exactly* her ship but the principle was what mattered.

The woman laughed, a throaty, huffing noise that revealed missing teeth and black ones that should be pulled. Her mouth must smell as foul as her fart, despite the lavender.

'Your guard Pietro?' she said. 'Didn't he tell you? I'm his mother.'

First the unpleasant brothers, now an equally unpleasant mother? Who looks old enough to be his great-grandmother! 'No, he didn't tell me! I paid good money to be the sole passenger on this ship so he *should* have told me. *He* works for *me*,' Hlif said, in case the woman had not understood that passage should have been requested, not taken for granted, whoever's mother she might be.

'I know.' There was neither embarrassment nor apology in the woman's tone. Her Frankish was fluent but now she was listening for it, Hlif could hear the hint of an Italian accent. Like her son's. The mother shrugged. 'I told Pietro I was coming.'

Hlif's opinion of Pietro dropped even lower. To accept being told what to do by his mother! And to assume that he could add somebody to their party without asking! She gathered her skirts closer as if to avoid contamination.

'He is a good boy but not very clever. He should have told you.' Pietro's mother shrugged. 'My name is Maria.'

Hlif contemplated acting on her threat, putting the old woman off the ship, abandoning her to whatever cutpurses, bandits and murderers might frequent the land route ahead. She couldn't do so until the next port anyway, so she might as well accept what she couldn't change, for now.

'He should have asked,' she said, hating how petulant she sounded.

The woman laughed again. 'We don't *ask*,' she said. 'But Pietro was right about you. I think we can do business together.'

Hlif opened her mouth to object but decided not to encourage the mad old biddy, who would be out of Hlif's hair once they disembarked. If she couldn't shake her off before the orange farm, Pietro could take his mother from there to the family home while Hlif negotiated with the farmer. Meanwhile she could just let the stranger witter on, and she would nod politely, if she stayed awake.

Now they were well out at sea, under sail and oars shipped, the sense of urgency had left the crew. The course was set and they could afford a moment to exchange tall tales. Hlif knew the routine of work and watches, alternating between troubled sleep and full attention.

Every item on board must be stored and secured, as tripping over a man's pack could cost a life. Hlif checked that her own pack was carefully stowed under the stool. Her companion had no belongings on show but this was a cargo ship so maybe she had a kist in the hold.

Taking up more of the space Hlif had paid for, she thought, with another flare of irritation.

As a result of its build, the cargo ship was slower than a drakkar, a lumbering cow with full belly, compared to the sleek sea-stallion that was an Orkneyjar dragon ship.

This more leisurely pace was reflected in the attitude of the crew. One even took the time to call up the steps, 'Mamma Maria, are you all right?'

Another brother?

'Don't you worry about me, Jehannes,' Maria called back. 'Everything that aches on land aches at sea too but I won't bring bad luck to your ship by dying on it.'

The sailor laughed. 'Always the same Mamma Maria!'

Apparently he had no interest in how the ship's paying passenger — other paying passenger? — was faring.

Maria turned her attention back to Hlif. 'There is so much you need to know,' she began. 'The oranges crop every year but in the same region you are heading to, the autumn gives far more valuable crops. Every two years in Catania are the pistachios — you know these nuts?'

Hlif did know these nuts and was intrigued, despite herself. Not that she would be in Sicilia in the autumn, but a woman's fate could change, and if the Norns should keep her on this island, there was no harm in knowing more about these delicacies that left both salt and sweetness on the tongue at the same time. Gentle for the teeth but with enough crunch to please with their texture. She did indeed want to know more about pistachios.

'And the best olives also grow in the foothills of Mount Etna,' continued Maria. 'Olive trees are like women. They do not thrive if they produce young annually. Every three years is better for their health.'

Hlif wondered idly how many more siblings Pietro had, produced every three years no doubt, but she thought it more politic to talk about nuts and olives.

In this manner, the voyage passed more pleasantly than Hlif had anticipated.

Catching them in conversation as he emerged from the hold before a port stop, Pietro told Hlif, 'My mother knows everything,' and bestowed one of his most disarming smiles on her.

Despite the smile, the comment chilled Hlif, as if more than nuts and olives were meant. What had Maria meant when she said 'I know why you're here.' Was it possible that she knew the truth?

Afterwards, she would ask herself repeatedly why she hadn't forced the old woman off the ship at the first port and the answer was always the same: Maria's wishes were somehow compelling. Whatever made this so, Hlif wanted to have that power, without waiting until she was widowed and withered. It seemed that witchcraft was not the only way of having influence and whatever the source of Maria's power, it must be far less dangerous than rune-reading or dream-walking. So Hlif thought then.

CHAPTER TWENTY-EIGHT

HLIF, SICILIA

Hlif's sense of anticipation grew as *La Nef* sailed into a busy harbour defined by a curved bite of sandy beach and a settlement above the waterline. Taormina, where *La Nef* would unload its Palermo cargo, leaving room in the hold for new purchases, including Hlif's oranges.

Hlif was looking shoreward to the group of locals gathering to meet the ship, when the bustle of preparation for docking changed to something more sinister. Men shouting and then, unthinkably, a woman's screams, drew her attention to the deck below, where the hold was being emptied.

With a sinking heart, she saw the 'cargo' stagger forward to the gangplank, linked by ankle and neck chains so they could only shuffle. What conditions had these people suffered, with foul water swirling past them in the dark, barrels and rats for company? And, occasionally, bad-tempered oarsmen or mariners giving them food and drink. At least, Hlif hoped they'd had food and drink.

Your cargo is fine, one of the brothers had told Maria.

Hlif turned to the old woman, who had taken no interest at all in the brouhaha below and was clearly not leaving the ship at Taormina.

'You're selling slaves!' She couldn't help sounding accusatory even though she knew such business was legal.

The old woman shrugged. 'Only in a small way. My family has many business activities. The ships bring them from Ifriqiya to Palermo, we invest in a selection and sell them in Taormina for a profit. You have a soft heart I think. Not good for business.' She shook her head. 'These people will be better off on the farms of Sicilia than they were in their Ifriqiyan huts.'

'But what about their families?' Hlif was outraged. She told herself this was quite different from what had happened to Fergus and Brigid. *Vastly different!*

The wailing from the slaves grew louder and two young women were uncuffed and separated from the rest of the group. They alternately clung to each other and made frantic, beseeching movements but were strangely quiet. This was even more evident when the large group of slaves was herded down the gangplank and swallowed up in the crowd of observers gathered on the shore.

At that moment, the same brother who'd spoken to Maria earlier yelled up to her. 'There is a problem, Mamma Maria.'

The old woman rose stiffly, leaning on her cane, as if the word 'problem' required that the full extent of her diminutive height be in view. She was even smaller than Hlif and might have been no taller even when her back was straight.

She didn't need to speak. Standing up was enough acknowledgement that she required information before action.

The deck below was emptying quickly so the two slaves in their huddle of misery were clearly visible.

'Watch,' said the mariner. He was holding the horn used as a signal by all ships in fog or difficulty, or to send messages in a fleet. He walked in a circle around the young women, blowing bright, brassy notes that made Hlif jump each time he set his lips to the instrument again.

There was no reaction at all from the slaves.

'See?' The mariner shouted. Even though he was right beside them, neither woman reacted to the noise.

He clapped his hands right beside a slave's ear.

The only response was an open-mouthed expression of horror from the other woman, who could see the mariner clapping his hands. She pointed at him, gestured wildly and then sat on the deck, rocking.

In the quiet that descended, Hlif realised the women were not silent. They were chirruping, like broken birds. Maybe that was their language, from their home.

'They're deaf,' rasped Maria with disgust. 'We've been cheated. Nobody will want deaf slaves and it would be bad for our reputation as honest businessmen to try to sell them.'

Hlif turned a snort into a cough.

'Put them back in the hold and we'll dispose of them at sea. It will be a kindness. They're better off dead.'

'No! I'll take them,' Hlif heard herself saying. A lifetime's experience of striking bargains with hard-headed traders made her add, 'Let me check what else is wrong with them before I decide.' She tried not to think about the fact she was buying people. Until she'd made her purchase, the seller could always increase the price beyond what she could pay, or back out of the deal completely.

She headed down the steps to the deck. Maria followed her and instructed the mariner, 'Show her the goods.'

Forced to stand, to raise their heads, the slaves looked younger than they had from above. They were mere girls, so alike they must be twins. Their hands still fluttered but Hlif had been mistaken. The gestures were not frantic. Nor were they random. The girls were watching each other's hand movements intently.

When the mariner laid a hand on one to show how well-fed she was, pinching her stomach and arm to show the fat, the girl flinched and Hlif's stomach churned. But she must play the game or risk Maria changing her mind.

Like buying a pig at market.

Maria opened the haggling. 'You can see how much they've cost us in food, in passage — they've taken the place of two healthy slaves, who would have brought a gold solidus each in the market, so that should be their price.'

Hlif walked around the slaves, inspecting them. She could not bring herself to prod them as if they were fruit but she feigned indifference, assumed an expression of vague disappointment, forced herself to say, 'But you will get nothing for them if you throw them in the sea. I thought they were older, more use to me. And how can I give orders to deaf slaves?'

Maria shrugged. 'You have come to your senses. I would not burden you with such slaves. They are of no use. Tonio—'

Hlif cut in before Maria could complete her order to Tonio. '— but they will grow into women. And they do not labour with their ears.' She screwed up her mouth as if deliberating. 'The outlay will be heavy and the risk is all mine. I'll give you half a solidus for the pair.'

Greed warred with business sense in Maria's eyes but she knew when she was ahead and when to stop bargaining. 'It's a deal. I have made a loss on these two but you are a special customer and we shall do business again. I have warned you of your foolishness so it is none of my doing when you regret your purchase.'

Hlif did not point out again that half a gold coin was a lot more than the alternative of 'nothing'. With the air of one who'd spent more than she intended, she withdrew her money pouch, counted the coins out and handed them over.

The slaves, her slaves now, looked from her to each other and their talking hands flew.

'Put them in the hold, Tonio,' ordered Maria.

'No!' said Hlif. 'It is unhealthy and I don't want them perishing below deck. Who knows what sailors might be tempted to do, out of sight. The sea air will do them good. They will sit beside me and learn their place.'

She held out her hand and the mariner passed over the chain which led to their cuffs. And then the key.

Without meeting the deep brown eyes that met hers in defiance, then quickly looked down again, Hlif led the girls up to the forecastle and pointed to the deck. Where they sat, like dogs. Except that they were holding hands. There was more than a familial resemblance in their broad faces, doe-brown eyes, shiny round cheeks and haloes of frizzy hair.

Definitely twin sisters, concluded Hlif, *by blood and by circumstance.* Rachel would tut at their appearance and recommend oiling their hair.

Only a few hours to the port of Saracena and then Hlif would change their world for the better, she vowed. And oiling hair would be only one of their options.

CHAPTER TWENTY-NINE

HLIF, SICILIA

'Two weeks and we sail,' Captain Lemercier warned Hlif as *La Nef* docked at the huge harbour known as Saracena Port, some sea-miles past the walled city of Catania which it served. A hundred or more warships could have laid anchor in this haven at the same time and she felt the ghostly presence of great events, those past and those to come.

No sooner had the thought come to her that Saracena Port had welcomed ships through countless ages, through the rule of Greeks and Muslims to the present-day Franks, than a second thought usurped the first.

Insidious at first, the notion that Saracena Port would not last long, grew into overwhelming horror as she glimpsed its fate. A road rolled forward, wide as the horizon, churning and sliding towards the sea. Grey mud erupted in flame, belched smoke and destroyed everything in its path. The dragon under Sicilia awoke, heaving up the land on its back, covering all trace of human activity, all life. The sparkling water filled with ooze, mud piled on mud, hissing as fire met water.

Impossible! Hlif blinked to clear her eyes and her head.

In the distance the cone of Mount Etna blew a plume of smoke. The dragon slept peacefully.

Hlif shivered. *May the dragon sleep until Ragnarok,* she prayed.

If the gods meant something by such a vision, they would reveal more when the time was right. Apart from her head aching, there was no vestige of the catastrophe. *La Nef's* entry to the harbour was under a cloudless blue sky, the sun glinting on ripples as it navigated a route through the peaceful ships of all sizes bobbing in its wake.

Hlif was standing on the deck, ready to disembark. Pietro had collected her personal kist from the hold and was waiting for the gangplank to be put in place. The two sisters stood behind their mistress, subdued, as if wearing invisible chains.

'I intend to be back here by the time those two weeks are up, with my cargo,' replied Hlif with composure. 'But if I'm not, and you sail without me, you'll forfeit the second half of your payment.'

The captain shrugged. 'There's always people wanting cargo shipped.' He grinned. 'And I'll charge them double for short notice.'

Reminding herself that Captain Lemercier had been recommended as trustworthy, Hlif ignored his bluster and addressed Pietro instead.

'Get us a cart, please, and load my kist. And two mounts suitable for the journey to the plain of Catania.'

Her manservant yelled at two mariners — brothers? — to carry the kist ashore and she saw them guarding it while Pietro disappeared, presumably about her bidding. The captain seemed comfortable with Pietro's ease on his ship and respectful to Mamma Maria, who was also leaving the ship at Saracena.

Two swarthy men in workers' leather tunics, much-repaired hose and worn boots came on board the ship to greet Mamma Maria, hoist her kist up and accompany her on shore.

Hlif marched after her down the gangplank, followed by the two sisters. She pushed her way through the usual crowd selling food to those leaving the ship, or seeking to buy whatever novelties might emerge from the crates being carried out of the hold. When she reached enough space to pause, she did so. As did her slaves, hard on her heels.

Too short to see over the heads of those around her, Hlif was looking for a boulder or box to stand on, when one of the girls made a gabbling noise and grabbed her arm. Instinctively, Hlif recoiled and saw hurt in the brown eyes, something darker in her sister's. Contempt?

The girl who'd touched her, pointed, and Hlif could see Pietro coming towards them. He looked cheerful, which no doubt meant he'd accomplished his mission. Although it might mean he'd been distracted by an agreeable flirtation and fancied a night in Saracena. You could never tell with Pietro. Hlif only trusted him as far as his interests aligned with hers.

'Good. Let's get moving.' She spoke aloud, then realised words were wasted on the girls. However, they seemed to understand the situation and followed her to meet Pietro. It dawned on her that the twins had 'told' her Pietro was coming, that they could reason and communicate. She flushed at her earlier assumptions. So much the better for her plan!

A drover stood beside his horse and cart beyond the crowded harbour, on a dirt track that skirted the settlement in the direction of the farms and mountains inland. Three mules were attached to the back of the cart, two saddled for riders and a third prepared for pack. Hlif felt oddly vulnerable at the thought of taking to the road with only Pietro and an unknown local for protection but she steadied her resolve with thoughts of oranges — and red stones.

First, she must free the slaves.

They were so close behind her, she almost trod on one, when she turned, and they took a step back, alarmed.

She took the proof of ownership out of her scrip, and removed a stub of charcoal from its linen wrap. Even though she knew words meant nothing to them, she looked each girl in the eye and spoke the formal words of manumission.

'I Hlif, ward of Jarl Rognvald of Orkneyjar, wife of Skarfr the Skald and Navigator, do abjure my rights as owner of two thrall-women.' Then she wrote the words in the space at the bottom of the parchment, signed it and put a broad charcoal cross through the rest of the document.

She showed the sisters, made cutting movements over the parchment, hoping they understood it meant nothing, that their chains were gone forever. She offered the proof of their freedom to them but they shrank back, unwilling to even touch the document, so she tucked it away in her scrip. Hlif had no evidence that *she* was free so why should they need any?

She fished in her pouch for the wherewithal to support them in their first steps as freedwomen, as karls in this new land. Careful to bring out only what she sought, and not to reveal what other treasures might be in the leather pouch, she tried to put a small pearl in one girl's hand. She had to pry open the girl's fingers and then close them again over the precious gift to force acceptance.

Then Hlif offered the onyx bead to the second girl, who opened her palm of her own accord, despite the apprehension in her eyes.

Hlif nodded, smiled to show approval, then turned each girl to face away from her. She gave each a little push.

'Go,' she told them. 'Make your own lives.'

The sisters took a few paces, stopped and looked back. Hlif continued to smile and nod, made shooing gestures with her arms as if they were a pair of scavenging cats.

The girls walked further away and Hlif turned back to the drover and Pietro, who'd been watching her with incredulity. As had someone who'd caught up with their party after disembarking from *La Nef*.

CHAPTER THIRTY

HLIF, SICILIA

'You are a greater fool than I thought,' sneered Mamma Maria. 'You don't really think they can live on their own?'

Hlif didn't deign to reply. 'I'm ready to go, Pietro,' she said, accepting his proffered hands to boost her into the saddle of one of the mules.

But instead of mounting the other mule, Pietro helped Mamma Maria onto its back and put her kist on the pack mule.

'I have business at the orange farm,' said Mamma Maria. 'Pietro thought it would be useful for me to travel with you.'

Unable to say why she thought this a terrible idea, Hlif spoke through gritted teeth. 'I'm happy to give you such protection as we can offer on the journey.'

'Oh no, dear.' Maria gave that knowing smile which was more irritating than a plain insult. 'Quite the reverse, quite the reverse. And it's my pleasure.'

Hlif did not thank her.

Pietro took his place, walking beside the drover, who held the carthorse's reins. With clicks and a flick of a whip, the drover urged the horse forward. Wheels rolled, the mules settled into a long-distance ambling gait, as did the humans on foot.

Their route was along the main road from the port, towards

Catania, its walls growing ever more imposing as they drew nearer. Hlif could see the guards at the watchtower checking each newcomer before permitting entry to the fortified town but before they reached the queue at the gate, Pietro and the drover turned left at an intersection.

Most of those who'd travelled from the port with them continued towards Catania. Hlif knew that the captain and most of the crew would also be heading for the town once they'd secured *La Nef*. Catania was the hub of activity in the region and any sensible person seeking entertainment or conducting business would be heading for the town. So it was with some disappointment that Hlif realised Maria was staying with the company and she really *had* meant the whole journey.

The town was out of sight when Hlif had the feeling that they were being followed. The hairs on the back of her neck rose. She looked behind her and, at a respectful distance, two familiar figures, on foot, kept up with the party.

'I told you so,' said Mamma Maria.

As soon as they found a suitable place away from the town, the party paused to eat. According to the sun, it was well after midday and Hlif was hungry. She'd been sailing from dawn at Taormina to Saracena Port late morning with only some dry bread and water on the ship to break her fast.

Hlif was never comfortable on horseback and even though she'd been riding for only a short time, she stretched her legs with relief when she dismounted. After one look at the deposits of ash on damp, grey earth, she chose to remain standing while she chewed on a hunk of stale bread and dry goat's cheese. There were no pastures in this region, so there were no cows, but goats thrived on their diet of what shrubs and herbs were available.

The cheese produced was best in summer but Hlif was hungry enough to appreciate its flavour, washed down with local red wine, well-watered. Another gift from the soil around Mount Etna, however unprepossessing it looked. The wine was good and plentiful in all of Sicilia, she admitted, although Orkneyjar's amber-coloured honeyed ale could hold its own. And could fell a man more quickly. She took another bite of bread and thought with longing of the mature orange cheese in her dairy, produced from the rich, creamy milk Fergus collected from their cow, the red one named for its colour, Rauðka.

Even her wool-gathering led her back to orange and amber! She brought her straying thoughts back to the present. Maria had said that appearances were deceptive. This grey land, showered as much by ash as rain, was so fertile men fought to farm on the slopes of the dragon-mountain. This was hard to believe, looking at the desolate landscape, but as Hlif kept telling herself, *We shall see.*

A movement in the middle distance attracted her attention and she realised with a pang of conscience that she'd forgotten all about the two slaves — ex-slaves — who had no qualms about sitting on the grey soil, waiting patiently.

They had no food!

Hlif waved an imperious hand, summoning them. If they *would* keep following, then they might as well be part of the group.

Hesitant, casting a wary eye on Maria and the drover, the two girls approached.

Hlif held out food to them and immediately one girl showed the pearl in her palm and offered it in payment.

'No, no!' Hlif shook her head, closing the fingers once more over the precious pearl.

The girl looked at her sister and some silent agreement passed between them. The onyx and the pearl were offered again but this time more was being asked in exchange. With gestures, pointing to Hlif and the cart, miming the journey with walking fingers, one girl made it clear they would stay with Hlif and her party.

The harsh voice of Mamma Maria put into words the girls' dilemma. 'They will be hung as thieves if they try to sell those baubles. If bandits don't find them first and slit their throats. Without a master, they have no proper place in the world. What did you think their fate would be when you cast them off?'

Hlif felt the heat rising around her neck. 'Freedom is not

abandonment,' she stated with hauteur, but she knew Maria was right.

'*Keep us,*' pleaded the girl's eyes, as clearly as if she'd spoken.

'You need names,' said Hlif. She pointed to herself. 'Hlif,' she said. Their eyes remained blank.

She took the pearl from an open palm, pointed to it and then to the person who'd held it. She made a circle with the thumb and first finger of her right hand and pointed to the pearl and to the girl.

'You are called Pearl,' she said.

Pearl made the same circle gesture and pointed at herself. Hlif nodded, pleased.

Then she picked up the onyx from the girl's hand. The twins looked at her, curious. Hlif looked at the bead, a black teardrop. She laid the forefinger of her left hand in a straight line below her eye, making a shadow, a black teardrop.

She pointed to the onyx, made the sign again, pointed to the girl and said, 'You are called Onyx. Now she'd named the twins, Hlif could sense the differences between them. Pearl was calmer, smoother in movement and Onyx sparkled more, was the leader. As she studied them, she could see their personalities in their eyes and mouths, similar but no longer the same to Hlif. She knew well the power of a name and felt the same rush of Freyja's *seithr* magic running through her, as when she cast the runes. The Norns had brought her Onyx and Pearl, and they would teach her how to speak with them.

As if reading her thoughts already, Onyx fluttered her hands, pointed to the remaining food and to her mouth.

Hungry.

Hlif gave them more food.

Pearl made a different shape with her hands, bowed her head.

Thank you.

Pietro interrupted the mime. 'It's time we were moving or night will catch us on the road.'

His concern, real or feigned, was unjustified and they had an uneventful ride across the plain, past fallow fields prepared for wheat and through leafy orchards. Remembering al-Idrisi's map and Rachel's directions, Hlif noted landmarks, especially what must be the tower of Paternò in the distance, so she could retrace her steps when she had the opportunity. March weather in Sicilia was fickle and she was glad of her woollen layers under a cloak that had served her well since she set sail from Orkneyjar.

Late in the afternoon, they passed orchards dotted with orange fruit and at last they reached the cluster of stone buildings that made up Gian's farm. Women appeared in doorways to assess the newcomers and dogs rushed around barking, with much the same intention. Welcome or warning depended on their findings. A young man with enough influence over the hounds to call them off approached Pietro and asked their business.

Hlif watched the exchange. She too could observe and make judgements before taking any lead in proceedings. The man clearly had some authority and the blue dye of his practical clothes suggested status higher than a peasant's but his youth made it unlikely he was the landowner described by the Palermo shopkeeper.

Son maybe? Or other relative? But then, wouldn't Gian leave him in charge while conducting business in Palermo, or indeed send the young man. Unless he didn't trust him. Or—

'The steward is going to fetch his lord.' Pietro cut into her thoughts with the answer to her question.

From the moment Gian appeared, his weathered face telling of a life outdoors and his smile making the visitors welcome, Hlif took charge. She introduced Pietro as her manservant and translator should one be needed, and the sisters as her maids. She even managed to speak for Mamma Maria, although she suspected the latter of indulging her by staying silent.

'Mamma Maria is Pietro's mother and has been a travel companion. I believe she has family business of her own here.'

'Mamma Maria is always welcome.' Gian swept a bow as if the old lady were visiting royalty but when he straightened, Hlif saw a shadow cross his face before the smile returned. *Worry?* And he had confirmed Hlif's suspicion that Maria was known here. And respected — or even feared. What was this family business? Whatever it was, Gian spoke to Maria at length, in private, with the feeble excuse that Hlif needed time to settle into her room and to recover from the journey.

When she was granted the interview she requested, Gian could not have been more agreeable. Indeed, he would appreciate an intermediary to take oranges to Palermo while he tended to his farm. The planting of new pistachio trees was a priority and he was open to Hlif's proposition of a second contract for the pistachios themselves, from the older trees of course, in the autumn. The first contract was quickly concluded, with minimal haggling over the price per hundred given to Gian, and with the proviso that he would ensure a cartload of oranges, twenty sacks in number, weighed and tagged, was harvested and bagged within two days. Hlif could check the weights herself and oversee his men loading the sacks onto the cart.

'I trust you,' she said, knowing that the future deal over pistachios was a guarantee of fair trading now and that Gian could not afford to sully his reputation in Palermo.

However, as she lay awake that night, despite her comfortable mattress and a stomach replete with Sicilian food and red-flushed orange segments for dessert, it was not the breathing of the sisters on their floor cushions that kept her awake. She was troubled by the ease with which business had been conducted. It had gone so smoothly, too smoothly.

Don't meet trouble halfway, she told herself, and directed her thoughts to her plan for the next day. While oranges were picked and stored, while Pietro flirted with the winsome teenager who'd been making eyes at him earlier, and while Mamma Maria did whatever she did, Hlif would slip out with a mule and her maids. She would leave a message saying she wanted to ride out for pleasure and explore the surrounding countryside. The sisters would be security enough in the countryside. She did not need Pietro. No need for anyone to worry. She would be back by nightfall.

As if Pietro would question a day off! And the sisters would not betray her with tattle.

When the first rumbling of thunder began, Hlif smiled. Thórr was blessing her project and would finish his hammer-work by morning. With that thought, she drifted into sleep, unaffected by the storm searing the skies white outside the thick stone walls of her windowless chamber.

CHAPTER THIRTY-ONE

HLIF, SICILIA

The crack of light around the doorway confirmed Hlif's instinct that it was time to rise from her bed. She poured water from the ewer into the basin kindly provided and washed her face, then roused the twins with a light touch on a shoulder. The girl, Pearl, flinched, then recognition dawned in the wary brown eyes.

Hlif gestured at their clothes and started to don her own. *Time to get up.*

Pearl nodded understanding, stretched and stood up, and her sister stirred, then followed suit.

As she'd hoped, her matinal routine had wakened her early and only the servants were visible, discreetly carrying out their domestic tasks. Hlif acquired food for their outing, tied neatly in a clean cloth, and a leather waterskin. After leaving a message for Pietro and her host, she headed for the stables, her maids in tow. All went as smoothly as the business agreements the previous day had done, which Hlif took this as a sign that the gods were with her.

In the time it took to saddle one mule, and establish that the sisters preferred to walk beside her, Hlif was ready to leave. She didn't need Skarfr's navigational skills to orient herself. The smoking peak of Mount Etna showed clearly to the north and the road they'd followed the day before led east. She would backtrack an hour or two until she could pick up one of the small trails leading to the river.

It must have rained heavily during the storm because the clay soil was sodden and dark, sucking at the mule's unshod hooves and at the girls' bare feet, on which a muddy tide-mark formed and dried as they walked, ash-grey on leathery-black. Hlif remembered her barefoot childhood and wondered whether she would be doing the sisters a favour if she bought them boots. Softened feet could be a disadvantage in whatever work the twins might find in the future. Hlif could not swear she would always keep them at her side.

But whatever happens, Mamma Maria was wrong and it will be better than slavery or death!

Every outline in the landscape was blade-sharp after the storm, from cone-shaped Etna to the fruit trees. Raindrops clung to twigs, sparkling as they plopped onto the ground or onto the rider of a stubborn mule, which took a detour to nibble branches. Onyx took the reins and led the creature back onto the road while Hlif licked the sky's tears from her lips. The freshness of the day was pleasant and the dampness underfoot caused no problems. It would be even wetter when they reached their destination.

Al-Idrisi had said that from its source in the mountains, the Someto matured in river-fashion, from a rushing stream to the stately broads that emptied into the sea south of Catania. But he had no idea that her interest in the river was motivated by anything other than geographical information for its own sake, an interest which he considered normal.

Rachel's instructions were more specific. The lower reaches of the river, where its slowness created silt and beaches, threw out the amber nuggets washed down from the mountains. Especially after a storm, when the river would rise, leave debris on the banks, then shrink back down.

Dull, hiding in plain sight like a princess disguised as a kitchen-maid, the gems could only be identified by somebody who knew what she was looking for. Somebody who had an example of such a stone in her scrip.

After stopping to break fast on the main road, sharing food and a swig of water from the leather bottle, Hlif directed the mule onto a smaller track heading south, which must surely lead to the river. She could only hope that this shore would prove fruitful as it seemed unlikely that she could cross the still-swollen river.

If she found nothing today, she would have to search further along the banks, downriver towards Catania itself, where there would no doubt be a ferry. She could venture out again the next day but would then be expected to leave the farm with her oranges. Her last chance would be to go beachcombing from Catania itself, during the last afternoon and evening, before the ship sailed. But it would be more difficult to get rid of Pietro.

The road had been deserted but there was a different quality to the isolation of the small track Hlif now rode, as if the possibility of travellers had left an imprint on the road that this untravelled path lacked. Something had kept the way clear, but whether human or animal, there was no telling. Broad daylight kept fears at bay but Hlif was glad of her maids' company all the same.

The mule showed no premonition of danger and picked its way along the path as if he could scent water and approved of the route. Soon, a glimpse of silver proved to be the river itself, where shrubs had drunk enough to grow into trees, solving Hlif's problem of where to tie the mule while she foraged.

She took off her boots and stockings so as not to spoil them and left them near enough the mule to find them again easily, but out of nibbling reach. Then she tucked her gown up above her calves, as she'd been accustomed to do on the Orkneyjar beach where she'd first met Skarfr. With her sample of raw amber in hand, she began to scour the beach. She defined an area with landmarks — a stone shaped like an owl, a stick with hound ears — and then methodically walked up and down between the river and its shrubby borders.

The sisters watched with evident curiosity, guarding the mule and boots, until Hlif gave an involuntary cry. They rushed to her side, touching her, making urgent noises in their bird-like manner, asking questions with their hands.

Too excited to hide her triumph, Hlif held up the unprepossessing rock she'd found, with its little hint of red glinting through dull striations. She showed the sisters her sample, placed the two pebbles side by side. There was no doubt. She'd found her first lump of raw amber. She had no idea whether it would be beautiful or mediocre once polished, but it was amber! Her back no longer felt weary and she set to, scouring the beach again.

When she glanced up from her work to check that the mule was in its place, she realised the sisters were no longer standing beside it. Looking around her, heart thumping, she saw them further along the shore, copying her, looking for the magical stones their mistress wanted.

The mule and boots were moved frequently throughout the day to search ever further along the river and the rewards were worth the back-breaking work. After what seemed days bending and screwing up her eyes, and several splashes into the river to fill the water-bottle and refresh her weary face, Hlif slogged her way back to the mule. She waved to the sisters, beckoning them.

'Enough!' she called and they read her movements, straightening and stretching, as if they'd been winnowing wheat all day. Work for which they were well-suited, thought Hlif.

All the food had been eaten and Hlif placed the empty cloth on the ground so the sisters could tip their collection onto it. Whether they knew what they'd collected or not, the pride of Pearl and Onyx shone from their eyes and Hlif knew they understood how pleased she was. Pearl, Onyx and amber. Gems indeed. She added her own trawl to the pile but before she could knot the cloth's corners, Onyx selected an amber stone with more red showing than most of the others.

She showed it to her sister and made the circle sign that Hlif had invented for Pearl's name. Then she drew a finger below her eye to make the teardrop, the sign for Onyx. She reached out and touched Hlif's face, then a strand of hair escaping as usual from the coif.

Pearl understood before Hlif did and smiled broadly as Onyx

pointed to the raw amber and to Hlif, while making a spiky sun shape around the stone, her fingers like sunbeams.

'Pearl, Onyx, Amber,' said Hlif, still not understanding.

Pearl pointed to herself and made the circle, then she signed the teardrop and pointed to Onyx. Light dawned on Hlif, as Pearl put both hands together in the spiky sun and pointed to Hlif. The twins had given her a name. She was now Amber.

After she'd satisfied Pearl and Onyx by repeating the spiky sun enough times to show she understood her new name, Hlif hid the stones beneath her cloak. She exaggerated the action, to show that this work was nobody else's business, but she was confident that her maids would neither steal from her nor show her collections to others, not just because they could not speak in words. Sometimes, a person's true character was evident to those who knew what to look for, and like amber, shone when polished.

CHAPTER THIRTY-TWO

HLIF, SICILIA

As anticipated, Pietro had shown no interest in Hlif's absence or activities. More than happy with the day's haul, which she had stowed in her pack without arousing suspicion, Hlif accepted Gian's invitation to visit the orange grove with him the following day.

'What about the rain?' she asked, wondering whether the evening's showers would spoil the harvest.

'Some were knocked down in the storm,' he told her, 'but we gathered those today and will make syrup and drinks with them.' He jerked his head towards the door. 'This is nothing more than an evening wash and the oranges won't take in any water now to weaken the flavour. I think we'll have a fair day tomorrow. He told her she could watch the entire process by which her oranges reached her sacks, from tree to the weighing table, then to tagged and sealed sacks.

The prospect of sampling oranges and learning which should be chosen to finish ripening on the journey, and which should be sent to the local markets as soon as possible, was irresistible. Whenever she bit into a blood orange in the future, it would taste of this harvest and this orchard.

The sun glinted through the previous evening's raindrops, watery at first then stronger as morning passed, raising mists until distant hills reappeared. The Frankish keep at Paternò started the day as a mystical tower above a white sea and by midday was square and solid, a stronghold on a scrubby knoll.

As the day brightened, so did the workers. An olive-skinned youth picking fruit up a ladder, smiled and called 'My lady!' before throwing a perfect orange down to Hlif. She sensed the sun-warmth of its dimpled zest and the filaments of pith as she dug in her nails, separated a segment. Juice squirted and dribbled down her chin as she savoured the rich sweetness. She should have been embarrassed at such messy eating but out here, among the dappled light of the trees, where everyone was picking or packing oranges, nothing mattered but the quality of the fruit.

Fruit-pickers stretched and bent, climbed and plucked, muscles working beneath their simple brown tunics and breeches. Choosing which to pick and which to leave, at an impossible speed, the workers up the ladders passed the oranges down to those below, who handled their precious crop with unexpected delicacy. No damaged or bruised oranges were placed to dry on the sacking laid out below the trees. There was a separate barrel for fruit destined to macerate as juice or wine.

The whole experience surpassed its promise and Hlif's compliments to Gian at day's end were genuine. She used his seal on each of her twenty sacks of weighed, tagged oranges, and left them to one side of the barn, ready for loading on the cart the next day. A convivial meal was the final seal on the partnership and laid Hlif's misgivings to rest

She continued in this sunny frame of mind after a sound sleep and an early start on the journey to Catania, with twenty sacks of oranges on the cart and two pounds of amber stones in her pack. Not even Mamma Maria's sour comments regarding Onyx and Pearl could affect her mood. She couldn't wait to tell Skarfr of her trading triumph. Maybe he and Sea-born would be home at the same time as she arrived back after circumnavigating the island. That too would be an adventure to tell.

She was daydreaming in this pleasant manner when the drover swore, the carthorse shied at something on the road, and the innocuous travellers, apparently making camp beside the road, revealed themselves to be eight men wielding clubs and daggers.

As they ran towards her, Hlif could see their faces, the stubble on their chins and dirt on their leather tunics. Only too conscious of their weapons, Hlif tried to identify them but she didn't recognise anyone. They all looked alike, olive-skinned, swarthy, black-haired, and dressed in scratched leather jerkins, typical of a minor lord's men-at-arms — or of outlaws who'd seen better days.

The ninth jumped to his feet from his position as roadblock and tore the horse's reins from the drover while the rest of his band immobilised all those in Hlif's party.

She kicked her mule into action but the beast was as lethargic as Pietro, who offered no resistance to the ruffian standing over him. She'd expected better even from him and she aimed a vicious kick at the bandit who'd made her his assignment. More agile than her mule, he dodged easily, cursed her loudly and waved his cudgel around the mule's head, no doubt to remain out of her reach while appearing violent. As contemptuous of the bluster as was Hlif, the mule placidly chewed his lip, waiting to see what the humans would do next.

Think! Hlif told herself. However inept these bandits might be, the ambush had worked and even stupid men were more than a match for two men and four women. Pearl and Onyx stood still, shaking and looking at the ground, no doubt reliving their days with the slaver. There would be no help from them. And as for Pietro!

Two of the men investigated the cart, spoke rapidly to each other, and called to the man guarding Hlif.

'Oranges,' they yelled predictably.

'Look in the packs on the mule,' ordered the man beside Hlif, evidently the leader, and her heart sank. She knew what they would find. From the knowing look in the bandit's eyes, she suspected he did too. The man nodded and went over to the baggage-mule, untied the rope securing Hlif's pack and dropped it on the ground.

Hlif needed a distraction. She spat at the leader, aiming for his face, hoping her expression showed her murderous intentions. Although the spittle fell short, the man flinched, which was satisfying. Hlif was just preparing mentally for the movement which would draw her knife from her belt and send it the same way as her spit, with more chance of hitting the target, when help came from the least expected quarter. Or what seemed like help at the time.

'Enough!' Mamma Maria's voice rasped into the silence, drawing all eyes her way. 'These people are protected. You should see this before you make a big mistake.' She pulled a tightly rolled parchment out of her bodice and waved it in the air then kicked her mule to ride towards the bandit leader. His men let her pass.

For a moment, Hlif wondered whether the nine robbers were some more of Maria's 'sons' and that was why Pietro had been so passive. He was in it with his 'brothers'. But no. Maria obviously did not know this man or his fellows.

'Can you read?' she asked as she unscrolled the writ. Hlif glimpsed the even writing of a clerk or notary — no monkish scribe, for sure! — and a seal which she recognised.

So, it seemed, did the robber, although he asked the question anyway. His tone had changed to that mix of respect and fear which Mamma Maria usually evoked — even from her mule, thought Hlif with envy. 'Whose protection?' he asked.

CHAPTER THIRTY-THREE

HLIF, SICILIA

'It is the king's seal.' Mamma Maria waved a dismissive hand. 'Tell your master he has no business here.'

The man made one attempt to execute his commission. 'This does not affect you. They are on my lord's land and have something which belongs to him.'

He did know about the stones. Hlif was sure of it! Whose land was hereabouts? She remembered a red-faced, sweaty man in the Tiraz, telling her she was not welcome there. Perhaps he had heard her conversation with Rachel and had been waiting for her. It would have been easy enough to hear gossip of a stranger, a red-haired trader-woman who wanted to buy oranges. Captain Lemercier and his men would have been garrulous in their Catania drinking-den.

'Your lord enjoys privileges at court,' Maria observed.

Visits to the Tiraz! Hlif was right. It *was* Rachel's client who'd set an ambush.

'And enjoys protection, for which he pays taxes.' She paused. 'For which he owes taxes. The king requires that they be paid. He is considering the whole question of your lord's privileges, protection, and the amount due. Now would be a very bad time to defy your king. Do you understand?'

The man conceded defeat and nodded.

'Then tell your lord.' Maria was sharp. 'I repeat, this party is under protection and you will let us pass without hindrance. Put the lady's baggage back on the mule and be off.'

Like naughty schoolboys caned by a strict monk, the robbers slunk away, heading off the road towards Paternò.

Hlif noted the direction: more confirmation that she was right. And if Rachel's patron was behind the attack, he knew or had guessed that Rachel had betrayed his secrets. What would he do to her? He was supposed to be in Palermo but what if he was here, on his estate? Her mind raced with horrible visions of what might have happened if he'd found her by the river. What if he'd been watching? What if he'd timed the ambush so as to reclaim all 'his' amber when she'd finished collecting it for him? Thank the gods he'd underestimated the power of this old woman, however she came by it.

'I know who's behind the attack,' she blurted out.

'Who?' Maria made her mule halt and of course, Hlif's beast did likewise. Pietro walked beside Hlif's mule; behind him came the cart and then the twins, who hung back nervously, following slowly.

'Lord Eudes. He owns an estate near Paternò and is in King Roger's court winter and summer. He won't give up. He'll come after me again. I need to get back to Palermo as soon as possible, to warn —' She'd already said far too much in the heat of the moment and she clammed up.

Maria narrowed her eyes, nodded. 'Don't worry about him. He will be taken care of.'

Hlif had seen the impact Maria's words had on the lowest of thugs and cutpurses and a flood of gratitude rushed through her at the prospect of Lord Eudes being constrained by the old woman's influence.

'I don't know how to thank you,' she babbled, annoyed with herself for having so underestimated this formidable woman, her saviour.

'Yes you do,' said Mamma Maria, 'I told you that you are under my protection and we are business partners and you will give my family one sack of oranges when we reach Palermo.'

Hlif's gratitude turned to lead in her guts. At least her amber was safe. And she didn't have to comply.

'Why should I agree?' she queried, defiant.

'Because you care about an ugly one-eyed cat. And a barbarian Northman who speaks without thinking, so nobody would be surprised by an accident. And about a brat whose lack of lineage shows in his uncouth manners. But you care about them.' She shrugged.

'Sea-born is my gods-given son!' *Twice over!* 'Don't you *dare* touch him!' Hlif could feel the rage explode in her and understood what Skarfr called 'unleashing the dragon' when he went into battle. Red-faced and black-hearted, she reached for her knife — and was blocked.

Pietro had caught her wrist in mid-air and deftly removed the knife from her belt before releasing it.

'I was like you once,' Maria observed before clicking at her mule to move on. 'All fire. It's a pity you're married already. But you will learn. Only blood counts. The cuckoo in your nest will do what all cuckoos do — usurp his brothers' place and drain his foster-parents dry.'

The runes had foretold that Sea-born would have no brothers, or sisters, so the curse missed its mark by a mile. Hlif's pulse was still racing but there was little she could do to gain the upper hand and her mind was clearing of the red rage. She indulged in sarcasm, while pondering her options. 'If blood's all that matters, I'm surprised you risk the rivalry of so many pretend sons.'

'You know nothing. They have bonded in blood, as sons and brothers. Such loyalty is to the death.'

Hlif had often heard such talk before, in the Jarl's *Bu* at Orphir or in his dragon ship. And she'd seen the same warriors who'd sworn loyalty take an axe to each other.

She sighed. There was always a price to pay for any gift from the gods and a sack of oranges was not too expensive for peace of mind, to be rid of this unwanted connection, this 'business deal.'

'As payment due to the king,' Hlif clarified, to salve her conscience.

Maria pulled her parchment writ out of her bodice, waved it at Hlif and kicked her annoyingly obedient mule into a turn so she could look at her.

'As payment to the king,' she agreed, holding a finger to her lips and then drawing a finger across her throat.

So that was what had happened in the fruiterer's shop. He had been late with his payment for protection, he'd said. Perhaps he'd even refused to pay and suffered the consequences.

It dawned on Hlif that King Roger would see none of the money nor feast on oranges. Maria and her 'sons' were no doubt selective in passing on the 'dues' they collected. And where did Pietro stand in all this, one of the 'brothers'? She kicked her mule, which only moved once it could follow the tail swishing in front of him.

Maria looked back over her shoulder, to add, 'And when the gems have been polished, we will have three of them in payment.'

Fuming, Hlif held her tongue. She could hear Loki, the trickster god, laughing at her for thinking how smoothly her venture had gone. What a fool she had been, thinking her activities had gone unnoticed, thinking a woman *could* go out for a day with only maidservants. Nobody had worried or commented because there had been eyes on her all the time. Pietro no longer seemed such an idle good-for-nothing. Nor did he seem harmless. And even if he *was* a spy, she dare not sack him.

CHAPTER THIRTY-FOUR

HLIF, SICILIA

The voyage back to Palermo seemed endless to Hlif, although somewhat enlivened by daily practice of hand signals with Onyx and Pearl. A cargo ship was so slow, made so many stops. On a fast vessel, Lord Eudes could be at the King's palace long before them and Hlif fretted over what he might have done to Rachel. She wouldn't believe that Maria had prevented Lord Eudes from harming Rachel until she saw her friend. She wished Rachel had never spoken to her in the first place. A woman's life was more precious than shiny stones.

Nevertheless, the moment they docked in Palermo, she clutched her pack tightly and instructed Pietro regarding transport and storage of her oranges. A trader's habits straightened her spine, gave her courage to face whatever might come. And if she wasn't too late, if Maria had been successful, Hlif would make sure Rachel stayed safe until Skarfr could spirit her away from her thralldom.

With the sisters stubbornly following, Hlif rushed up the winding streets from the harbour to her home, where she told Amina that the two women were new maids who could neither hear nor speak but could communicate very well with hands and faces. Ignoring Amina' horrified expression, she demonstrated speaking with only hands and face, and gestured to Onyx and Pearl to stay put, to do what Amina told them.

Then she stowed her pack safely in the clothes kist, checked with Amina that One-eye was well, that her menfolk were not back yet, and that no domestic disasters had occurred, then dashed off to the Tiraz.

Without oranges, she had to argue her way in to see Rachel but, emboldened by the implication that Rachel *was* there to be seen, Hlif negotiated a future orange deal with the guard and walked past the other silk workers until she reached her friend.

Not even to warn about murder did she dare interrupt Rachel as she sewed fine beadwork onto a ceremonial tunic so Hlif waited, watching the pattern form, gold thread and seed pearls on stiff red damask.

Finally, Rachel snipped a thread, sighed with satisfaction, and turned to Hlif, eyes wide.

She whispered, 'I don't know what you did but he's dead and I'm safe again. Did you get the amber?'

Hlif nodded, dumbstruck. Dead? He had looked to be choleric. Perhaps he'd died of an excess of exercise.

'I didn't know,' she stammered. 'I didn't do anything.' She should tell Rachel that his men had tried to attack them but not now, not here. Not when there might be somebody eavesdropping. Not when someone in the Tiraz might have told him about Hlif's voyage in search of the amber.

'Knifed,' said Rachel, looking at Hlif sceptically. 'Are you sure you didn't know?'

Hlif shook her head. Not apoplexy then.

Trying to take in what Eudes' death meant, Hlif asked, 'Do you still want to go home?'

Rachel nodded. 'But it is no longer urgent. I can cope with the other clients. I do the king's bidding — and his son's, as do all who work in the royal Tiraz.'

They could not speak freely among so many people and they could not convey all they needed to by nodding and shaking heads.

All this mute communication reminded Hlif of the sisters, which gave her an idea. She needed a way to communicate with Rachel, without coming to the Tiraz, where she was less and less welcome.

'I understand,' she said. Then in a louder voice, 'On my travels I came across two maids seeking work and I brought them back with me. But I don't have enough for one maid to do, never mind three, and I wondered whether they could earn their keep here?'

'Silk-making is skilled,' Rachel objected.

So that was a no. But Rachel considered the matter further. 'But the silk workers who are most valued as musicians and entertainers do need maids for personal care. Are these girls discreet?'

Hlif smiled. 'Very,' she replied and explained why.

Unlike Amina, Rachel could see advantages in the girls' silence. 'You said they are free? Legally freed?' she asked wistfully.

'Yes, they have the documents,' said Hlif, reminded that she needed to get two manumission forms from al-Idrisi, for Fergus and Brigid. They would be formally freed the instant she and Skarfr set foot again on Orkneyjar.

'Then why would they want to work here?'

'They are alone, a long way from home and a document won't feed them. "Free" means nothing to them.'

The silence spoke of how much 'free' meant to Rachel.

'Bring them here,' she said. 'There is work for them and they will have food and board.'

'Thank you.' Hlif held Rachel's gaze, willing her to understand the hidden meaning. 'I will talk to Skarfr about our project. The pistachios will be ripe in *autumn.*'

'Autumn,' said Rachel, with longing. 'I can wait till autumn — *pistachios* are worth the wait.'

The code was clear enough between them.

Hlif pointed to the embroidered tunic. 'Is that for Prince Guillaume's coronation?' she asked.

'Yes. The idea of him becoming king while his father is still alive seems so strange. Two kings at the same time.' Rachel shook her head.

'Not so strange to me, said Hlif. 'It is our way to have two Jarls, our rulers. There is a saying in my home country. *One jarl rules for himself but two jarls must heed their people.*' Rognvald could never have gone on pilgrimage if he hadn't trusted his co-ruler Jarl Harold. With the undeniably astute Thorbjorn to advise him. But she didn't want to think about Thorbjorn. The point was that Orkneyjar would be absolutely fine while Jarl Rognvald was away and she would return, with her family, to find nothing had changed. 'King Roger is making the order of succession clear and avoiding dissent. As a ruler, he must worry over the deaths of his heirs and as a man, his heart must be breaking.'

A hullabaloo broke out in the adjacent chamber. If only the row had happened earlier, they could have spoken openly without any chance of being overheard!

'I don't think he'd have married again if his other sons still lived.' Rachel had to raise her voice over the noise. 'He has women enough in the Tiraz and is still wed in his heart to his dead lady.'

'Poor Queen Sibylle, to know nothing but duty in a marriage. But when her son is born, maybe the king will warm to her.'

'Perhaps. In the autumn.' Rachel's mind was clearly on what else the autumn might bring.

'More work for you,' teased Hlif, 'another ceremony—' She broke off. 'What is that noise all about?'

She popped her head through the archway, saw curtains flung open and their occupants talking ten to the dozen in the hallway, Tiraz workers and clients equally caught up in discussing the news.

Guimbarde looked at her, doe-eyes sparkling and his mouth tilting in fun. 'The Emir's fleet has returned safely,' he said, 'with treasures from Ifriqiya. Gold, jewels, spices and hunting leopards! And a giant grey unicorn!'

Safely. May it please the gods, safely. Without a backward look, Hlif rushed past the gossiping workers, down the stairs and out onto the street, where she picked up her skirts and ran. When she reached home, her husband and son would be there. She knew it, could feel their return in every beat of her heart.

CHAPTER THIRTY-FIVE

SKARFR, PALERMO, SICILIA

Skarfr rested his chin on top of Hlif's head, which was buried in his chest. He held her so close that she complained, 'You're crushing me,' without making any attempt to free herself.

Had it only been two months? He moved her gently to arm's length so he could study her face. She looked different. New worry lines under sea-grey eyes, which read his face in the same way he did hers, reconnecting. A new cluster of freckles on her right cheek, shaped like a bear.

He traced the outline on her skin with his forefinger, said, 'Like lace constellations, brown on cream.'

Cream flushed a becoming crimson. Hlif took the wandering hand in hers, pressed it against her heart and he felt the drumbeat of homecoming. And he felt her attention go to the third person in this homecoming.

'Sea-born,' she said, her tone warm honey.

Sea-born hung back, standing awkwardly on one leg, a habit of his that made Skarfr envy his balance while feeling protective of his vulnerability. Skarfr opened his embrace to the boy, invited him into the circle they formed.

I have become the ring-breaker, the generous lord, he marvelled. 'Our son was brave and skilled,' he told her.

Sea-born flinched. Again that strange reaction to praise, which Skarfr had noticed during their voyage, as if he felt he had no right to it. And this gauche behaviour was more noticeable if George of Antioch was in hearing distance or, worse still, giving the compliments. It could be just the awkwardness of boyhood but Skarfr was relieved that he could talk to Hlif about the lad when they had a moment to themselves. Sometimes Sea-born was like other lads but at other times a shadow lurked beneath his shuttered expression, the residue of past experiences at which Skarfr could only guess.

'Our son,' murmured Hlif, her eyes smiling at Skarfr as she hugged the boy. She'd noted the words, the change in his acceptance of this gift from the sea.

'You've grown,' she accused Sea-born, whose face was nearly level with her own.

He stood on tiptoe. 'I'm a man now. And I'm taller than you.'

'So you are.' Hlif laughed and released him. 'Now, Amina will fetch wine and sweetmeats, and you can tell me all about your adventures.'

'Well-watered wine for Sea-born and me,' she instructed Amina and then the three of them sat down before starting the crossfire of questions and stories, each trying to outdo the other in amazing the listeners.

Skarfr and Sea-born passed the tales between them, encouraged by every, 'No! I don't believe you!' or 'You didn't! It's a miracle you're alive!' from Hlif, whose expressions of suspense, shock and relief were everything her menfolk could want.

Skarfr relived every moment in the telling of it, adding refinements and a lot of poetic licence to Sea-born's input. Amid the thunder-clouds of Thórr and a deluge at sea, Sea-born had climbed a mast as high as Sicilia's fire-spouting mountain, while it swung low and perilous over the white teeth of the whale road. Then the gods had dyed the Sicilians blood-red to rout the terrified Almohads, and Sea-born had raised the sky-blue standard that flew above the battlefield, announcing the victory to Sicilia and Mahdia.

Along the Ifriqiyan coast, word of their triumph had flown ahead of the fleet, fast and ominous as Óðinn's ravens, Huginn and Muninn, so that wherever the Sicilians laid anchor, treasure and luxuries were offered in hopes of their speedy departure.

Sea-born's heroic role in the saga was emphasised by Skarfr and the boy's eyes were shining when he tried to claim his reward. 'Father says I can watch the hunting leopards work,' he said.

'Maybe,' said his mother, giving Skarfr a reproving look.

'The king won't go hunting until the autumn, so it's a while away,' Skarfr pointed out, hoping to get back in Hlif's good graces.

'Autumn,' she said in a dreamy way, her eyes losing focus. Vision? Or something more down-to-earth that she knew and he didn't?

'I'll be a year older in the autumn,' persisted Sea-born and both his parents decided to let him have the last word on the subject.

'And is there *really* a grey unicorn?' asked Hlif, her scepticism obvious.

'Yes,' chorused the two adventurers.

'Only it's not a horn,' admitted Skarfr.

'More of a very long bendy nose,' added Sea-born. 'You can go and see it if you don't believe us. It will be in the king's menagerie at La Favara.'

Almost as fabulous as the grey unicorn were the camel caravans and chests of gold, spices in all the colours of the desert, sand for so many miles that the only water came from your eyes, making pictures of trees and lakes that disappeared when you blinked.

Finally Skarfr said, 'So we're rich. Our share of the plunder has been unloaded and Pietro helped put it into the cellar. There was just about room beside your oranges.'

His smile should have told her he was teasing but, for a fleeting moment, her eyes creased with worry.

He tried to reassure her. 'Pietro has added a bar to the door inside the cellar, and a lock outside.'

The worry deepened.

'What did you do while we were away?' he asked, preparing himself for a boring account of how much per hundred Hlif had paid for oranges and how she had secured storage for them to get them back to Palermo. But there was no reason to bore the boy, who was hopping on one leg again. 'Sea-born's been waiting patiently to tell his friends about Ifriqiya. If it's all right with you,' Skarfr carefully included the proviso, 'we'll let him go?'

Hlif nodded. And when she told her tale, without embellishment, he was stunned into silence. Sailing to Ifriqiya had presented fewer problems than those facing him here! However, a man did not marry a völva and expect her to grind corn all day.

'Speak to me,' she said, taking his hands. 'Will you help Rachel escape, like you did for Inge?'

Forced to consider only one of the terrifying dangers Hlif had faced without him, Skarfr gave the matter his attention. 'It's not the same,' he objected. 'Inge's life was at risk and she is a free woman. If Rachel works in the Tiraz, she is the king's thrall. He owns her. You can't free every thrall you take a fancy to!'

Hlif flinched at his harsh words and his conscience stung at the memory of his own thralls, like Rachel and the twins, kidnapped and taken far from their home. He'd promised them their freedom and never got around to it. He brushed the thought away. Fergus and Brigid would be fine. They were as good as owners of the longhouse and farm. Thinking of them made him soften towards Hlif's actions and he didn't want to be at odds with her.

Hlif's eyes pleaded but she said nothing, let him think things through.

'We talked about finding Jarl Rognvald in Jórsalahcim,' he began slowly, 'and we have Ifriqiyan wealth.'

'And money from my orange trade and amber,' said Hlif quietly.

Skarfr harrumphed. 'You should never have accepted this bargain with a woman for a few beads! And now you say the man is dead? She would be better off staying in the Tiraz. But—' he carried on quickly, '—you did make a bargain and your honour is my honour.'

Her eyes filled with tears and there was a tremble in her voice when she said, 'Thank you.'

'How can marriage be otherwise? And as I cherish your honour, so you do mine. We cannot leave this island before I've fulfilled my duty to King Roger so we will attend his son's coronation and I must join in this *mattanza* the men find so important.

'I swore to sail with the Emir against Constantinople and I will keep to my word. Until that time, I will be his loyal servant.' He paused. 'Maybe staying here in Sicilia is best for our family. Sea-born is getting a good education from the monks. You can establish trade links which will benefit Orkneyjar in the future. Some of the king's most respected men are foreigners like us, who found a place here and stayed. We could gain so much.'

Her face fell so he took her hands, said earnestly, 'I yearn for our home in Orkneyjar just as you do but maybe it is a longing for the past, not for the future. I am no longer sure. Since Ifriqiya, the Emir respects me. He is an honest man and an experienced leader.'

'What does your heart say, for yourself, not thinking of us?' asked Hlif.

Skarfr sighed, 'As a warrior, I have a place here and to sail against Constantinople would bring me great honour and more riches. Moreover, this country has fine poets. Sometimes I think I could become so skilled in Arabic that I could be one of them.'

He paused. 'But my heart sings in Norn, with the skaldic training I had from childhood. Their Sicilian verse is nothing like Óðinn's mead and leaves me always thirsty. Truly, I will never be one of them, and that grieves me.

'Also, despite his treatment of us, my fealty remains with Jarl Rognvald and the day might come when I can ask — no, *demand* to be reinstated. I *should* be there to tell his saga, as he wished. He was wrong to exile us and I want him to admit this and right the wrong.

'The only curse on you came from Rognvald himself and we have proved him wrong. It does not matter who your father is! In Jórsalaheim, among his saints, he will see this is true.'

'In the autumn, *elskan min*, we will go to Jórsalaheim and change his mind. I feel it,' she told him fiercely.

'Then Sea-born and I must impatiently await the autumn. One of us is going to be disappointed.' He smiled at her. 'What kind of reunion is this, full of so many difficult decisions? These lame ducklings you bought and freed can go to the Tiraz tomorrow and you can tell Rachel we will let her know if we are sailing for Jórsalaheim. If that happens, we can consider then what should be done as recompense for the King. Maybe I shall have earned a reward. Let the Norns weave their pattern and show what must be done. And you can pay this Maria person her oranges and her amber beads, then forget about her.'

She returned his smile, still a little tearful, and he drew her onto his lap. She could not see his face as he planned the conversation he would have the next day with Pietro. That man would not spend another day abusing his master's trust. But tonight belonged to Hlif.

Skarfr was pleased with himself. He'd restored order to his home and his life within a few days of returning. Pietro had reacted badly when Skarfr told him to go but had not dared to challenge his master with more than threats, the most foolish of which was implying that One-eye would not live long. As the irascible cat had welcomed Skarfr home with a sudden attack on his ankles, this menace fell short of its intended effect. But Skarfr did not mention One-eye at all to Hlif when he told her the man was out of their lives.

She was happy with Pietro's replacement, Jasim, who was a distant cousin of al-Idrisi. Skarfr was sure he could be trusted. Moreover, he did not flirt with Amina, which Hlif considered to be an advantage, even if her maid did not.

The ambiguous 'help' from Maria was now paid for so Hlif could forget the woman. Jasim had delivered a sack of oranges to her, along with a small velvet pouch containing three polished amber beads. The jeweller had finished these as a favour to Rachel, whose beadwork always featured his artistry with stones, and he promised the others would be done once he'd finished commissions for the coronation ceremony.

Pearl and Onyx had accepted their move to the Tiraz with good grace and a flutter of hands that, according to Hlif, meant they hoped to see her again.

'At least they're together.' Hlif had wiped her eyes, reporting to Skarfr on the welcome Rachel had given the girls. 'Their hands said thank you, over and over, to me, to Rachel, to Mikael, who showed them to a curtained chamber of their own. It's wrong that they should feel grateful for what we take for granted. I can think of a few people whose manners would improve if they were taken as thralls!'

'You care too much and it makes you vulnerable,' he told her and took the opportunity to give a gentle warning. 'Which is why you should not risk using your powers. What if your feelings overwhelm you in the otherworld and you can't come back to me? I could not bear it.' That was the simple truth and she must have heard it was so, although she said nothing, merely leaned against him.

'Who is Mikael?' he asked, suddenly remembering the Emir's insinuations about Hlif visiting the Tiraz and his own unease. Was that really only two months ago?

'I forgot to tell you, with all that's happened! He's an acquaintance of yours.' And so Skarfr learned that the young man he encountered back in Narbonne as Guimbarde was an entertainer in the Tiraz. All his reservations about the propriety of the silk works vanished at the prospect of playing his flute with a fellow-musician. Disappointingly, Hlif had no idea what instrument Mikael was playing now or whether he'd replaced the guimbarde he'd given to Skarfr. What's more, she didn't seem to care, so he stopped the interrogation and moved on to something about which she did care, very much.

He had finally talked to Hlif about Sea-born, opening up his heart to her about the contradictions in being a warrior and a good man, in dealing death and in controlling bloodlust. How hard this was to live with and even more so when trying to steer their boy on a true course to manhood. He told her how his heart had hurt for Sea-born on the ship, how the Emir had tested both Sea-born and him, how impossible it was to hold back when Sea-born was in danger or suffering, and yet how essential it was that he had. *That* was how he'd earned George's trust, as much as in battle or by navigating the ship.

And that was also how Sea-born had earned his place among the crew. He'd never once asked Skarfr for help.

'Pride and worry fight in me every day and Sea-born is turning my hair white,' he concluded.

She combed his hair with her fingers, inspecting it. 'Maybe one or two white hairs,' she teased, and then more seriously, 'That is our lot as parents: pride and worry and hard decisions. But we are lucky in our boy, that we do feel pride. Not all parents do. Maybe,' she told him wryly, 'you care too much and it makes you vulnerable.'

He hung his head, knowing it was true. His son was his weakness in battle. But that doom was laid on him now and what mattered was raising the boy as a man, as the right kind of man. 'Growing to manhood hurts,' he told Hlif. 'I must shape Sea-born and this is a heavy responsibility. I can see he has worries but he doesn't share them with me.'

'*We* must shape Sea-born,' she'd corrected, 'and if we wait, this demon on his shoulder will either leave him, a boy's worry, or will grow too big for him, and he will tell us. Meanwhile, try to share *your* feelings with him. Set an example.'

Skarfr considered this advice from his wise woman. 'I shall take him swimming with me,' he decided. And the next day, he did so. Sea-born and he swam in the warm water of the Middle Sea. They kept stroke in the companionable silence of men and returned to the shore well-exercised. Hlif's counsel had been good.

Yes, Skarfr congratulated himself, *everything sorted out*. A bird's shadow flew between him and the sun, reminding him that the gods do not like vainglory. He touched his hammer amulet to ward off evil consequences and listened for Loki's laughter. Nothing but seabirds' shrill cries and sailors' gruff exchanges reached his ears.

Alone this time, he walked past the docks and around the headland to a sandy cove. Waves lapped peacefully, within easy reach, Stripping to his smallclothes, he accepted the sea's invitation and skidded down the softly shelving sand until the water reached his belly. He slipped into the rhythm of the stroke, arms dipping in and out like oars. Far out from the shore, he floated, buoyed up on salt waves, so different from the freezing lochs of Orkneyjar.

Middle Sea indeed, between heavens above and the world beneath the ocean. What did he matter, a mere man, in the immensity of such worlds? He felt weightless, floating light-hearted.

But a tree weighs nothing until it falls on a man. Just because Skarfr did not hear the gods' laughter does not mean there was none.

CHAPTER THIRTY-SIX

HLIF, PALERMO, SICILIA

The Emir summoned Skarfr to stand beside him and Philip in the front row. Unthinking, Hlif followed with Sea-born. The boy was dragging his heels, no doubt chafed by his new clothes and lacking interest in the ceremony. But she remembered Skarfr's perception that the Emir had some kind of adverse effect on Sea-born and she would stay alert for any signs of odd behaviour.

Skarfr made room for the two of them and she found herself beside Philip of Mahdia, a man she knew only from a distance and from Skarfr's description. The palatine chapel was filling up and in the crush, Philip's hand brushed hers. He politely excused himself. There had been no lewd intention yet she felt unsettled, as if the light contact had left a scorpion crawling up her sleeve.

Silly. The man can't help what was done to him. She didn't use the word *eunuch* even to herself.

Angels soared over her head and flew in the gold mosaic dome around the glittering figure of Christ, who looked out from his position above the altar with an expression of benevolence. His right hand was raised in blessing and his left hand turned the Holy Book towards the churchgoers. The figure of Mary in the group below him was equally serene and nowhere in the magnificent artwork was there any depiction of Christ's passion and suffering. The cross on the altar was a simple wooden symbol. In such a setting, a woman could believe in a better, more beautiful world.

Even the wooden ceilings, with their pendulous Muslim carvings, told of the brotherhood of men, of a sanctuary in which the faiths mixed in architectural harmony. The best of Sicilia was in this Christian building ,created in stone, wood and tile, and Hlif let the feeling of peace flow through her.

A hush spread over the crowd and the great doors banged shut. King Roger and Prince Guillaume had entered. Hlif was curious to see this fourth son, who'd never expected to be king and who'd grown up as befitted his status as a younger son. A fighting man with the strength of ten, it was said, with claims that he could break an iron bar in two with his bare hands and that once, when he'd seen a horse stumble on a bridge, he'd righted horse *and* rider without any aid. Others said it was a mule he'd picked up, with its heavy burden still on its back. Whatever details were disputed, all agreed that his strength was exceptional. And that he was as uncouth as his bestial appearance suggested, with shaggy black hair all over his body.

The only reported resemblance to his father was his frequentation of the Tiraz, and not in order to buy silk. Married young, he showed the same attention to duty as his father, and the same preference for taking his pleasure with more sophisticated partners. Rachel knew both of them intimately but was not among King Roger's favourites. Now that her friend's possessive protector was dead, Hlif wondered whether Rachel would see more of the new king. Or be forced to see more of him.

Autumn, she promised silently. *Hold on until then.*

Hlif had seen the king many times but never in full panoply. As Rachel had predicted, he was wearing the red silk mantle he'd had made a few years after his own coronation, as if he'd wished for a garment more opulent than the richly embroidered cream kurta he had worn, one similar to what his son wore now. The red mantle was the Tiraz' finest work, bearing the type of embroidered band which had given the silk works its name.

When the procession passed Hlif, she saw the back of the mantle and gasped. The gigantic design was all executed in gold and silk threads; either side of a palm tree, a huge lion dug its claws into a camel's back. The tiraz band along the immense length of the lower edge was of Arabic letters in gold as Rachel had described; Hlif had not expected them to look like runes, so tall and twig-like.

What had Rachel said the inscription meant? A paean of praise to the royal workshop in which it was made, and then the final proof of provenance, place and date. *Sicilia in the year 538.* Even the numbering of the year showed the Muslim culture which King Roger had not only inherited but which he seemed to have embraced in so many ways.

Slight and solemn beside his towering son, King Roger still surpassed the latter in regal presence. His pace was matched to Archbishop Hugh's, a beat appropriate to such an occasion. Prince Guillaume strode out as if training his hunting dogs, then stopped short to avoid bumping into the Archbishop.

'The Pope will not be pleased at the king crowning his son without requesting papal permission,' murmured Philip.

'He should have thought of that when he gave Archbishop Hugh the Pallium and the right to anoint a king,' replied George.

'Nevertheless, he will see it as an insult, as one more reason to join forces with Germany against our lands in Italia.'

George sighed. In agreement, Hlif thought, as she identified the nobles around her, Sicilia's most powerful men and women, displaying the Kingdom's wealth in their jewelled robes. A glitter of gold, silver and jewels in a sea of silk. The Pope had reason to cast covetous eyes towards Roger's realm and to fear its power and prominence.

The Queen's gown was an equally sumptuous example of the Tiraz' work, studded with rubies in tribute to her birthplace in Bourgogne, known for its red wine. Her growing belly was only perceptible if you knew she carried a child, hidden beneath the rich gathers under her breasts. The woman beside her was in the same interesting condition but had already proved fruitful so there was less speculation about whether Prince Guillaume's wife, Margaret of

Navarre, could bring another heir to term, than there was about Queen Sybille.

With due formality, the coronation service followed the prescribed ritual. The king and the king-to-be were seated on the carved wooden thrones and, as the Pope's authorised representative (regardless of whether the Pope approved of the ceremony), the Archbishop named the new king. Guillaume then gave his oath to govern justly, in compliance with the law and the traditions of Sicilia.

After anointing the monarch with holy oil on his hands, chest and head, the Archbishop placed a very large crown on the shaggy black head and pronounced Guillaume to be king, co-ruler of Sicilia.

Could any men truly co-operate as rulers? wondered Hlif, wondering how much power King Roger would actually delegate. Orkneyjar's history attested otherwise. *With the exception of Jarl Rognvald and Jarl Harald.* It seemed she was not alone in her scepticism about men's co-operation but Philip was not looking at the two kings.

'There can only be one bear in that forest,' murmured Philip, observing two courtiers nearest to Prince Guillaume, one wearing a turban and cream robe with gold embroidery, the other in garish finery: a long scarlet tunic with wide yellow braiding on sleeves, neck and hem, along with sky-blue stockings to show off his sculpted calves. The cap he'd doffed had more feathers in it than on the duck Hlif had plucked the previous week.

George stifled a chuckle. 'I'll lay a bet on Maio of Bari,' he said.

'His clothes are dull,' objected Philip. 'No, I say it will be the Englishman who stays when the king… when the time comes. May it be many many years hence.'

Hlif understood *that* at least. One day, Guillaume would be the sole king.

'*William* Brown?' George pronounced the foreign name with scorn. 'You will lose your bet.' Then his tone suddenly became gloomy. 'But I shall not be alive to collect my winnings.'

'Nor will I,' said Philip cheerfully. 'The Hautevilles live into their seventies.'

And King Roger is only fifty-six, was the unspoken thought.

Hlif shuddered. They should not have spoken of their own deaths.

The scorpion under her skin from Philip's touch had not gone. At first she only felt the alien brush of the creature, a wrongness raising the fine hairs on her skin, moving up her arm. Even though she knew there was no scorpion, it felt so real she wanted to cry out. As it moved, the evil creature grew hotter, scorching her skin in spreading patches. She bit her lip, felt each slither and pause, until it reached her throat — and burst into flames.

The venomous wildfire shrivelled her skin to ash, raced through her body, filled her throat , which burned inside and out. When she tried to speak, nothing came out but a dry cough. She doubled up with an overwhelming urge to vomit.

Not real she told herself, fighting the vision, repeating *chapel, coronation, Guillaume* in her mind to anchor her to the present, until she could straighten up again. Nobody had noticed her odd behaviour as all eyes were on Archbishop Hugh at the altar as he held a crown over King Guillaume. The newly-anointed ruler looked uncomfortable, his huge thighs hiding the throne...

Another wave of nausea swept through Hlif, emanating from the powerful eunuch. This was not her scorpion but Philip's. She could see him beside her, amongst the stone and stained glass, relaxed and observing the ceremony. But, through swimming eyes, she also saw Philip writhe in agony — not now, not here. A traitor's death, worse than any scorpion.

She tried to block the pain, to lose consciousness, but the gods pounded her with more pain: the raw burn of the rope around her hands, her skin flayed, the terrified horses galloping, dragging her through the choking dust. A stone building, so hot. A lime kiln, the flames waiting. Searing heat, the smell of burning flesh...

She could not bear such agony and broke away, pulling Sea-born with her and pushing through the crowd to stand near the entrance at the back, away from Philip.

Muslim, apostate, traitor, the words echoed in her head, as the same voice proclaimed his son a king and demanded loyalty from all his subjects to King Guillaume as to himself. While Hlif struggled to return to her own mind and body, the shouts of *Long live King Guillaume* mingled with the jeers of a mob avid for blood, yelling King Roger's judgement *Muslim, apostate, traitor* as they watched a man die.

Gradually, Hlif returned to herself, to puzzle over the meaning of what she had seen. She shuddered at the thought she'd witnessed the doom of Philip of Mahdia. But it made no sense. King Roger condemning his loyal general, and to such a death? For the crime of being Muslim? If it were a crime then it was being committed daily in this kingdom by most of the population. The very walls around her in the king's chapel displayed Muslim holy words in Arabic writing, carved by Muslim architects.

Was Philip to be condemned for being a traitor? Unthinkable, from what Skarfr had said. Philip's loyalty to the kingdom was as unshakable as George's had been. *Apostate*. She didn't know what the word meant but she would find out. There was a message here about the king, about Sicilia, and not just about Philip.

'...loyalty to my son is loyalty to me and vice versa,' King Roger was saying, as the echoes of *Muslim, apostate, traitor* faded from Hlif's hearing. She knew all too well that visions could be trickier than Loki and she shook her head to clear it.

'...pay homage to the king who will succeed me one day and who will keep our kingdom as a force to be reckoned with, throughout Christendom and all of the known world,' concluded King Roger.

And then the ceremony was over. Archbishop Hugh led the two kings out of the church, passing so close to Hlif she could smell their sweat and see a loose gold thread in the palm tree on King Roger's mantle.

If I pull the thread will the tree of life unravel? she wondered. She didn't pull the thread. An embroiderer at the Tiraz would no doubt repair the symbolic palm tree as a matter of urgency.

Daylight flooded in as the great doors were opened and a huge cheer rang out from all the crowds waiting outside for a glimpse of the royal family.

Inside the chapel, the shuffling of feet, murmured commentary and subtle use of elbows preceded movement towards the exit. Skarfr forced his way towards her, looking anxious.

'Are you all right?' he asked.

'I was taken ill,' she said, 'and needed some air. I'm fine now.'

'She went green,' observed Sea-born.

'Let's get out of this press,' Skarfr said. He forged ahead through to the door and through the crowd to find a clear space. Sea-born and a grateful Hlif followed in his wake, the latter cursing how small she was, as she focused on Skarfr's broad shoulders and made her way through the jostling throng.

A man suddenly blocked that reassuring view. Pietro, hissing at her, his face a gargoyle's, ugly in hate. 'Maria has a message for you. Soon you'll realise just how much a widow needs protection.'

Then he was gone, just as Skarfr appeared, come to get her, anxious. 'Was that Pietro?'

She nodded.

Skarfr swore but Pietro was long gone, vanished into the crowd. 'What did he say to you?'

Ashen-faced, she repeated Pietro's words to Skarfr. 'She didn't mean herself. She means to have you killed. You must be careful.'

Skarfr laughed. 'Pfff. *They* should be careful.' Despite his contempt for such idle threats, Hlif's worry made him concede, 'I will wear a leather jerkin when out and about, and I'll make sure I'm armed.'

'Don't underestimate these men, Skarfr. They don't challenge you outright because they would lose. But a knife in the back would cause them no shame.'

'Then they are not men.' Skarfr dismissed such cowardice as beneath his consideration. He remembered something Jarl Rognvald had said, when asked what he was afraid of. He'd said he was not afraid of losing his honour because *that* was within his control. And the rest of his doom was in the Norn's deft weaving.

'Don't worry,' he reassured her, 'I have nothing more dangerous than training planned for months ahead. Oh — and a fishing expedition.'

'Fishing expedition?'

'The *mattanza*.'

'Oh, yes, the tuna run,' she clarified. 'What does the word *mattanza* actually mean in our language?'

He hesitated but she could find out easily so he told her. 'The slaughter.'

CHAPTER THIRTY-SEVEN

INGE, STRJÓNSEY, ORKNEYJAR

Inge had been straining her eyes looking out to sea from the moment Erlend's ship was sighted off Strjónsey. It was now at anchor in a show of good faith but also of restraint. Erlend and his chosen men would not leave their ship until the man they were waiting for appeared.

She knew what the message would be long before the watchman ran up the slope to where she stood outside the longhouse, and gabbled, 'Sweyn is approaching!'

Thank the gods!

She could see the familiar red sail coming closer, until, if she squinted, she could make out the plain prow. He had left the dragon-head stowed under a bench. A show of good faith from the other side in this parley — he was not coming to make war but rather to plan one.

In their attempts to get Sweyn and Erlend to meet they had suffered months of delay. After stealing Jarl Harald's tribute money from the Hjaltland ships, Sweyn had taken refuge in Skotland, where the charming sea-rover always found a welcome and a chance to stir up trouble. Erlend was still in Norðvegr, biding his time and building up strength to stake his claim to the jarldom in Orkneyjar with enough force to overcome any opposition. Getting secret messages between the two — three if you included Finn, who was to be the honest broker at the meeting — had been a logistical challenge but Finn and Inge had achieved their first goal: the meeting itself.

Now their work would really begin. Would Erlend put aside his blood grudges against Sweyn? Inge thought so, as Erlend had made an approach to Sweyn the previous autumn. But would her capricious brother throw his weight behind Erlend?

Finn joined her in the doorway and together they watched Sweyn and his shore party march up the slope, confident as always. Behind them, hanging back a little, came Erlend and his equally small band.

'I hope the food's ready,' Sweyn greeted his sister. 'Giri sent this for you.' He gave her a bundle and nodded to his brother-in-law.

The patterns! thought Inge, promising herself time with her tablet loom as a reward for getting through this meeting without swearing at her brother.

'Weapons go there,' Sweyn instructed his men, unstrapping his axe and dagger as he walked into Finn's hall. Inge heard the clank as the men followed suit and she heaved a sigh of relief. Sweyn could have been awkward, insisted on a ritual disarming that kept the two sides equally ready to fight but he'd set the tone for the discussion with another show of trust. Finn would not need to intervene, risking his own life or those of his hand-picked men, who were going about mundane tasks with hammers, pitchforks and hand-axes, useful tools that would easily convert to weapons if need be.

Following Sweyn's example, Erlend set his own weapons down at the back of the hall, on the other side from the pile already there. He and his foster-father Anakol joined Sweyn at the top table and the karls Inge had recruited from the settlement for the occasion rushed to serve ale, as men settled onto the benches.

Randomly, noted Inge. *Not according to allegiances*. And soon the hall hummed with talk of tides and treasure, which suggested that the followers were relaxed. She sent word to the kitchens to bring the fish stew and trenchers, then she took her own place at the top table, beside Finn, who was next to Sweyn, as his supporter as well as the host. On Sweyn's left was Erlend and beside him was Anakol, whose grey beard added weight to his approval of this alliance.

As the negotiations began, Inge listened and studied the two men she knew only by reputation. Anakol was exactly as she'd expected: transparently loyal to his foster-son, backing Erlend's just claim to the jarldom, prepared to wage war but not keen on doing so, past the age where he would be an asset in battle and without subtlety.

Erlend however was more of an enigma. *Jarl Erlend*, as she must remember to call him. On the surface, he was outgoing and likeable but whereas her brother's exuberance was natural, Inge sensed that Erlend's sociable manner took effort. As if a little boy inside the man had not been at ease with his fellows, not at all. Perhaps she was reading too much into the way he didn't quite meet Finn's eyes, or perhaps she was influenced by his family history. Not everyone grew up knowing his great-aunt had murdered his father with a poisoned shirt intended for his uncle. Not everyone could break bread with the sea-rover who'd burned his great-aunt alive in her hall. His great-aunt, the witch Frakork, who was also Thorbjorn's grandmother.

She tested the waters. 'I believe Jarl Harald and his advisor Lord Thorbjorn swore they would accept you as Jarl if you gained backing from Norðvegr. In which you have been successful. Surely all will be plain sailing now, with Lord Thorbjorn's backing. Jarl Harald will follow his counsel.'

There it was. A shadow, a flicker of hesitation, fear. He was afraid of Thorbjorn.

Unlike her brother. 'I can take on Thorbjorn, if he challenges us,' bragged Sweyn.

So it's 'us' already. Could he? wondered Inge. Could Sweyn fight Thorbjorn and win? They had never faced each other and she hoped they never would. The only certainty was that one would die and the other would be sentenced to an exile that would never be repealed. The only other warrior she thought capable of defeating Thorbjorn in battle was oceans away. *If* Skarfr was still alive.

One thing was certain. Erlend could not take on Thorbjorn. Without her brother, he was not strong enough to claim the jarldom.

'I don't doubt it,' she told her brother. 'You're twice the man Thorbjorn is.'

Sweyn preened. Then he deigned to say, 'I told you not to marry the man but you were young and headstrong.' He cast an approving look at Finn. 'You've done better this time, despite your reputation after being cast off.'

The blood rushed to Inge's head in a storm of memories. Herself at eighteen, with doubts about this arranged marriage. Sweyn on a beach, explaining why the alliance was important to him and why she must go through with it. The celebration feast, where Sweyn and Thorbjorn out-bragged and out-drank each other, The wall outside Rognvald's *Bu*, where Thorbjorn took his frustration out on Sweyn's sister, his affianced bride, his possession as much as any thrall could be. She wanted to scream at her brother, throw the lie in his face. She had married Thorbjorn for *his* sake.

Her stomach heaved. The men were so deep in talk of their next meeting and of calling a Thing Council that they didn't notice her mumbled excuse as she rushed out of the hall, made it as far as the midden and vomited.

She was doubled over, her head pounding, tears in her eyes, when she felt a large hand on her back, steady, caring. One of the men *had* noticed her undignified exit.

'He might be your brother but I will hold a knife to his throat if you want me to,' Finn said calmly. 'Or just throw him out for lacking respect to you.'

Inge straightened and turned to face him, then buried her face in her husband's best tunic, which smelled of the cedar chips her mother had given her to keep moths away. A comforting scent.

'No,' she said, her voice muffled in linen, 'you can't defend me against all the stupid men in the world as well as the dangerous ones.'

Finn lifted her chin and promised, 'I will, whenever you say the word.'

She laughed weakly. 'It's a tempting offer but — no. We can use the stupid ones against the dangerous ones. I am myself again.'

He offered his arm and escorted her back into the hall, back to her place at the table.

'Inge felt unwell,' he said, 'but she's fine now. Do you have a plan of action?'

Sweyn shrugged. 'She never could take her ale but she insists on drinking it. We are in agreement,' he confirmed. 'The King of Norðvegr endorsed Erlend's claim to Harald's share of Orkneyjar, which he will not give up willingly. So we make him.' He grinned.

Startled, Inge glanced at Finn. *Not Rognvald's share of Orkneyjar but Harald's.* This would indeed pit Erlend against Thorbjorn. She looked down to hide her reaction. Not that the men would notice.

Erlend showed more courtesy than her brother had, addressing Inge before returning to the matter in hand. 'Thank you for being such a gracious hostess. I hope you are feeling better now, my lady. Thanks to you,' he included Finn in his gesture, 'with Sweyn's help and God willing, I shall take my rightful place as Jarl of Orkneyjar. After forcing Harald to cede Orkneyjar, we,' he looked at Sweyn, 'will call a Thing Council to confirm it.'

Anakol had been following the discussion intently and his question was to the point. 'What do you gain from fighting for us, Sweyn Asleifsson? Why should we trust you?'

Inge watched her brother carefully put his cup down on the table, flexing his arm muscles as he did so. He changed from affable to menacing in one movement but, when he spoke, the threat was not aimed at Erlend, not for now at least. 'Harald should not have exiled my brother Gunnr. Nobody slights my family.'

Nobody slights the men in our family, thought Inge bitterly, biting her tongue.

This was the most dangerous moment of the day, when any man there could mention the blood debts that lay between Sweyn and Erlend, worse than any slights. Sweyn's murdered father. Erlend's murdered great-aunt.

'Gunnr can join us. His unwarranted sentence will be revoked at the same Thing which confirms me as jarl,' promised Erlend. The tension lifted. 'I'm sure the jarl's coffers can afford some practical recompense, both for Gunnr and for yourself. Your reputation will grow even bigger. Harald will learn his lesson and no man will show disrespect for your family.'

He continued smoothly, addressing Finn, 'Your family, who enabled this alliance. Is there a boon you would ask of me for all you have done for me?'

'Yes.' Finn and Inge spoke together.

Her husband let her make the request. 'Would you declare a lawsuit against Lord Thorbjorn for the Thing to judge, at that same Council meeting? With regard to Thorbjorn's theft of two thralls.'

'It would be my pleasure,' said Erlend.

CHAPTER THIRTY-EIGHT

SKARFR, SICILIA

When Sea-born was at school, no doubt learning by heart Latin stories of diligent ants, and red-cloaked girls in wolf-riddled woods, to recite at their next meal together, Hlif told Skarfr that her illness in the chapel had been something more worrying than feeling ill.

After she'd told him her story of skin crawling, torture and flames, all connected with Philip, he was silent, thinking. Such visions frightened him, had always frightened him, but not for what was in them. He worried for Hlif, that one day he would lose her into such a vision, that the otherworld would claim her. It was easy to face your own death without fear but not that of one you loved.

'The gods never speak simply to you,' he said. 'I have seen you read runes for the Jarl and more lay in the interpretation than in the letters themselves. This vision could mean different things. The scorpion you felt — I have felt like that too about Philip, about what was done to him. His touch is different from other men's touch. But when we work together, he is Philip and I don't think about him being a half-man.'

'Maybe that is part of it,' admitted Hlif. 'But I feel there is some message here for us. This crime, *apostasy*, I have found out the meaning.'

Skarfr knew what it meant. He remembered conversations between George of Antioch and Philip, George warning the eunuch to be careful that his words matched his profession to be a Christian. 'Apostasy means pretending to follow the White Christ.'

She nodded. 'And isn't that what we do, pay lip service to the White Christ but respect the old gods? What defence do we have if King Roger accuses us of being hypocrites, says that we profane his religion, condemns us to—' she swallowed '—such a death?'

'He wouldn't.' Skarfr spoke before thinking. He felt confused. 'We respect the White Christ and His saints. We are on a pilgrimage to Jórsalaheim with Jarl Rognvald and Bishop William. The bishop married us in the Christian way.'

'And we pray to the old gods, I carry a wand and read the runes. *Have* read the runes,' she amended quickly before he could object. 'You wear a hammer amulet and you touch that more often than you make the sign of the rood.'

He could not deny any of that. 'But even Bishop William does no more than grumble about Orkneymen who pay respect to the old gods.' He laughed. 'He threatens hellfire for so many sins I lose count.

Hlif did not smile. 'The fire for apostasy is in this world, not hereafter. And Sicilia is not Orkneyjar. I listen too. The Franks say that the Byzantines are heretics and yet they too believe in the White Christ. Muslims and Jews are called heathens, and allowed to worship their god freely, but they pay higher taxes for following the wrong religion. Traders from the east have other beliefs and they are considered strangers who know no better. But worst of all in their eyes are those who do not follow the White Christ in the manner that they say is the true faith.'

Skarfr felt the dragon stirring in anger at such nonsense. 'None of this matters between men on a ship, in battle or even in the baths!' He remembered he was supposed to be helping her interpret her vision and controlled his irritation. 'If some doom is on Philip, this is for the Norns to decide and not our business. What you have seen will be clearer as time goes on.'

'Should I warn him?' she asked in a small voice.

'No!' Skarfr was sharp. 'He will not believe you. And if it *is* a prophesy — which is not clear — no man would wish to know of such a fate.'

'Be careful, Skarfr. Don't talk of the old gods and don't touch your amulet all the time. Please.'

Her tone was so earnest, he said, 'I'll do my best.'

'I mean it,' she said, her gaze fixed on some future he could not see. 'What if religious tolerance is like Mamma Maria's protection? A hold over non-Christians that is profitable but can turn overnight into violence and expulsion of particular communities?'

Skarfr vaguely remembered being criticised by George regarding his pagan habits when under duress. But George was an extremely strict follower of the White Christ so no man would live up to his expectations and example. Maybe Jarl Rognvald would become like George one day but that was not his manner with the company on fifteen dragon ships, even when he'd had to deal with one captain sacrificing a man to make the weather change. Skarfr wondered how George would have dealt with *that* incident. Then he put such lawyer's analysis out of his mind and got on with his life, carefully of course.

'That will never happen,' he said firmly.

When word came at the end of May that the tuna were running and Sea-born pleaded with him to go fishing, he thought Hlif would be pleased that he'd said yes. Instead, she berated him for a mutton-headed shit-for-brains. Not very ladylike at all, as he pointed out. But she did not ask him to take back his word so Skarfr and Sea-born joined the hundreds of men on the two day journey from Palermo to Favignana on the west coast where fishing boats were waiting for them. More fishing boats than Skarfr had ever seen in one harbour.

With quiet efficiency, the trawler captains organised their crews and added some Palermitans, until gradually there were more men on the boats than on the quayside.

If he didn't act soon, there would be no seagoing space for him and Sea-born so Skarfr approached the nearest boat, which seemed to still have some space for crew, and asked, 'Can we come aboard?'

'Can you fight?' asked the captain, his eyes taking the measure of Skarfr and apparently approving.

'I can,' Skarfr replied, finding it an odd question. 'And the boy can help on deck.'

The captain jerked his head, which Skarfr took as an invitation and he jumped aboard, along with some fellow Palermitans, who pushed their way past him. It looked like they were known to the captain. Sea-born followed, as sure-footed on the rocking deck as on land. Skarfr smiled at the thought of all the unnecessary promises he'd made to Hlif about keeping Sea-born out of danger. The boy was as much at home on a ship at Skarfr himself was, and adept at keeping out of the way of rigging, beams and belongings.

Keeping out of the way was all that was required of them for now so Skarfr looked around him. His shipmates were a mix of regular fishermen and Palermitans here specially for the *mattanza*, distinguished by their clothing more than by any uncertainty about what to do. They were probably all old hands but those who were fishermen by trade wore oiled leather jerkins over their rough-woven brown tunics, and those who didn't wear turbans wore oiled caps, hair tightly confined. The stench of fish emanated from the jerkins and no doubt radiating from the stains on them.

Even though the Palermitans wore workday tunics and had bound their leggings or breeches to avoid them flapping, they looked and smelled different. Not from each other, however. To Skarfr, they resembled each other too much to tell apart. Black hair, olive skin, brown eyes and muscular bodies.

But as he studied them, he noted small differences and he started to give them nicknames, in Orkneyjar fashion. Bandaged-Knee was obvious, as was Hairy-Bear, who was bald. And there was one man with a dour expression, flattened face and snub nose, whose one long bushy eyebrow was as straight as his set lips. Skarfr hesitated between Misery-Guts and One-Brow. He'd have liked to ask Sea-born to play the name game but didn't feel it set a good tone for camaraderie with Sicilians in a small fishing boat. It was their loss that they didn't know the brotherly fun of giving and accepting such names.

None of the Palermitans seemed eager to speak to him so Skarfr turned his attention to the wider organisation of the *mattanza*. Some of those staying ashore were setting up trestle tables and buckets in anticipation of the biggest fish market Skarfr had ever seen. Others were standing beside the fishing boats, ready to cast them off.

'We'll be last to sail and then we'll have the longest wait,' said a shipmate, who would have been called Bent-Nose in any Orkneyjar crew. The rest of his appearance also suggested he was no stranger to an ale-fuelled brawl and his weathered face was as stained as the leather apron of his trade. Everything about him suggested he was a regular crew member.

'Why's that?' asked Skarfr.

'The nets were put in place a week ago.' Bent-Nose leaned over the wale, apparently at ease, in the manner of a hardened soldier before a battle, prepared for action but knowing there was time to pass first. 'There's a system of nets we call the *tonnara*. See those buoys out at sea?'

Skarfr obediently shaded his eyes and looked, spotted the wooden floats bobbing along the line of invisible nets below the surface.

'That's the beginning of the net wings which start out there, where the fish are running. They make a long funnel, a mile or two in length and the tunny have already swum into that funnel.'

Skarfr pictured the teeming fish, driven by instinct to their breeding-grounds, herded by the nets into—

'Where does the funnel send them?'

'Into the next bit of the *tonnara*, a net tunnel so big they don't realise they're trapped. The tunny swim into the next tunnel like going through a maze. Our leader, the *Rais* — see him on that boat—'

A man wearing exactly the same kind of waxed tunic as the other fishermen was on the next boat but one.

'—the *Rais* decides when there are enough fish in the nets and he says it is time for the *mattanza*.'

The outermost boats were peeling off in order from their mooring points, linked by ropes to keep them close without working the oars. When they stopped, Skarfr could see sunlight glinting on filaments of fishing net and, as the two lines of boats turned to come back closer to shore, they were linked in two long chains of netting.

'There are five net chambers with gates, each one smaller than the one before. The other boats will herd the tunny through the chambers by closing each gate and raising the nets, driving them closer together until they reach the final chamber. That's where we will be.'

'What do we do?'

Bent-Nose gave one of the most unpleasant smiles Skarfr had seen. 'It is called the *camera della morte*. When all the tunny are in the chamber of death, the *Rais* gives the word, the last gate will be closed and we will raise the net, until there is nothing to see but fish. We close up our boats to make a pen around the net and we do what we came here for.' He grinned again.

'Until then we wait. And sing.'

The boat jerked and left the jetty. The oarsmen pulled without strain and the captain steered the boat out to sea, not far at all, and barely two oars' distance from the next boat.

'The nets must start far enough out to be where the tunny swim but not so far out that the sea destroys the nets. And for the *camera della morte*, the shelter of the harbour is good.'

Skarfr barely heard the fisherman's last words because the singing had begun. Started by the *Rais* himself and his crew, the deep voices of hundreds of men joined in an Arabic chant, ceremonial and solemn. As sunlight glinted on swirling water, disturbed by the race of fish, one song followed another in a tradition so ancient Skarfr felt his dragon respond.

Silver-blue fins leaped in the passages of death.

The *camera della morte* began to fill up with giant fish. Taller than a man and twice as heavy, the confused tuna had nowhere left to run to. They bashed against the sides of the boats and swam deeper, trapped in the net. Sea-born leaned over to see them better and Skarfr hauled him back.

He told him fiercely, 'Stay behind me.'

And then the *Rais* raised his arm and the singing stopped and the sea-gate to the net was dropped and escape was closed off. Twenty boats end-to-end now circled the *camera della morte*, In the eerie cessation of human sound, the thrashing of the enclosed tuna grew louder as the net was raised, reducing their space in increments until fish were piled on flapping fish.

The boats circling the *camera della morte* rocked as men rushed to the sides nearest the fish. Fast, shallow-keeled vessels such as dragon ships would have capsized from the uneven distribution of weight but the fishing boats were sturdy and merely bobbed about, secured to each other by ropes. The men leaning over the wales, armed with oars, were packed as close as the tuna below.

Beside him, Bent-Nose said, 'Now we fight together as brothers against the tunny. You must look into the eyes as you kill, show respect, be a man.' He gave Skarfr an oar and it was clear that this must be the only weapon used. A moment's regret for his spear, a memory of harpooning a shark, all flitted through Skarfr's mind, then vanished in the knowledge he must wrestle these monsters onto the deck, for honour's sake. This was why the captain had asked if he could fight.

Skarfr picked up another oar, gave it to Sea-born behind him, told him. 'When the tuna are landed on the deck, club them with this. It is a kindness to kill fish quickly.'

Wide-eyed, the boy took his weapon.

A mournful horn blew and there was a roar from hundreds of battle-ready fishermen. The true *mattanza* began.

Slippery and strong, each weighing as much as three men, the tuna fought to escape the hands clutching and the wooden blows rained on them.

Skarfr saw Bent-Nose struggling with his chosen target and instinct took over. The two men clamped the fish between their oars and grabbing whatever part they could, a fin, a toothless mouth, a tail, they swung the creature over the side of the ship onto the deck, to join three of its fellows.

There had evidently been enough looking in its eyes during the fight as Bent-Nose returned to the fray straightaway.

'Your turn, brother,' he said.

Skarfr was already adapting his technique to the strange adversary, and it wasn't long before he too could claim a catch. Exhilarated by the duel, he thought nothing strange of One-Brow's intense stare. Probably wanted to learn from his own skills, he thought.

He heard Sea-born's words without understanding what they meant, shrugged them off for later and turned back, intending to claim another tuna.

Someone swung an oar carelessly. It caught him hard in the back and carried him over the wale into the seething, frenzied mass of giant bloodied fish.

'Watch out!' Sea-born had shouted.

As Skarfr thrashed among the tuna, merely one more man-sized panicking creature among hundreds, he gulped in some air and caught a glimpse of his boat. And wished he hadn't.

'Father!' yelled Sea-born, getting onto the wale ready to dive. One-Brow was behind the boy and for one heartbeat Skarfr thought he might pull the boy back. Instead, he pushed him onto the mass of crazed fish.

CHAPTER THIRTY-NINE

SKARFR, SICILIA

A silvery tail caught Skarfr on the head with the impact of a pikestaff and he dropped below the surface again, his head swimming even if his body couldn't. *A witty thought.* It was manly to joke while dying, his scrambled brains pointed out. What a pity that nobody would know.

There was little water but it was enough to drown in, and although the beasts had no teeth — thank the gods! — the power in their flailing bodies, and the sheer volume of tuna, would knock him unconscious. Perhaps that was for the best. His oar had dropped with him so he had nothing but bare hands and booted feet as weapons.

He shut his eyes, holding his breath from the instinct to stay alive even when he knew the sands had run out in his hourglass. The blue fins rasped along his skin like shards of glass and he tried hanging on, surging through the shoal with his scaled mount.

No, he'd have to ride on the tuna for it to be a mount. And he couldn't do that so his line of verse didn't work.

He wished he was wearing scales. *Silvery fish-armour,* he thought, pushing upwards to take another gulp of air, surrounded by monstrous bodies that thwacked and clubbed and pecked.

Pecked.

No, that wasn't right. Kicking and punching to tread water, or at least keep a place for his head above the surface, Skarfr felt the drill of a beak in his leg, then felt feathers brush against his face. He opened his eyes.

'*Aark, arkk, Fight for Sea-born!*' cawed the cormorant, black among silver, breaking the surface and soaring into the sky, with a tiny silver tuna in his mouth, which he dropped. It grew bigger and bigger until it became a full-grown tuna, which landed on Skarfr's head, knocking him underwater again.

Throwing out his arms to keep space for his body, Skarfr touched something that was cloth not fish. Afraid he would rip the garment, or that it was only a piece of his missing son, he flung his arms wide, punching tuna with all his strength and throwing his arms around whatever was wearing the cloth. He had an armful of boy and he didn't hesitate to follow the cormorant's order.

Fight!

The tuna wanted to go down as much as he wanted to go up and he had never battled so hard in a shield wall as he did to force a way to the surface, holding his precious burden to his chest with one arm and lashing out with the other.

Fight! the voice urged, with a dragon's roar, giving him the extra strength he needed to breach the surface once more, to lift his limp son's head out of the water, to pray.

When something wooden hit the water beside them, he flinched. He almost dived down below to escape being clubbed by a fisherman. Then he realised he'd been seen. He'd come up so close to the boat that someone was reaching out to him.

'Grab it and hold on!' yelled Bent-Nose.

Skarfr clutched at his only hope of rescue, battered and bruised by the desperate tuna. He was starting to shake with the strain of holding on and he'd run out of words for prayers so he thought only, *Please, please, please.* And he held on.

The men beside Bent-Nose continued using their oars against the fish around Skarfr, hauling them one at a time onto the deck until there was enough space to land a man and a boy instead of a fish.

Dragged up the side of the boat, Skarfr tried to protect Sea-born's lolling head and finally he was over the wales, standing, shaking, holding his son in his arms. This was how a man acknowledged his son, he thought. He holds the baby in his arms and speaks the words.

Hoarse from swallowing water, he rasped out, 'I Skarfr Kristinsson do acknowledge this boy child Sea-born Skarfrsson as my son and heir. You are my witnesses.'

A man in a turban stepped forward, tried to take Sea-born but Skarfr resisted. He would hold on as long as he had to.

'Put him down on the deck. Let me see if I can help him.' the man said, pity in his eyes and authority in his voice. *Gentle-Eyes* thought Skarfr.

Skarfr laid his son down on his back so the sun could wake him. *So pale, still sleeping.* The crew members crowded around, curious, perhaps waiting to see if whichever god they followed would demand payment for the exceptional catch they'd landed this *mattanza*. And the catch *was* exceptional. Dozens of tuna lay in a shining heap in the middle of the boat, the latest additions still flapping. If the other boats were equally weighed down, hundreds of tuna had been caught.

Gentle-Eyes said, 'Trust me. If he has drunk too much water and has not yet left us, this might bring him back.'

Numb, Skarfr watched as the man rubbed Sea-born's chest on the left-hand side, intoning a prayer, asking for the boy's heart to beat again and be strong.

'I don't like this,' the captain said, pulling Gentle-Eyes away from Sea-born. 'It is against God's will to bring someone back from the dead.'

Skarfr felt the word like a blunt tuna nose hitting him in the guts.

'*Inshallah*,' said Gentle-Eyes, making no attempt to return to his nursing. 'As God wills.' He looked at Skarfr and shook his head.

Too dazed to act, Skarfr stood, wooden as the useless oar he'd picked up.

'Watch out!' yelled a sailor and Skarfr was propelled into action by the memory of an oar hitting his back. Instinctively he jumped to one side and crouched, just missed by a tuna which had flipped its way off the pile.

Sea-born was not so lucky. The tuna hit him, rolling him over onto his side and the fish bashed against this human barrier with its blunt nose. Three times Sea-born's back took a battering and then Skarfr was on his feet, dragging the fish away from his son. He raised the oar and brought it down on the tuna, looked into its eyes as he delivered the killing blow. And he saw the ineffable power of Njord the sea-god looking back at him before life ebbed away and the eyes dulled.

At the same moment, he became aware that Sea-born was convulsing. Then the boy groaned and vomited.

Thank you, said Skarfr, to the dead tuna, to the gods. His knees gave way and he sank to the slimy deck beside his son. He put his hand on Sea-born's shoulder, afraid of breaking such a fragile and precious being.

'You should have stayed on the boat, son,' he said gruffly. 'But we shall have a story to tell your mother. A story fit for a saga.'

Sea-born waved his hand vaguely.

Skarfr got to his feet. It had not been an accident. 'Where is One-Brow?' he asked. 'The man who pushed me overboard?'

'He dived off harbour-side and swam back towards the quay,' said one of the men.

'It can wait,' said Gentle-Eyes. 'You and your son need care.'

Within the time it took to summon a small boat, Skarfr and Sea-born were heading back to shore, where an old man insisted they stay in his daughter's house, that she would tend to them. Too exhausted to argue, Skarfr and his son stumbled along the rough path to a fisherman's cottage on the rocks overlooking the bay. The woman of the house was as welcoming as promised. Clucking around them like a mother hen she ushered them into a curtained chamber, where they collapsed together onto a simple straw mattress and fell into a blue-silver sleep.

Skarfr's sleep would have been more troubled if he'd known what Hlif was doing.

CHAPTER FORTY

HLIF, SICILIA

Hlif should have insisted she go with Skarfr and Sea-born, for her own sake not theirs. She couldn't get anything done for her presentiment of disaster. She'd reduced Amina to tears and driven Jasim to reciting surahs to himself, from the Muslim holy book, all advocating patience. There were enough of these to drive Hlif to the Tiraz when she heard Jasim murmuring yet another, 'Be patient. Surely Allah is with those who remain patient.'

In the Tiraz, Rachel complained that Hlif's nervous jiggling was making her stitches uneven and told her to go home before she upset Pearl and Onyx or put Mikael's lute out of tune. Mikael himself showed no such concern but, as was his custom, stayed within earshot in case he could be of use. However, not even Mikael's attentions could reduce Hlif's anxiety and she gave up seeking distraction. She might as well pace up and down in her own rooms.

It could not have been more nerve-wracking to be there on the quayside in Favignana, watching the *mattanza*, than in Palermo, knowing nothing about what was happening. Skarfr had made it sound as if they would go out on a fishing boat, cast a line and catch some fish but she knew that hundreds of men would not get excited about small fry. She tried to mend a pair of hose and pricked her finger, spotting the fine beige weave with blood.

An ill omen she thought, dabbing water on the stain and rubbing bigger the tiny hole she'd been repairing. She had not felt this uneasy when Skarfr and Sea-born were at sea or in Ifriqiya. What was wrong with her?

She would get nothing useful done at home in this state so she sat on a stool and stared inward, seeking her menfolk. Barely using her powers at all. Merely behaving as an ordinary woman would if she were worried about her absent loved ones. Nothing the gods might find presumptuous.

The sudden pain rocked her on the stool, a blow to her back followed by confusion. Holding her breath to bursting point, battered and beaten, water, not enough water... No visions came but she could feel Skarfr struggling, as she'd once watched him near-death in a fever, when his wild words were all of drowning.

That's it! Water, holding his breath, he's gone overboard. Drowning. No, she would not believe that. How could Skarfr the cormorant drown, a creature at home underwater as in the air?

Cormorants die underwater if they're trapped there. Or caught by a pelican.

No, not Skarfr. She would not believe it until she saw his dead body and even then she would follow him to Valhalla itself and drag him back to their hearth. It was not his time yet!

But *something* had happened. What had Pietro said outside the chapel? *A widow needs protection.* Hlif had told Skarfr to be careful, had warned him the menace was real, and now Maria had carried out her threat. Not personally of course but through one of the brothers, in some cowardly attack from behind. She remembered the man outside the fruiterer's shop, one finger to his lips then across his throat. Who'd been with his 'brother' to threaten a tradesman, and then her, a woman. He was a bully and a coward. Nobody would have got the better of Skarfr in any honourable fight.

Enough of payments in oranges and amber. Enough of looking over her shoulder, worried about Skarfr, Sea-born and One-eye. She, Hlif, was no coward. This was between her and Maria, the spider-widow whose lethal web entangled men, and Hlif would not be trapped any longer.

Daughter of a saint-murderer, wife to a warrior, mother to one Sea-born, Hlif was more than all of those things. She was a völva, wielder of words and power over men, stronger than Maria. She'd said she wouldn't use her *seithr* unless there was need. Now, there was need.

This night, Maria would face the worst nightmare of her life and Hlif would be that *mare*, the demon that crushed her chest, riding her to madness.

She spent the rest of the day preparing. First, she went to the potter's, whose face showed his surprise when she took no interest in his fine ceramic ware from Caltagironi at 'knockdown price, just for today' but was willing to pay for a small lump of clay, wrapped in a damp cloth. From the colours of clay on offer, each from a different part of the island, she chose red from Santo Stefano di Camastra.

Earth, she thought, and called on the goddess Freyja. *Be with me, Lady.*

Next, she bought a length of fiery red ribbon in the haberdasher's, resolutely ignoring the temptation of pearl buttons and turquoise braid with gold bees worked into it.

Fire. Be with me, Lady.

She took her purchases home and dismissed Amina, told her to spend a few days with her family. Then she took a sack and scavenged along the lines of sea-wrack on the shore, collecting some green salty strands; creamy cockle shells and long dark hinged ones with pearlised interiors; driftwood smoothed into the shape of a bird; seven feathers.

Sea-gifts and wind, from a bird in flight. Be with me, Lady.

Satisfied with her trawl, she returned home and took off her coif, shaking free the unruly ripples of red hair, then studied the woman in the mirror on the wall. *More fire.* She used the red ribbon to bind and plait her finds into her hair, weaving in strands of seaweed, poking holes in the shells so she could thread them onto pieces of ribbon, making a headdress of looped hair and feathers.

Feathers, to conjure up the Lady's feathered cloak.

Now when she looked in the mirror, a völva looked back at her. She never wore red as a rule because it clashed with her hair but the last light of the sun gilded her strangely-dressed locks in startling shades of flame. If al-Idrisi had thought her unbound hair shocking, he should see her now! She laughed, a harsh, dangerous sound with no mirth in it.

She opened the damp sack and dipped her fingers into the red clay, drew three interlocking curves on each cheek, the symbol of the All-father, the Rune-bringer, to show respect. She hoped to please him with her use of *seithr* this night in the otherworld. From the kist where she'd hidden it, she retrieved her wand and menaced her reflection with it. The effect was satisfying.

But one thing was missing. A völva should wear fur. As night fell, Hlif opened the door and called softly from behind it. If a passer-by heading home late glimpsed a witch in a doorway, nobody would believe it was not a wine-vision.

'One-eye,' she called, and the great cat who pleased only himself yowled and came running. When she bent to him, he leaped into his place around her shoulders, purring. Carefully, stroking her black-and-white neck-fur with one hand and her wand in the other, she walked to her bed and sat down.

One-eye adjusted his position, became a furry torque below her chin as she slowly stretched out full-length on the bed, her hands clasped around her wand. In the position she would adopt in her tomb one day.

Lady Freyja, you shall know me as your völva by these symbols that I wear, for fire, wind, earth and sea. For your love of cats and völvas, take me to the woman known as Maria; Lord Óðinn father of the gods, bringer of seithr *and the mead of true poetry, take me to the woman known as Maria, the mother of too many brothers, wherever she stands or lies, in this world or another.*

One-eye purred against her throat and chin, a necklace less opulent than Freyja's magical Brisingamen but perhaps equally pleasing to the Lady of the cats. Hlif had done all she could to enlist the gods' support and avoid their displeasure. What ensued would be as the Norns decreed. She shut her eyes and walked into the dreamworld.

Like a hound on a scent, she followed an invisible trail, ignoring the shadows and echoes that flitted past her eyes and ears.

Irrelevant. She had not come for them. She had come for this woman, so shrivelled and shrunken, sleeping under her silk patchwork coverlet. Maria had one hand curled under her chin, a child's sleeping habit. So vulnerable. Hlif should have felt pity. She felt no pity.

Implacable, she stood beside the bed, her wand held above the woman's chest, said her name for all the demons in the dreamworld to hear, dragging out the syllables. 'Ma-ri-a.'

The old lady's eyes snapped open and widened.

'Stay still,' Hlif hissed, 'and you won't get hurt. Your worst fears are on top of you. Feel them, a weight that will crush you if you move, breathing your air, suffocating you. Look at them, how keen they are to have their revenge.'

Maria made a small choking noise and her eyes fixed on something in front of her, something far worse than a wand that only she could see. Hlif could sense their presence though. Maria's demons had come to her summons.

'You're dead. You have no place here.' Maria's tone was a plea and she was not speaking to Hlif, who concentrated on the iron wand-tip, on the *seithr* of words.

'You are accountable for many deaths but that is between you, your victims and your God. I am here to settle the debts between you and me. I know what you have done to Skarfr.'

Maria raised a trembling hand, slowly made the sign of the cross. 'Begone, phantom,' she told Hlif, her voice shaking.

Hlif laughed, felt invincible. She wanted to hurt this woman who'd attacked her family. *He is not dead.* 'Where is your protection now, coward? Hear this: if you touch me or mine again, be it so much as a shopkeeper who sells me oranges, you will know only red eyes and parched mouth, no sleep. The moment your eyes shut, I shall find you. *We* shall find you.'

The darkness spoke for itself, forced Maria to turn towards Hlif, who stooped over the bed. One-eye dug in his claws to avoid slipping and gave the old woman the full impact of an enraged cat spitting in her face. Maria screwed her eyes up to avoid seeing.

Sometimes, what a woman sees behind closed eyelids is worse than with eyes open. Hlif straightened.

'Should your 'protectors' kill me in the day world, I will have even more power in this one, and show less mercy. All the false debts you created are settled. And now *you* owe *me*. What is my Skarfr's life worth? Beg for *my* protection or I will demand payment.'

'You will go to hell,' Maria told her, quavering. 'Witch! And the lord you had me kill will weigh on *your* chest.'

'You should be afraid I will go to your hell, for I will see you there and not hold back!' spat Hlif. 'And I will answer to my gods not to yours. Now, beg!'

The woman's body bucked in a futile attempt to rid herself of whatever held her down and then a chill swept up the wand and into Hlif, something so dark she felt Maria's terror. She broke into a cold sweat. What had she summoned?

'Please protect me.' The old woman began to sob.

Hlif and the darkness spoke with one voice. 'This will remind you in the morning of what we can do.' Hlif's hand took the wand, scored a line up Maria's cheek with the sharp black tip as the old woman whimpered. The cut was beading with blood as Hlif lost herself in an ancient force, so much bigger than she was, so welcoming. Was this death?

Skarfr returned home the day after the *mattanza* to find Hlif on their bed, laid out as if it were her last resting-place. Her cream skin was painted red, as if with desert sand, for battle. Her hair was full of shells, seaweed, red ribbons and feathers, wild and salty as any of the nine underwater daughters of Rán. Her hands were clasped across her chest, holding her wand and One-eye was wrapped around her neck, hissing and spitting at him.

'What have you done?' Skarfr asked, his stomach convulsing with dread, a worse feeling than the seawater had given him. He was drowning again.

CHAPTER FORTY-ONE
FINN, HROSSEY, ORKNEYJAR

Bondsmen and community representatives had come from all over the islands to attend the autumn Thing. Finn was not the only Thing-goer to choose to drop anchor in the big harbour of Kirkjuvágr and walk for four hours to the assembly, rather than compete for space in the small coves near Thingwall. Kirkjuvágr also offered all the attractions of a market town, so why not combine business with pleasure after the meeting? Boats of all kinds jostled along the quayside and demonstrated the prosperity or otherwise of their owners.

Finn, however, would not be seeking entertainment in town after attending the Thing, and he was one of the few to have sailed there in a longship with full crew. He had also come with his wife, whose eyes expressed the anxiety her clasped hands sought to conceal. This was the day their plans would come to fruition — or fail.

He walked along the well-beaten path around St Magnus' cathedral, where the building work was finished in the north-east corner and had progressed to roofing over the middle section. Once through the town he headed north-east, joining a band of fellow Orkneymen heading for Thingwall, excited at the prospect of formally appointing a new jarl.

The public acknowledgement of Erlend at the Thing was almost guaranteed but its consequences were unpredictable. Finn had plenty of time on his journey to mull over the events of the previous months and to rehearse his own lawsuit. Since forging their alliance at Strjónsey, Erlend had garnered support from all those he'd nurtured the previous year, in readiness for this second attempt at gaining the jarldom. This time he had Sweyn with him and, together, they were invincible. Secure in the goodwill of most Orkneymen, Sweyn and Erlend attacked Harald at Michaelmas. He fled from his ship, left in this very harbour, in a doomed attempt to seek refuge in one of the old round towers near the town.

Harald was only released after relinquishing his share of the jarldom in Orkneyjar and he promptly set sail for the land in Ness over which he still ruled as Jarl. As far as Finn knew, Harald was still in Ness, licking his wounds, but Thorbjorn had been detained in Hrossey by the notification of a lawsuit against him. However much he wished to avoid the humiliation awaiting him at a Thing which would laud the new jarl, Thorbjorn's currently low reputation would fall even further if he did not answer the case against him. He would also lose the suit by default if he did not attend the Thing and pride would not allow that. His arrogance would ensure his belief that he would win.

So Margaret and Inge had counselled Finn. He had been in two minds about leaving Inge on the ship.

'You would be better at all this dancing with words,' he told her. 'There will be other women there, some landowners and widows.'

'And those whose husbands are absent or infirm, which you are not,' she replied. 'It would make you look weak if I spoke for myself in such a case, unless it was against another woman. You are not weak. And you know that my words would not be taken seriously.'

Because she was a woman. It was true. Usually with good reason, thought Finn, though he would never say so to Inge. Other women could be so silly.

'He will provoke you,' Inge reminded him, 'and if you insult him at the Thing, you give him the right to avenge himself. Nobody will care if the fight is fair or not, if he is wronged in an assembly where respect is due and sanctuary given to all who attend.'

'And if he insults me?' Finn asked. Nothing could please him better than to have an excuse to kill this man who had hurt Inge in the most unforgivable way.

She shook her head. 'He won't. He's more devious than that, unless he completely loses his temper — and that would set you both outside the law. The insults will be indirect, to make *you* lose your temper. When he pokes you with words, remember we have already tumbled him from political power and we want to win this case for Fergus and for Brigid.'

The Irishman was standing beside them, his body so full of tension Finn could have strung him as a bow.

'I should come with you,' said Fergus, his eyes hollow with the agony of waiting and hope.

'We have talked of this,' said Finn. 'I will have to say things about you which are disrespectful and I would rather you did not hear them.'

Fergus' gaze was steady on his. 'There will be nothing I have not heard before.'

'But not from me,' insisted Finn. 'And if I hold back because you are there, we might lose the case.'

Fergus' eyes darkened. 'You will not lose,' he said.

'He will not lose,' asserted Inge stoutly. 'Thorbjorn is clever and a fine warrior but you, Finn of Strjónsey, are a good man, and that will count in the eyes of the voters.'

'I think Margaret's cleverness will count more,' he said. 'But I will do my best.'

'May the gods go with you,' Inge told him, then she kissed him in the most immodest manner he had ever experienced in public. There were some vulgar comments from the crew, along with noises and gestures he construed as envy. So much for Inge's cold reputation. The memory of her mouth on his warmed him as he walked and filled him with courage.

CHAPTER FORTY-TWO

FINN, HROSSEY, ORKNEYJAR

From a distance, Finn could see across the heathland to the assembly mound, which was surrounded by a packed circle of Thing-goers. The day was dry and sunny but the ground and air were fresh from overnight rain so people were warmly dressed. Cloaks, or warm jerkins and bonnets, in various shades of brown, gave the gathering the appearance of some gigantic beast undulating on the invisible turf. On the outer perimeter, some enterprising vendors had set up pie-carts and ale barrels. The Thing would continue for two or three days, if necessary, but those matters pertaining to high-ranking men would be dealt with on this, the first day, when attendance would be highest. Thorbjorn was unquestionably a man of high rank, so Finn carved a route through the crowd, up the slope to the top of the mound where only those in authority stood — and those engaged in the morning's lawsuits.

Here, the cloaks were in expensive shades of blue or green, and, like Finn's, trimmed with braid. The red, blue and yellow tablet-weave border edging his deep blue cloak was in a chevron design. It was Inge's most recent creation and he was sure it was as fine as any king's. He need not worry about his attire being equal to the occasion. A flutter of nerves lodged in his gut and he took a deep breath, blew it out into the westerly wind. His pre-battle ritual.

Take my fear, he told the wind. *Breathe it into my enemy.*

'Finn!' The first person to greet him was the man who stood out from all others on that mound. Tall and sunshine-haired like his sister, Sweyn wore victory like the finest gold-threaded raiment, bestowing his radiance on the man beside him. Jarlmaker indeed. And a veteran of lawsuits at the Thing, many times accused of pillage or murder, sometime resulting in his exile, never dampening his spirits or hampering his exploits.

Despite his air of confidence, Erlend — soon to be Jarl Erlend officially — stood very close to Sweyn.. He had dressed for his coronation in a fur-lined cloak with ermine trim on its hood and hem, surely of Norwegian fabrication, a gift from the king perhaps. When he raised his arm to welcome Finn, his cloak fell back, revealing three thick silver arm-rings. Every inch the jarl and yet, he faded to ordinary beside Sweyn, however careless the sea-rover was about his appearance. Finn doubted whether Sweyn ever needed to breathe out his fear on the wind but he suspected that Erlend did.

Anakol, the loyal greybeard, was also at Erlend's side. He too must be looking forward to the formal proclamation of his foster-son as jarl.

'We will hear the case of Finn of Strjónsey against Thorbjorn Klerk. Are these two men present?' asked the Lawspeaker, a grizzled official with downturned mouth and exaggerated diction, both probably the results of years of pronouncing the complex codes of civilised society.

Finn took his place in the centre, among the Thingmen of highest status. He knew from the way a hush traversed the crowd that his opponent had arrived. On the opposite side from Erlend and Sweyn, Thorbjorn came through the inner ring to face Finn.

'Good-day, Thing-goers,' he said, his gaze glancing off the new jarl and his supporters, to rest on Finn. If Sweyn was like the sun, Thorbjorn was the wolf, ever chasing, the wolf which one day would reach its prey. Of a height with Sweyn, above that of most men, Thorbjorn had a warrior's ease in his own body, coiled and ready to strike, lightning-fast and trained. He too showed respect for the assembly in his attire, wearing a fine cloak of green wool, with braiding almost as skilfully executed as on the one Finn wore.

In an echo of Erlend's gesture, he raised a hand, not in greeting but to flick his thick black hair out of his eyes, and his cloak fell back. There was a gasp from the men around him. Four wide silver arm-rings glinted in the sunshine. An insult to the new jarl so subtle there could be no offence taken and yet clear enough to *be* an insult, a breathtaking act of defiance. With one silver arm-ring more than Erlend wore, Thorbjorn declared himself to be of higher rank than the new jarl. He had not come to the Thing as Harald's advisor, tail between his legs, but as Thorbjorn Klerk, a force in his own right, whoever ruled Orkneyjar.

Finn almost admired the man, even while knowledge of what he'd done to Inge sent a venomous spurt of jealousy and hatred through his blood. He felt like a clumsy bear faced with weapons beyond his ken. The enemy showed no sign of having contracted fear blowing on the wind. Thorbjorn turned to Finn, his blue eyes frank and faintly puzzled. 'It is a while since we last talked, Finn of Strjónsey. I had not expected us to meet again over some trivial misunderstanding.'

Before Finn could take the initiative as instructed beforehand, Thorbjorn spoke in a soothing, reasonable tone, man to man. 'To save time, let me explain the dispute and the misunderstanding, so we can get on with more important matters.'

'Please do,' said the Lawspeaker. Finn was rendered mute.

'Lord Finn disputes my ownership of two Irish thralls, a male and a female.' Thorbjorn looked at Finn and paused.

What could Finn do but nod? Already, he was dragged too fast in Thorbjorn's wake and soon he would surely drown.

With a flourish, Thorbjorn produced a piece of parchment from his pouch and waved it in the air, allowing his arm-rings to catch the sunlight again. 'Let me read you this letter from Botolf the Skald, written just before he died, signed and dated, leaving two Irish thralls to me in his will.'

He paused again, consulted Finn. 'You agree that these are the two thralls concerned?'

Finn nodded, helpless.

Thorbjorn's voice was commanding, without hesitation at first. Botolf's words clearly identified the two thralls as a death-gift to Thorbjorn, who broke off in embarrassment after reading this part. 'I don't think the next part is appropriate for the Thing,' he stammered. 'After that comes the signature, Botolf Begla, Renowned Skald to the courts of Snaeland, Norðvegr and Orkneyjar.'

There was no way the Lawspeaker would let him off so easily and Thorbjorn knew that, thought Finn uneasily.

Sure enough. 'Read the missing part,' ordered the Lawspeaker, his decision popular enough to gain the first clatter of weapons from the audience.

With every show of reluctance, Thorbjorn said apologetically, 'Botolf was an old man, dying when he wrote this, and no doubt thought he was flattering me.' He quickly read the part of the letter he'd omitted.

'You who are Jarl of Orkneyjar in all but name, my Lord Thorbjorn, you who are a foster-father too – and who understand what is due to one who has raised a child not his own – I know you will not let such unnatural, ungrateful behaviour spread its evil contagion.'

Finn was sweating despite the chilly wind, desperately trying to find one of the chinks in Thorbjorn's armour for which he had prepared. This could not be the only part of the letter Thorbjorn had not read aloud. Finn knew the letter had revealed Skarfr's role in Inge's escape from Thorbjorn. Had Thorbjorn skipped that part? It reflected badly on Thorbjorn so he would not make it public, and it would do Inge no good to stir up the past, so Finn must let that go. Was that the trap, one he'd avoided? Or was there another?

Thorbjorn flashed the letter at the Lawspeaker, who agreed that the signature was Botolf's. Then he looked at Finn, his blue eyes so honest and appealing that a man must be suspicious indeed to mistrust him. 'Would you like to read the letter yourself, to see the words with your own eyes?'

He held out the parchment and Finn's natural instinct was to reach out and take it.

Thorbjorn added, 'If you can read.'

He will try to provoke you, to make you retaliate. Finn's habit of thinking before acting so often made him slow but this time it saved him from a grave error. As he searched for the right response, the increasing tension warned him. If he took the letter, he was calling Thorbjorn a liar. That would give his opponent the right to call for character witnesses, three probably for such a minor offence, and Finn would lose the case. The insult would also give Thorbjorn the right to seek him out after the Thing, to attack him, to kill him.

Finn smiled, his hands at his side. He projected his deep voice so it carried and he tried to keep any sarcasm out of his tone. 'I have no doubts about Lord Thorbjorn's honour or his letter. This is indeed a misunderstanding and once we receive the correct legal advice, I am sure he will happily restore the two thralls to their rightful owner, as will I. Or rather one thrall, as the second one is already attending my wife while the case is judged. Let me explain.'

For the first time, there was a tiny flicker of doubt in Thorbjorn's eyes, quickly hidden.

'Please do.' The Lawspeaker was evidently not pleased at a turn of events likely to prolong the hearing but he held up a hand, indicating that Finn should proceed and Thorbjorn must listen.

And so the tide turns. 'Botolf could not will the thralls to Lord Thorbjorn because they do not belong to him. They belong to his foster-son Skarfr Kristinsson, who had already come of age and into his inheritance when this parchment was written. Skarfr is on pilgrimage with Jarl Rognvald so cannot speak for himself. Sadly, his house was razed to the ground just after his ship left and the thralls he'd left tending it found themselves homeless.'

Skarfr's name was murmured in the crowd, along with the rumours regarding the mysterious burning of his longhouse.

'Is the thrall here as witness?'

'No. His word cannot be trusted. I'm sorry to say he bears some grudge against Lord Thorbjorn.' Finn left a moment for his listeners to guess what Fergus might have witnessed.

The implication was not lost. 'Are you accusing me of setting fire to Skarfr's longhouse?' Thorbjorn was no longer so equitable.

'Of course not.' *Even though you did and now everybody here wonders whether you are a liar. Apart from those who know you are.* 'Why would you do such a thing?' *Let them wonder about that too.*

'Then why did Botolf think the thralls were his?' asked the Lawspeaker.

This was dangerous ground. Botolf knew full well the thralls belonged to Skarfr, as did Thorbjorn, none of which could be said without an implicit accusation. Everyone knew that Botolf had no house and squandered his money, living from his prizes as a skald until the Thing awarded him Skarfr as a foster-son. From then on, he'd trained his apprentice skald with beatings and used Skarfr's inheritance as his own until the boy became a man.

'This is exactly the point of law I needed to bring to you,' Finn said humbly. 'If a man is responsible for a child's upbringing and his inheritance for many years until he comes of age, do these possessions become his? His house, his cow, his sheep, his thralls?'

Thorbjorn could contain himself no longer. 'This is ridiculous,' he said. 'Botolf bought these thralls, so they were his. Nobody's suggesting he owned Skarfr's house!'

'Which has burned down,' pointed out the Lawspeaker, frowning at the interjection and pulling at his beard as he mused. 'Botolf must have bought the cow too,' he told Thorbjorn, 'using monies he'd acquired from the estate he was managing on the child's behalf. Yet Botolf didn't mention these valuable animals in his will, only the thralls. Under the law, he had no right to any of Skarfr's possessions once the boy came of age, be they sheep, cow, horse or thralls. Ergo, he had no right to bequeath them to another person.'

Finn's insides loosened. He had won. Fergus and Brigid were Skarfr's by law.

'But—'

Finn's stomach clenched again.

'—there remains the question of temporary ownership until such time as Skarfr returns, complicated by the burning down of the longhouse.'

Thorbjorn looked contrite. 'I have erred in claiming ownership,' he said, 'but I'm happy to make amends by offering the thralls a home and work on my estate in Ness until my friend Skarfr returns. One thrall is already part of my household and it would be a pity to change her situation once more.'

No, no, no. Finn felt sick.

'That seems reasonable,' declared the Lawspeaker. 'Do you agree, Finn?'

'Very reasonable,' said Finn, his mind scrambling for a way out. Then it came to him that two could bend the truth. 'Unfortunately, I am honour-bound to keep the promise my lady wife made to Skarfr, that should anything happen to leave his thralls in need, she would take them in. Since the longhouse burned down, I have been seeking a way to keep this promise without causing offence to Lord Thorbjorn, when he clearly sought only to do what was right.'

'Ah, if honour is involved...' The Lawspeaker's face cleared at the light shed on the case. 'If only Skarfr's house hadn't burned down, the thralls could have continued to live there and look after his farm.' He sighed. 'As things are, the law gives temporary ownership of the thralls to Finn of Strjónsey and his wife Inge Asleifsdottir until Skarfr returns.'

Nobody wanted to go into the ramifications of what would happen if Skarfr didn't return. Finn breathed thanks to the gods.

'If I may speak?' The interruption came from an unexpected quarter. Erlend stepped forward, gave Thorbjorn a hard look and then broke off an arm-ring. 'As today is an important one for me, let me show the people of Orkneyjar what manner of jarl I shall be if they acknowledge me today. I give this silver to Finn of Strjónsey for the rebuilding of a longhouse for Skarfr Kristinsson.'

'An important day indeed,' said Thorbjorn, throwing his cloak back and baring one arm, his four rings flashing. 'I accept the judgement and will add to funds for building Skarfr a new longhouse.' He broke two silver bands from his arm and handed them to Finn.

'That is most generous,' stammered Finn, as the crowd went wild, clattering weapons and showing their approval of Thorbjorn's action. The enemy had turned himself into the hero of what should have been Erlend's day, and there was nothing Erlend, or even Sweyn, could do about it.

Thorbjorn leaned close to Finn under cover of the noise, whispered, 'Tell your lady, she will pay for this. Remember the last time we met, you and I, and how I seal bargains outside the Thing.'

Then he stepped back, raised his arms in farewell to the Thing-goers and stalked off, leaving a sense of anticlimax as people dispersed for a pie and a piss before the spectacle of Erlend becoming jarl.

Finn left quietly, walking in the opposite direction to that which Thorbjorn had taken. He remembered the last time they had met. Finn had been one of Harald's party in the meeting with Erlend last summer, when Harald had conceded Rognvald's share of Orkneyjar on the condition that Erlend gained support from the King of Norðvegr. And when Thorbjorn had slit the throat of one of Erlend's men, to show how he sealed a bargain.

The further he walked away from the Thing, the less Thorbjorn's threats meant. Finn shook off the menaces as spit in the wind and began to realise what he'd achieved. Only Sweyn or Skarfr had any chance of matching Thorbjorn as a warrior, sailor or sea-rover but he, Finn of Strjónsey, had bested him in a Law Thing, thanks to his shieldmaidens, Margaret and Inge, whose words were more cunning than Thorbjorn's. Finn's weapons and shield. Together, they had protected Fergus from Thorbjorn and now they would rescue Brigid.

He ran the last part of the way to his ship, whirled Inge into his arms and thumped Fergus on the back, until they begged him to stop and tell them properly what had happened.

'Then there's no time to waste,' said Inge. 'We set sail for Ness.'

'Only if you stay at Lambaburg while we sail on to Thorbjorn's estate,' insisted Finn. It was a mark of how impressed she was at his victory that she did not argue.

What nobody mentioned was that Thorbjorn was indubitably sailing for Ness, too. If he put politics first and headed for Wick, to rejoin Harald and plot against Erlend, they could reach Brigid before he did. If he put vengeance first, Brigid would be dead when they reached her and Finn would face Thorbjorn in his own stronghold. There was no way Finn could out-sail Thorbjorn. He could only pray the gods would not desert him.

CHAPTER FORTY-THREE

BRIGID, NESS

Brigid was by the midden, sluicing out the night soil from the old woman's pail. Despite the foul odours from the bedridden woman's imminent encounter with death, Brigid preferred tending to Thorbjorn's mother than to the children. Her loss was so raw that a small hand touching hers gave rise to an inner scream that blocked all reason.

Fásach is alive, and so is Fergus, she told herself every day. As if in promise, the late sunrise of a November morning splashed gold, crimson and violet across the sky. Then she remembered what shepherds said about a red sky in the morning. *Shepherds' warning.*

Across the yard, by the big house, Ellisif was talking to a man who must have arrived after the women had gone to their beds the previous night. As she carried the pail out of the big house, Brigid had noticed him, sleeping on a bench in the great hall.

She watched the conversation, which seemed amicable enough, then the man walked off towards the stables and Ellisif looked around, saw Brigid, and walked towards her at a pace fast enough not to draw attention but with urgency. The chickens and dogs scattered, complaining that their usual source of food ignored them, intent on reaching Brigid.

'He's coming for you,' gasped Ellisif.

Thorbjorn.

Brigid's heart stopped. The pail dropped from her hands and she knew this was her end coming. She could not evade That One forever but at least little Fásach was in safe hands. Maybe one day Fergus would return, speak to Ellisif and find his daughter. When Skarfr returned.

But Ellisif was smiling.

'Fergus,' she said. 'Fergus is coming. Thorbjorn's man is here, with news from Orkneyjar. The master is in Wick with Jarl Harald for now, licking his wounds and plotting, but he might turn up at any time. And he won't care what the law said, so he won't. You need to go somewhere safe, and wait.'

Brigid's head reeled. 'I don't understand.' She tried to take in Ellisif's explanation of a lawsuit, and Lord Finn winning, the one who married Lady Inge, the one Fergus had said would protect him. So she belonged to this Lord Finn now and he would be coming to get her, with Fergus. Unless Thorbjorn came home first, which would mean trouble.

Fergus is coming.

She should be glad but she felt numb. She could not trust that all would be well. But she could hope.

'You must go to the bothy,' said Ellisif.

The bothy, the shelter known only to the women on Thorbjorn's estate, was accessible only across the bog.

'I won't go without Fásach,' Brigid said. The words came without thought but their truth anchored her to the spot.

Ellisif looked at her a long moment, must have seen the futility of argument and came to her decision. 'I shall get her,' she said. 'Find Wulfhild. She will know what you must pack in your panier, so it looks as if you are just picking wild berries and herbs when you go out this afternoon.'

'The woman, Ada, will not let her go,' said Brigid. This too was truth.

'I know,' said Ellisif. 'I will do what I have to.'

Wulfhild's fey habits meant she could come and go from the estate into the peat bog without question, singing snippets of incomprehensible songs and chanting a litany of herbs. But there was nothing fey about the way she found all that was needed for Brigid to survive with her baby in the bothy. Wulfhild had planned for this many times, and now a woman did need sanctuary, she quickly laid hands on the essentials for survival, including smoked fish, bannocks, water-bottle, goat's milk and a knife. There was even a fire-starter but Wulfhild warned her that she should avoid using it. If one of the peat-cutters wandered further than usual into the bogland and reported a fire, someone might risk investigating.

All the treasures fitted neatly into the sort of panier used to forage in the wilderness surrounding the estate. Then Brigid passed the rest of the morning trying to work. She attended to the dying woman, tried to make her comfortable by plumping up a pillow and changing her position — an easy task now, as if the body was already metamorphosing into air. She threw some grain to the chickens and found stale bread for the dogs, to make up for Ellisif's omissions earlier. She forced down some stew at midday, knowing this would be her last hot food for the foreseeable future.

When Wulfhild came to find her, said, 'It is time,' Brigid wrapped her shawl around her, tucked her arm through the handle of her panier and walked through the settlement to the far wall where the dead baby was buried. Where Ellisif waited for them, hidden by the wall, a blue and white woollen bundle in her arms. Brigid's stomach lurched and the imperative to hold her baby rushed through her.

Ellisif shook her head, gestured to Wulfhild.

'Swop baskets,' said Wulfhild, passing her own to Brigid. 'I know you want to carry your baby.'

Puzzled, Brigid did as she was told and then understood. Wulfhild's basket was lined with a soft wool blanket and a linen cloth over that.

Ellisif gently placed the baby on the blanket and covered her with the cloth. 'Just till you're past the peat-cutters,' she said.

Brigid took the strain of the added weight. The baby was so heavy now! All those lost months changing, growing, while Ada mothered Fásach. Jealousy stabbed her as she pictured Ada with her baby. Then pity.

'How did you...?' Brigid looked at the tiny pucker where a baby's breath moved the linen, in and out, in and out.

'I took her,' said Ellisif grimly. 'There's no time to talk of that now. She is your baby. Godspeed. Go!'

Ellisif went out from the wall into the open, headed for the big house. Brigid heard her saying yes, she'd been tending to a woman with a baby in the village, and all was well. She'd ordered provisions too, as the master was on his way 'some time'. How was a housekeeper to organise food for such a household, if a hundred starving men could turn up from one moment to the next?

'Come,' said Wulfhild and they took the path out towards the bog, where all paths would cease. Brigid had to change arm frequently, aching from the weight of the baby but she bore it past the men cutting peat, who barely looked up from their work.

Just another day foraging on the heath.

The tiny pucker of cloth moved in and out, and finally, they were onto the open heath, nobody in sight. Just miles of low shrubs and glittering crisscross waterways, treacherous moss, and life-saving tussocks. Heather was blooming purple and some of the moss was red-tinged. A year ago, Brigid had faced death in this lethal landscape, abandoned by Wulfhild and tested on what she'd learned by the harshest teacher she'd ever known, a landscape that punished one wrong step by dragging you down to die. Now, she knew and loved the sucking mud and gilded reed-beds. These were her defences against the man who would kill her.

With trembling hands, she put the basket down, lifted her baby out and looked at her. Her heart broke again.

'This isn't my baby,' she said. 'Ellisif has switched her.'

Wulfhild's guileless expression showed only sympathy. 'Be at peace, dear heart. This is your Fásach. Ellisif says that a baby grows and changes in nine months, blond hair to black, and from lolling head to sturdy explorer on all fours. Blue eyes can even turn brown but not with your blue-eyed bairn. Ellisif has watched over your baby when she had reason to go to the fishing village, watched her grow strong and healthy. Ada looked after her well.'

'I never meant to hurt the woman so much.' Brigid could not take her eyes from this small stranger, who looked back at her with Fergus' eyes and waved sturdy limbs in the air. Fásach didn't cry as Brigid picked her up, fitted her into the curve of breast and hip, secured her with the blue and white shawl and continued walking, the panier on the other arm and the weight better distributed.

'I know,' said Wulfhild. 'You should bless her in your prayers.' Like a flicker of cloud reflected and fractured in the myriad puddles around them, Wulfhild's lucidity vanished and she was once more singing one of her strange songs.

In such otherworldly company did Brigid cross from one safe tussock to another, following Wulfhild, as she had the first time she'd ventured onto the heath. From Wulfhild, she'd learned of the natural traps that killed. What looked like rosemary was poisonous. Red or green, the moss would take you down through quaking mud if you trod on it. She'd lost her shoe in that lesson and Wulfhild had thrown the other one to join its partner, a sacrifice to the spirits of this place.

Where grass, shrubs and heathers grow, you can walk. Peat at a pinch, but it's so soft it'll scare you to death. Rushes are your friend, following the crisscross paths of the water, which always flows downwards

Among the many water-birds gossiping out of sight, the two notes of a curlew's whistle rose and echoed in the blinding mist. When the top of the bothy came into sight above the swirling white, Brigid could only thank God and all the saints for the unknown marshmen of ancient times who'd built this solid stone shelter in the middle of nowhere, a dome shape with peat-filled cracks as waterproofing.

They had to stoop to enter the low doorway. The only light came from the open door and the ceiling inside curved down to the floor so they could only stand up in the middle section. On one side, taking up the whole length of the tiny building, was a long, raised stone slab like an altar, with a thick straw-stuffed mattress on top, a blanket and a pillow. On the opposite wall was a low ledge, on which Wulfhild placed all the contents from the panier.

Brigid sat down on the bed, Fásach in her arms, while Wulfhild completed her task, arranging the dried fish and bannocks on a cloth as if this was a feast for a queen, adjusting the position of the two bottles beside the food to make some pattern that pleased her.

Then in her abrupt manner, she said, 'I must go. I'll bring food tomorrow.'

Brigid nodded. 'Dark comes early now.' She reached out to touch the young woman, not knowing how to thank her enough but, like a startled rabbit, Wulfhild bolted.

Jiggling Fásach in her arms and crooning to her in Irish, Brigid watched from outside the doorway as Wulfhild skipped from tussock to tussock, choosing each short path along the edges of the patchwork pieces that made up the watery world of bogland. Long after the sky and the pools turned crimson, she stood there until finally she could see the stars against the darkening sky. She was so small in such vastness and yet she was part of it. She shivered, suddenly feeling the cold, and she went inside.

She fed her baby with goat's milk, dunking the cloth in the bottle and letting Fásach suckle a corner, then dipping in a finger so she could feel the suction and the small teeth. Reassured that her baby was hungry and well able to take the milk, Brigid controlled some drops straight from the bottle to that avid mouth. Fásach gulped it down, stopped to belch.

Then Brigid shut the door, lay on the bed with her daughter and wrapped the blanket around them both, with two shawls on top of that. She slept cocooned in the kindness of women and protected by the uninhabited bogland from the man she feared. The *who-who-who* call of an owl sang her to sleep and no ballybogs or shape-shifting *Púca* disturbed her dreams.

She woke once and carefully left her daughter tucked up in bed while she slipped outside to relieve herself in the moonlight. An infinity of stars winked in the black velvet sky and the ground had not yet pulled its morning blanket of mist over the rivulets and clumps of greenery. The grass-blades were tipped with tiny dew stars and all the world around Brigid glittered, as if she were being drawn into a fairy dance. As if she saw through her daughter's eyes the newness of it all.

'Fásach,' she murmured. 'Wilderness.' And with a sigh, she returned to bed, let the wilderness care for her as tenderly as any mother, while she slept and began to heal.

CHAPTER FORTY-FOUR

BRIGID, NESS

Two or three days had gone by and already Brigid was losing track of time, lulled into the small sections of wakefulness that suited Fásach during the day. Each small discovery was a joy. She could stay upright, even though she was wobbly, and take a few steps if Brigid held her tiny hands while she tottered forward. But she far preferred speeding along on all fours, gurgling and waving her small bottom in the air.

Each discovery presented new dangers. When Fásach fell down and sobbed, Brigid felt every tear as an accusation. The baby was smiling again within moments but Brigid's shock and guilt lingered until Wulfhild made her daily appearance and distracted her.

While Brigid took some food and water for herself, the open door proved too big a temptation for an inquisitive baby. Fásach was crawling full-speed ahead towards the sparkles she saw in a black puddle, when Brigid scooped her up, heart pounding. How could such a small being get up to such suicidal devilment? And yet, she envied her daughter too. Had she ever been so fearless, racing towards adventure, trying to catch the sun in a puddle?

They sang pitter-patter songs together when it rained, Brigid in Irish and Fásach in a babble that her mother thought more melodious than any nightingale. Brigid thought her child must be the most intelligent ever born when Fásach added the sophistication of clapping hands.

Brigid had almost forgotten what she was waiting for, in the endless present of minding her baby, when she heard voices outside. Although it was daytime, the door was shut because of Fásach's last escape bid. The game was only fun if Brigid watched her all the time to make sure she didn't reach any of those tempting glittery pools outside.

This was probably Wulfhild's usual time to visit but that was not what made Brigid's heart pound. One voice was Wulfhild's but she had brought a man with her. What if That One had returned, had threatened Ellisif? Wulfhild could not have borne that. Nobody could. The fear she'd forgotten flooded Brigid. She grabbed the knife off the shelf, picked up Fásach and settled the child on one hip. She faced the door as it was pushed open.

Maybe she could have barricaded it with her own body. Too late now. This time she would kill him. Through the heart. If he had one.

The door swung inwards and Wulfhild stood there, inches away from the knife. Brigid hesitated.

'It's Fergus,' the young woman said, clasping her hand, removing the knife, putting it back on the shelf, then moving it a little so the handle was at right angles to the wall, ready to be picked up.

'I don't believe you.' Brigid had to prepare herself for the worst. It was the only way to keep herself and Fásach alive for the day when Fergus would come.

'Brigid? *Mo chroí*, sweetheart,' said the familiar voice outside the bothy. 'Are you all right?'

Brigid pushed past Wulfhild and out into the soft light under a cloudy sky.

'I don't believe it,' she kept saying, as she stepped into open arms, felt Fergus' strength enclose both her and Fásach, who wriggled and complained, ending her parents' embrace.

'This is Fásach,' Brigid told Fergus. 'This is Dada,' she told the baby, passing their daughter to Fergus.

His blue eyes widened and he held her in his outstretched arms, kicking and gurgling.

Please don't cry, thought Brigid. She'd had her own moment worrying that Fásach would see her as a stranger and miss the woman who'd been her mother for nearly a year. But it was as if Fásach recognised her mother's smell and had settled as easily with Brigid as if they'd never parted.

'Fásach,' said Fergus. 'Sure and that's a perfect name.' He swung her up in the air and Brigid resisted the instinct to tell him off, to tell him to be careful. Fásach chortled and babbled so he did it again.

Wulfhild emerged to join them, carrying the two shawls. 'We must go,' she said. 'You can talk on the way.'

'One thing first,' said Fergus, taking the small shawl and wrapping the baby in it as if he'd been doing so for decades. He tucked the baby in one muscled arm and Brigid realised that she would no longer have to carry this weight alone, no longer have to carry any weight alone. Something in her gut eased and she twisted her hands in the soft comforting wool of her shawl.

Clumsily, Fergus fished around in his pouch and brought out a small object, held it out towards her.

Her ring. Silver with a blue stone Fergus had been told was sapphire when he'd bought it for her. She didn't care if it was sapphire or glass. It was from Fergus and it was *hers*. The ring she'd left for him to find when That One burned down their house, the one he'd tried to give back when he'd found her a year ago and had not been able to stay. When it had not been safe for her to keep the precious token.

'Hold out your hand,' he told her and she complied.

So wrinkled and vulnerable her hand looked, withdrawn from its warm hiding-place.

Awkward, one-handed, he fitted the ring back where it belonged. He kissed her hand and said, 'We're going home.'

She shook her head. Home was ashes. But as they followed in Wulfhild's steps, following the invisible, indirect path of tussocks and safe footing, Fergus told her the whole incredible story. Their house would be rebuilt. When Skarfr came home, they would be free in every way. Until then, they belonged to Lady Inge and to Lord Finn, who was waiting for them at this very moment at Lord Thorbjorn's home. Finn would escort her to the ship, with his band of armed men, and they would sail for home.

Her head buzzed with questions, with new fears. She could not so easily accept that all would be well.

'So we're still thralls,' she said, bitterly. 'All three of us.' She held up her ring so the stone gleamed in the silvery light. 'I don't even have the right to own this. It belongs to your man, your Lord Finn.'

'It's not like that,' insisted Fergus. 'There is no shame in working for a good man, who treats us well. *Thrall* is their word, not ours, and I promise you our family will have the same honour and respect Skarfr gave us.'

'If Skarfr had written the papers before he left, we would be free now.'

'And the house would still have been burned down, and we would still need work. Freedom does not keep you safe or put food on the table. The protection of a good lord does that.'

Brigid looked at her husband and the child he carried. Could she still believe in a good lord? She would wait and see. 'I do believe in the Good Lord who brought us together again,' she conceded, leaving it open to Fergus to apply the term to Finn or to God.

It was true that even free women needed protection. 'Wulfhild,' she said. 'I don't want you and Ellisif to suffer for having helped me. If That One finds out.' She would not call him master.

'Ellisif has weathered his moods before,' Wulfhild replied. 'She has a cunning tongue and he trusts her. She will hide her friendship for you when you leave with Lord Finn, and you must act the same way. Everybody knows I'm harmless so I do what I like. ' She started singing to herself and stopped to pick some heather to put in her panier.

Fergus persisted, echoing Brigid's concern. 'This time might be different. If you or Ellisif feel you are in danger, flee to Lambaburg in the north, on the coast. It's the family home of the Asleifssons. Lady

Inge is waiting for us there now and I'll tell her what you have done. She'll make sure you find shelter there, if ever you need it.'

There was no sign that Wulfhild had taken in his words and soon they reached the abandoned heaps of cut peat. Then the yard, where an imposing man in padded leather leaned on a long-handled axe, his warband supervising all the estate workers they had rounded up. Among these was Thorbjorn's man, who showed no sign of resistance.

Finn greeted Fergus with a clap on the back and bowed his head stiffly to Brigid.

A woman at the front of the gathered people yelled, 'Go back where you belong, treacherous bitch!' *Ellisif*. She was close enough for Brigid to see her eyes dancing.

Brigid felt tears coming, could think of no words that could safely be spoken, could think of no words big enough. She glared at Ellisif and tucked her arm through Fergus'. Let everyone else think she was being defiant. Ellisif would see the family she'd reunited.

'Heather is for coughs,' sang Wulfhild, brushing against Brigid to tuck a sprig of purple-flowered luck in her hair.

Brigid whispered into the ear conveniently close to her mouth. 'God bless you both. I owe you my life, my baby, my Fergus. Tell her for me.'

Wulfhild danced away and was shooed towards the rest of the workers by the frowning men-at-arms.

'There's no harm in her,' Ellisif told them, taking a sprig of heather from the panier and holding it tightly.

That was Brigid's last sight of the settlement where she'd arrived as a prisoner in the summer of the previous year. Her last sight of Wulfhild and Ellisif. All three sporting purple heather.

Heather is for coughs — and for friendship.

CHAPTER FORTY-FIVE

SKARFR, PALERMO, SICILIA

Had she come for him in his need, through the dreamworld, Skarfr wondered? Was she lost there? He reached out to touch her, and quick as a blade, One-eye's claws raked Skarfr's hand.

His blood boiling, Skarfr lunged for the cat's neck, picked him up by the scruff, yanked him off his mistress and dangled him in the air, where One-eye yowled his frustration for a few highly satisfying moments.

'What,' asked Hlif, enunciating each word carefully, 'Are. You. Doing. With. My. Cat?'

'Letting him go for a walk,' said Skarfr. Without changing his grip, he walked to the door, opened it with his free hand and, with excruciating gentleness, deposited One-eye on the ground outside. The door was firmly shut, with Skarfr inside and One-eye outside, before the cat had time to consider his options.

Hlif was sitting on the bed, observing him through narrowed eyes.

He knelt beside his wife, stretched out a hand and laid it on her heart, which beat as strongly as a passionate man could hope.

'I thought you were dead,' he told her.

'I knew you were not,' she told him. 'Where is Sea-born?'

He hesitated. 'I sent him swimming with his friends so I could speak freely to you.'

'What happened?' she asked, knowing and not knowing the answer.

After Skarfr had given her the first account of what would become the *mattanza* saga, she looked at him with disbelief.

'And you just sent Sea-born *swimming?* After he nearly *drowned!"*

Women never could understand what was so obvious to a man. 'That's why. To make a good memory so fear has no chance to take hold. He will tell his bold story to his friends as I tell mine to you and this bad thing will change into an adventure, something to be proud of.'

Hlif shook her head at him but her mouth tipped upwards.

He remembered he should be stern with her. 'What happened to *you?'* he asked, looking her up and down to make it clear that her decorated hair and face had not gone unnoticed, even though he had forgotten about the state she was in when he lost himself in his own saga. He thought he could improve on the kennings for tuna in his recital. Maybe *steel-clad hordes of the whale's way.* They'd certainly felt like armoured enemies and they *were* grey.

He could feel quizzical grey eyes waiting for his attention. *Enough skaldic distraction!* Hlif was going to tell him something important.

'I did something which will change into an adventure in the telling, something to be proud of,' she said and there was something dark in her tone, beneath the teasing. 'Maria will trouble us no more, nor will her dogs, the brothers.'

He knew from her mien that she was troubled by what had passed but she didn't allow him to probe.

'She is not dead, merely frightened. There is no more to tell,' Hlif said. 'And besides,' she ran her fingers up his arm, inside his tunic, 'we should make better use of Sea-born being out. Amina is visiting her parents and Jasim will be at prayers for hours. We are alive, despite our enemies. We should celebrate.'

He knew he should press her further on what he guessed she had been doing, and on its cost, but she could be very persuasive. And he felt *very* alive. The more dishevelled she became, the more shells and seaweed came unfastened from her hair, and the tang of the sea made Skarfr recoil. It was not only Sea-born who needed to face his fears before they took hold and what more pleasurable way to drown than in a woman?

> *Skin-shell, spiralling inwards to*
> *salty spume...*

Thought left him.

Sicilia was too hot in summer to make trade wars or military ones, so neither Hlif nor Skarfr put themselves in harm's way and each was pleased that the other was being careful. They were both waiting for autumn but the novelty of nights in warm nakedness, and days swimming or serenaded by cicadas, made waiting a pleasure.

Small things make no sagas, yet they matter, Skarfr realised.

He renewed his regular visits to the map-room, where al-Idrisi grilled him about the coastal settlements of Ifriqiya, checking that Skarfr's description matched previous information, making corrections and adding details that were new.

In al-Idrisi's chamber, surrounded by shelves full of books, parchment and inks, Skarfr's head whirled with new ideas as the scholar and the king switched topics from the grain harvest in Sicilia to the Pope's latest insult, from feeding a camel in the menagerie to King Guillaume's failings in diplomacy. And King Guillaume's diplomacy consisted only of failings, in his father's judgement. Skarfr could feel his mind expanding to make room for all this new information, listening intently to King Roger and al-Idrisi as they debated the views of the ancients and the actions of those in power now.

He worried about the secrets he heard. Was it treason even to listen to a father despairing of his son, when the two were co-rulers of Sicilia and he was— What was he? Not a subject exactly, maybe a foreign mercenary. Certainly one who owed loyalty to both kings, although he never saw King Guillaume and was unlikely to warm towards him if King Roger's anecdotes were true. Overfond of the Tiraz girls and fonder still of food and drink. A lecher, a glutton and a drunkard: that was the impression Skarfr gained of him. A man who shone on the battlefield and embarrassed in any other setting, where his famous strength became rustic clumsiness, likely to cause accidents and offence. Provision of heirs was not mentioned, a sore subject while Roger's queen was within two or three months of producing a rival to Guillaume's sons.

Tactfully, al-Idrisi dwelled on Guillaume's undoubted skills in battle and the likely need of them. 'Conrad has sent to Rome and to Constantinople, vaunting his plans to campaign in Italia in the autumn.'

Skarfr knew these were all inimical to Sicilia. Conrad, the self-styled King of the Romans and therefore the military arm of the Pope, had been ill following the disaster that was the Second Crusade, but had spent the winter recovering and was now plotting against Sicilia. The Pope in Rome considered King Roger to be overreaching his authority, with power he never should have had in the first place, and had not forgiven him for refusing to join in the Crusade. Pope Eugenius had indeed been offended by the anointment of yet another Sicilian king without his authorisation. Which would have been withheld. And Komnenos, the Emperor of Byzantium, wanted back the territory King Roger had taken from him.

The king studied a section of map pages from al-Idrisi's newly-named *Tabula Rogiana*, the *Book of Roger*, laid out on the tiled floor. To the east of the isle of Sicilia were its vast mainland territories in the south of Italia, once belonging to the Byzantine Empire and now threatened by all these enemies. If the Pope, Conrad and his allies supported Komnenos of Byzantium to take these lands from Sicilia, King Roger would have to deploy forces to defend them.

'And no doubt Venezia and Genoa will pitch in. Byzantium only regained Corfu after we'd taken it because of Venezian aid. Everyone except King Louis of Francia wants a piece of Sicilia. But they will not take one town from me. Guillaume can hold Monte Cassino, even against the forces of the Apocalypse, and they will never pass south.'

'There would be an attack by sea?' Skarfr asked hopefully. Land battles held no interest for him and his heart sank at the prospect of defending the border between Sicilia and Italia.

Al-Idrisi and the king looked at him, impatient at his ignorance. 'No,' they said in unison.

'Conrad has no navy. Venezia will want trade benefits from conflict without committing her own ships. Genoese ships are pirates and there is no love between Genoa and Venezia.'

It was all too complicated but Skarfr grasped the essential. 'So Byzantium and other Sicilian enemies would attack our regions on the mainland. But if our navy took the initiative, sailed against Constantinople, we could force Byzantium to defend its own shores and weaken them too much for any such attack? The others, the Pope and Conrad, could not take on Sicilia without Byzantium.'

This suggestion was not greeted with derision.

'That is the Emir's view,' said King Roger. 'He would like nothing better than a reprise of last year's attempt on Constantinople. He wants to split our forces, sending Guillaume to hold out against Conrad and any allies he can drum up, while he leads the navy against Constantinople.'

'I would make it succeed!' Skarfr saw no arrogance in stating a fact and apparently, neither did the King, who nodded, serious-faced.

'That also is what the Emir said, about himself and about you.'

Skarfr's hopes rose. The combination of George's experience and judgement, with his own prowess and creative strategies in sea battles, could not fail. And against Constantinople! That would be a legendary victory, a saga story to make Jarl Rognvald beg him to return to his side.

King Roger continued, 'But I think it will stretch our forces too thinly and risk us losing on both fronts. King Guillaume is the perfect leader for land battles but he needs enough men in his armies to win.' He sighed. 'However, the Emir is adamant that he can do such damage to Constantinople that Komnenos will not dare sail against us. And the Emir is not foolhardy. He has reinforced our strongholds in Ifriqiya and dealt with threats from that quarter, thanks to you,' he acknowledged. 'There is merit in both plans so I am undecided. Nothing will happen until the autumn, and events in the coming months will bring counsel.'

Al-Idrisi pointed out, 'Our enemies are also threatened by *their* enemies. As in the past, the Seljuk Turks might rise in force against Byzantium, in which case Komnenos will have no thought — or men — to attack us.'

The King nodded. 'The enemies of my enemy are my allies. And both Venezia and Constantinople want trade monopolies, each with envious eyes on the other. Any temporary unity against Sicilia will fall apart at the least dispute over silk or steel from the east.'

'Speaking of silk, Sire, I have added some more details to the description of Tunis, thanks to information Skarfr gleaned during his travels.' Al-Idrisi flicked through the pages on his lectern to find the section he wanted.

'There is fresh water in many wells but the water in two of them is sweeter and more abundant. They were dug according to the wishes of two Muslim women who wished to carry out benevolent acts.'

'Remarkable!' King Roger's eyes gleamed at such an unexpected addition to the city's description and al-Idrisi continued reading.

As always, the king left the map-room in better humour than when he entered, as did Skarfr. George would prevail and the fleet would sail against Constantinople in the autumn, whatever happened on the Italian border. Hlif would be disappointed but another year or even two in Sicilia would be no hardship.

Everything depended on the Emir, thought Skarfr cheerfully, as he headed for the Tiraz. And George of Antioch was an exceptional commander, who always persuaded the king to take the action he favoured. The Emir had brought Sicilia only honour and his sole remaining ambition was to humiliate Constantinople more thoroughly than by the one salvo he'd sent into the palace a year ago. Skarfr intended to make sure that ambition was realised.

CHAPTER FORTY-SIX

SKARFR, SICILIA

Playing duets and singing with Guimbarde, whom he must now call Mikael, was a relief for Skarfr after discussing politics, geography and science in the map-room. Skarfr had the king's permission to visit the rooms in the Tiraz above the silk works and had met Mikael there on several occasions. As well as the large chamber intended for entertaining the men who visited the Tiraz with music, poetry and dance, there were alcoves quite big enough for two musicians to rediscover the joy of conversing through strings and flute. With Mikael playing his lute and Skarfr his pipe, or even the guimbarde that was a private joke between them, they would turn a familiar melody into a voyage of discovery.

What was expected and what was allowed had no meaning in the world they created with their fingers and breath. Sometimes, Mikael would sing, his voice as high as the flute on which Skarfr accompanied him, and sometimes Skarfr took a turn, deep and gravelly as the ocean floor.

Just as in the public square in Narbonne, their performances attracted listeners, including the two maids Hlif had rescued and freed. This puzzled Skarfr. Why would two deaf girls want to watch music being made? Certainly, Mikael *was* beautiful to watch, lithe and graceful, his eyes dancing along with his supple fingers. When he glanced at Skarfr, sharing amusement at a musical phrase or an interpretation of a line in a love song, the understanding between them was tangible. It pained Skarfr to think about Mikael's encounters in the bedchambers behind the curtains.

'Why did you come here?' Skarfr asked Mikael. 'And why do you stay?'

Mikael's gaze was intense, his luminous brown eyes fixing Skarfr's. 'I love where I should not so I take pleasure where I can.' The long black lashes swept down, their tiny shadows the only blemish on the olive skin.

When he looked up again the impact was startling, like a doe's gaze through leaves. Skarfr had almost grown used to the make-up worn in the Tiraz, the black-lined eyes and lip-paint, but Mikael's appearance, enhanced in this way, made him uncomfortable. He knew the word that would have been used in Orkneyjar.

Mikael's eyes sparkled again. 'Let's play *Summer's Sun is Fleeting*,' he said.

> *Summer's sun is fleeting,*
> *be joyful while it lasts.*
> *Think not of tomorrow*
> *nor of the guiltsome past.'*

And so they played together.

Another time, it was Mikael who had something difficult on his mind. 'Rachel has been dropping hints,' he said. 'Dangerous hints. About autumn. And about you.'

Skarfr said nothing but he could hide nothing from someone who knew the mood of every note he played, any more than he could from Hlif.

'Do not do it, my friend,' said Mikael. 'Rachel is bound to the Tiraz, as am I, by the secrets of silk and by promises made to our patrons. Dreams of freedom hurt nobody.'

'I dream of leading a ship against Constantinople,' said Skarfr

'That is a good dream,' said Mikael. 'The only people who will kill you for it are a million Byzantine warriors.' He laughed and Skarfr laughed with him. It was good to be audacious, to forge your own fate. But Mikael's meaning was clear. Any attempt by Rachel to forge her own fate was doomed.

Neither of them referred again to autumn or to Rachel. *Summer's Sun is Fleeting.*

Skarfr found out he was wrong about Pearl and Onyx. They were not attracted to the musical performances by Mikael's beauty but by the instruments and in particular the guimbarde. When Pearl — or Onyx (he couldn't tell them apart) — reached out to touch the flute he was playing, he recoiled and the girl withdrew. But Hlif had told him that touch was important to her so he put the flute back in his mouth, guided the girl's hand back onto it and played a few notes.

Her eyes were wide in amazement. She withdrew her hand, put it back again. What did her fingers sense? He touched the flute himself with his free hand but his fingers were dulled by his hearing and there was nothing.

Soon, both girls were touching the lute and the pipe, discovering whatever music from these instruments became to their senses. Skarfr tolerated the touching for a while but when it became too disconcerting, he thought the guimbarde might distract them. This succeeded beyond anything he could have foreseen. Even Skarfr could see that the vibration made by the instrument between Onyx — or Pearl's lips could be felt by the girl playing.

With clumsy signs, he managed to tell them they could keep the guimbarde and take it away with them. Mikael nodded and smiled, added his own fluttering hand messages and, making their strange grunting noises, the girls took their precious new toy away out of hearing to experiment.

'The guimbarde works its magic again,' said Mikael, with that intensity Skarfr found discomforting.

'Out of hearing, thankfully,' said Skarfr.

And the summer music continued.

The balm of summer was not without flies, however. George of

Antioch's illness was now written in his grey face, wasting body and a mortal fatigue that took him to his bed most of each day.

As if he'd caught some lesser version of this malady, Sea-born too was pale and morose, but every time one of his parents asked, 'Are you all right?' the answer was, 'I'm fine.' He wasn't, but Skarfr and Hlif could do nothing but love him and wait.

When the Emir died, Sea-born was blank-eyed and said nothing.

Then he refused to go to the funeral.

'Why?' asked Hlif gently.

He stayed silent and would not meet her eyes.

Skarfr could not stand the impasse any longer. Love and patience had not been enough and he had to find a way to prise open this clam of a boy. In desperation he looked around the room for inspiration. The metal boss on his shield caught a ray of sunlight and winked at him.

He pondered this message, then fetched his shield and gave it to Sea-born, who looked at him, puzzled.

'This is my shield,' began Skarfr and was rewarded with the usual look of contempt a boy bestows on a patronising parent, 'and it protects me. Hold it up, as if I was attacking you. No, hold it with one hand — you would have a weapon in the other. Keep holding it until I say you may drop it.'

After endless moments, Hlif opened her mouth to protest but Skarfr shook his head. He watched his son, eyes shut and face screwed up, bravely holding the heavy shield until the tremor in his arm reached the shield. Before the boy reached breaking point, Skarfr said, 'You may drop the shield.'

Sea-born held it in place a defiant heartbeat longer, then lowered it to rest on the ground, his hand touching the rim. *And the rune for both their names*, noticed Skarfr. It was a sign that the gods were with him.

'When you hold a shield too long, it becomes heavy beyond bearing. Your mother and I are your shield-brothers and it is time you let us share the weight you carry. Whatever it is, we are on your side.'

The silence stretched out. Then Sea-born spoke in a small voice. 'I killed the Emir.'

Skarfr did not laugh, nor did Hlif. She said, 'This is a serious weight you carry. Share all of it, my son.'

'I didn't mind being treated badly but the Emir said terrible things about you, mocked you and said we were not—' he choked and couldn't continue.

'I know what he said. That we were not family,' said Skarfr. 'And everyone knows that is a lie.'

'Yes but I hated him so. I cursed him and prayed to God to kill him.'

Skarfr could see it all now. 'And when the Emir came back from Mdina in Melita he was ill. You thought God had answered your prayers. When the Emir was taken ill on the battlefield you took it badly because you thought you'd caused it.' Why hadn't he realised at the time? How blind he had been!

'I thought he was going to die there.' Sea-born's eyes were brimming. 'And that's when I knew I'd been wrong. I didn't want him to die and I prayed every night for him to live but it made no difference. He died anyway. And I killed him. God wouldn't let me take the words back.'

'Words have great power and such heavy words should not be spoken lightly,' said Hlif. 'I have killed a man with words.' She paused and Skarfr knew she was thinking of Maria, who turned light words into heavy actions. 'And I have learned to weigh words carefully. But you were not the cause of this man's death. The women of the Tiraz knew of his illness more than a year ago, when it was so bad for a month that he could not hide it from them. He seemed better for a while but that is the way of this sneaky malady. It comes back and kills. You had nothing to do with it. But,' she took his chin in her hand to make him meet her eyes. She didn't even have to tilt his face upwards as they were of a height now. 'You will not be so ready to wish a man dead from now on. You cannot change your mind about killing.'

'I misjudged him,' said Sea-born. 'I am glad that I am innocent of the deed if not of the thought.'

Maybe the monks' teaching *had* sunk in after all, thought Skarfr, his own heart lighter for clearing the air.

'You killed a man with words?' Sea-born was looking at Hlif with awe, which was probably not the result she'd intended.

Skarfr sighed and picked up his shield. 'Let's have no more talk today of killing. A warrior has died and deserves our respect. We are going to the funeral of a great man, the Emir of Sicilia, and we will tell stories of his courage, how he led his men even when this illness was eating him from inside.'

'Wash your face and change your tunic,' said Hlif, giving Sea-born a hug. He disappeared behind the curtain into his bedchamber and made splashing noises that were too enthusiastic to be authentic.

'What does George's death mean for the attack on Constantinople in the autumn.?' Hlif asked.

'Philip will be the new Emir,' Skarfr told her, 'and can lead an attack. But who the King wishes us to attack, if anybody, will depend on what the Pope, Germany, Venezia are up to, and gods know who else, as well as Byzantium. Politics!' He made a rude gesture, luckily before Sea-born emerged in his best tunic.

The Emir's death left its mark on King Roger, who turned to maps and charts as a different man, such as George himself, might have sought comfort from the church. Melancholy suffused the conversations on the wonders of science and the natural world, which had given all three men such pleasure. The king was listless, dutiful, and Skarfr soon understood that George's death changed everything.

However experienced and competent Philip of Mahdia might be, he was unproved as Emir, and he was no George. King Roger did not have the same confidence in him and there would be no attack on

Constantinople. The fleet would provide men as required for any defence of the border with Italia. *If* the King could rouse enough energy to order such a defence. King Guillaume merely continued in his usual pleasures, ignoring any crisis that did not slam him in the face.

September came and the atmosphere at court grew as heavy as Queen Sybille's belly, approaching term, and Skarfr could no longer deny that he felt the same sense of foreboding as Hlif.

'I will seek my release and ask a boon, that he sell me Rachel, for the service I have given,' he told Hlif, who had not asked aloud the question he answered. She was not one to nag or force a man to a conclusion he did not come to willingly. And for that too, he loved her. That, and the way she stood on tiptoe to reach his lips. There were so many things to love and he had not discovered them all yet. *May the Allfather give us many more years together.*

When he spoke to the King in the map-room where they had shared so much speculation on the nature of the universe, the response came as if from the bottom of a deep well of indifference. If Skarfr had not known this was the melancholia speaking, he would have been insulted.

'Yes, you may leave Sicilia. You have given good service and if this slave has taken your eye, you may have her as a gift. I will not take payment.'

Skarfr was offended at the very suggestion he might want any woman other than Hlif but such were the ways of Sicilia. 'Thank you, Sire,' he said, sketching a very passable Frankish bow.

'Al-Idrisi, do you have the necessary form I should sign? A transfer of ownership? To save me getting a clerk to write a new one.'

Al-Idrisi searched among some papers, pulled one out.

'And two forms to free a thrall — a slave,' Skarfr added. Brigid and Fergus would have their status made official. He'd had no idea that it mattered so much, when so little changed on the surface. Pearl and Onyx behaved as thralls more than did Rachel. Whatever Mikael might think.

'Two?' queried al-Idrisi, finding the necessary papers nevertheless.

King Roger frowned. 'If you *must* free her, make her earn it,' he advised. 'Or she will not be grateful to you and there will be no loyalty.'

Rachel will be grateful enough, to be spared the boorish demands of King Guillaume.

'I've changed my mind,' said the King, with almost a twinkle in his eye.

Skarfr held his breath.

'You *can* pay me. If you return to Orkneyjar as you plan, you will likely travel to the court at Constantinople. Belittle Komnenos. Let him know the court in Sicilia is more civilised than his.' The thought evidently pleased him.

'Consider it done.' Skarfr bowed again, wondering how he would avoid being executed in Constantinople, while insulting its Emperor. Truly, these people were too subtle for him and he would be glad to be among Orkneymen again.

Al-Idrisi was even less gracious in his parting words. 'You should stay,' he said, irritated. 'Until I finish the *Book of Roger* and the planisphere. We haven't finished the section on Ifriqiya. Even your wife was useful, for a woman, and could check some sections when I've finished.'

'Your remarkable work does not need this humble Northman,' Skarfr returned and the compliment worked long enough for him to take his leave, with genuine regret. He would never forget the great minds that had brushed against his in Sicilia.

On September 19th, all the bells in Palermo tolled and Sicilia went into mourning. Queen Sybille had died in childbirth. As had the baby.

Armed with all the correct paperwork, Skarfr waited while two Tiraz guards searched Rachel, Pearl, Onyx and Mikael, who insisted he was coming with them.

'I have the king's permission to visit my people's Holy City,' he'd said, 'and I will see you arrive safely in Acre.'

Amused at the thought of Mikael protecting him, Skarfr accepted the additional member of his party.

The guards were meticulous in examining the contents of the small kists those from the Tiraz were taking with them, and finally pronounced their owners innocent of any attempt to smuggle silk-making secrets out of the Tiraz. Rachel's needles and samples of embroidery gave the guards pause but she presented each of them with enough gold-stitched braiding to edge sleeves and hem on a tunic — or to sell — and they pronounced themselves satisfied.

Skarfr paid the extra to add one more passenger to the merchant ship on which he'd booked passage for five adults and a child. Hlif and Sea-born were already on board, with their own belongings and a cat. Skarfr thought it unlikely that Jarl Rognvald would welcome Hlif returning with five kists instead of one, or the cat, but he knew better than to say so.

The ship set sail for Crete, under heavy clouds but with a following wind and no rain. Skarfr watched Palermo's harbour growing smaller, until it disappeared from sight as the ship continued eastwards. Was it really only a year since Hlif and he had been married by Bishop William and exiled on those shores? Now he knew every cobble in Palermo and was carrying more knowledge gleaned from savants and scientists than would fit comfortably in his head.

As he stared over the steerboard wale, towards his past in Sicilia, the northern coast rolled past in a stately farewell of beaches, rugged rocks, and hilltop settlements, where houses were stacked on each other higgledy-piggledy. The ship was following the same route as Hlif had taken to Catania, skirting the Sicilian coast east and then south.

A pleasant day's sailing brought them to Messina, where the ship laid anchor for the night and those accustomed to sleeping on a rolling deck slept better than those discovering what sea-legs meant.

Dawn arrived through a grey filter. If anything the cloud cover was heavier but it was still dry and the Sicilian coast was all the reassurance the captain needed to set a course south.

Skarfr had not expected the leaving of Sicilia to be so long-drawn out but the course was the captain's business and he was in good company. Hlif retold the story of her previous voyage, of how she'd found Pearl and Onyx, while the girls' hands fluttered in their own account, sharing past horrors and present happiness, to judge by their faces.

While Mikael played softly on his lute, Rachel made word-pictures of the fabulous treasures of Jórsalaheim, sacred to their people as well as to the Christians. The red silk scarf wound around her lustrous black hair fluttered loose in the breeze and her eyes shone as she spoke of *Har haBáyit*, Temple Mount, and its holy history. She told them of underground marvels dating back to King David's time, water tunnels so big a man could walk them upright, and temple ruins that made the palatine chapel in Palermo seem primitive. And she would find her cousins in the Jewish Quarter. She planned to earn her keep with some sewing work, and live a simple life.

The lute conjured up the majesty of the Holy City and the warmth of family and a home, as the ship sailed towards Rachel's dreams. Skarfr put his arms around Hlif and Sea-born, feeling that he too was making the first leg of the voyage home.

'Catania.' Hlif pointed out the massive harbour and beyond it, across the Catanian plain, Skarfr saw the grey breath coming from the conical mouth of the monster which rumbled in its sleep beneath the island. The monster they called Mama Etna. Skarfr had heard so many stories about the mountain and the monster but what he saw was the dragon of Sicilia, a capricious and deadly overlord. With future-sight, Hlif had seen the dragon wake, breathe rivers of fire across the fertile plain and stone villages, claim its tithe of lives and land in return for the riches Sicilians took for granted.

Skarfr shivered and touched his amulet, then looked around furtively in case his gesture had been seen. *Pfff.* In leaving Sicilia, he could leave behind him words such as *heretic, pagan, heathen,* and above all *apostate*. How easy it would be in future to endure one of Bishop William's sermons, with no risk of a vile death for being the wrong kind of Christian. Or indeed not Christian at all. There was much to be said for Orkneyjar's more tolerant God. Long might it remain so.

Hlif was staring towards Catania, her gaze distant.

'What are you thinking of?' he asked her.

'Pistachios,' she said. 'All that we are leaving behind.'

'Regrets?' he queried.

'No. Just memories and threads dropped from the loom.' She turned to Rachel, who was also looking towards the coast. 'And we sail to a bright future, where Rachel will be free.'

Rachel flushed and excused herself, going down the steps to the main deck, as if to use the bucket behind a blanket down below. However, she could be seen leaning over the landward wale, her back hunched.

'Perhaps she feels sick,' said Hlif. 'I'll go to her.'

Skarfr watched the women. Hlif put her arm around Rachel, spoke to her. Rachel turned to Hlif, must have replied. Then Hlif recoiled, grabbed Rachel's hand in a less friendly manner and towed her back up the steps to Skarfr.

'Tell him!' she said. Two red spots in her cheeks showed how angry she was.

Eyes large as a doomed rabbit's, Rachel said, 'I paid the guards to delay but now they will have told King Guillaume I have gone. It is their duty. And he has sent his ship after us.' She cast her eyes down at the deck. 'He has threatened all the workers. If one of us takes the secrets of silk making out of the Tiraz she will be dragged back and her tongue cut out. But he has become…' she searched for a word, '… possessive about me. And brutal.'

Skarfr's thoughts buzzed. 'But we have King Roger's permission. You were mine to claim and now you are free.'

Rachel shook her head. 'King Guillaume is not King Roger. There will be a ship after us. Believe me, his ship is on its way. He will stop at nothing to get me back.'

Hlif battered Rachel with reproaches. 'Why didn't you say all this beforehand! We could have left Sea-born in Palermo in safety, we could have used a decoy person or a decoy boat. Now we can do nothing!'

'You would have left me behind,' said Rachel, 'and you said Skarfr was unmatched as a warrior and a navigator.'

Hlif retorted, 'Not even Skarfr can outrun a warship in this cumbersome collection of planks!'

Mikael was looking at Skarfr with 'I told you so' in his eyes. And pity. Because they both knew Hlif was right. When King Guillaume's warship caught up with the merchantman, Rachel's escape bid was over. And if they didn't die in the confrontation, the King would show no mercy afterwards.

CHAPTER FORTY-SEVEN

SKARFR, THE WHALE ROAD

Óðinn said:
"How will there still be a sun
when the wolf has eaten the one
that now flies in heaven?"

Riddle-weaver said:
"The sun
will have a daughter
before Fenrir eats her.
And that young sun
will travel on her mother's path
when all the gods have died."

The Poetic Edda

Skarfr made his way aft to talk to the captain, instinctively reading the weather and the wind. The sky grew ever more leaden, cloud piled on cloud with no trace of sunlight, but still dry. The wind was now gusting south-easterly, frustrating their progress as they sailed south along the Sicilian coast. Too far south, Skarfr realised. Hlif had recognised Taormina and their course should have been south-eastwards long before that. The ship was a sitting duck for King Guillaume's warship.

The captain's words confirmed his fears. 'Lord Skarfr, we might take longer over the journey and need an overnight stop, at port or at anchor. We can't head eastwards against this wind so we'll sail further south and hope it changes. I don't like these clouds, either. Without the sun, we could get lost in the open sea between us and Iraklion. We can't lose sight of the coast without some waymark.'

Knowing that a warship was after them changed all their options but Skarfr had no intention of testing where the captain's loyalties lay by telling him.

'I can save time,' he said. 'Northmen sail in open sea all the time.' He hoped the captain had not seen Hlif's amusement at his exaggeration. 'Let me navigate.'

'Saving time' won favour with the captain and two gold pieces convinced him that Skarfr was as good a navigator as he claimed, although he blenched and muttered to himself when Skarfr set a south-easterly course against the wind, leaving the safety of the coast behind. This was not a dragon ship running before the wind so Skarfr used the advantage of the lateen sails and sailed as close to the wind as he could. Little by little, tacking in a great zigzag, he took the ship further east and south, taking his direction from the wind tell on the nearer mast, which streamed out towards the steerboard side of the stern. Turning a big ship like this through the wind was too dangerous but he made gradual adjustments, being careful not to let the sails luff. The crew were well-trained and at the first sight of a flap in the sail, sheets were tightened and the rudders turned enough to avoid hitting the wind head-on.

And then the ribbon on the mast fell, limp. No wind, no shore in sight, only clouds ahead. Becalmed and lost.

'I think the shore's that way — we have to go back to Sicilia! Man the oars!' The captain's voice rose in panic as the merchantman wallowed, turning. The oarsmen took their places, stabilised the ship with a slow rhythm. But in which direction, the gods alone knew. The going was so slow as to be hardly perceptible.

Skarfr ignored the captain, thought for a minute. He heard an encouraging *Waark* from a black bird hidden by cloud and he knew what he had to do. A Sicilian warship would never take such a risk and they would be free and clear. If he was successful.

He swept his hair out of his eyes. A breeze had started up again and the wind tell streamed again but where was it from? The Middle Sea was known for fickle winds that could change ten times in as many moments, and the dancing ribbon on the mast teased his navigation skills. The currents were as unreliable as the wind. So that left one constant—

'I can find the sun,' he told the captain, 'with this tool.' He held up the pouch around his neck. 'Hold a course that keeps the ship steady, long enough for me to find which way is east.'

Then he spoke to the steersmen 'How long do you reckon it is since we left Messina? About three hours?'

They concurred.

Skarfr visualised the sun chariot's race across the sky, as he'd last seen it in Palermo. It was late afternoon. 'Then the sun would be in the south-west now?'

'Yes.'

Skarfr extracted the sunstone from the pouch, prayed, *Mighty Thórr, now glorious Sol is veiled, may the wily wolf Sköll catch her chariot, to show an unworthy pilot which course to steer. Let Skarfr the Navigator see the wolf chase Sol.*

Then he held the instrument up towards the clouds, turning it until the two black spots were one. The wolf-hunting Sister Sun had caught its prey.

'There!' he said. 'The sun is there, above the clouds!'

Eyes gleaming, the captain said, 'Then that's south.'

As one, he and Skarfr looked at the wind tell and announced in triumphant unison, 'The wind's north-westerly!'

'That'll be the Mistral getting up,' said a steersman. 'If it stays gentle like that, we'll reach Crete easily enough.'

The captain needed no further instruction to set a course east for Iraklion. Order was re-established, the crew took their watches and trusted to Skarfr's readings with the sunstone to confirm that the wind remained favourable and that they were heading in the right direction. The inscrutable rise and fall of the sea, in every direction, told them nothing. A man could easily imagine himself sailing in circles until the flesh dropped from his bones and only skeletons manned a ghost ship, a warning to all sailors.

They would have to sail through the night and another day to reach Iraklion and even Skarfr was on edge as the sky grew darker. Not storm clouds but twilight. Could the sunstone find Brother Moon? He hoped he wouldn't have to put it to the test.

The wind dropped as night fell but there was still enough breeze to keep them moving. For want of other guide, Skarfr assumed the wind was still in the same direction. Even when oil lamps were lit, the wind tell was invisible from the steerboard so messages were passed along the ship to verify orientation.

The sky grew so dark, Skarfr did not notice that the clouds had lifted until sparkling dots appeared, growing ever brighter.

'Stars.' The pilot's teeth gleamed yellow in the lamplight. Any pilot worth his salt could steer by the stars and Skarfr felt his burden lift.

The captain clapped him on the back. 'Sleep. You've earned it. Pilot and I will take alternate watches until morning then you can take over. I'm betting it will be fine tomorrow.'

It *was* fine.

As a trading ship, the merchantman was welcome in Byzantine Iraklion, where they anchored overnight. The next morning they sped on their way.

By the time they arrived at St Jean d'Acre and stepped onto the soil of the Holy Land for the first time, Skarfr and Mikael had exhausted their musical repertoire and Rachel was composing new lyrics for them, based, so she said, on traditional Arabic poetry. Very lewd poetry, in Skarfr's view, but as Hlif showed no sign of fainting from offended modesty, he joined in with enthusiasm.

Boosting the crew's morale, he told himself.

Fifteen dragon ships were not difficult to spot in the harbour at St Jean d'Acre. Hlif and Skarfr left their entourage on the quayside and boarded Rognvald's *Sun-chaser*. The nickname given to Rognvald's ship in the fog had stuck. Like the gods, a ship could have many names during a voyage, different avatars from the many stories they'd lived.

As expected, only a few men had been left to guard the ships, while the majority of the company completed the pilgrimage to Jórsalaheim. Skarfr and Hlif were greeting with raillery and questions, as prodigal shipmates. Who was in favour and who was out mattered little to men who remembered Hlif's efficient provision of victuals, and Skarfr's skills in battle and skaldcraft.

Rognvald's party had been delayed by shipworm damage. Skarfr could imagine how pleased the Jarl must have been at discovering that these voracious sea-creatures had been eating their way through some planks. Their bodies were worm-like but their heads were like tiny clam shells and there was no sign of the attack until holes appeared inside the ship — or the pier.

While repairing and tarring the ships affected, the party had spent months laying to off the coast of Crete, where the Orkneymen were well enough received to linger until spring. Then they had sailed to Acre without mishap. When the first pilgrims returned from the Holy City, those sailors who'd drawn the short straws and stayed with the ships, would have their chance. Then the ships would be cleaned and re-proofed to Rognvald's satisfaction before starting the long homeward journey when the weather was calm enough.

'We'll be heading for Mikligard first,' said Crick-neck, who had gained his nickname from a wound while laying siege to a castle, when Skarfr was still with Rognvald's party.

Hlif and Skarfr exchanged glances. 'I've been hoping to see Mikligard.' Skarfr's tone was mild, revealing none of his ambitions to captain a Sicilian warship.

'You could bide here till they come back. And Hlif — sorry, *Lady*

Hlif — could take over the provisions for the ships,' suggested Crickneck, with hope in his voice.'

'Just Hlif will do fine,' she said, smiling. 'But no, we've time to catch up with the Jarl and Skarfr has a yen to see the place we've come so far to reach.'

'Aye, he'll want his pilgrim's palm badge to pretty up that leather,' joked Bandy-legs.

'Just so,' agreed Skarfr.

'But we can't take One-eye.' Hlif unwound the cat from her neck and he stalked along the deck, urinated against a thwart and then pounced on an imaginary rodent, just for practice.

'No,' said Bandy-legs.

'Yes,' said Hlif calmly. 'He stays on the ship and you give him some water and scraps of fish every day. Apart from that, he can look after himself. And, if any harm comes to him, I hold you personally responsible and Skarfr will render you suitable for a guard's duties in the Sicilian Tiraz!'

Bandy-legs looked pained and said to Skarfr, 'Does she talk like this all the time now?'

'Yes,' said Skarfr. 'And what she means is that, if the cat is missing so much as one whisker when we return, I'll chop off your manhood and you'll piss through a straw.'

Bandy-legs winced. 'You wouldn't.'

Straight-faced, Skarfr said, 'There is no limit to what I would do for One-eye's sake.'

He received such an approving look from Hlif, he almost felt guilty.

Defeated, Bandy-legs said with resignation, 'Water and scraps it is, then.' He added, 'Watch out for Eindridi. He's a mean bastard and even if Rognvald forgives you, Eindridi won't.'

Skarfr shrugged. 'Eindridi hates anyone stronger than he is.' But he had not forgotten the Norðvegr captain who sailed with Rognvald and thought himself better than the Jarl. Better than everyone, not just because he'd been to Jórsalaheim before.

Mean bastard, indeed. Eindridi had killed a pilot to get the sunstone which was in Skarfr's pouch and was unlikely to forgive Skarfr for having survived a botched attempt to murder him too. Nor would Skarfr forgive Eindridi.

As if his thoughts had been turned into actions, a high-pitched scream on shore made Skarfr whip round and leap from the ship onto the quayside. Hlif too had recognised their son's cry and was only a few steps behind him.

Heart thumping, axe in hand, Skarfr had difficulty interpreting the scene in front of him. At first he didn't see Sea-born, but then he realised that Pearl and Onyx had wrapped themselves around the boy, hiding his eyes so he could no longer see the person fallen to the ground.

Mikael stood like an avenging angel with a bloody dagger in his hand. Had he intervened?

'Are you hurt?' Skarfr called to him, still not understanding.

Hlif put an arm on his. 'Rachel,' she said, rushing to the huddle of clothes on the ground and turning the body. Skarfr saw the ripped fabric, the blood, looked at the knife in Mikael's hand again. Realisation dawned.

'Don't come closer,' said Mikael, his voice breaking. 'I *warned* you.' He was backing away from the group and the gawking spectators stayed out of the circle he made, swinging his knife, switching it from hand to hand.

'She's dead,' Hlif pronounced, gently closing Rachel's eyes, and unwinding the red silk scarf from the long black hair, to cover the still face. Then she joined Skarfr again, laying a hand on his axe arm. He jerked as if waking from sleep but it was into nightmare not from one.

'Why?' he asked, taking a pace forward towards Mikael, his axe readied.

Mikael kept moving backwards with small steps, agile as an acrobat, knife swinging.

Behind Skarfr, crew members from his ship had come ashore to ascertain what had caused the commotion, to see if he needed help.

One word, one gesture from Skarfr and they would bring Michel to justice. Alive.

Did Skarfr want Mikael left alive? The dragon roared for blood to pay for that spilt. But a guimbarde played in his mind and so he listened, held back the judgement that must come.

'For you, Skarfr,' Mikael said, lingering tenderly over the name. 'I report to the King and hide what I can, to keep the women safe. You made no secret of leaving, or about buying Rachel. King Guillaume told her what would happen if she left. He wanted you killed too. I made a bargain. If his ship didn't catch up, her life for yours. You are free,' he said, his eyes filling. 'And so is she.' He looked down at Rachel.

Skarfr took another pace forwards, the axe still readied. 'You could have gone to King Roger. He sold Rachel to me, gave his permission for her to leave.' He could have thrown the axe to end the murderer's words. But Hlif's hand cautioned patience and still he listened.

'Don't you see, Skarfr? It's King Roger I report to, made the bargain with. He knew what his son would do. He would never have let a silk worker leave in case others followed, all of them carrying the royal secrets of silk. Not in any chest they carry but in their skills and knowledge.'

King Roger. To whom Skarfr had shown only loyalty. Wily King Roger, who had thought to rely on his predictable son and keep his hands clean. As he relied on Maria and the brothers to ensure compliance from his citizens. Skarfr felt sullied by association.

'Will you kill me, Skarfr?' asked Mikael, tears flowing freely now. 'If you don't, I must go back. I will find a ship. Don't return to Sicilia. Remember me as Guimbarde.'

'Why go back?' Skarfr asked, as if there could be sense to any of this.

'For the women,' said Mikael. He smiled weakly. 'Don't you see? The King will punish them if I'm alive and don't return. I too know the secrets of the Tiraz.'

'Don't,' said Hlif, holding onto his axe-arm with all her might. 'Let him go. He spoke true.' Was that compassion in her voice? 'We do not want kings for enemies or a blood feud that tracks us wherever we go. It was all my fault. I should have seen the consequences. I thought it would be as for Inge, that we would help this poor woman.'

As Skarfr hesitated and Mikael stood, watching him, wings beat overhead and like one of Thórr's bolts, a cormorant dived at Skarfr, stirring his hair as it flapped just above him, echoing Hlif, '*Craaaaark*. No!' Then, beating heavy wings, she — for surely it was Skarfr's cormorant — flew over people's heads, clumsy until she dropped into the sea in a graceful arc.

Skarfr let his axe drop to his side, defeated. 'Maybe Mikael was right. She'd have been safe in the Tiraz.'

Mikael whirled around, scattering the people nearest him, and fled.

'No!' Hlif was fierce although her eyes were red and her face shone with tears. 'She chose this risk rather than that life without honour. A woman has the right to *kill* a man who forces her and all she did was try to escape.'

An unwanted memory of Thorbjorn forcing Inge and assaulting Hlif came to Skarfr.

But some men believed such behaviour was the right of a husband, or of a thrall-owner, and the law agreed with them. Did King Guillaume even know his attentions were abhorred? Weren't the Tiraz women skilled in making a man believe he was the best of lovers?

What a tangle of contradictions. Skarfr would never understand a woman's concept of honour but he would give his life to protect Hlif. That was simple enough.

And now Rachel was dead. That too was written in stone and must be accepted.

'She wanted to be with her own people,' Hlif said. 'We will send to the synagogue and she shall have her wish in death, if not in life. And she will wear the finest silk, embroidered with tiraz.'

CHAPTER FORTY-EIGHT

THORBJORN, NESS

Thorbjorn's stay with Harald in Wick had been hard work but constructive. It was even possible that Harald's political nous had progressed from non-existent to embryonic. He could no longer be considered the young jarl now Erlend was the even younger jarl, so it was about time he showed some maturity. And nothing hastened maturity more effectively than unexpected defeat, even if Thorbjorn had to take the blame for it being unexpected. The accusations were lengthy.

'It was *your* idea to postpone war by telling Erlend to get the support of the King of Norðvegr. You said if he did get it, then it would be for Rognvald's share of the islands, not for mine!

'*You* said Erlend was so weak, as a leader and in supporters, that either of us could defeat him personally, and that, with our allies, we could defeat any army he gathered.

'*You* said Sweyn would never side with Erlend because of the blood feuds between them.

'Now Sweyn supports Erlend, and they've stolen my jarldom and I'm stuck in this godforsaken hole. It's all right for the hunting season but there's nothing to do here the rest of the time! Nothing! *And* Gunnr's is back on Gareksey fornicating with my mother. It's disgusting at her age. If I can't exile criminals then I'm not really a jarl at all. It's humiliating.'

And if you hadn't exiled Gunnr for a crime that exists only in your head, Sweyn wouldn't have supported Erlend, we would have been the stronger force and you would still be Jarl of Orkneyjar.

Swallowing the words that could not be spoken, Thorbjorn admitted, 'There were mistakes.' *I didn't take your stupidity into account and I should have.* 'But what's done is done and the only question is, what do we do now? I have some ideas…'

His suggestions brightened Harald's eyes, as the prospect of action always did, and soon they were drinking toasts to the future.

Thorbjorn didn't have long to spend on his own estate, when the jarldom itself was in jeopardy, but he would have time for a duty visit to his mother, who surely couldn't last much longer, and he could decide what to do with the thrall. His revenge against Skarfr lacked savour, with the other man in ignorance and away for years. What satisfaction there had been in burning the house, in stealing an old thrall, had long gone.

With so much of more importance to think about, he was tempted to comply with the Thing's decision, to let Finn have her. That would save him trouble and lull his enemies into a false sense of security. For he had no doubt that Finn was his enemy, harried by the harpy he'd married — that they'd both married. Thorbjorn had no doubt that Inge was behind the lawsuit and he would pay her back when the time was right. But for now, he was busy.

And, although he'd lost the legal case, he had not come out badly from his public appearance. More than one bondsman had congratulated him on his bearing, on being such a gracious and generous loser. The more he thought about it, the more he thought he had used the hearing to his advantage. That didn't mean he would forgive Finn and Inge, but thralls were irrelevant.

He was in good humour, joking with his men, when he beached the ship and left some of the crew on guard. He took the rest with him on the march inland to his estate. He felt so benevolent that he stopped to listen when a fisherman and his wife ran into his path in the village, asked him for justice. He smiled, thinking that carrying out justice was now one of his reputed virtues.

'What is your grievance, good man?' he asked.

'Our baby has been stolen, whisked away from her cot while my wife sorted the morning's catch.'

The woman's face was tear-stained and ugly, and she smelled of gutted fish, even if she had removed her working apron. Thorbjorn stepped back as she took over the story from her husband, with far less coherence. 'Little Farsight, sleeping she was, and she always sleeps long enough for a full catch. Scales and guts, heads and tails, see.'

'You didn't have farsight?' prompted Thorbjorn, already regretting his kindness.

'That's her name. Farsight. I didn't name—' The woman flushed and rambled on, until she said something that caught Thorbjorn's full attention. 'She was hanging around and I didn't think nothing of it, she helps with babies you know, she helped with my baby, but I know she took Farsight. That Ellisif who works for you. I knew she couldn't be trusted. She as good as said that one day—' Once more she cut herself off and glanced at her husband.

A stolen baby. Ellisif, his housekeeper. A woman he trusted. Ellisif, who helped deliver babies, who'd shown him a dead baby. Said the thrall's baby had died. Now a baby was stolen.

'How old is Farsight? he asked. What sort of name was that for a child? Not Christian and not Northman either.

'Two month short of a year,' said the man. 'Ada, my wife, was took poorly and thought she might lose the babe so she was took in a cart to this Ellisif, on your estate.'

'Two month short of a year,' repeated Thorbjorn, thoughtfully. 'Be assured, good people, I will look into this and try to find your child. If anyone is guilty of misdeed they will be punished.'

'Thank you, Sire. Thank you.'

Thorbjorn's good mood had vanished. If the thrall was still there and there was no sign of a baby, then there might be some other explanation. If the thrall and baby were there together, or if the thrall had gone, and a baby with her, Ellisif was guilty.

CHAPTER FORTY-NINE

THORBJORN, NESS

The effect of Thorbjorn's arrival on his labourers was pleasing. They stopped work in mid-task as if a paralysing wind had swept through the settlement. Then they laid down tools and came to the yard in front of his house to greet him and ask what instructions he had for them. The women servants also materialised. Like beetles fleeing smoke they came out of their cottages and out of his house, shaking down their work aprons and patting their hair into place.

The man Thorbjorn had sent ahead from Wick, to make sure all was prepared for him, stood before him, looking wary. 'My Lord,' he said, then swallowed hard and confessed, 'Lord Finn came with his warband and took the thrall...' Courage failed him and he stuttered, 'You know, the thrall that... the Thing... the one...'

'I know which one!' snapped Thorbjorn. Why was he always surrounded by idiots?

The man flinched and then looked puzzled. Presumably, he'd expected to be hit and God knows he deserved to be but Thorbjorn was playing a longer game.

He scanned the buildings. They all appeared to be undamaged. Maybe there had just been looting. 'What else did they take? What did they destroy?'

'Nothing, my Lord. They marched in, waited until the woman was found.' Here, the man looked a little evasive. No doubt there was a longer story demonstrating his shortcomings but Thorbjorn was no longer interested.

'And they left,' the man finished lamely.

'How noble of Lord Finn.' *What a weakling.* In Finn's shoes, Thorbjorn would have expressed his feelings in fire and pillage. He smiled at the man, who stepped back. What *was* the matter with the fool?

'Lord Finn had every right to reclaim his property and I am very disappointed that he and his men were not offered hospitality.' More than a few faces expressed confusion but he ignored them and looked at the women who'd come out of his house.

The thrall had gone. If he asked, he'd be told a child had gone with her. He didn't need to ask. He *knew*.

Yes, there she was. *Ellisif.* Coming towards him as she always did when he came home, a fake welcome pasted on her plain face and treachery in her every act. The same duplicitous pretence as the previous autumn, when he'd come home to find that an Irish male thrall had come calling. 'Chased onto the bog,' Ellisif had said, 'That'll be the end of him,' she'd said.

Liar. The thrall hadn't gone onto the bog at all because Finn said that he was alive.

'It's good to see you home, my Lord,' the liar said. 'Your mother is nearing death but she can still speak. You have time yet to hear her last words.'

'Have you killed her too?' asked Thorbjorn and silence fell among his people.

Ellisif went white but stood her ground better than his man had. 'I don't know what you mean, my Lord. She is very old and has had a long illness. We've tended her well.' As if to spite him, knowing he'd hate such a detail, she added, 'We've emptied her soil bucket and cleaned her body of all the leaking fluids, three times a day, for weeks.'

Disgusting. He spoke for all to hear. 'I have submitted willingly to the justice of the Thing. Justice must always be served. Here, I represent justice for this community and however unpleasant my duty, I will perform it.'

The silence became oppressive. Ellisif stood stone-still. She didn't even lower her eyes respectfully. She knew what was coming. Or she thought she did.

'A fisherman and his wife in the village brought me their grievance, accused this housewife of a terrible crime.' He looked around at his audience. 'You thought she was a healer and a midwife and so you trusted her. I trusted her.' Never again. Never would he trust a woman, not even a plain, ageing spinster.

He addressed Ellisif directly. 'As God is your witness, answer these questions truly and make no attempt to pervert justice with excuses.'

She could not control the fear that suddenly shadowed her eyes. 'As God is my witness, I shall answer with the truth,' she replied, a tremor in her voice.

'Did you take a child from the fisherman and his wife?'

'I did.'

'Did you bury their dead baby?'

Ellisif paused, then whispered, 'I did.'

The crowd erupted, hurling insults and even sods of earth, although that stopped before it could become popular as the missile-throwers realised how close to Thorbjorn their target was standing.

He raised a hand, called for quiet. 'She is condemned by her own words. This woman killed a baby.'

Ellisif's attempt to speak was silenced by a blow.

'You've said enough. Justice must be done for this terrible crime. I sentence this woman to death.' Support for his verdict was enthusiastic. Once again he held up a hand for quiet, which came quickly. People were always avid for the details of how a death sentence would be enacted. Even, perhaps, Ellisif herself.

'You will run onto the bogland,' he told her, 'where none can survive. As you were a competent housekeeper for many years, I give you this mercy.' His new reputation as a man who upheld the law would benefit from reports of mercy, even if there was mild disappointment from his household. 'You have a head start and then I will set the dogs on you. They have never failed me in a hunt. Your death will be quicker than you deserve.'

He lunged at her, ripped a piece of cloth from her sleeve and shouted, 'Start running!'

Ellisif picked up her skirts and fled, flanked by Thorbjorn's men-at-arms, in case she ran in any other direction than the heath. One of the other women, the mad one, ran part of the way with her, singing and twirling two bits of rope she'd picked up from the pile for mending. She put them in the panier she always carried and gave this to the fugitive. As if a basket would be any use to Ellisif where she was going.

Thorbjorn watched her run out of sight. His men would make sure she headed onto the bogland and kept going. He whistled for his hounds, who came eagerly, always keen to go hunting. Too keen sometimes. He didn't want the work of getting them all back from the moors so he kept two with him and had the rest chained up.

The two young boarhounds he'd chosen were tenacious and deadly. Once they'd sunk their teeth in their prey, they would die rather than desist. Harald had offered to buy them more than once, increasing his bid each time. Maybe Thorbjorn would concede when he took them back to Wick with him. After they'd carried out justice for him. And after he'd spoken to his mother.

With one hand, he held them by their collars, increasing their frenzy by restraining them, by urging them, 'Seek and attack!' He waved the cloth fragment, with Ellisif's scent on it, in front of their noses.

'Seek and attack!' he shouted again, and unleashed them. Like avenging Valkyries, they flew in the direction of the excitement, of people running, and of their prey.

Thorbjorn went into the house to watch his mother die.

The stench was near unbearable but he took the stool beside the bed. Death would be a blessing. *May mine be long before I am a bedbound bag of stinking bones*, he prayed. But a man had a duty. This too would be good for his reputation.

'Mother?' he said quietly and the crabbed hand lifted slightly on the blanket, then fell again. 'I am here.' He took the hand in his own, let them rest entwined, guessing this was what people called comfort to the dying. He wouldn't know. He'd watched many die, usually at his hand, but never before of old age.

'Thorbjorn, son.' The voice seemed to come from beyond the grave, a wind whispering through autumn leaves. 'Something to tell you.'

Ah, the famous last words, which would inspire him and give him a mission. *Let's get it over with.*

'What is it, mother?' he asked gently.

'Erlend...' she began.

He waited.

With an effort, her breath rattling between words, she said, 'They say he's jarl now. Promise me you'll treat him well. His life has been hard. He's your cousin, you know. And he's a good boy.'

Thorbjorn squeezed her hand and hoped it hurt. She was too far gone and he couldn't tell. But promises made to the dying were heard by the gods so you had to be careful. As careful with words as Loki himself. 'I promise you that I will make sure Erlend is treated as he deserves,' he said.

As if she'd stayed alive only to see him, to deliver her pathetic message, she said nothing more. He sat with her in silence, listening to the rattling breath as it grew fainter, had more hitches in rhythm. A man could think of many things while at his dying mother's bedside. He was *not* a good boy but he was there.

When her mouth fell open, he knew it was over. He watched carefully but he did not see her Christian soul leaving her *hamr*, the form she had taken in this world. And if her departing luck, her *hamingja*, passed to a descendant, he was happy for good cousin Erlend to receive the tainted gift, or some girl relative. His mother's luck was not a legacy he wanted. He shook off her limp hand, wiped his own on his breeches. Duty done. She could rest in peace and he would keep his promise. Erlend would indeed get his just desserts.

He and Harold intended to kill the upstart at Christmas, when Sweyn would be otherwise occupied and nobody would expect ships to sail the rough winter seas from Ness to Orkneyjar. At Christmas, everyone would be celebrating Yule in the season of peace and goodwill. The plan was perfect. One jarl killing another would not even attract a charge of murder once the deed was done. Who would want to offend the living Jarl for the sake of a dead one? Not even Sweyn.

Thorbjorn called for the housekeeper, then remembered he didn't have one. He'd have to replace her. Some other woman came and started wailing. He left the corpse for her to deal with and went outside.

His dogs should have returned by now but there was no sign of them. His men told Thorbjorn Ellisif had disappeared into the mist, then they'd heard the baying of the hounds as they caught up with their prey. Then silence, as was natural. The dogs would have made short work of the woman, who had neither tusks nor other weapons.

But what if they'd been too stupid to negotiate the sinking mud of the bogland? Chased some game bird and lost their way? He regretted his choice of punishment for Ellisif, which now seemed unsatisfying and might have cost him two expensive hounds. But then again, if the dogs were that stupid, he didn't want them. They too were replaceable.

As soon as a hasty funeral in the Christian style was over, Thorbjorn sailed back to Wick, to join Harald. His dogs had not returned, which was annoying, but Harald's fewterer knew of an interesting litter, six months old and each already showing a a good nose and a grip like an iron trap.

It never crossed Thorbjorn's mind that his hounds would greet the hand that fed them with wagging tails or that the hand in question was Ellisif's. Whether they even considered him to *be* their master was a moot point as the hunting season was short and when Thorbjorn was away in Orkneyjar, the housekeeper was the most important human.

When she heard them baying with the excitement of closing in on her, Ellisif turned to face them and stood still, so there was no risk of them mistaking her for prey on the run. They barrelled into her, almost knocking her over in their joy at finding her. She recognised them straightaway.

'Lap-it-up and Pat-a-paw!' When they heard the pet names she'd given them, the dogs wagged their tails so hard, their entire hindquarters shook. Ellisif stroked their long ears and told them what good dogs they were, gave them the expected titbits — dried fish from the provisions in the panier. There was something else in the panier and she drew out the two lengths of rope.

Clever, clever Wulfhild.

Ellisif made running nooses and slipped a rope around each of her self-appointed guardians. Keen to explore this unknown terrain, the hounds happily continued with her, noses to the ground. With the sure instinct of animals, they picked their way across the bog to the bothy faster than she could have done alone.

That was where Wulfhild found her later and after sharing the rations Brigid had left, along with those in the panier, the two friends nestled together on the narrow bed, while the hounds snored on the floor beside them.

'What if he takes it out on the others?' murmured Wulfhild. Somehow, this place demanded that voices be hushed.

'I have tried for so long.' Ellisif's voice broke. 'But there comes a time when saving yourself from such a man is the most you can do.'

'And saving me,' whispered Wulfhild, snuggling into her friend, savouring their first night of freedom.

The next day, four runaways set out for the haven offered to them in Lambaburg.

CHAPTER FIFTY

SKARFR, JÓRSALAHEIM

They named her Heith
when she came into their homes,
a sorceress who foresaw good things.
She knew magic,
she knew witchcraft,
she practised witchcraft.
She was the pride
of an evil family.

The Poetic Edda

The journey to Jórsalaheim was sombre. Skarfr and Hlif were full of self-recriminations, speaking only for practical needs or for Sea-born, who had shown no sign of perturbation since the scream that still vibrated in Skarfr's innards. It was Sea-born's equanimity that worried his parents, reminded them that their son thought nothing of a woman's death. Perhaps because this death lay on his parents' consciences, not on his. Perhaps because of his past, about which they knew nothing.

Finding hundreds of Orkneymen in Jórsalaheim was easy enough, despite the crowds of visitors and residents.

Finding what to say, after a year's exile, was not so easy. Even after Skarfr knew where Jarl Rognvald was lodging, in the guest quarters of the hospital run by the Knights Templar, he walked past the forbidding stone building and put off the meeting until the next day. He found accommodation for his family near the hospital at a price Hlif reduced to a third of what he was asked. The Holy City was adept at profiting from pilgrims but Hlif had honed her own skills to the sharpness of Palermo's international trade and was more than a match for the souvenir peddlers.

There was so much to see and do. Streets filled with relic-sellers and food vendors, essential sites and shrines a pilgrim had to visit so, the next day, Skarfr postponed meeting Rognvald until the day after. This was the Holy City after all and they should visit the Basilica of the Holy Sepulchre and pray to the saints. When they had begun this journey, nearly two years ago, they had hoped to lift the curse on Hlif so Rognvald would bless their marriage. It made sense to pray to the saints before meeting with Rognvald.

The day after that, Skarfr opened his mouth to speak and was cut off.

'I did not tell you all,' Hlif said, her eyes cloudy, 'of my journey into darkness against Maria. I have no words for the mysteries of Óðinn and Freyja that only a völva knows but I came back changed. You know this.'

She looked at him intently, read acknowledgement in his eyes and continued. 'You were afraid for me, wanted me to hide what I am, even from myself. I don't blame you for that. But I do not hide. Nor do I run.'

Rachel ran, he thought.

'I have grown into what I am, what I have always been, and I accept it. I am a völva.'

She was not wearing seaweed, shells or feathers, and her cat was annoying Orkneymen on a dragon ship in Acre, but she exuded that same power and presence he had felt when he saw her body lying on the bed while she dream-walked.

Then she smiled at him and was his Hlif again. He suddenly

realised that she was dressed in Orkneyjar fashion again, although with Sicilian decorative touches. The straps of her dark blue wool gown were pinned with matching brooches, amber ovals set in engraved silver. Strung between them was a row of perfect amber beads from the Catanian plain, polished and set by a Sicilian gemsmith. The gleaming jewels reflected sunlight onto the hair peeping out from a cream coif which matched her linen undergown.

He scanned her from head to foot, trying to see her as she would appear to someone who had not seen her for a year, someone who had never truly seen her. His gaze lingered on the woven band, tiraz embroidery, slung low across her hips, matching the band above her hem. Shot with gold and patterned in roundels. Rachel's work.

He should have known from her clothes that his procrastination was over but there was no doubt possible, and his fate was sealed, when he noticed her footwear. Below the richly embroidered hem of her gown, her scuffed Orkneyjar leather boots were a reminder of the housekeeper and trader who'd travelled across half the world with fifteen Viking ships. He remembered the barefoot girl on a beach and thanked the gods who brought them together.

She took his hand. 'I need no blessing from saints or even from an Orkneyjar jarl to be Hlif, the völva, and to be your wife. Today we will speak to Jarl Rognvald, offer to renew our allegiance to him as a gift, not as a plea. He would be a fool to turn away such a gift.'

The words of Ibn Hamdis, the exiled Sicilian, ran through Skarfr's mind. *Chain yourself to the beloved homeland.* Orkneyjar was his homeland however far away he might roam.

Skarfr squeezed her hand. 'He is not a fool.'

And so, after a year in exile, Skarfr put on his best silk shirt and walked with Hlif along the cobbled streets of Jórsalaheim to kneel before Jarl Rognvald and offer homage once more.

EPILOGUE

AL-IDRISI, PALERMO, SICILIA

Al-Idrisi ripped up four pages of the *Book of Roger* and threw the pieces into the crucible in which he made medicaments. Then he set fire to them. He'd become attached to the Northman despite Skarfr's untrained mind and pagan beliefs. His way of seeing the world had been refreshing. Even the woman had brought new details for the book, mixed in with the usual female trivia and embroidery of facts. In truth, he would miss her warmth, her vivacity.

But they had not stayed to see the completion of his great work. In three or four years, the book and the planisphere would be complete. There was nothing like either in the world and never had been. A wonder. And yet they had not cared enough for such work to stay.

He had been foolish to grant them the privileges of discourse, to let them contribute in any significant way to his book. Truly, their home country lacked any importance.

He began writing a new version of the section he'd burned, which had been full of wide skies and oat fields, ancient stones held to be sacred, sea-harvests and dragon ships. After more time gazing into the distance than writing, he read back the two paragraphs he'd written in *The Seventh Clime, Section Two, England.*

Skotland stretches to the north of the great island. There is nothing of value there, no towns or villages. It is one hundred and fifty miles long.

Between the northern tip of Skotland, which is a deserted island, and the tip of the island of Írland, takes two days sailing towards the west.

Al-Idrisi placed his quill in its stand. No more words were needed for such empty places. The original pages were ashes but his heart and his eyes still burned. Lines from Ibn Hamdis' work ran through his mind. *This is Allah's country. Abandon its spaces and your aspirations on earth will be shattered.* How could anyone leave Sicilia and not miss it forever?

> *My soul yearns for Sicily*
> *and the laughing days of my youth there.*
> *In exile from Paradise, I remember*
> *the noblest of people*
> *and my tears add salt to*
> *the rivers I cry for my homeland.*

In exile, a man discovered his home.

Dipping his quill once more in black ink, al-Idrisi wrote on a piece of parchment he kept for thoughts that were inappropriate to a work of science.

Allahu akbar. Siqilliya sana-hallahu. God is great. May God protect Sicilia.

AUTHOR'S NOTE

The more I research the 12th century, the more I realise how skilled people were, as sailors, craftsmen, warriors, weavers –– the list is long –– and the modern experts who recreate those skills are a vital link between us and a way of life with much to recommend it. Thanks to two passionate experts at the Viking Ship Museum in Roskilde, Denmark, who dedicated two hours to answering my naïve questions, I learned as much about how it *felt* to sail a Viking ship as I did about the practicalities. With unfailing kindness, they helped me aboard a reproduction merchant knarr, so they could show me the hold full of stones, to provide ballast in the absence of cargo, and also the strain on the ropes, which fray all the time. I had no idea so much water sloshed around *inside* a boat.

I have always wondered how on earth oarsmen managed to row a Viking ship if their shields were hung on the sides of the ship (the *wales*). So I asked. I nearly cheered at the answer. My experts exchanged looks and smiles, and told me, 'We've tried every way we could think of and never managed it. We think the shields were stowed away.' *Yes!*

Mentioning a sunstone will also start an argument among historians. One saga mentions a 'solar stone' that can find the sun on a cloudy day but no 'sunstones' have been found on Viking sites. However, one such crystal (Icelandic calcite) was discovered three feet from a pair of navigational dividers when the wreckage of *the Alderney* was explored. This Elizabethan warship sank off the Channel Islands in 1592, much later than my period, but it suggests that navigational sunstones did exist.

What's the science? I bought an Icelandic calcite crystal (also known as Icelandic spar) so I could check out how it worked. Because it's a rhomboid shape, if you look through it at an object, or at a spot painted on the sunstone, there is a double image because light is refracted through the crystal. This property has long been used in optics and to study light. But if you hold it in just the right position, the two images merge and you know the crystal is pointing east-west. So you *can* find the sun, even when it's behind clouds, fog or at twilight. All you have to do is let the wolf catch the sun, as Skarfr would say. I had fun navigating my way around my garden on a cloudy day but I'm no expert!

One of my favourite discoveries in researching this novel was the history of Sicilian silk. The workshop known as the Tiraz *was* staffed by the Jewish women silk workers George of Antioch had kidnapped and enslaved during a raid on Byzantine Thebes.

Silk workers were mostly skilled women, often slaves (either officially or, as nowadays, entrapped by poverty and lack of residency status), who did indeed have to provide sexual services. For centuries, in many European countries, working in the silk trade was a euphemism for such services, and the sensuality of silk as a motif in literature is one of the rabbit-holes I dived into, fascinated.

My interest in silk is personal. There are two white mulberry trees in our garden, and the people who lived in our house over a hundred years ago would definitely have kept silkworms and made silk thread. They might also have spun it and woven it, as a cottage industry. Mulberries can live up to two hundred and fifty years and, every spring, I imagine the thousands of silkworms which have munched on the leaves. The only munching these days is when the mulberries fall and the dogs tuck in but what an amazing history those two trees could tell.

I loved not just the Tiraz but all of my imaginary visit to 12thC Sicily! Today, it's a sunny holiday destination but in the 12th century, the Norman Kingdom of Sicily was an extremely rich world power. Strategically placed in the Mediterranean, with primarily Muslim citizens, King Roger showed respect for their skills and apparent tolerance for citizens of all faiths.This multicultural integration went beyond the similar cohabitation taking place in al-Andalus, as King Roger even defied the Pope by refusing to join the Christian crusade. He was accused by Bernard de Clairvaux of behaving like a sultan, in his robes and eastern habits. This makes the fate of Philip of Mahdia, who became Emir after George's death, even more of a mystery. Historians can only guess at the cause of King Roger's 'Christian' cruelty to Philip.

Like any medieval king, Roger *was* demonstrably capable of great cruelty but he was also passionate in his patronage of great thinkers from different faiths. Many such did indeed stop over, en route to somewhere else, and never left, including al-Idrisi, who is known to this day as 'the Sicilian map-maker' although he was not born on the island. There doesn't seem to be an English translation of *the Book of Roger*, which is such a pity! so I read this remarkable Arabic work in French. All extracts from it are my own translations, from the French, of what al-Idrisi actually wrote.

Sicily today is also known as the home of the corrupt, violent family-based network known as the mafia. Mamma Maria and the brothers could star in a medieval version of *The Godfather* but they are not anachronistic. In his article *The Mafia, Part 1: From Roots as Feudal Enforcers to Modern Gangsters*, Joe Goia pointed out that *Mu'afa* is an Arabic word meaning protection, and *Ma'afir*, the tribal name of Palermo's former rulers. 'Both are seen as possible roots of the word *Mafia*. It first appears as the name of a Palermo group that led the bloody 1282 uprising against the despised Angevins. In the aftermath, the word *mafiusu* came to mean a swaggering, boastful, proud individual.'

It seems to me perfectly credible therefore that, in 1151, Lombardy settlers from mainland Sicily could run a protection racket with the king's blessing, to collect debts for him and ensure a nice income for themselves on the side. Some things don't change. As for the 'godmother', Mamma Maria, her power comes from wealth and widowhood, always given a special status in medieval societies. Never underestimate old ladies!

If I start talking about 12thC attitudes to women, I will never stop, but one of my best 'I *see* you' moments came when I met a völva in Copenhagen. Her story was told in an exhibition centring on the preserved body of a 1othC völva, buried with artefacts including very large, heavy wands and a pouch containing henbane seeds, probably used to send herself into a trance. She was still wearing her toe-rings, a detail which really brought her to life. What struck me then was something I'd only half taken-in previously. In medieval Norse culture, witches were wise women, gods-gifted and respected. Powerful men consulted them and considered them to be a force for *good*.

The verse from *The Poetic Edda* that heads the last chapter of *Hunting the Sun* fits Hlif perfectly. Her family is considered evil but she wins respect for her wisdom and skills. I can't wait to spend time with her and Skarfr again in Book 4, the climax of the series.

ACKNOWLEDGMENTS

Many thanks to:

my brilliant editor Lorna Fergusson of Fictionfire Literary Consultancy;
Babs, Jane and Kristin for your invaluable critiques and support;
The Sanctuary writers' group for providing exactly that and for all your expertise;
Dr Jackson Crawford for sharing his expertise in Old Norse and for permission to quote his translation of *The Poetic Edda* in chapter headings;
The staff at Roskilde Viking Ship Museum, Denmark, for treating me like a VIP and sharing their expertise with passion and patience;
Ryerson and Paul for being my specialists on boats, sailing and rowing – all mistakes are mine, not yours;
Patricia Long, Orkney guide, for sharing her knowledge and love of Orkney;
Lesley Geekie for being my woman at the scene;
Fran Hollinrake, Custodian/Visitor Services Officer, St Magnus Cathedral for information on the history of the building and on masons' marks;
Staff of Historic Monuments, Scotland and of Maeshowe Visitor's Centre for information and support;

Midwinter Dragon maps © Jean Gill, created using Inkarnate.com, a base map of Orkney from Ordnance Survey Open Data with inset derived from File:Scotland location map.svg by NordNordWest, created by Wikipedia User Nilfanion; a base map of Sicily and of the Mediterranean both from d-maps.com

and Jessica Bell Cover Design for the amazing covers for all my books.

SELECTED REFERENCE WORKS

Selected reference works
Extracts *from The Poetic Edda* translated and edited with Introduction, by Jackson Crawford. Copyright © 2015 Hackett Publishing Company, Inc

The Orkneyinga Saga – Project Gutenberg (Public Domain)

John Julius Norwich – *The Kingdom in the Sun, The Normans in Sicily Vol II*
Egbert of Liège (translated by Robert Gary Babcock) – *The Well-Laden Ship*
William Granara – *Ibn Hamdis, the Sicilian, Eulogist for a Falling Homeland*
Robert S Lopez and Irving W Raymond (translators) – Medieval Trade in the Mediterranean World
Pierre Aubé – *Roger II de Sicile*
Henri Bresc et Annliese Nef, traduction du chevalier Jaubert – *Idrisî, La première géographe de l'Occident*
Neil Price – *Children of Ash and Elm*
Ian Crockatt – *Crimsoning the Eagle's Claw*. The poetry of Rögnvaldr
Ian Crockatt – *The Song Weigher*. The poetry of Egill Skallagrimsson
Jamina Ramirez – *Femina*
Jóhanna Katrín Friðriksdóttir – *The Women of the Viking World* (Bloomsbury)
Judith Jesch – *Women in the Viking Age*
Grace Tierney – *Words the Vikings Gave Us*

Fiction
Tariq Ali – *A Sultan in Palermo*, Bk 4 of *The Islam Quartet*
Erik Linklater – *The Ultimate Viking*

A.D. Howden Smith – *Swain's Saga*

Historical Articles
E. Jane Burns – Sea of Silk: A Textile Geography of Women's Work in Medieval French Literature, University of Pennsylvania Press
Judith Jesch – 'The Nine Skills of Earl Rögnvaldr of Orkney'
Judith Jesch – 'Earl Rögnvaldr of Orkney, a Poet of the Viking Diaspora'
Lucy Collings, R. Farrell and I. Morrison – 'Earl Rögnvald's Shipwreck' (Viking Society for Northern Research)
Debbie Potts – 'An Introduction to Skaldic Poetry'
Brenda Prehal – 'Freyja's Cats: Perspectives on Recent Viking Age Finds in North Iceland'
R. W. Reid – 'Remains of Saint Magnus and Saint Rognvald, Entombed in Saint Magnus Cathedral, Kirkwall, Orkney' (Oxford University Press)
Albert Thomson – 'Masons' Marks in St Magnus Cathedral' (An Orkney Miscellany 1954)

Online
www.vikingeskibsmuseet.dk especially the articles, logs, diaries and videos about the voyage of the reproduction longship *Sea Stallion* from Denmark to Dublin, via Orkney.
https://skaldic.org/ The Skaldic Project, especially the compilation of indexed kennings

Nidavellnir Nalbinding on Facebook and YouTube, for information and practical demonstrations of this pre-knitting technique, and for the expertise on Viking textiles of Emma 'Bruni' Boast, a Viking-Age Archaeologist and Nalbinding Specialist based in York, UK. Member of the Guild of Mastercraftsmen UK.

ABOUT THE AUTHOR

I'm a Welsh writer and photographer living in the south of France with two scruffy dogs, a beehive named 'Endeavour', a Nikon D750 and a man. I taught English in Wales for many years and my claim to fame is that I was the first woman to be a secondary headteacher in Carmarthenshire. I'm mother or stepmother to five children so life has been pretty hectic.

I've published all kinds of books, both with traditional publishers and self-published. You'll find everything under my name from prize-winning poetry and novels, military history, translated books on dog training, to a cookery book on goat cheese. My work with top dog-trainer Michel Hasbrouck has taken me deep into the world of dogs with problems, and inspired one of my novels. With Scottish parents, an English birthplace and French residence, I can usually support the winning team on most sporting occasions.

www.jeangill.com

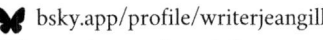

- bsky.app/profile/writerjeangill
- youtube.com/JeanGill
- bookbub.com/jean-gill
- facebook.com/writerjeangill

Join my Special Readers' Group

for private news, views and offers

with an exclusive copy of *How White is My Valley*

as a welcome gift.

Sign up at *jeangill.com*

From award-winning author Jean Gill, exclusive to her Special Readers' Group, the follow-up to her memoir *How Blue is My Valley* about moving to France from rainy Wales.

How White is My Valley tells the true story of how, now living in France, Jean

- nearly became a certified dog trainer.
- should have been certified and became a beekeeper.
- developed from keen photographer to hold her first exhibition.
- held 12th century Damascene steel.
- looks for adventure in whatever comes her way.

Praise for *How Blue is My Valley, a memoir*

'Laugh out loud ... such a picture of the fields of lavender, sunflowers and olive trees that you could almost be there with her.' Stephanie Sheldrake, *Living France Magazine*

THE TROUBADOURS

The adventures of Hlif and Skarfr continue in
Book 4 of The Midwinter Dragon.

Stay in the 12th C and discover the Troubadours, Dragonetz and Estela, in *Song at Dawn, Book 1* of the award-winning *Troubadours Quartet.*

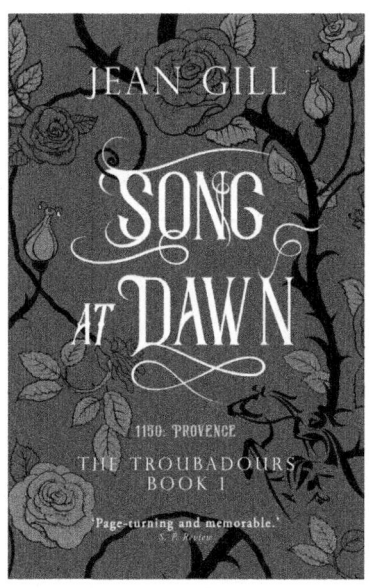

Printed in Great Britain
by Amazon